Murder at Hatteras

A novel by

Joe C. Ellis

Upper Ohio Valley Books

Upper Ohio Valley Books
Joe C. Ellis
71299 Skyview Drive
Martins Ferry, OH 43935
Phone: 1-740-633-0423
Email: joecellis@comcast.net
www.joecellis.com
Copyright © Joe C. Ellis, 2010

ISBN : 978-0-9796655-3-0
Printed in the U.S.A.
First printing, May 2010

PUBLISHER'S NOTE
Although this novel, *Murder at Hatteras*, is set in an actual place, the village of
Buxton, NC, on the Outer Banks, it is a work of fiction. The characters, names,
and plot are the products of the author's imagination. Any resemblance of these
characters to real people is entirely coincidental. Many of the places mentioned in
the novel—Buxton Village Books, the Cape Hatteras Lighthouse, the Sandbar and
Grille restaurant, etc. are wonderful places to visit on the Outer Banks. However
their involvement in the plot of the story is purely fictional. It is the author's hope
that this novel generates great interest in this wonderful region of the U.S.A., and
as a result many people will plan a vacation here and experience the beauty of this
setting firsthand.

CATALOGING INFORMATION
Ellis, Joe C., 1956-
Murder at Hatteras by Joe C. Ellis
ISBN 978-0-9796655-3-0
1.Outer Banks—Fiction. 2. Buxton, NC—Fiction
3. Mystery—Fiction 4. Suspense—Fiction 5. Inspirational—Fiction.
6. Martins Ferry, OH--Fiction

Attention Filmmakers, Editors, and Publishers:
If you are interested in Film/Television Rights, Foreign Rights, or
American Publishing Rights to *Murder at Hatteras*, please contact:
Joe C. Ellis
71299 Skyview Drive
Martins Ferry, Ohio 43935

Acknowledgments

The author would like to thank the following people for their help:

Gretchen Snodgrass has done an excellent job carefully editing this novel. This is the fourth book she has edited for me, and I am always amazed at her ability to catch errors, both in grammar and plausibility. She also offered suggestions that helped develop the plot and characters. God bless you, Gretchen.

My family and I vacationed on Hatteras Island in the village of Buxton in June of 2009. We enjoyed this wonderful area and spent time at many of the places mentioned in the novel. While in Buxton, it was my privilege to meet Gee Gee Rosell, the owner of Buxton Village Books. Gee Gee is a real Hatteras gal. She shared great insights concerning the region and told wonderful stories about her experiences on the island.

I would also like to thank Outer Banks Bookstore owners who have been selling my novels for the last three years. Because of them, *Murder at Whalehead* has become a regional bestseller. Hopefully, *Murder at Hatteras* will follow suit. Who knows? Maybe there's another town along the Outer Banks where another murder will take place in my imagination. Manteo? Nags Head? Kitty Hawk?

A Note to Readers

All my novels are now available in ebook form from Amazon.com (Kindle) and Barnesandnoble.com (Nook). If you enjoyed *Murder at Hatteras*, please email your friends and tell them about it. Also, I would like to hear from you. Email me with any comments or questions at joecellis@comcast.net and visit my website at www.joecellis.com.

Thanks for checking out my other novels,

Joe C. Ellis

The Healing Place by Joe C. Ellis

The rural community of Scotch Ridge on the outskirts of Martins Ferry, Ohio is a safe haven from the dangers and corruption of the world until the day Nathan Kyler arrives. He has envisioned a diabolic plan—an obsession to sacrifice another human being. His target is Christine Butler, the preacher's daughter. Soon after Christine disappears, the community rallies to find her. A mile from the Scotch Ridge Church deep in the Appalachian woods is a spot known as the Healing Place. Here something incredible happens. Available in hardcopy and ebook for Kindle and Nook.

Murder at Whalehead by Joe C. Ellis

On the northern Outer Banks looms an old hunting lodge known as the Whalehead Club. During the roaring twenties Edward and Marie Knight entertained prominent guests at this isolated Mansion by the Sea. Now it has become one of North Carolina's leading tourist attractions. Less than a quarter mile away deep in the marsh along the Currituck Sound lies the body of a young woman. Someone has killed and craves to kill again. The Butler family never expected to cross paths with a homicidal maniac while vacationing at the beach.

Available in hardcopy and ebook for Kindle and Nook

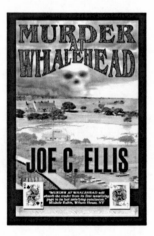

The First Shall Be Last by Joe C. Ellis

Two young lovers separated by war cling to hope and sanity by exchanging passionate letters. As Howard heads for his first battle on the Pacific island of Peleliu, Helen fulfills her call of duty by working at a local factory. They discover they have more to worry about than the Japanese forces deeply entrenched on the island. A platoon member, Judd Stone, seeks revenge against a black Marine named Josiah Jackson. Howard fears Stone may go to any length to get what he wants, even murder.

Murder on the Outer Banks by Joe C. Ellis

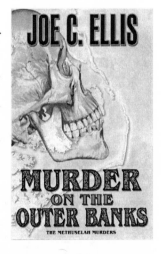

Newly hired deputy, Marla Easton, and Sheriff Dugan Walton are amazed at the performance of Dr. Sylvester Hopkins in a local 5K footrace. At sixty-five years old, Hopkins posts a world class time of 17:35, two minutes faster than he has run in the past few years. Walton suspects Hopkins has concocted some new performance enhancing drug. A trail of bodies from Frisco to Nags Head lead Deputy Easton and Sheriff Walton to the discovery of the Methuselah serum—a new drug designed by Hopkins that reverses aging in human cells. A nefarious triumvirate of pharmaceutical CEOs known as the Medical Mafia wants the formulae at any price. So does the FBI and the President of the United States. But Sheriff Walton believes that he and Deputy Easton have been divinely chosen to guard the formula and serum. Like the angels posted in Eden to guard the Tree of Life, they take their mission seriously. That mission turns perilous when Marla's seven-year-old son, Gabe, is kidnapped.

Chapter 1

The nylon rope felt good in his grip. When he pulled it taut, it constricted his hands causing that pin-prickly feeling in his fingertips. He closed his eyes and imagined tying it around a slender wrist and lashing it to a bedpost. The vision excited him. He drew in a deep breath, the salty air filling his lungs, and exhaled slowly. The fantasy faded as the breeze from the ocean picked up and cooled his face. He opened his eyes and scanned the shoreline. The Cape Hatteras Lighthouse shot a beam above the waves out to sea. Night had arrived.

He let go of one end of the rope and reached on top of his head for the mask. His fingers brushed over the horns, grasped the forehead, and tugged slowly downward until he could see through the eyeholes. The papier-mâché felt rough against his cheeks. Sliding his hand over the jaw line, he sensed grape forms and the grooves of the beard. *Dionysus.* He had just downed a bottle of Mogan David. The smell of the sweet wine intensified as he breathed against the mask.

At his feet two ghost crabs scampered towards the surf. The full moon's glow lit the leading edge of the water as it rushed up the bank engulfing the crabs, then withdrawing, dragging them into the ocean. He turned away from the black and white striped tower and headed north along the shore towards the apartments. The stretch of beach before him was empty. *Good. No one to notice me. This could be the night I tie a few things up.*

1

He snapped the rope like a whip. An ache of desire quivered through him. *I'm tired of watching someone else have all the fun. I'm ready to rope and ride.*

It was warm for early October, mid-sixties. The short walk up the beach caused beads of sweat to trickle down his forehead and cheeks. The black warm up suit didn't help. "It's like a sauna under this thing," he said. His voice sounded creepy, distorted by the electronic device he had inserted into the mouth opening. The oddness of its tone stirred his wicked frame of mind even more. He slid the mask up and wiped the sweat from his face. The sea breeze refreshed him. When he peered across the dunes he saw the four-unit apartment house, its walkway zigzagging through the sea oats to the beach. He twirled the nylon towrope, allowing it to slap the sand at intervals as he approached the walkway.

At the steps he grabbed the wooden handrail then hesitated to peer down the narrow boardwalk that traversed the dunes. He focused on the downstairs apartment about forty yards away. The bedroom window glowed in the shadows under the second-story deck. The blinds were wide open. *She's stretched out on that bed. And he's gone.* For a moment he considered walking away, denying this dark craving that had been growing ever since the couple had arrived. He'd crossed that line only once before, but oh, what a charge it gave him. Was it too late now that he'd done the deed, forced himself on an unwilling woman? Lately, fantasizing about it consumed him, especially with her—a girl he wanted so badly but could never have. His hands trembled, so he wound the end of the rope around his free hand and yanked it tight. The nylon dug into the latex. The pain steeled him. After snapping the rope several times, he mounted the steps and headed down the walkway.

He descended the steps to a sandy path that cut through sea oats and ended at the lower section of the house, which served as a laundry room for all four apartments. No one had turned on outside spotlights yet; the darkness under the lower deck made it hard to see the laundry room entrance. *The darker the better.* The back decks didn't have stair access. To ascend he had to climb the two-by-six crossbeams that created X-es between the deck's supporting posts. Climbing wasn't his specialty, but he'd manage as quietly as possible. He hung the towrope around his neck and tied with a simple knot to free his hands. Grabbing an upper crossbeam, he tested its soundness. *Should hold me.* He lifted his foot, placed it halfway up the board, pulled himself up, and secured his other foot where the boards crossed. *Halfway there.* Repeating the maneuver, he rose to deck level and scissored one leg over the railing. He shifted his weight, hearing a plank creak, and carefully pulled the other leg over.

2

The bedroom window was only three feet to his left. He pressed his back to the wall and edged to it, then craned his neck to take a peek. She sat on the bed, back propped on a pillow against the headboard. Her short, black negligee clung to her svelte body, red panties slightly exposed. In her hands she held a book, a thick paperback that rested against her knees. She wore blue-framed, chic glasses, and a tress of her dark brown hair had caught on the rim's corner and slashed across her cheek. Her beauty stalled his desperate lust the way light stuns unprepared eyes. He stared for many seconds without thinking.

When his hands began trembling again, he grasped the towrope and untied the knot. Wrapping it around one hand then the other and pulling tight sent a bite of pain across his knuckles and snapped him back to the task at hand. He eyed the space of the open window and the bottom of the frame where he could grasp and lift. But the screen still blocked his entrance. With the window open he could plow through the screen like a monster out of the darkness. *Get ready.* He slid his hand along the frame and lifted slightly. The window budged a fraction of an inch.

She glanced up from her book and yelled, "Gabe is that you!"

Now! Now! He stepped closer to the window to get better leverage. *Get ready. One. Two Three. Now.* He lifted the window and it moved about an inch.

She laid the book at her side. "Gabriel! Is that you?"

"Yeah. It's me, Sweetcheeks!" A voice called from somewhere beyond the bedroom door.

He withdrew his hand and listened.

Chapter 2

"Why ya home so early?" she hollered. "Did someone get pissed off again? Those wannabe writers are so sensitive."

"No. Everyone got along fine tonight," Gabe yelled from the kitchen. He opened the cupboard above the dishwasher, fished the last granola bar out of its box, stripped off the wrapper, and took a bite. He closed the cupboard door, thinking Marla would scold him later when she found that empty box. "We talked about character development for a little while and then decided to exchange chapters and head home. I've got a lot of critiquing to do for next week. What you been up to?"

"Reading. Harry Potter. I know you think it's kids stuff, but I like it."

"It's not Faulkner or Conroy."

"You and your Southern writers."

"You want something to drink?"

"Yeah." She hesitated. "A homemade milkshake."

"Chocolate?"

"Of course. And use the skim milk."

Gabe snagged a tall glass from the top rack of the dishwasher, twirled to the fridge, and snatched a bottle of Gatorade and the carton of skim milk from the top shelf. He crouched to open the freezer and tugged the ice cream out from under a box of frozen shrimp. As he prepared his

4

wife's milkshake, rapidly stirring the milk and two scoops until it became a chunky concoction, he chuckled to himself about her latest craving. *She wants a baby so bad she's adopted a mama's appetite.*

When he entered the bedroom, Marla removed her glasses, smiled, and stretched her arms. She shifted to the edge of the bed and reached for the chocolaty mixture. Gabe admired the way the silk negligee clung to his wife's body, just enough cleavage to make him want to see more.

"You must have something on your mind wearing that skimpy thing tonight," he said.

She took a gulp of the milkshake and licked her upper lip. "I do."

"Let me guess. You can't wait to get your hands on this fine body of mine."

Her grin widened. "Distance runners aren't known for their bodies, but that's okay. I still need you to get what I want." She slid her hand under his T-shirt to his chest and then raked down, grasping his belt, pulling him towards her.

With his fingertip Gabe traced the rim of her ear, along her jaw line to her chin then lightly across her lower lip. "And what is it you want so badly?"

Marla sucked in a quick breath, her eyes closing. "You know."

"You'd like to see Private Happy come to attention."

Marla burst out laughing and shoved Gabe.

He backed into the dresser. "Hey! I almost spilled my Gatorade." He took a long drink.

She took another swig of her milkshake. "Private Happy better be ready for night maneuvers. I'm ovulating. It's baby-making time."

"Baby-making time!" Gabe downed the last of the Gatorade, placed the bottle on the dresser, and walked to the other side of the room where an acoustic guitar leaned against the wall by the window. He picked up the guitar and sat on the end of the bed, slowly picking through the strings of an E chord. "I stopped by the clinic today to make a deposit."

She set her glass on the nightstand and stretched out on her stomach facing the foot of the bed, the side of her arm brushing against the guitar. Gabe stopped playing, reached to his right, and combed his fingers through her hair to the middle of her back several times with long slow strokes.

"I don't think it's you, Luuvums," she said.

"We'll find out. They'll let me know in a few days."

"No. It's got to be me. It's the stress—teaching first graders for the last five years. That's what Dr. Corby told me. He said a couple months down here would do the trick. I think he's right."

"The Outer Banks are incredible." He gently massaged her shoulder. "I think more clearly here. More creatively. I've finished five chapters already— one a week since we've been down here. Don't know if it's the waves, or sand, or that striped lighthouse out there. Maybe it's the sea and sky meeting on the horizon like God took his finger and traced that long flat line right before our eyes just to remind us He's around. It's hard to pinpoint, but the words seem to flow down here."

Marla turned onto her back. Gabe slid the negligee up to her breasts and placed his hand on her belly. Her skin felt wonderfully warm.

"I know what you mean," Marla said. "I love it here. Working at the bookstore is a blast. Me and Mee Mee get along great. When things are slow we gab a lot. She doesn't even mind if I sit and read. I think I'll be fine here. Won't be long and I'll have a baby bump."

"A baby bump?" Gabe circled her navel with his fingertip.

"You know. Preggo."

He widened the circle, skimming across the top of her panties.

Marla quivered. "You're getting me a little shook up there, Elvis."

"Yes, ma'am. All shook up."

She cupped her hand over his, intertwining their fingers. "So tell me. Were you able to . . . you know . . . put a few of your . . ." She snaked her free hand through the air. " . . . tadpoles into the test tube at the clinic?"

"Without you it was incredibly difficult, but I managed."

"Did they give you any visual aids?"

Gabe paused and met Marla's gaze. He sensed a tinge of resentment in her voice. "They offered me a *Playboy*, but I didn't want it. Kept remembering what Pastor Byron said at our counseling sessions—you know, lust for other women is a sin and all that."

"You're such a Puritan. Pastor Byron would have understood your circumstances."

"Anyway, I had all I needed in my wallet—a picture of you in your white bikini."

"Really!" Marla sat up eyes wide, smiling again.

Gabe nodded. "Within three minutes—kaboom, the cannon exploded."

"Three minutes. That sounds about right." Marla giggled. "I guess my picture lit the fuse."

"You're my inspiration. Hey, that reminds me. I wrote a new song today." Gabe picked through the strings of a D minor chord.

"A song for me?" Marla asked as she lay down again and clasped behind her head.

"You inspired every word." Gabe worked through a series of simple but beautiful variations of D minor, D, and A chords. When he sang, he expressed each word with subtle emotion, his voice nicely textured on the low notes and smooth in transition to the higher notes: "Do you believe in love so strong, it melts your fears away? Makes you want to sing, makes you want to pray. Do you believe in love so good, it lifts you to the sky? Makes you want to laugh, makes you want to cry. I do. I do, because I found you. I'll never be the same, ever since you came into my life."

As his fingers picked through the next series of transition chords he glanced at Marla and smiled. She gazed at the ceiling, her blue eyes the color of sapphire, the nostrils of her petite nose widening as she drew in a breath. Desire charged through him, an overwhelming need to make love to her. He leaned the guitar against the dresser.

"I love it," Marla said. "Is there another verse?"

Yeah, but I'll sing it to you later. Time for night maneuvers."

He crawled on top of her, his hands pressing the mattress on each side of her head, his knees digging in by her hips. She grasped the bottom of his t-shirt and pulled it up his torso to his neck. He leaned back on his haunches, allowing her to peel it from his head and arms. She tossed the shirt onto the floor.

When he lowered himself to kiss her, she said, "No. Don't start that way. You know what I like."

Gabe knew the routine well. Supporting himself with one hand, he traced the outside of her ear with the forefinger of his free hand. She closed her eyes and inhaled deeply. He continued along the contour of her jaw, up the middle of her chin, and across her lower lip. Her breathing accelerated slightly. After crisscrossing her lips several times, she grabbed his hand and kissed his fingers. This was how she liked to start their lovemaking. He didn't mind the ritual. Not at all.

"Kiss me now," she gasped.

As their lips met, the sound of glass breaking on the deck tinkled through the open window. Gabe pushed himself erect and heard footsteps pounding across the deck.

"What the hell?" he said. "Did you hear that?"

Marla's head angled to the side as she glared at the window. "Someone's out there."

Gabe tumbled off the bed and charged to the window. Darkness enshrouded the deck, so he hurried into the living room to the sliding glass door and flipped on the deck spotlight. His heart pounded, echoing in his ears. Not seeing anything, he turned the lock and slid open the door. The smell of salty air and a brisk breeze accosted him. He edged open the screen slowly at first, then more firmly sliding it along its track. He listened but heard nothing except the distant rumble and crash of surf.

The baseball bat. Should have brought that with me. He shook his head, trying to decide whether or not to go back to the bedroom closet to retrieve the bat. *No. Not enough time. Get out there. See what's going on.* He stepped onto the deck and looked both ways. Nothing. Glancing down, he noticed a broken glass, one he'd left on the table next to the window yesterday after he'd finished his run. *The footsteps. Someone was watching us, knocked over the glass, then took off running.* To his right he saw the railing at the end of the deck, the most logical place someone could ascend and descend.

He stepped to the rail and scanned the dunes. The full moon gilded the sea oats with a ghostly sheen; they flowed in the wind like ripples sent from the waves at the shore. Other than their movement, he saw nothing unusual—no deer hopping through the scrub between the dunes and house or even a vacationer on a night beach walk. Whoever it was must be hiding nearby or perhaps took off to the front of the apartments.

Marla appeared at the door in her red robe. "Do you see anyone?"

"No. The pervert skedaddled. Must have climbed over the rail and jumped to the ground. That's about a nine foot fall, but it's a soft landing if he hit the sand next to the sidewalk."

Marla stepped onto the deck, keeping the robe tight against her despite the breeze. She peered in the other direction. "Could they have gone that way?"

"Maybe." Gabe walked to the wooden divider separating their side of the deck from Mr. Payne's. "It's only about three feet tall. Wouldn't be too hard to get over. But then the jerk would have had to jump from that side. Either way it's a long drop."

"Unless . . ." Marla pointed towards Mr. Payne's door.

"You think it might have been Old Man Payne?"

"He's not that old. Late forties, early fifties."

"Yeah, but why would he do something like that?"

Marla shrugged. "He gives me the creeps. Not very friendly. Always has that far-off look in his eyes."

Gabe stood on his toes to get a good look in his neighbor's window. "There's a light on in the kitchen. Can't see much else. The blinds are half closed."

"Listen," Marla said.

Gabe could hear a woman's voice coming from inside Payne's apartment but couldn't make out what she was saying. "He must have company tonight."

"And his wife's in the hospital."

"Maybe it's a relative."

"Should you call the police?" Marla asked.

"Not much they can do about it now."

"At least they'd know we've got a Peeping Tom in the neighborhood."

"Might just be some high school kid getting his jollies. Who knows?" Gabe took her hand. "Come back to the bedroom. I want to show you something." He led her to the bedroom closet and pulled his shirts to the side, the hangers sliding along the rod to expose a baseball bat in the back corner. He grabbed the bat and held it up. "This is the only weapon we've got in this house—my good ol' Louisville Slugger." He flipped it, caught the thick end, and then extended the handle to her. "Try it. Whack the pillow."

Marla stepped back, hands up, refusing to take it. "You expect me to crack some maniac on the head with this thing."

"Give it a swing."

Marla took the bat and held it in front of her as if gripping a sword.

Gabe grasped her shoulders and turned her towards the bed. "Raise it over your head and aim at the pillow."

Unsteadily, she raised the bat and brought it down with a mild thump, missing the pillow by several inches. To Gabe she resembled a dysfunctional lumberjack. "You just need some practice." He took the bat and demonstrated by whacking the pillow several times. "Try it again."

Marla chopped down onto the pillow, but her effort failed to match the loud whop of Gabe's connection. "I want you to practice every day. Build those arms up," Gabe said.

Marla raised an eyebrow and handed the bat to him.

He leaned it against the wall near the bed. "It's right here if you ever need it."

Marla crossed the room to the window, closed it, locked it, and twirled the rod to shut the blinds. "I'm crawling into bed and pulling the covers over my head."

"I'll be back in a minute," Gabe said. "Got to make sure all the doors are locked."

"Good idea, Luuvums," Marla said, sliding under the covers. "And Gabe . . ."

"Yes, Sweetcheeks."

"Hurry back. I need you. I still want that baby tonight."

Chapter 3

In the shadows under the deck, pressed against the laundry room door, he had removed the mask so he could better detect any movement above him. The porch light sent weak rays filtering through the cracks between the deck boards. The couple had entered the house, but he decided to wait several minutes before he took off in case one of them came back out. *That was close.* He breathed deeply, trying to slow his heartbeat. *Bad timing. Luuvums hurried home to Sweetcheeks sooner than I expected. Lucky for Sweetcheeks. Damn, I was ready to go for it. Now what? Go to a bar? Pick up a slut?*

He took two steps forward into the slices of dim light and listened intently. No sound but the waves lapping the shore sixty yards away. He moved to the edge of the deck's shadow. As he prepared to peek around the corner of the building, he heard footsteps. *Shit. Someone's coming.* He flattened himself against the wall. The footsteps grew louder. He held his breath. To his right a young woman with long blonde hair passed under the glow of the porch's spotlight. She wore a lime green tank top and tight hip-hugger jeans. He recognized her—that round face with luscious lips, well-defined biceps, and hot body. *I know you, but you aren't familiar with my new face.* He lifted the mask and waved it slowly in front of him. *You're not Sweetcheeks, but you'll do for tonight.*

She turned left at the corner of the deck post and angled towards the walkway that crossed the dunes to the beach. He watched her climb the steps and disappear into the darkness as she progressed down the boardwalk.

He positioned the mask on top of his head, wrapped the towrope around his hands and yanked it tight. *Think I'll do some ropin' and ridin' after all. Lead the way, Miss Muscles. We'll see how strong you are.* He waited another thirty seconds before hurrying across the open space between the deck and the walkway. Crossing the boardwalk, he tried to stay light on his feet in case she had slowed her pace or stopped along the way. He didn't want to scare her . . . not yet.

On the beach he spotted her fifty yards ahead, going north. *That's a lonely stretch. Walk as far as you want, Miss Muscles. I'll be tagging along not far behind.* She meandered near the edge of the surf, so he hugged the dune line, blending in with the blackness of the mounds of sand.

After twenty-five minutes he lost his patience. *Didn't mind you leading us away from civilization, but I wasn't planning on a marathon. I'll be too worn out to perform.* Just when he decided to cross the beach and surprise her, she stopped, turned around, and headed in his direction. *Perfect. I'll catch my breath right here until you pass.* He crouched at the base of a dune.

She walked directly in front of him, and he noticed how the moonlight lit the tresses of her wind-tossed mane. *Nice. I'll make sure I get a handful of those golden locks when I'm trying to keep you under control.* Once she passed, he took off across the beach, hoping the waves would drown out his footsteps. As he neared, he pulled the mask over his face. He came to within a few feet and stopped.

She whirled around and gasped, her eyes wider than a frightened filly. "Who are you?"

With his voice eerily distorted by the mouthpiece, he said, "Don't you recognize me?"

"Tony? Take off the mask. You're scaring me."

"I've got a knife. Do exactly what Tony says or I'll gut you like a sixty-pound tuna."

Her voice wavered as she spoke. "Okay. Okay. Please don't hurt me. My father made me break up with you."

"Turn around. Put your hands behind your back."

As she complied, she whimpered, her breaths coming in quick, short huffs. "Tony, is that really you?"

"It's me all right." He lashed the towrope around her wrists. *This might be easier than I imagined.*

Chapter 4

Gabe stepped onto the front deck clad in his favorite workout attire—black Nike racing shorts and a yellow Pittsburgh Steelers t-shirt with the sleeves cut off. For a clear, fall morning it was warm, probably near 70 degrees. He plopped down on an Adirondack chair and tightened the laces on his Saucony Triumphs, threading a shoestring through his apartment key and securing it between the laces before double knotting each shoe. Marla would head off to her job at the bookstore in Buxton before he got back. After last night's scare, they decided to keep the doors locked at all times.

Today he worked the late shift at the Lighthouse Souvenir and Gift Shop—1:00 P.M. 'til 7:00 P.M. He didn't mind not having a fulltime job. The six-hour shifts left him more time to write. Money was tight, but they got by. When he had worked as a reporter for *The Times Leader* back in Martins Ferry and Marla taught school, money was rarely a problem. But Gabe would rather live frugally on the Outer Banks with plenty of time to write than comfortably anywhere else. Even if it meant no cell phone, daily newspaper, or cable TV.

Glancing to his right, he saw Sonny Keys coming around the corner of the building twirling a yellow rope. Sonny lived in one of the two upstairs apartments. Gabe's twin brother, Michael, lived in the other directly above Gabe and Marla. Sonny was caretaker of six beachfront apartment complexes along the Hatteras Island shoreline. Everyone liked him, although his shaved head and intense blue-gray eyes often generated an intimidating first impression. When Gabe had met him, Sonny asked Gabe to guess his age. Gabe had guessed twenty-eight, which made Sonny shake his head and laugh. Nope, nope, nope. I'm thirty-six," he'd said, rubbing his tanned dome. "Most people think I'm in my twenties. It's 'cause of this Yul Brynner look I got." Sonny, about six feet tall with muscular arms and a noticeable paunch, took great pride in maintaining the apartment complexes. Whenever Gabe needed anything repaired or replaced, Sonny made it a priority to get to it within twenty-four hours.

"How goes it, Sonny?" Gabe asked.

Sonny, standing in bright sunshine, shaded his eyes to focus on Gabe in the shadows of the deck. "Just another day in paradise, Mr. Easton."

"What's with the rope?"

Sonny motioned him to come over. "Check this out."

Gabe descended the steps to the driveway and walked to the corner of the building. "That young live oak there in need of a little help?"

Sonny tied the rope to the top of a sapling. "Three days ago I strapped this tree to the post here to keep the wind from bendin' it. This mornin' I come out and the rope's gone."

"Maybe you didn't tie it tight enough."

"No, sir. Watch this." Sonny brought the loose end of the rope around the deck post twice then fed it through the first loop and pulled it tight under the second loop. "That's called a studding sail knot. It'll hold a lot better than a reg'lar overhand knot."

Gabe marveled at his speed and efficiency with the rope. "You sure know your knots."

"I might not be the smartest puppy in the pound, but I know the wind didn't pull that rope loose. Someone untied it."

Gabe tugged on the rope. "That's strong stuff. What is it? Nylon?"

"Yeah. Fishermen use it to tow stranded boats. You can even tow a car with it. Got a whole spool back in my storage shed if you ever need any."

"Why would someone untie it?" Gabe asked.

"Don't know. Probably some teenage troublemaker, some rebel without a cause."

The word *troublemaker* triggered Gabe's memory of last night's intruder. "That reminds me. Did you see anyone wandering by here last night just after dark?"

"After dark?" Sonny's bottom lip curled into an upside-down U and a dimple formed on the middle of his chin as he gazed into the sky. "As a matter of fact, I did. Pretty blonde gal came by here 'bout half past nine. Her family's stayin' in one of the apartments I look after. She told me she had a big fight with her daddy over a boy—the Trenton boy, the one that works at the Citgo station. No good SOB. Always causin' trouble. Anyways, she told me she was walkin' it off. I asked her if she wanted company, but she said no. Not that I'm interested in teenage girls, mind you."

Gabe tried to read his expression, to detect salacious hints in his eyes or mouth but didn't notice any. "You don't go for younger women?"

"Nope, nope, nope. Just wanted to help her out. She's probably eighteen or nineteen. Just a kid."

"Do you date much?"

"Now and again." Sonny raised his hands as if juggling a slinky back and forth. "I'm partic'lar, Mr. Easton. Lookin' for a partic'lar kind of gal. Late twenties. Early thirties. Pretty. How old's your wife?"

"My wife?" The question surprised Gabe. *Is he infatuated with Marla? Enough to peek in our bedroom window?* "She's twenty-eight. Why do you ask?"

Sonny glanced at his feet, his face reddening slightly. "Well, if she's got a sister that's half as nice and pretty as your wife, I wouldn't mind meetin' her."

"'Fraid not, Sonny. Two big, ugly brothers."

Gabe heard a door open and turned to see Martin Payne leaving his apartment. He wore casual clothes, a navy polo shirt and beige pants. Not quite six feet tall and somewhat flabby, Payne wasn't physically intimidating, but his constant perturbed countenance made Gabe uncomfortable. He had thick salt and pepper hair combed back like the popular singers of the fifties. His dark eyes and thick eyebrows added to his stern disposition. He walked down the steps and turned towards them, stopping at the edge of the driveway.

Payne cleared his throat. "Mr. Keys, just wanted to remind you about the leak under my kitchen sink. It's got everything soaked under there." His voice was gravely.

"Yes sir, Mr. Payne. Hope to get to it sometime this afternoon."

"I'd appreciate that." Payne nodded to Gabe and climbed into his little blue Honda.

As the car backed out Gabe asked, "Do you know Payne very well?"

Sonny nodded. "He was livin' here when I got hired five years ago."

"What kind of man is he?"

"Don't like sayin' nothin' bad 'bout anyone, but he's a strange feller, 'specially since his wife went into the hospital. She's in a coma, you know."

"So I've heard."

"I could tell you some stories." Sonny tilted his head and fluttered his fingers. "Twilight Zone-weird stories."

"Sounds interesting." Gabe wouldn't have minded listening but was pressed for time. "Hey, Sonny, I've got to get my run in and do a few things before I'm due at the gift shop. I'd like to hear a little more about Mr. Payne though. Marla and I don't quite feel at ease living next to him. Maybe we could get together later."

"Sure thing. I'll catch you some time tonight."

"Sounds good." Gabe slapped Sonny on the shoulder and then jogged around the corner of the house and headed towards the beach.

Gabe wondered about Sonny's admiration of Marla. He doubted Sonny was the Peeping Tom but wasn't sure. He seemed guileless, forthright, a man who could be trusted. As Gabe padded along the shore, he noticed a dead horseshoe crab that had washed up a few yards ahead, the smell of decay smarting his nostrils. *You never know what's inside a man. The shell can hide a foul interior. But then there's Mr. Payne. What does a foul exterior have to hide? Can't get much worse than the rumors about his wife.* According to Gabe's brother, Michael, Payne tried to kill her, push her down the Cape Hatteras Lighthouse steps. But he was never prosecuted for any crime. Sometimes Michael exaggerated, stretched a story for entertainment purposes.

Thinking about Michael's ability to spin a good yarn from a few strands of truth set Gabe back on the track of refining the plot of his novel. Running usually got his creative juices flowing. The story involved an old man embarking on a cross country bicycle trek for charity. The latest chapter focused on an encounter with a black motorcycle gang. Gabe wanted to create something special with this scene, something the reader would remember. Unfortunately, he was creatively constipated. He tried looking out to sea and then gazed into the sky at a flock of gulls, but nothing helped. Maybe last night's incident had thrown him off, knocked his writer's mind out of the groove.

When he raised his head to peer down the shoreline, he glimpsed a man sitting on a beach chair about a hundred yards away. Was he fishing? An odd object stood in front of him, and behind him sat some kind of vehicle. As Gabe neared he recognized the man by his girth and sombrero—his brother Michael had arisen early, loaded up his ATV with his easel and paints, and headed down the beach, probably to capture a sunrise seascape.

"Hey, Michael!" Gabe yelled. "Glad I ran into you. I need to pick your gray matter."

Wearing flowered, baggy shorts and an orange tank top, Michael lifted his sombrero slightly, then drank from a golden can. "Brother Gabriel, you've been exerting yourself again. Would you like some refreshment? Got plenty of Michelob in the ice chest." Michael was an expanded version of Gabe—same height, same thick black hair combed straight back, same dark brown eyes and Roman nose, but weighing about fifty pounds more. Everything was slightly wider, especially his belly.

"Why in God's creation are you drinking beer at nine o'clock in the morning?"

Michael lifted his paintbrush from a palette of various blues and golds. "Because, dear brother, I'm still asleep at seven o'clock." He dabbed a heavy stroke of light blue into a Van Gogh-style sky. "Besides, it loosens me up, helps me to express myself."

"It's going to put you into the fertilizer business if you keep it up."

Michael chuckled. "Good ol' Gabe. Always worried about my mortality."

"I've got a splendid idea. How about tomorrow morning bright and early you and I go for a three-mile walk on the beach. We'll work our way up to five, and then eventually get you jogging. Before you know it you'll be a lean, mean painting machine."

Michael patted his belly. "I like my six packs the way they are—on ice. We may be twins, but our passions are very different. You write; I paint. You run; I drink." Michael downed the rest of the beer and belched loudly. "Now, how do you like my latest masterpiece?"

Gabe had to admit it was quite good. A yellow and gold sun sent rays into a sky painted so thickly with dabs of blue that the colors seemed to vibrate. The ocean portion was about half finished, the gold reflecting on the crests of the waves in thick strokes.

"You painted all of this today?"

Michael nodded. "That's what I like about my style. Whip out a painting in two hours. Sell it for four hundred bucks. Gallery gets two hundred. I get two hundred. Everybody's happy."

"No wonder you love it down here."

"How about you and Marla? Getting used to the surroundings yet?"

Gabe sat down on the sand next to his brother. "We're so glad you convinced us to move to this Eden. Marla loves it—working at the bookstore, walking on the beach every day, meeting the locals. She's convinced her nerves will settle down and she'll finally get 'preggo,' as she calls it."

"How about you?"

"I think she'll get pregnant too, if I'm not the problem. I stopped at the clinic yesterday to get my baby batter tested. I want to make sure it's not me."

Michael laughed. "I'm not asking about your special sauce status. How do *you* like living down here?"

"Oh, my bad." Gabe grinned sheepishly. "It's great. I feel energized down here, creatively alive. I'm averaging a chapter a week on this new novel. Today's the first day I've felt a little backed up. That's what I wanted to pick your brain about."

"Okay. Set me up a little. What's happening in the story?"

Gabe talked about the scene where the old man encounters the black motorcycle gang. He was convinced it could be one of the most powerful chapters in the book considering the visual contrasts: an old timer on a Schwinn with saddlebags full of donated money surrounded by young, intimidating black men on Harleys. Gabe liked the combination but struggled to envision the outcome.

"Meet me at the Lighthouse Sports Bar at noon for lunch," Michael said, rubbing his chin. "That gives me a couple hours to think about it. I guarantee you I'll come up with something that'll work."

"Sounds good. I better take off if I'm meeting you for lunch. Got to get my run in and do some chores before then."

Michael raised his can of beer. "To you and your running."

Gabe spread his arms. "You should try it, especially here on the Outer Banks. It makes you feel alive."

Michael grinned. "This *is* paradise."

"Yeah. That's what Sonny Keys told me this morning." Gabe felt a slight vexation remembering Sonny's adoration of Marla. "Sonny's an all right guy, isn't he? I mean, he can be trusted, right?"

"Sonny the 'Keyman' Keys? Of course. Why do you ask?"

"Someone was on our back deck last night looking through our bedroom window. The pervert was about to get an eyeful when he knocked over a glass and took off running."

"You think it was Sonny?"

"I don't know. This morning he mentioned to me how pretty Marla was."

"I guarantee you it's not Sonny. He's a saint. Spends all his spare time helping his handicapped buddies, Wyatt and Frank. Not a lecherous bone in his body."

"How about our next door neighbor?"

"Payne?"

Gabe nodded.

"I wouldn't put it past Payne. I told you about what he did to his wife."

"What you *think* he did to his wife. He hasn't been convicted of any crime."

Michael shook his head. "For an innocent man he acts awful guilty. Just look in his eyes. Watch the way he comes and goes, always looking over his shoulder, as if someone is watching him."

Gabe was about to speak when he heard a motor. Glancing up, he saw a man cruising towards them on an ATV. The man wore a black ball cap, black shorts and a light gray collared shirt with the glint of gold on the left side of his chest. He had to be from the sheriff's department. In his five weeks on the Outer Banks, Gabe discovered these guys made their presence noticeable in town and throughout the vacation rental neighborhoods—appreciable appearances Gabe didn't mind at all. As the officer neared, Gabe saw red hair edging the hat and recognized the familiar face of Dugan Walton, another Martins Ferry transplant.

Dugan skidded to a stop in front of Michael's easel and cut the engine on his Suzuki King Quad.

Michael stood and tilted back his sombrero. "Well, I'll be a son of a cross-eyed whore, if it ain't the renowned Deputy Dugie."

"Howdy, boys," Dugan said. "Good to see a couple Purple Riders enjoying this spectacular morning."

"Indeed." Michael raised his hand to slap Dugan's. "Once a Rider, always Rider."

Dugan's smile widened as their hands collided.

Gabe stepped forward and shook Dugan's hand. The young deputy was slightly taller than Gabe, about six-two and had developed some muscles since high school. "To what do we owe this audience with one of Dare County's finest?" Gabe asked.

Dugan's expression sobered. "Missing person. Young gal disappeared last night. Been trolling the beach checking with anyone I see." He reached

19

into the front pocket of his shirt and pulled out a photograph. "Name's Julia Hungerman. Either of you see her in the last twenty-four hours?"

"I recognize her," Michael said. "Hard to forget a blonde beauty like that. She was hanging on Tony Trenton's arm the other night at the Lighthouse Sports Bar."

Dugan nodded. "I need to question Trenton. The girl's parents told her to stay away from him. 'Course that made him all the more desirable to her. And you know the Trenton boy. Thinks he's a bad ass and doesn't mind proving it. Once the parents told him to get lost, he kept showing up anyway."

Gabe thought of his conversation with Sonny. "You might want to talk to Sonny Keys. I think he talked to her last night."

"Will do," Dugan said.

"What's your theory, Mr. Deputy?" Michael asked. "Think she and the Trenton boy took off together?"

Dugan shook his head no. "I called the Citgo station. He's scheduled to work later on this morning. I'll stop by and see him."

"She's probably hiding out somewhere," Michael said. "Trying to force her parents to cut her some slack on that leash they got her on."

"I truly hope you're right," Dugan said.

Michael reached and gripped Dugan's elbow. "How 'bout a beer before you go? Got some cold Michelobs in the cooler."

"No sir-ree. I can't drink on duty."

Michael kicked the sand creating a small crater. "Come on, Dugan. For old times sake, just like we used to in high school after the games on Friday nights."

Dugan straightened up and pointed at Michael's four-wheeler. "Is that your vehicle?"

"You know it is," Michael said.

Dugan's eyebrows knotted, and his jaw stiffened. "You really shouldn't be drinking and driving that thing."

Gabe felt uncomfortable seeing Michael press Dugan on what was surely a sensitive law enforcement issue, as if testing their friendship. He wanted to tell Michael to ease up and back off. But it was hard to tell his brother anything.

"Ah, come on, Dugan." Michael stepped back and surveyed the shoreline. "This is October. Very few people around. If I run into anything on my way home, it'll be a beached whale."

That brought a smile back to Dugan's face. "Guess you're right. I'm just saying to be careful and don't drive that ATV intoxicated."

"Believe me. I'm far from intoxicated. Now tonight at some bar in town you might see me intoxicated."

Dugan lifted the bill of his cap slightly, then pulled it tight. "Boys, I hate to break up this hometown reunion, but I've got work to do." He mounted his black Suzuki King Quad and started the engine.

Gabe waved as he pulled away, but Michael belched out the words: Dugie Walton, Texas Ranger.

"Cut him a break, would you, Michael? He's got to do his job."

Michael laughed. "I know. I'm having a little fun with him. Don't you remember back in junior high when he would strut around thinking he was Chuck Norris? Telling everybody he knew karate and his body was a lethal weapon."

Gabe remembered the young, insecure Dugan. His parents had divorced, and his father rarely came around. His karate claims were literally a defense mechanism. He grew out of it, though, and became a pretty good guy in high school.

"Dugan always claimed he'd go into law enforcement," Gabe said.

Michael sat down on his beach chair and picked up his palette and brush. "Right. He said he was going to become an FBI agent like his father. Then we found out his old man was a used car salesman. A Dare county deputy sheriff is a long way from an FBI agent."

"But it's a start," Gabe said. "I admire him."

"You would, Brother Gabriel. You would."

Gabe stared at Michael as he applied thick dabs to the canvas. Why was Michael so jaded? They grew up in the same house with the same mother and father. Maybe it was the car accident six years ago that took their parent's life. Did Michael blame God? The good Lord had blessed Michael with incredible talent, but he never pushed himself, never came close to his potential. Gabe worked hard for everything he accomplished. He possessed something Michael never could grasp—a driving desire to succeed. Maybe he didn't have the talent his brother possessed, but perhaps desire was more precious than talent.

"I've got to go," Gabe said. "Lots to do today."

"Hey, it's Karaoke Night at the Sandbar and Grille. You and the old lady interested?"

"I'll have to check with Marla and get back with you on that one. Take it easy on the Michelob, would you?"

Michael lifted the bottle and drained it. "Take it easy on that run, would you?"

Gabe shook his head and took off.

Gabe had started out at a good pace down the beach in objection to Michael's words and attitude. He refused to take it easy when it came to the things that benefited his life. Running kept him sharp mentally and physically. If only Michael would open his eyes and confront the consequences of his lifestyle. Gabe had hoped to have a positive influence on his brother when he moved to the Outer Banks but never anticipated the frustration Michael caused him. He loved his brother and didn't want to see his health and talents dissipated through indulgent living. Now Gabe's legs grew heavy, his breathing labored. He slowed his pace. *Patience. Michael will come around. Give him time.*

Gabe's frustration moved through him physically, tiring him, upsetting his stomach. As he progressed along the deserted beach the rumbling in his digestive system increased. *Oh no.* A cramp almost doubled him over. *I feel a big crap coming on.* He scanned the beach, looking for a good place to climb the dunes and hunker down in a secluded dip between the mounds of sand. Luckily his route had taken him along the seashore preserve north of Buxton. No one was in sight.

He headed in the direction of a dune with a gradually sloping approach. Climbing it wasn't an easy task. His feet sunk and slid, his leg muscles burning as he struggled to ascend; but with great exertion, he crossed the summit and skidded down the other side. After a quick inspection of his surroundings, he lowered his shorts and briefs and then squatted. Glancing up he saw something sticking out from a thick patch of sea oats about twenty feet in front of him. He blinked. *Is that what I think it is?* A chill cut through him as he focused on the red-painted toenails, foot, ankle, and calf of someone's leg.

Chapter 5

Gabe stood slowly and pulled up his shorts, eyes fixed on the leg. *Please, God, let her be alive.* He tried to detect movement, but only the sea oats waved in the wind. Fear gripped him, spurring him to run like hell, but he controlled the urge. *Get a hold of yourself. She may need your help.* He edged towards the leg, craning his neck to see above the oats. As he angled to his left, the body came into view, a young woman completely nude. It was the girl in the photograph but no longer smiling and attractive. Her blonde hair fanned out from her head, tangled strands snaking through the bent and broken reeds. Her skin had the gray cast of the dead. She stared blankly into the sky, her mouth a gaping hole frozen in the agony of a last gasp. Bluish-purple bruises discolored her neck like an oddly tattooed collar. One arm stuck out akimbo, the hand forming a rigid claw. A gash scored the wrist, and the dark red of dried blood crusted the wound. *Did she slit her wrist?* The gash was wider than the cut a knife or razor would make. Her other arm was tucked awkwardly beneath her, arching her belly.

She had been a beautiful girl with an athletic build, but now her exposed, lifeless body sickened Gabe. He turned away, and his stomach cramped, causing him to wretch. Several dry heaves followed. He was thankful he hadn't eaten breakfast yet. Knowing it was too late to help her, he no longer fought back fear but allowed it to energize his body, to propel him away from that scene. He scrambled up the dune and down the other side towards the beach.

He plowed through the soft sand onto the firmer footing near the water's edge then turned south, increasing his stride. If Michael was still finishing his painting, he could catch a ride back to the apartment complex. Hopefully, Dugan would be there, questioning Sonny. After three minutes of hard running, he spotted Michael about a half mile away. His lungs heaved, not able to take in enough oxygen to keep up with his body's demand. A wave rushed up the slope, and he splashed through it, slowing to a pace he could maintain for a couple more minutes. Now he could see Michael more clearly. His brother was loading his canvas and easel onto the back of the ATV. Gabe wanted to yell but realized his effort would be futile, knowing Michael was more than a quarter mile away. He waved his hands instead, hoping to catch his attention.

As Michael climbed onto the vehicle, Gabe tried to pick up his pace again, but his breathing was out of control. *Damn it, Michael. Look back.* He heard the engine start, muffled by the surf. Now he was only about two hundred yards away. The ATV thrust up the slope, Michael leaning forward. When he turned it towards the lighthouse, Gabe's heart sank into the pit of his stomach. *Didn't see me. He's leaving me behind.* Now Gabe would have to run another mile to get home. He slowed his pace and tried to get control of his breathing. Up ahead something large and round flew into the air, and the ATV's brake lights flashed on. Michael's sombrero had blown off. As his brother sprang off the vehicle to chase his hat, Gabe waved his arms again. *Look up. Look up.*

Michael picked up the sombrero and stared directly at Gabe.

"Wait!" Gabe shouted.

Michael waved.

Gabe picked up speed and yelled again.

Michael positioned the wide-brimmed hat back on his head, slipped the bead up the cord under his chin, and crossed his arms.

By the time Gabe arrived, he was totally exhausted like an Olympic runner expending every ounce of energy to cross the finish line. He staggered to a stop and leaned on his knees. His head spun, and his harsh breathing made it difficult to formulate words. Finally he huffed, "Girl . . .back . . . there."

"Girl?" Michael said. "What girl?"

"Back there . . . . . .found her . . . . . .dead."

"The missing girl? She's dead?"

"Yes." Gabe pointed over Michael's shoulder. "Take me back." He took several deep breaths. "Got to find Dugan Walton."

Michael raised his hand. "Wait a minute. You actually saw her? You found her body?"

Gabe nodded. "About a mile up the shore."

"On the beach? Drowned?"

Gabe shook his head sideways. "On the other side of the dunes." He stumbled to the ATV and climbed onto the seat. "Come on. Take me back."

"I hope you're not hallucinating." Michael mounted the crimson Kawasaki 4 x 4, causing Gabe to back into the folded easel. "Maybe you were on one of those runner's highs, making you see things that aren't there."

"Just get moving. I know what I saw."

Michael started the engine and shifted into drive. Within seconds they were flying down the beach, Gabe's arms wrapped around his brother's substantial belly.

"How close did you get to the body?" Michael yelled over his shoulder, the sides of his sombrero flapping.

"Close enough," Gabe yelled back.

"How'd she die?"

"Don't know. Her wrist had been bleeding, but I don't think she killed herself."

"Why not? People do it all the time."

Gabe thought about it. She had fought with her parents over a boy. They insisted he stay away from her. At eighteen everything gets dramatized, blown out of proportion. Maybe she failed to grasp the inconsequential nature of the circumstances—the fleeting infatuations of youthful romance. Could she have killed herself over a boy she had known less than a week? No way. Why would she strip naked before slicing her wrist? Besides that, it wasn't a slice. More like a gouge. Then Gabe remembered her bruised neck.

"No," Gabe said. "I think . . . I think she was murdered."

"Murdered!" Michael shouted just as they flew over a ridge of sand.

Gabe's stomach rose into his throat as his rear end came off the seat. He held onto his brother tightly as they rumbled over several smaller ridges. Up ahead a few hundred yards he could see the apartment complex.

When they neared the walkway that traversed the dunes, Michael hollered, "Hold on for your life!" Then he swung right, curling the ATV so that they would approach the dunes head on. Michael steered the vehicle to a small gap between mounds, and they charged up and through, becoming momentarily airborne. Gabe's arms ached from clinging so intensely, and his head bounced off his brother's back as they plunged and lurched over the remaining dunes. Finally, they slid to a stop beneath the deck near the entrance to the laundry room.

"Thank God we're here!" Gabe gasped, releasing his hold on his brother. He shifted his weight to his right foot to rise off the seat, hoisted his left leg over the easel and jumped to the ground. For the first few steps his legs felt like linguini. As he headed towards the driveway, his muscles began to function with some coordination. Rounding the corner, he glimpsed Dugan Walton's ATV near the front of the apartment complex.

He made a sharp right at the corner of the front deck and skittered to a stop, almost colliding with Dugan Walton. The deputy studied a small notebook as he slid an ink pen into his breast pocket. Sonny Keys waved from the cab of his blue Ford pickup truck as he pulled out of the driveway onto Old Lighthouse Road.

"Hold on there, partner," Dugan said. "You look like you just stepped out of a hurricane."

"I found her," Gabe said.

Dugan lowered the notebook. "The missing girl? Julia Hungerman?"

Gabe nodded.

"Where is she?"

"Down the beach about two miles."

"Is she okay?"

Gabe glanced into Dugan's mirrored sunglasses, seeing his own reflection. His hair stood straight up from the windy ride, accentuating his shocked mien. He took a deep breath and let it out slowly. "I'm afraid she's dead."

Chapter 6

The ride back to the body was much less harrowing. Michael had removed the canvas and easel, giving Gabe more room on the seat. They drove along the shoreline at a moderate speed, missing the more severe dips and ridges left behind by the receding tide. Dugan followed twenty yards or so behind. Gabe wondered why Dugan didn't contact the sheriff and request a forensic team. Did he doubt Gabe's story? Maybe Dugan thought the girl might still be alive. Gabe pictured the scene in his mind: the leg sticking out of the sea oats, the blank eyes, the gray complexion, the frozen horrified expression. No way could she be alive.

Now Gabe wondered if he should have touched her, shaken her to make sure. The thought repulsed him. He remembered when he was seven years old, finding his cat, Snowball, in the back of his bedroom closet. She wouldn't come out when he called her. Finally, he reached in and grabbed her by the collar. She was stiff, her legs extended and unyielding as if protesting his efforts to pull her out. After dragging her into the light, he noticed her eyes were open yet unseeing, and her mouth was ajar exposing her small, sharp teeth. He shook her, but when she didn't respond, he became frightened. This was his first close encounter with death. His mother told him cats find hiding places when they are ready to die. She wanted him to understand death was a natural process, but that moment of

27

fright when he realized he had touched something dead remained imprinted on his memory.

Gabe looked to his left, studying the rise and fall of the dunes along the wide beach. Would he recognize the place where he climbed over the top? What if he couldn't find it? "Slow down, Michael. We might be getting close."

Michael let up on the gas and pulled away from the shoreline to give Gabe a better look at the dunes. The soft sand gave Gabe the sensation of riding over a mattress. Ahead he saw footprints, more like dips in the sand, leading up a hill that sloped less severely. "I think that's it. Over there." He released his grip on his brother's belly and pointed. "That's where I climbed up to take a crap."

Michael slowed to a stop in front of the slope to which Gabe had pointed. Dugan pulled up beside them, and they cut their engines.

"I think this is it," Gabe said.

Michael stepped off the ATV. "Figured you wanted to walk it from here."

Dugan bobbed his head. "Less chance of disturbing the crime scene." Dugan motioned to the sand hill. "These your footprints?"

"Yes. I'm almost sure that's where I went up."

"Lead the way," Dugan said. "We'll try to follow in your footsteps."

Gabe took his time climbing the slope, planting each foot solidly before proceeding. That terrible sense of dread returned, making his stomach quiver. He forced himself to face the fear, to prepare for the jolt of seeing the lifeless body of that poor girl. This time the surprise element would be gone. Now it was a grim task, one that had to be done for the sake of justice, for the girl's family, and the good of society. Still, Gabe didn't look forward to it.

At the top Gabe pointed down the slope to the left. "That's where I relieved myself. From there I saw the leg."

Halfway down the incline the leg came into view, the red toenails vivid in the sunshine. Gabe stuck his hand to the side, motioning Dugan and Michael to stop. "Over there." He pointed to the right.

"Hold up," Dugan said. "Let me lead. There might be evidence between here and the girl.

Dugan took his time moving towards the body, inspecting every inch of ground. "Look there. The weeds have been trampled. Someone cut across farther up." He stopped and stared in the direction of the tramped sea oats. "I see some clothing—jeans, I think, and panties."

Gabe peered in that direction and saw the blue fabric of the jeans and what appeared to be a pink thong lying nearby. He hadn't noticed them the first time there. When he turned to see Michael's reaction, he noted his brother's solemn face, a rare expression for the usually glib man. Michael wasn't used to confronting death either, Gabe thought.

Dugan moved down the incline until the full body came into view. He cautiously approached it, reached, and gently shoved the knee. Rigid with rigor mortis, the whole body slightly moved. He unsnapped a flap on his belt and withdrew a cell phone from its holder. "You were right, Gabe. She's dead. I'm calling the sheriff."

Gabe wanted to say *I told you so* but fought his prideful attitude, knowing Dugan didn't want to cry wolf to his superiors concerning something as serious as finding the corpse of a missing girl. He remembered back in grade school Dugan often exaggerated various claims in an effort to impress his classmates. Of course, the effect was a loss of credibility. The young lawman had grown up a lot since then. Something must have happened to shape his character, to establish the importance of accuracy and truth in his conduct.

Gabe forced himself to view the girl. Flies buzzed above her face, a few alighting on her lips, cheeks, and forehead. He wanted to rush at them, shoo them away, make them respect the dead. The scene forced him to recognize his own mortality. He too would one day die. What if Marla, the person he loved most in this world, were murdered? The thought made him shudder. He shook his head and fixed his eyes on the marshy land towards the Pamlico Sound.

"Morning, Sheriff," Dugan said into the phone. "Deputy Walton here. Got good news and bad news. We found the Hungerman girl." He bobbed his head, listening. "Yes sir, a friend of mine found her when he was out for a run this morning." He paused again. "The bad news is not too pleasant." He nodded. "That's right. She's dead."

Dugan spent several more minutes talking to the sheriff, pinpointing the location and getting instructions. Then he snapped the phone closed and slid it into the holder on his belt. "Sheriff Johansson wants you to hang out until he and the investigation team arrive. Got some questions for you."

Gabe turned to Michael. He had climbed back up the dune and was looking out to sea. *Doesn't have the stomach to look at the girl either.* "Hey, Michael, do you mind if we stick around until the crime scene people get here?"

29

Michael turned and skidded down the dune to where they stood. "That's fine. My work is done for the day. We can stay as long as you need us."

"Terrible thing, ain't it?" Dugan asked, motioning towards the body. "That some monster would squeeze the life out of a pretty young gal."

Michael glanced at the body and then at his feet. "It must have been horrifying for her."

Dugan took a couple of steps towards the body. "You can see by the bruises the murderer choked her to death."

"Obviously," Michael said.

"Do you think he raped her?" Gabe asked.

"We'll certainly find out," Dugan said. "Hopefully the perpetrator left a DNA sample behind: hair follicle, body fluid. Maybe she dug into him with her fingernails. If we get his DNA, then it's a matter of finding a match."

"Any immediate suspects?" Michael asked.

"I'd say Tony Trenton, the boyfriend. He's been in trouble before. Nothing major—possession of marijuana, drunk driving, roughing up a girlfriend—the kinds of things that could escalate into something like this."

"What information did you get from Sonny Keys?" Gabe asked.

"Sonny saw her last night about 9:00 heading to the beach. Sounded like she opened up to him: told him about the fight she had with her parents over Trenton. Sonny offered to walk with her, but she turned him down. He told me he thought she was real pretty. Seems unlikely that he would do something like this, but you never know. I've got to consider him a suspect too."

"Sonny Keys? Are you kidding?" Michael said. "Come on, Dugan. You've known Sonny as long as I've known him. He's the neighborhood do-gooder."

Dugan placed his hands on his hips. "Murderers don't always fit the evildoers' profile. Sometimes they could be the person you least expect."

Michael said, "Yeah, but Sonny doesn't know how to lie. If he murdered that girl last night, would he be stupid enough to tell you how pretty he thought she was?"

"Everyone knows how to lie, Michael. I don't think Sonny did it, but I can't count him out as a suspect."

Michael spit into the sand. "I'll tell you who you ought to question."

"Who's that?"

"Martin Payne. Right, Gabe?"

Dugan eyed Gabe.

"I forgot to tell you something earlier today." Gabe rubbed his chin. "Last night someone was on our back deck peeping through the window."

"You think it was Martin Payne?"

"I don't know. There's no stair access to our back deck. From the ground you'd have to climb the crossbeams. Payne lives next door. He'd just have to step over a three foot railing that separates our decks."

"Besides that," Michael said, "Payne's a wacko, a real nut-job. Everyone knows what he did to his wife."

"I'll make sure I question Mr. Payne," Dugan said, "but I don't put any stock into rumors. He had his day in court. No strong evidence against him. No witness accused him."

Michael lifted his hands, palms up, as if holding an invisible tray. "That's because the witness was in a coma."

"Good point, but no evidence is no evidence." Dugan turned and peered at the dead girl. "Let's hope we find substantial proof here. If we do, and Payne's the man, he'll get a small room with no view at Central in Raleigh."

"And, hopefully," Michael said, "a big roommate named Bubba."

Sheriff Johansson and the crime scene investigators arrived in a white Chevy Tahoe followed by an ambulance. Gabe, Michael, and Dugan watched them approach from the top of the dune. The vehicles cut across the beach and parked beside the ATVs. Johansson stepped gingerly from the driver's side door and walked with a slight limp towards them. He wore a black ball cap with a gold star embroidered on the front. When he reached the base of the sand hill, he said, "Oh hell. These ol' legs surely'll get tested today." He peered up at them. "Deputy Walton, you got a rope you could throw me? You and your buddies there could tow me to the top."

"No sir," Dugan said. "Old Jim there will have to carry you up."

Johansson glanced to the right. Beside him stood a large man, six three or four, with thick gray hair and a bulbous nose, carrying equipment boxes. "Old Jim's got his hands full."

A muscular blonde woman dressed in black knee-length shorts and a white uniform shirt stepped from behind the big guy. She held a clipboard in one hand and a black case in the other. "Get on my back, Sheriff. I'll haul ya on up."

31

Johansson chuckled. "Jessie Lou, I believe you could. But I'll do my damnedest to make it on my own. You lead the way."

"Follow me, boys," the woman said.

She climbed the slope with ease, the muscles in her legs rippling with each step. Gabe wondered if he should extend his hand to help her to the top, but figured she might take offence. She sported silver-rimmed sunglasses. Her tanned and narrow face was graced with a slightly turned-up nose and full lips. He guessed her age at thirty-five or forty.

A younger man with brown, close-cropped hair and carrying camera equipment came next. Big Jim and Sheriff Johansson took their time but eventually ascended the hill. At the top Johansson turned and eyed the two men at the back of the ambulance. "Just bring up a stretcher and body bag for now, boys."

"Yessir, Sheriff. Be right with ya," one of them said.

The sheriff faced the group. "Okay, Deputy Walton, where's the body?"

"Down the hill about twenty yards, Sheriff."

Johansson held out his hands. "Everybody stay put." Johansson was a rugged looking man with bushy, steel-gray sideburns and eyebrows, deep lines in his forehead and cheeks, and a wide nose with large nostrils. His ample paunch hung over a thin black belt holding up black trousers. "Perry, get some video before we start tramping around too much." The sheriff circled his arm like he was twirling a lasso. "Back, front, sides, everywhere."

The brown-haired guy immediately pulled a hand held video camera out of a shoulder bag. As Dugan introduced Gabe and Michael to the team, the cameraman began filming, working his way around the perimeter of the crime scene.

"Your turn, Mr. Easton," the sheriff said. "Tell us how you found the girl."

Gabe tried to relax, but his heart was thumping into his throat. He had to swallow just to speak. "Well, sir, I was out for my usual morning run when I felt a BM coming on."

"A BM?"

"I'm sorry. A bowel movement. That's what my wife calls it."

"You had to take a shit?"

Gabe nodded.

"That's what my wife calls it." Johansson smiled and Jessie Lou shook her head, her full lips suddenly tight and curling into a smile. "So tell me, Mr. Easton, exactly where were you . . . conducting this movement?"

Gabe felt his face flush. He turned and pointed to the left. "From there I could see the leg sticking out of the sea oats."

"That was quite a place to scare up a tater, eh, Mr. Easton?" Johansson waved his finger through the air in the direction Gabe had indicated. "To be flexing your cheeks twenty-five feet from a corpse?"

Gabe didn't quite know what to think or say.

"Purely coincidence?" The sheriff asked.

Gabe shrugged. "I had to go, so I looked for the easiest approach up over the dunes."

"Makes sense." Johansson raised his eyebrows. "Sounds like someone had the same idea a few hours before you got there." He craned his neck to find the cameraman, who was now filming near the body. "Perry should have plenty of video by now. Okay, Deputy Walton, lead the way."

Dugan shuffled down the slope, careful to remain along the same path they had taken earlier. The team followed close behind, the two ambulance guys trailing. Gabe decided to hang back and observe from a distance. He didn't want to get in their way.

"I'll be over there if you need me," Michael said, thumbing towards the top of the sand hill. "I'd rather watch CSI on television than experience it up close and personal."

"That's fine," Gabe said. "I don't blame you, but I'm going to stick around and try to hear what they have to say."

"Here." Michael handed Gabe a folded piece of notebook paper.

"What's this?"

"Some ideas for that chapter in your novel—the one about the black motorcycle gang. Pretty good stuff if I have to say so myself. It's chicken scratch, though. I jotted it down while you were on your run."

"Thanks, man." Gabe stuck the folded paper into the pocket of his running shorts. "I'll rewrite it into my plot notebook later if I think it'll work."

"Consider it my contribution to your masterpiece." Michael smiled and walked away.

Gabe scooted down the hill to where he could see the team at work. Big Jim unrolled crime scene tape while Perry got out another camera and snapped still photographs of the body. Jessie Lou and Sheriff Johansson pulled on latex gloves and then circled the corpse. Jessie Lou jotted notes onto the clipboard. The sheriff rubbed his chin, the corners of his mouth drooping, deepening the lines in his face as he took in the details. The mood of the crew had definitely sobered—no one joked or smiled.

Sheriff Johansson knelt next to the girl's claw like hand. "My God, O Lord, Almighty." He took a deep breath and let it out audibly. "This poor gal suffered tremendously. Choked to death. Terrible way to go."

Jessie Lou hovered over him. "Look at the laceration on her wrist."

The sheriff wiggled his finger over the crusted blood. "Almost looks like a burn, a deep rope burn."

Jessie Lou walked to the other side of the body. "I've got a feeling, Sheriff, about this other hand. The one tucked under her."

Johansson glanced up and nodded. "I'll heave and you ho." He leaned and placed one hand on the dead girl's shoulder and the other on her hip. While he lifted gently, Jessie Lou bent over and slid the arm from under the body.

Gabe stepped forward to get a closer look. Something dangled from the uncovered wrist—a yellow towrope, the same kind Sonny used to support the sapling. Gabe's mind jumbled with the possibilities. *Sonny? But wait. He told me someone had stolen the rope. Some teenager. Sonny was replacing it.* Gabe pictured Sonny strapping the tree to the post, remembering the efficiency and speed with which he had tied the knot.

"See what happened here, Sheriff?" Jessie Lou asked.

Johansson bobbed his head. "The murderer hogtied her. Probably wanted to rape her. But she wasn't going to spread her legs and make it easy for him."

"Not at all." Jessie Lou lifted the end of the rope. "That's nylon. It'll cut ya good. Bet she severed a ligament or two getting free."

Johansson said, "Make sure you get under every fingernail. Hopefully she clawed him good."

"Will do, Sheriff." Jessie Lou headed towards Gabe, their eyes meeting momentarily, but then she scanned the ground until she spotted the black case she had carried. She crouched and fiddled with the clasps.

Johansson rose to his feet. "Deputy Walton!"

Dugan stood in a patch of sea oats about twenty yards from them. He held a strange shaped object in his hand. "You want me, Sheriff?"

"Come over here. I want to get your two and a half cents."

Dugan took his time, inspecting the ground as he made his way through the scrub. Gabe noted the object he carried looked coiled, almost like a fat snake.

"Take a gander at that rope," Johansson said.

Dugan bent slightly and studied the recently uncovered arm. His bottom lip tensed, thinning.

34

"What do you think so far, Deputy?" Johansson asked. "Give me your best slant on how this killing unfolded."

"I interviewed Sonny Keys this morning. He talked to the girl last night about nine p.m. Sonny said she wanted to be alone, upset about the fight with her parents over Tony Trenton and all."

"So what do you think happened?"

"Well, I think she moseyed on down the beach by herself, but someone followed her. About two miles down the perpetrator rushed her, tied her up, and hauled her over this dune. Wanted to have his way with her. Looks like she broke loose, so he rung her neck."

"We're on the same page, son. You think he went through with the rape?"

Dugan scratched his freckled cheek. "Hard to say. He's a sick hombre. Sick enough to rape a dead girl? Don't know. Maybe he did the deed before she broke free."

"We'll find out." Johansson eyed Jessie Lou as she approached. "You ready to get some samples?"

"That's my job, ain't it?" She said.

"Yes, ma'am, and you certainly do it good."

Dugan held up the coiled object.

"What you got there, Deputy?" the sheriff asked. "Looks like a ram's horn."

Dugan pointed to its base. "Check out the edges. They're frayed. It's been torn off of something."

"What's it made of?"

Dugan rubbed the side of the object. "Feels like papier-mâché."

Johansson touched it. "Papier-mâché?"

"Yeah. Like the papier-mâché masks we used to make in art class."

Chapter 7

Marla had forced herself out of bed and into the shower after Gabe took off on his run. She'd wanted to lie there and dream of the baby she hoped now dwelt inside of her, so small, yet possessing all the necessary chromosomes to develop into the perfect blending of their union. She imagined holding him or her—it didn't matter, the infant nursing at her breast. It had to be. She prayed and pleaded with God that last night was the magic night. It felt so good, the lovemaking, so intense and electrifying. Maybe the incident with the Peeping Tom had made her want Gabe's physical intimacy even more. Rarely had she reached such a level of ecstasy. She was ninety-nine percent sure she had conceived. *Please, God, let it be.* But lying in bed and enjoying the lingering afterglow was not an option. She was due at Buxton Village Books by 9:30 and it was already quarter 'til nine.

She showered quickly, toweled off and stepped up to the mirror. Leaning on the sink, she examined the slight crow's feet around her eyes. It didn't seem fair: not even thirty yet and lines were appearing. Gabe didn't seem to notice. If he did, he wouldn't mention it anyway. He loved her unconditionally. But Marla didn't want to take advantage of her husband's big heart. Knowing Gabe appreciated her body, she kept the pounds off, even firmed up with daily Pilates since they had married three years ago.

She felt attractive and vibrant. Can't stop the wrinkles of time, but I'll do my best to cover them up, she thought as she applied her makeup.

After blow drying and brushing her hair, she stepped into some white capris and funneled into a retro flower-power, sleeveless t-shirt. She snagged her purse, hurried to the front door, and opened it to check the temperature. *No need for a jacket.* She slipped on her favorite thong sandals, stepped onto the deck, and checked to make sure the door was locked.

They had only one car, a red Chevy Cobalt. Gabe walked, jogged, or biked wherever he went. The souvenir shop where he worked was less than a half-mile away, and if he needed the car, he could always hike the mile over to the bookstore to get it. Marla stuck the key in the ignition and turned it. The engine sputtered, giving her an uneasy feeling. After four tries it finally started. Usually it rumbled to life on the first attempt. She turned off the radio, backed out, and proceeded down the access lane, listening to the engine. Something didn't sound right. At the stop sign she turned right onto Old Lighthouse Road and then left onto Route 12. She made it about a half mile when the engine conked out. Fortunately she managed to drift onto the shoulder before stopping. When she tried the ignition, the battery had plenty of juice, but the engine wouldn't kick over. After multiple attempts, the battery struggled to turn the starter.

She stepped out of the car and walked to the front. Facing the hood, she wondered how in the world to open the thing. *Does it matter? I wouldn't know what to do if I did get it open.* A green mini-van sped by. *At least if it were open, people could see I need help.* About a half mile from the bookstore, she considered hoofing it. By the time she got there Gabe would be back from his jog. *I could call him when I get to work, but what about the car? A note. I'll write a note and stick it on the windshield.*

She climbed back into the car and dug into her purse until she found a pen and pad. What to say? How about: *Car broke down. Tow truck on the way. If you need me, please call* . . . As she wrote the words, she heard the sound of a motor getting nearer. She turned to peer out the back window. A black Jeep convertible pulled up behind her driven by a young man with short bleach blond hair. She'd seen him before. Where? The Citgo station a few hundred yards back. He stepped out of the vehicle and walked towards her wearing tight jeans and a blue denim shirt. He leaned against the car door and gazed through the open window at her. She could see his name embroidered in red on the breast of the shirt: *Tony.* He was young, about twenty-one, with muscular arms. He hadn't shaved for a couple days, giving him the Brett Farve look.

"Good morning, pretty lady," he said with a smooth voice. "Having troubles?"

She didn't like the I'm-checking-you-out look in his eyes. She dropped the pen and notepad next to her purse and held her hands near her face so that her wedding ring would be hard to miss. He didn't seem to notice. *Just stay in the car. Think of something to get rid of him.* He thrummed his fingers against the door.

"The car just died," Marla said, "but I'm fine. Help's on the way."

He raised his chin and smiled, a cocksure smile. "I'm a mechanic. Pop the hood. I'll take a look."

"I have no idea how to do that."

"What?" he snorted. "You don't know how to pop the hood?"

"I'm sure there's a button here somewhere, but that's okay. You don't have to . . ."

He yanked the door open and reached for the hood release under the dash, his arm brushing her leg. The strong whiff of cheap aftershave assaulted her nostrils. Before she could voice any protest, he scurried to the front and lifted the hood. Pissed off, she stepped out of the car, juggling words of reproof on her tongue.

"Might be a fuel pump gone bad," he said.

She felt blood rising to the surface of her face. "I told you help's on the way."

He propped the hood with the support rod and stepped back. "Just trying to help, ma'am."

"I appreciate the offer, but I'm fine. Please shut the hood."

He rubbed the stubble on his cheeks. "I know who you are. I've seen you around . . . at the bookstore in town. Moved here a few weeks ago."

Like you actually hang out in bookstores, Marla thought. "Yes, my husband and I live and work here now. Gabe should arrive any minute."

"I can hang out 'til he gets here." His eyes moved up and down her body. "A sweet looking babe like you shouldn't be left alone for long. Too many sex offenders around nowadays."

And you're probably one of them, she thought. Although he was good looking, his presence repulsed her—the same feeling she had last night when she discovered someone had been watching Gabe and her through the bedroom window. Could it have been him? Was he stalking her? "I can take care of myself. Now please leave."

He stepped closer and touched her shoulder. "I love that shirt. Kind of a throw-back, ain't it? Sixties or seventies. Flower power and free love."

"Please, don't touch me." She backed away and edged around the fender towards the door.

He kept pace. "Why are you afraid of me? I don't mean you no harm." He reached and grabbed her shoulder. "Hold on now."

His strong grip startled her, making her suck in a fearful breath. She stared at his hand. The pressure eased, and his fingers slid lightly down her arm.

"There, see. I'm just a friendly Southern boy. You've got nothing to worry about." He grabbed her hand firmly. "Come on back to my Jeep. We'll wait for your husband there."

She tried to pull her hand away, but he held it tight. "Please . . ." She swallowed. "Let me go." She stood fast, but he tugged her towards the Jeep.

"Come on, now. Relax. I'm just looking out for you."

She felt her feet slipping, half-stepping towards his vehicle as he kept her off balance. "No! Don't you understand the word 'no'?"

A small blue pickup truck skidded to a stop beside them on the road. "Is there a problem, Mrs. Easton?" a familiar voice said.

Marla managed to look in the window and see Sonny Keys. "Yes, Sonny. Please help me. This man won't let me go."

Sonny bolted out of the truck and flew around the rear end. "Let her loose, Trenton. Now!" he demanded.

Trenton released her and raised his hands. "What's up with you people? I'm just trying to help her."

Sonny stepped in between them. "She don't need your kind of help. Get lost."

Trenton stuck up his middle finger. "Go screw yourself, you moron."

Sonny's eyes narrowed and face reddened. His hands, at his sides, formed fists. His lower lip trembled slightly before speaking. "I'm gonna count to three," he said deliberately. "If you're not out of here, I guarantee you, I *will* kick your ass."

The cocksure sneer returned. "Yeah, right."

"One." Sonny raised his fist.

The smile instantly faded.

"Two"

Trenton pivoted and walked quickly towards his car.

By the time Sonny said three, Trenton had the engine started. As the Jeep peeled out onto the highway, he shouted, "I'm surprised you can count to three!"

With his hands on his hips, Sonny watched the car disappear around the turn. When he faced Marla, she hugged him, and he patted her back.

"Thank you so much," she said.

"That guy's a real asshole, pardon my Latin."

They stepped back from each other. "He wouldn't leave me alone," Marla said. "I told him not to touch me."

Sonny shook his head. "He's been in trouble before for pickin' on girls. The truth is the gal he's been with this week is missin'. Just talked with Deputy Walton about her. Wouldn't surprise me if he did somethin' real bad with her."

Marla put her hand to her mouth. "Oh my God. Really?"

Sonny bobbed his head.

"I don't know what would've happened if he had gotten me into his Jeep. I'm so glad you showed up. You're my knight in shining armor."

Sonny smiled and glanced at his feet, his face reddening again, his shaved dome glistening with beads of sweat. "Well, Mrs. Easton, how can I help you? I'm not much of a mechanic unless you want your oil changed. Can I give you a ride down the road?"

"That would be great."

"Joe 'the Tow' Sacco is my mechanic. We were on the football team together in high school. He was an all-star kicker. Best engine guy around, and he's got a tow truck to boot. Want to stop by and see him?"

Marla patted Sonny on the shoulder. "Great idea. Let's go."

As Sonny's pickup rumbled onto Route 12, Marla said, "I thought you were actually going to knock Trenton's noggin off."

Sonny smiled. "I don't like fightin', but kickin' the shit out of that boy would have been pure joy, pardon my Latin."

Marla laughed. "You don't like him very much, do you?"

"Nope, nope, nope. He's incorrigible. That's my new word for the week."

"Incorrigible?"

Sonny nodded.

"What's it mean?"

"Incapable of being corrected."

"Very impressive. A man with strong arms and a good vocabulary."

Sonny gave Marla a quick glance. "Don't want to give you the wrong idea. I'm not too smart. Back in school I was in the slow learner class. But I'm a believer in workin' hard on my weaknesses. Every week I learn a new word. I bet a smart gal like you already knew what incorrigible meant."

Marla felt a little embarrassed for playing along. Sonny seemed so open and sincere. "You're right. I read a lot. I did know that word. Sorry."

"No need to be sorry. I like it when people test me on a word."

"But I was somewhat disingenuous, acting like I didn't know."

"Disingenuous—not straightforward or candid. That was one of last month's words."

"Do you remember all the words you learn?"

"Most of them. I try to review. That's one thing Frank Nolan taught me. Review, review, review. He'd say, Sonny, repeat the definition out loud. You'll learn it faster that way. Frank Nolan was my favorite high school teacher."

"You don't seem like a slow learner to me."

"I might not be the smartest puppy in the pound, but I'm not dumb. Back there Trenton called me a moron. That's a terrible thing to call someone, I don't care how slow you are."

Marla sensed a quivering in Sonny's voice, a subtle hint of how words can hurt. "I agree. Usually a person with a poor self-image will put down someone else in an effort to make himself feel better."

"Trenton must have a terrible self-image. A few weeks back at the Sandbar and Grille Restaurant he passed by our table with one of his buddies and said, 'Table for three—an idiot, a moron, and a cripple.' It took every bit of strength I had not to go after him."

Marla noticed Sonny's jaw becoming rigid and his eyes narrowing, possibly reliving the scene in his mind. "Are your friends handicapped?"

"Yeah. Frank's paralyzed from the waist down. Got hurt in a car accident about ten years ago. I grew up with Wyatt. We were in class together. He has some severe learning disabilities, but he gets along fine. The three of us go out a couple nights a week, have some dinner, go bowling, maybe see a movie."

"Do they have jobs?"

"Frank Nolan's a teacher at Cape Hatteras Secondary School."

"Your favorite teacher?"

Sonny nodded. "That's right. And Wyatt gets social security. He lives with his mom. It's important that Wyatt gets out of the house. He and his mom can drive each other nuts."

As Sonny talked about his friends, Marla began to see more deeply into his character. He was a caregiver, a protector of those less fortunate or more vulnerable. His hard-working approach to life also made him an overachiever. Marla admired him. "It's nice that you take care of Wyatt and Frank."

A pickup truck stopped in front of them. Sonny braked his vehicle and raised his hands, as if protesting Marla's comment. "I wouldn't put it that way. I just want my friends to feel like normal human beings. That's why we go out—to do things everyone else does, to meet people and have fun. I'd never try to help Frank into the car. He does it himself. Opens the door, lifts himself in, folds his wheelchair, hauls it in to the back seat. We don't think twice about helping him. Doing it himself makes him feel normal. Independent. That's all handicapped people really want—to feel normal."

Sonny drove for several hundred yards then turned into his mechanic's parking lot. The shop looked like a green metal barn with four garage doors, all of them open. On the right side was a small office with a sign over the entrance, the logo showing a large toe with the words *Joe the Tow Sacco* arced around it. A yellow tow truck sat in the far corner of the lot, rusty and patched.

Joe walked out wearing green coveralls, his name clearly embroidered on the left side of his massive chest. He had a round face, buzz-cut dark hair, and a neatly trimmed black mustache. "Sonny the Keyman Keys!" his low voice boomed, and then he went through the motion of placekicking a football. "How goes it, Keyman?"

"Hey, José. Got some business for you," Sonny said. They stepped out of the pickup and walked to where he stood by the office door. Sonny introduced Marla, and she gave Joe the rundown on the car problem

"I'll head out there and haul her in here within the next half hour or so," Joe said. "Not to worry. Doesn't sound too serious. Let's hope not anyway."

Marla explained that she worked at a shop in town and would call later that afternoon to check on the car. After giving Joe the keys, she and Sonny climbed back in the truck and drove to the bookstore about a half-mile away. Tony Trenton kept appearing in her mind, the snide smile, the ogling, the unwelcome touch. The image kept coinciding with the memory of glass breaking and the realization that someone had violated her and Gabe's privacy. She wanted to call Gabe as soon as possible and tell him about the incident.

Sonny slowed to a stop in front of the bookstore. It looked more like a cottage than a store, light gray with white trim, shutters and neat wood scrolling in the apex of the entrance overhang. A quaint sign hung between two posts in the middle of a patch of holly bushes and hibiscus plants. An American flag waved from a holder attached to one of the posts.

"Well, here we are," Sonny said.

Marla popped open the door. "Thanks again, Sonny. You truly are a great guy."

Sonny glanced at his lap and smiled. "It's too bad what your husband told me."

"About what?"

"Your two big ugly brothers."

Marla laughed. "He's exaggerating. They're not that ugly. Why did he mention my brothers?"

"I was hopin' you had a sister or two. And they'd only have to be half as pretty as you to please me."

Marla felt her face flush. She stepped out of the pickup and shut the door. "You really know how to make a girl's day, Sonny. You really do."

Sonny waved and drove away.

Mee Mee Roberts, the bookstore owner, glanced up from the register at the checkout counter and let out an audible sigh of relief when Marla entered the shop. "Where have you been, Marla May Easton? You're usually here ten minutes early. I called your house a half hour ago. Nobody home." Mee Mee, in her early fifties with sandy blonde hair, peered over wire-rimmed glasses, raising her eyebrows. She was thin and pretty with that wiry look of someone who worked out regularly. The sun coming through the window behind her lit the rows of books with a golden shimmer and set her yellow turtleneck aglow on the edges. Her usual enthusiastic smile and mirthful eyes were now edged with concern.

Marla closed the door. "I'm sorry I'm late."

"Don't worry about that. It's been slow here. Are you all right?"

"I've had a trying morning. My car broke down about a half-mile back." Marla hurried to the counter, set her purse down, and took a deep breath. "I thought I was in big trouble."

"Big car trouble or real life danger?"

"A big time scare." Marla felt fortunate to have a female friend on the Outer Banks to whom she could pour out the ups and downs of life, especially one like Mee Mee, who sincerely cared about her. Mee Mee's insight, wisdom, and warmth made it easy to open up. After last night's intrusion and this morning's drama, Marla needed an attentive ear.

She started with what had most recently frightened her—the encounter with Tony Trenton. Remembering the scene vividly, she covered every detail from the time he pulled up behind her to his hasty getaway. Mee Mee confirmed Sonny's opinion of the scoundrel: Trenton was a bully who took advantage of his good looks to seduce any young gal who was naïve enough to fall for him. He'd grown up in Buxton, a small coastal town where everyone knew each other's business whether they wanted to or not. Familiar with his reputation, Mee Mee recalled several girls over the last couple years who had stepped into his snare. One had even had him arrested for physically mistreating her. Mee Mee told Marla to consider a restraining order against him.

Then Marla recounted Sonny's rescue. She couldn't get over how valiant he had been, without hesitation rushing to her side to protect her. His overachieving attitude and honest and open approach to life amazed her. Mee Mee didn't know Sonny well but had only heard good things about him.

Finally she related last night's episode with the Peeping Tom. At first she felt hesitant to share how the intruder's invasion interrupted her and Gabe's lovemaking, but over the last five weeks Mee Mee had won her trust. Once she had started the story, her reservations disappeared.

"So you think Trenton was the pervert on your back deck last night?" Mee Mee asked.

"I'm not sure. He's definitely a prime suspect. Sonny told me Trenton's most recent girlfriend is now missing. Maybe he does have criminal tendencies."

Mee Mee leaned on her elbows, hands positioned under her chin. "Any other suspects?"

Marla shrugged, tilting her head. "There's our next door neighbor."

"Mr. Payne?"

"Yes. I feel very uncomfortable around him. Do you know much about him?"

Mee Mee sat back and clasped her hands behind her head. "Payne's a strange one. He and his wife, Loretta, were history professors at the community college in Manteo. Of course, he still is, but his wife is in a coma at the Outer Banks Hospital in Nags Head."

"Gabe's brother, Michael, claims that Payne put her there."

Mee Mee nodded. "A lot of people think that's true. They were arguing publicly that day. Some people thought Loretta was having an affair. No one knows for sure. They had walked to the top of the lighthouse, a regular trek for them. Then he came storming down all 282 steps shouting that his wife needed help. He claimed she'd fallen down the top flight of stairs to the landing. A lot of people believe he knocked her down those steps. But there were no witnesses. No proof. The authorities had to let him go."

"I can see why people think he did it," Marla said. "He seems distant, cold-hearted. Our back deck doesn't have stair access to the ground level. All he would have to do is step over the railing that divides our side from his."

"I'm not sure what to think about that possibility. I've known Martin Payne for about five years. He's a regular customer. For most of those years he seemed like a normal guy. Then the rumors started about his wife and other men."

"More than one affair?"

Mee Mee nodded. "She was seen with a series of different men at different places. But the relationships could have been platonic. You know how people spin tales. It just seemed unusual. At that same time Payne's personality changed. Usually when he entered the store, we greeted each other and talked about the weather or the latest book he'd read. Once the rumors started he seemed unapproachable, as if something was weighing upon him, and the last thing he wanted was to interact with another human being. This odd temperament intensified with Loretta's unfortunate fall. But he still comes in here regularly and orders the strangest books."

"What kind of books?" Marla asked.

Mee Mee looked beyond Marla to the door, her jaw dropping. "Speak of the devil."

Marla glanced over her shoulder to see Martin Payne mounting the steps to the store entrance. He opened the door and entered, his features strained with a sense of great vexation.

"Good morning, Mr. Payne," Mee Mee said.

He glared at them as if trying to see through a fog. "Did the books I ordered come in yet?"

"Yes sirree, they did. Yesterday afternoon. I have them right here under the counter."

Payne inspected the rows of bookshelves to his left then right.

"Can I help you find something?" Mee Mee asked.

"I think by now I know my way around this bookstore." He turned left and marched to the back, veering down the aisle marked History.

Marla met Mee Mee's gaze, seeing the same trepidation in her eyes that Marla felt. Mee Mee stood, reached under the counter, pulled out two books, and set them near the register, close enough for Marla to see. Then she waved her finger at the books, a gesture Marla took as a prompting to check them out. The title of the top one was easy to read: *Jack the Ripper's*

Copycat Killers. The cover featured a gleaming knife and blood splatters. The subject matter repulsed her, but knowing Payne was a history teacher, she considered the work to be related to his realm of expertise. She looked up to make sure Payne wasn't coming and then nudged the top book until she could see the second title. This one, *Walk-ins—the Real Body Snatchers,* struck her as eerie.

She heard footsteps and knew Payne was approaching. She sidled towards the mystery section to get out of his way and pretended to rearrange several of the novels. Payne placed a book on the counter and reached for his wallet. Marla craned her neck to see around him but couldn't make out the title. The thought that the man standing near her might have been the one watching her and Gabe last night agitated her. If she made eye contact with him, maybe a hint of guilt could be discerned by any subtle change in his expression. He paid for the books, waited for Mee Mee to bag them, thanked her, then turned, almost colliding with Marla.

"Good morning, Mr. Payne," Marla said, studying his face.

"Excuse me," he said, not looking at her at first. When he did meet her gaze, a flash of recognition entered his eyes. "Miss . . . I mean Mrs. Easton. Good morning." He glanced around the shop. "Do you work here?"

"Yes. Been here more than a month."

He nodded, that look of irritation momentarily fading. "It's been about that long since I've been here. Well . . . I guess I'll see you at the apartments."

Marla tried to smile but didn't know if her effort appeared genuine. "Yes. I'll see you around."

Payne nodded and smiled, an odd uncomfortable smile, then left the store.

"Well, I'll be a fool at a funeral," Mee Mee said. "That's the first light I've seen in his eyes in more than a year. Shows you what a young pretty face can do to a man."

Marla approached the counter. "I won't take credit for that, but he did seem affected by me, as if he were glad to see me. I'm not so sure that's a good thing."

"You think he's been spying on you?"

Marla shook her head. "I don't know what to think any more. It might have been him at our window last night."

Mee Mee touched Marla's hand. "Did you see those books he bought today?"

"The first two. What was the title of the third?"

"*Nineteenth Century London's Ghosts.*"

"Hmmmm." Marla rubbed her chin. "Makes sense. You said he's a history teacher. Even the gory book about Jack the Ripper wouldn't be considered unusual for someone like him. But that third one freaked me out—the one about the body snatchers."

Mee Mee sat straight up in her chair, her eyes widening behind her wire rims. "That was the one about walk-ins."

"What are walk-ins?"

"He's ordered several books on the subject. I've glanced through them. A walk-in is a person whose soul has been taken over by a disembodied spirit."

Marla raised her shoulders. "That's a little spooky. Why would he be reading about walk-ins?"

Mee Mee glanced at the ceiling, eyebrows knotting, and then met Marla's gaze. "Because of his wife. She's brain dead." Mee Mee fluttered her fingers through the air. "But her spirit is trapped in the realm of the living. Maybe she's looking for a body to possess."

Marla pictured Payne's usual expression, distressed and antagonized. Did he feel oppressed by her? Perhaps guilty? "So you think her spirit is tormenting him? Maybe getting revenge for pushing her down the lighthouse steps?"

"I don't know that much about the spirit world. But for some reason he won't let her go. He refuses to pull the plug."

Chapter 8

Waiting for their sandwiches, Gabe and Michael sat at a table near the big screen television at the Lighthouse Sports Bar. Sunshine poured in from a cupola's windows above them, casting the shadow of a ceiling fan across their table. ESPN commentators were previewing the upcoming NFL games, but Gabe, even though he enjoyed pro football, couldn't concentrate on their banter. That morning's events kept replaying in his mind: finding the dead girl and hearing the conversations of the investigators. With all the excitement, he had to skip his chores and miss out on his usual writing time, two hours in front of the computer screen slowly pecking away at his novel. That creative zone would have been too difficult to enter today. He needed his brother's company.

Michael stared at the TV, a bottle of beer in his hand. "Steelers play the Ravens on Sunday. Should be a bloodbath. You coming over to watch?"

"What?" Gabe had heard the words but his mind had been on the wrong track to respond with coherency. "Oh, yeah. The Steelers. We'll see. I don't know what Marla has planned."

"Geesh, Gabe, do you have to check with Marla on every move you make? You might as well keep your dingleberries in a box at home and give her the key."

Gabe sipped his iced tea. "She's a priority in my life. You're single. One of these days you'll understand when the right girl comes along."

"Not if I can help it. Bachelorhood suits me. I do what I want to do when I want to do it."

"When you love someone it's not me, myself, and I anymore. You learn to become one with another person."

Michael waved his hand. "You've been watching too much *Oprah.*"

"Besides that, I'm worried about her."

"Because of the Peeping Tom?"

Gabe fingered the condensation on the outside of his glass. "The Peeping Tom, the murdered girl, and something else that happened to her on the way to work today. She called just before we left."

"What happened?"

"The car broke down, and Tony Trenton stopped and gave her a hard time. Acted like he wanted to help, but Marla's sure he was trying to make a move on her. Luckily, Sonny Keys came along and scared him off."

Michael slapped the table. "The Keyman to the rescue. You know, he's a helluva guy. You may not have to worry about that Trenton boy for long if they pin the murder on him."

"Trenton's the obvious suspect for sure, but don't forget about Martin Payne. He came in the bookstore this morning and actually spoke to Marla. She said he looked her in the eyes and went from scowling to smiling, as if she had some kind of mood-swing power over him."

Michael gulped down the last of his beer and set the bottle in front of him. "Interesting. Here's my take on it: Trenton's a bully; you've got to protect your women when he's around. But Payne's the real psychotic. When a nut-job like Payne loses it, anything can happen."

Smiling coyly, the waitress, a pixie-cut blonde, approached the table with their food. She wore a pink sleeveless top and snug jeans. Michael's attention immediately riveted to her generous cleavage. He reminded Gabe of a Labrador Retriever waiting to be tossed a bone. Talk about mood swing, Gabe thought.

"Ah, the beautiful Mona Lisa has arrived. What a mysterious smile you have, young lady," Michael said theatrically.

Gabe noticed "Lisa" on her nametag. She held the tray at a slight angle, balancing the two uneven plates. She delivered Gabe's first, turkey on rye with a few onion rings. Feigning great strain, she lowered Michael's foot-long Philly-beef-and-cheese sub with fries and coleslaw.

After setting the platter down she said, "Whew. Glad I've been pumping iron. That's quite a load."

Michael's grin widened. "May I say I'm quite impressed with your . . . gazongas. That's Spanish for biceps."

Lisa stuck her hand on her hip. "I know what gazongas are, Michael. I may be blonde, but I'm not stupid. What I want to know is why you have twice the food on your plate than your buddy here."

Michael held out his hands, imploringly. "Obviously, I'm twice the man."

"Oh, I agree," Lisa said, winking at Gabe, "literally you are twice the man. Can I get you boys anything else right now?"

Michael raised his finger. "Another Michelob for me please. Brother Gabriel, anything for you?"

"I'm fine," Gabe said.

Lisa shook her head, eyes fixed on Gabe. "He's your brother?"

Gabe nodded.

"My twin brother," Michael said.

She compared their faces. "Now that you mention it, you do look exactly alike, except Michael is . . ." Her mouth twisted as her eyes narrowed.

Michael's hands seesawed in front of him. "Robust? Brawny? Strapping?"

"No. More like super-sized." She slapped Michael's shoulder, pivoted, and sauntered away, hips swaying.

Michael raised an eyebrow. "Now that is one hot honey muffin."

"Would it be too much to ask for you to keep your tongue in your mouth when she's serving us?"

Michael had already picked up half of his Philly sub, cramming it into his mouth.

Gabe snagged an onion ring. "I guess there's not much we can do about Trenton or Payne. Better let the law handle things."

Michael, talking with one cheek stuffed, said, "You're wrong, dear brother. There's something we can definitely do."

A red light flashed on the control panel of Gabe's mind. Michael could come up with some outrageous schemes. Gabe preferred the conservative approach to problem solving—think it through and make wise decisions. His brother thrived on impulse.

Michael swallowed and swiped his mouth with his napkin. "Listen to this. We get in my car and head over to the Citgo station, pull right up into the garage. I've got a Smith and Wesson thrity-eight special in my glove compartment. He comes over to ask what we want and I aim my piece at

50

his pecker and say, 'Mess with Marla Easton again and you'll be minus two cobblers.'"

"Where do you come up with these things? And I'm sure you don't have a thirty-eight special in your glove compartment."

Michael leaned forward. "Are you really that sure?"

Gabe reconsidered, studying Michael's eyes. "You really do have a gun in your car, don't you?"

"Damn straight I do." He tapped his finger on the table. "And I'll make sure Tony Trenton knows I have one too. Now, what do we do about Martin Payne?"

Gabe didn't want to create unnecessary enmity with Payne, knowing he lived next door. "Hey. Don't do me any favors with Payne. As of now, we have nothing on him. He could be totally innocent."

Michael pointed at Gabe. "That's what we need to discover. Why does he walk around like a constipated wolverine? What's he hiding?"

"Why are you so convinced he tried to kill his wife?"

Michael sat back and popped a fry in his mouth. "Two summers ago Payne's wife, Loretta, informed me she was giving a series of lectures on Greek gods. You know me. I've always been interested in mythology, so I signed up for the class. She offered to drive since she had to make the trip anyway. It's about an hour from here to the community college in Manteo. We got to know each other well, became pretty good friends. Payne didn't like it at all. One hot night I was out on the back deck, enjoying the breeze. I could hear them arguing in the apartment below. It got quite heated. He accused her of having an affair with me."

Michael leaned forward to pick up a handful of fries. Gabe examined his face, thinking he wouldn't put a fling with an older woman past his brother.

After gobbling the fries Michael said, "Of course, she denied it. The arguments continued the rest of that summer like clockwork. Several times he threatened to kill her. I tried to keep my ear attuned whenever the fights erupted, just in case Payne did something rash. He never got violent in the apartment. That never happened 'til early September at the lighthouse. Unfortunately, I wasn't around on that occasion, but I swear to you, Gabe, he knocked her down those lighthouse steps. I know it like a sailor smells a hurricane."

Gabe folded his hands in front of him. "I'm going to ask you a question, and I want you to tell me the truth. Did you have an affair with Payne's wife?"

"Geesh, Gabe, she was almost twenty years older than me. What kind of guy do you think I am?"

To Gabe's right the front door opened and Sonny Keys ambled in.

"The Keyman's here!" Michael said. "Sonny, come over here and have a seat. My brother wants to buy you lunch."

Sonny glanced up, his tanned dome catching a ray of sunshine from the cupola window. He waved and headed in their direction with a gleaming smile.

Gabe stood and extended his hand to Sonny before he could sit down. "You are the man of the hour, Sonny. My wife told me all about your courageous intervention on her behalf. You sent that bum Trenton packing like a rump-shot jackass out of the carrot patch."

Sonny gripped his hand tightly. "I don't have much tolerance for shit heads who pick on nice ladies. Pardon my Latin."

Gabe pulled out a chair. "Have a seat, my friend. Lunch is on me."

Sonny sat down just as Lisa returned with Michael's beer. Sonny ordered a burger with everything and a salad. Gabe instructed her to put it on his bill then gave Lisa a condensed version of Sonny's heroics.

"That calls for a beer on the house," Lisa said.

"Better make it a Coke," Sonny said, shaking his head. "I don't like myself when I drink."

"What's not to like?" Michael said, patting him on the back. "One beer won't hurt you."

Sonny held up his hand. "Better not."

"If the man doesn't want to drink, so be it," Gabe said.

"I'll be back with your Coke in a jiff." Lisa twirled and headed towards the kitchen.

"Listen, Sonny," Michael said, "You've been around even longer than me. Don't you agree that Martin Payne is a total lunatic?"

Sonny bobbed his head. "He is a little flaky."

"Do you think he's nuts enough to kill someone?" Gabe asked.

Sonny shrugged. "That's a tough one considerin' what happened to his wife. Not that I'm convinced he tried to kill her, mind you. But it is possible. The whole incident was awful suspicious."

"See what I mean?" Michael said. "Even Sonny, the nicest guy in town, thinks it's possible."

"Well . . ." Sonny eyed Michael and then Gabe. "There's somethin' else I know about Payne that's really strange."

Michael leaned forward, jarring the table with his belly. "Something that might incriminate him?"

52

Sonny appeared disconcerted as if the conversation had made a wrong turn, his eyes wary and mouth unusually stern. "I haven't told this to anyone before."

"Better to get it off your chest then," Michael said. "You can trust us."

Lisa delivered Sonny's Coke to the table. He smiled and thanked her but waited until she left before he continued. "'Course you know I live directly above Payne. Sometimes when I'm standin' near the return air register in the kitchen I can hear voices."

"Voices?" Michael said. "He never has any visitors."

"That's what so weird. He'll talk for a while as if someone is sittin' there listenin' to him. Then I'll hear a lady's voice answerin' him."

"A lady's voice?" Gabe said. "Maybe he has a girlfriend on the side you don't know about, Michael."

Sonny glanced around the bar and then lowered his head. Speaking in almost a whisper he said, "It's Loretta."

"Get out of here," Michael said.

Sonny nodded, eyes moving from Michael to Gabe. "I swear the woman sounds exactly like his wife. I know it can't be, but that's who it sounds like."

"What kind of things do they talk about?" Gabe asked.

"He'll say somethin' like, 'Honey, I'm sorry this happened. I wish I could take it all back.' And she'll say, 'You can't change the past. I just want to be free. Let me go.' I've even heard him use his wife's name. He'll say, 'Loretta, I can't let you go. Please don't ask me to do that.' And then she'll plead with him. I know he's mimickin' his wife's voice, but it still gives me the heebie-jeebies."

Michael pounded the table, making the silverware jump. "You see what I mean, Gabe. The guy is off the chart of the normal bell curve. What if he got into a murderous mood again last night and followed that teenage girl down the beach?"

The thought of a maniac living next door, spying on Marla and him, perhaps about to slip off the balance beam again and commit an egregious crime sent a wave of cold prickles over him. He crossed his arms and drew in a measured breath. "But there's nothing we can do about it."

"The hell there's not," Michael said.

"What?" Gabe said. "Call the sheriff and tell him that Payne talks to his brain dead wife, and sometimes she answers him back?"

"No." Michael stabbed his finger into his coleslaw. "We break into his house when he's not there and find evidence. If he killed that girl last

53

night, there's got to be some shred, some clue, some sliver of evidence in that apartment."

Gabe glanced at his watch. He was due at the souvenir shop in twenty minutes. Michael's crazy notions were beginning to chafe his already stressed mental state. Having an out offered some relief. "I'd gladly help you break into Payne's apartment and perform a full investigation, but I have responsibilities to attend to—it's called a job."

"We don't have to break into Payne's apartment," Sonny said, his face beaming.

"What do you mean?" Michael asked.

Sonny pulled a ring of keys out of his pocket. "Mr. Payne insisted that I repair a leaky pipe under his kitchen sink this afternoon."

"Boys, I'm not sure about this," Gabe said.

"It's perfect," Michael said. "You go to work, Gabe. Don't worry about a thing. Sonny and I will handle this.

Chapter 9

Armed with a cell phone, digital camera, toolbox, and master key, Sonny Keys turned the lock and entered Martin Payne's apartment. He knew the layout well, the same as his apartment one floor above. The front door opened into a large combination room, the kitchen, dining, and living areas separated only by the arrangement of furniture. To his left stood the refrigerator followed by a small counter space then the stove. Straight ahead was the dining room table, covered with a sand-colored tablecloth with several whelk shells stacked in a bowl in the middle. Beyond the table sat a crimson loveseat facing the opposite wall where a small television perched on a stand next to a window offering a view of the ocean. A matching couch sat against the right wall. A large bookshelf filled most of the space on the other side with a leather recliner, and reading lamp nearby. Sonny turned left and headed to the sink to deposit his toolbox.

He opened the cupboard under the sink and noticed a bucket catching a steady drip from one of the feeder lines. Quickly he undid the clasp on his toolbox and laid out several wrenches and fittings on the floor. Then he stood, reached into the pocket of his baggy green workpants and retrieved a digital camera. Peering out the window above the kitchen sink, he could see down the access lane clear to Old Lighthouse Road. No cars. *If Mr. Payne went to see his wife at the Outer Banks Hospital in Nags Head, then I've got all the time in the world.* Sonny took a deep breath. *But if he's on his way home from town then I'm out on Shit Bay in a leaky skiff without a sail.* He dug into his pants pocket, clasped the cell phone, pulled it out, and flipped it open to make sure it had plenty of power. *Michael, you better be out there on guard duty and not taking a beer break.* He slipped the phone back into his pocket. *Guess I'll start here and work my way around the kitchen.*

He stepped back, facing the refrigerator and stove, and snapped the first photograph, the flash blazing the surfaces of the appliances. He pivoted to his left and noticed a large framed poster of the Cape Hatteras Lighthouse. On the balcony a medium built woman stood and waved, long black hair blowing in the wind. He zoomed in and took the photo. On closer inspection he guessed the woman to be Loretta Payne, although the distance made it difficult to be positive. Sonny remembered how she used to flirt with him, always wanting to rub his shaved head for good luck. He didn't mind. She was pretty for a middle-aged lady, but not his type. Besides, he'd never go after a married woman. Then he envisioned Marla Easton's face. A pang of guilt edged through him. *No. Not even her. I couldn't do that to a good guy like Gabe. Besides, Marla doesn't think of me like that.* He moved on, trying to force her attractiveness out of his mind.

A large oil painting of two wild horses walking along the beach hung on the wall in the middle of that side of the room. The artist had used thick strokes of color and texture on the waves and had captured the forms of the horses beautifully. Sonny reminded himself he didn't have time to admire good art and snapped the picture. He proceeded around the walls of the living room area, photographing the sofa, loveseat, television and spectacular view of the dunes and ocean out the back window. He saw nothing unusual, nothing suspicious, nothing he could possibly conceive to be used as evidence in solving a murder.

Then he came to the bookshelf by the leather recliner. He counted six rows and tried to get several good pictures, ones sharp enough to make out the titles. If Payne was responsible for the girl's murder, perhaps some of the books influenced him in some sick way. Most of them were history books, a whole section on England and the Middle Ages. One row held an extensive collection of World War Two biographies—Churchill, FDR, Patton, Eisenhower, Montgomery, MacArthur, and Hitler. Another row seemed out of place with titles like *Talking to the Dead, Walk-ins and the Spirit World, Conducting a Séance,* and *When the Departed Return.* Sonny recalled the times he'd heard Payne speaking with his wife's voice, and a prickly sensation ascended his spine. He wondered if the books had something to do with it. *That man is creepier than a shoebox full of tarantulas.*

At the end of this row Sonny found a large scrapbook. He pulled it out and examined the cover. "Our Life Through the Years" had been hand printed on it in a flowing, calligraphic style, probably with a permanent marker. The image on the front depicted a beach with a cliff rising up from the sand. A tall tan lighthouse was perched on the edge of the cliff as several seagulls floated through a blue sky patched with wispy clouds. Sonny photographed the cover then turned to the first page.

A large picture of a young Loretta and Martin posing with arms around each other took up most of the space. They leaned against a black railing with a blue sky and the ocean as a backdrop. Loretta's youthful beauty stirred Sonny, her long black hair, green eyes, bright red lips, and lean but curvy body. She wore a tight black tank top and pink shorts. Martin definitely looked older than she, maybe six or seven years, but his hair had no gray streaks like it did now. Below the picture someone had written: *July 2nd, 1985—Our first time on the gallery of the Cape Hatteras Lighthouse.* Sonny clicked the camera and turned the page. He quickly worked his way through the scrapbook photographing a few images he thought might be significant. Every few pages he noticed another picture from the top of the lighthouse. He reasoned this was their favorite spot, perhaps the place they came back to every summer to capture that nostalgic feeling on film. Eventually they must have moved to the Outer Banks to live in the surroundings they cherished. The lighthouse photos revealed the toll time had taken on their faces and bodies. In the last one Mr. Payne especially appeared weathered with gray streaks in his hair and an added forty or more pounds to his waistline. Loretta remained trim, but her face acquired the wrinkles of a woman in her late forties who spent a lot of time in the sun.

At the end of the scrapbook Sonny found a folded newspaper clipping of Loretta's tragic tumble. The headline read: *Local College Professor in Coma After Fall.* Her picture, a head and shoulders shot, appeared to the left of the article. Sonny skimmed the story to see if he could find any mention of accusations directed at Martin Payne. When he unfolded it to read the bottom half, a piece of paper fell out and floated to the floor. It looked like a page torn from a book. He picked it up and read it:

> *It is most helpful when contacting a departed*
> *loved one to secure a common item, something*
> *that intimately connected you to the deceased,*
> *for example an article of clothing,*
> *photographs, or a cherished handwritten*

Sonny stared at the scrapbook. *This is what Mr. Payne uses to bring his wife back.* His hand trembled, and the page slipped from between his fingers and drifted to the floor. This is bullshit, he kept telling himself, but the scrapbook felt energized as if it were some kind of conductor. He placed it on the floor then carefully spread the article next to it and adjusted the zoom on the camera to get the best picture. After clicking the photo he picked up the torn-out page and put it on the newspaper, folded the article, placed it back in the scrapbook, and slid the scrapbook into its slot on the end of the shelf. His nerves had tightened like a twisted beach towel, but he felt glad to be done with the photo album.

He walked to the window above the sink and peered down the access lane to Old Lighthouse Road. Still no cars. The last thing he wanted was to get caught snooping around Mr. Payne's apartment. He brushed the outside of his pants pocket and felt the cell phone. *Don't let me down, Michael.* Hopefully he had time to investigate the two bedrooms and bathroom. *This detective work is exciting, but I don't know if my stomach could take more than a day of it. I'll stick to maintenance.* He glanced across the room and noticed the two bedroom doors. *Better get it over with.*

He decided to enter the bedroom nearest the kitchen first. The queen bed was unmade, the covers and sheets whirled into a heap. Boxer shorts and several pairs of dark socks were scattered here and there on the floor. *This must be where Payne sleeps.* Systematically he worked his way around the border taking pictures. He opened the closet and carefully inspected it, thinking it may be a good place to hide evidence. But he didn't see anything odd—shirts, pants, and suits hanging on the rod and sweaters folded awkwardly and stacked on the shelf above. Various types of shoes were scattered across the floor. He clicked the camera a couple of times and moved on.

He entered the bathroom via the bedroom. The first thing he noticed was a yellow towrope strung above the tub with a couple of towels, a swimming suit, and a washrag hanging on it. Mr. Payne had approached him about two years ago, asking for some kind of cord to be used for drying things. He remembered giving him more cord than what hung there but guessed that he must have used the rest for other purposes. Sonny snapped the picture of the rope. Next he opened the medicine cabinet and captured an image of its contents. With a couple more flashes of the camera he completed his tour of the bathroom.

The spare bedroom also had access to the same bathroom. When he entered and smelled stale air, he figured Payne rarely used it. He walked to the window, peered out onto the back deck, and then focused on the ocean beyond the dunes. The air seemed suffocating, and the temptation needled him to open the window, but he knew that would be a mistake. He took a quick picture of the view then turned to inspect the rest of the room.

The queen size bed had a shiny black bedspread and pink pillows. Sonny wondered if Payne and his wife had slept in separate bedrooms. On the wall above the bed hung four odd looking masks. Between the third and fourth mask he noticed a blank space where a fifth mask had been removed. Over time, the morning sun shining through the window had faded the paint on the wall creating a stencil of the missing mask, its shape slightly darker. Sonny guessed the shape to be some kind of animal or half-human because its edge revealed two curving horns.

The one in the middle appeared to be a king with thick curly hair and beard, wearing a crown. The eyebrows formed a V over black eye holes, and a wide nose led to a mustache that framed an angry mouth. To the left was his queen, her rippling hair parted in the middle below a similar golden crown. Then came one Sonny recognized from a movie he'd seen when he was a kid—Medusa, the woman with snakes for hair. He was glad the mask had holes instead of eyes, remembering how she had turned people into stone with her stare.

The final mask on the far right resembled a devil with a large nose, wide grin, and pointed ears. Leaves rimmed the top of the head where two stubby horns protruded. To Sonny it was the most grotesque of the group. No way would that thing ever hang above my bed, he thought. Ever since watching *The Exorcist* years ago, he feared the possibility of being possessed by a demon. As he gazed at the mocking face, his upper body tensed and shuttered. The sudden anxiety spurred him to finish his investigation. He took a quick photo of each mask and the empty space of the missing one, then stepped back to get all of them in one shot.

As he turned to exit the bedroom his cell phone rang. He almost dropped the camera. His hand shot into the deep pocket and fished out the phone. He flipped it open, raised it to his ear and said, "Yes."

"He's coming," Michael said. "The car's about fifty yards away."

Sonny snapped the phone shut and dropped it into his pocket followed by the digital camera. He opened the bedroom door and stepped into the living room, thinking he needed to stay low in case Payne spied him through the windows. He crouched and walked around the couch to the dining room table where he dropped to the floor and crawled to the sink.

Hands as fast as a gunslinger, he located his flashlight and positioned it under the sink at an angle to illuminate the pipes. He shut off the water valves and slid the bucket to the side. The sound of his own rapid breathing and the thumping of his heart reminded him to get control and try to appear as normal as possible. He took deeper breaths in an effort to relax. When he picked up a crescent wrench and ducked his head under the sink, he heard the front door open, followed by two steps, and a loud clamor at his feet.

What the hell? Sonny eased out from under the sink to see Payne standing near the door with a heap of groceries on the floor. "Are you all right?" Sonny asked.

"Mr. Keys," Payne gasped. "It's only you."

"Sure it's me. Told you I'd fix the leak this afternoon."

Payne looked pale, his hands in front of him, fingers spread and frozen.

Sonny forced a smile. "Didn't mean to make you drop your groceries. Think I was a ghost?"

"I don't know what I thought." Payne glanced at the split paper bag at his feet overflowing with cans and vegetables. "I wasn't expecting to see someone."

"Need help pickin' those up?"

Payne shook his head. "No. Keep working. No harm done here. I'll put them away." He dropped to his knees and began picking up the groceries, cradling them in his other arm.

Sonny crawled back under the sink and organized his thoughts. *Get the damn leak fixed and get out of here.* He adjusted the crescent wrench and loosened the compression fitting to the cold-water feeder line. *Who did he think I was? His wife?* While he worked, he heard Payne walking around the kitchen opening the refrigerator and various cupboard doors. Sonny kept thinking about the scrapbook, trying to remember if he put it back exactly where he'd found it. Payne's footsteps exited the kitchen. Sonny heard a door open and guessed Payne entered his bedroom. He backed out of the cabinet and searched in his toolbox for the right length feeder line.

He heard the bedroom door open again, a few footsteps, several moments of silence, and then Payne saying, "What the hell?"

Oh no, Sonny thought, I must have put that scrapbook back upside down or moved something I shouldn't have. His hands trembled as he tried to get a good grip on the fitting. He crawled back into the sink cabinet and steadied himself, focusing on the task in front of him. Finally, the compression nut settled onto the thread of the valve, and he finger-tightened it. As he reached for the wrench, he heard Payne walk towards him across the kitchen and stop within a few feet. A prickly feeling like a tarantula crawling up his back froze him. He held his breath and listened to Payne breathing heavily, as if he were trying to control his temper.

"Mr. Keys," Payne said harshly.

Sonny slowly backed out from under the sink and peered up.

Payne's furrowed brow and dark eyes sent a piercing jolt through him. "Y-yes sir, Mr. Payne." He swallowed, trying not to stammer, trying not to look guilty. "Is something wrong?"

The corners of Payne's mouth twitched slightly before he spoke. "My wife's bedroom door was ajar. There's something missing. Did you go in there?"

Chapter 10

Marla and Gabe mounted the steps to the second floor of the Sandbar and Grille Restaurant. The wonderful smell of freshly baked pizza wafted up from the pizzeria on the first floor. She would have been happy to pick up a large pepperoni and head home after the day she had, but Gabe insisted they eat dinner with Michael. Gabe was in the mood for seafood and wanted to know what happened with Michael's scheme to send Sonny into Payne's apartment earlier that day to find evidence. Marla had to admit she was curious too.

The restaurant had a wonderful atmosphere and good food, lots of fishing nets and gear suspended on the walls and ceiling to give patrons that fresh-out-of-the ocean expectation of the meals coming their way. Michael, sitting by himself at a table for four in the back, stood and waved. The place was crowded and a little festive, not unusual for a Friday karaoke night. Marla and Gabe took their time navigating the maze of packed tables to get across the spacious room. Two empty beer bottles sat in front of Michael as he chugged a third. He sat the empty bottle down next to a manila envelope and tried to stifle a burp with little success.

"'Scuse me," Michael said. "Never gulp too fast on an empty stomach. The carbonation joins forces and riots."

"You've already drunk three beers?" Gabe asked.

"I've been here since 7:30, brother Gabriel. That's one every fifteen minutes. I'm a little behind my usual pace."

Gabe pulled out the chair next to Michael for Marla and said, "You're going to end up killing yourself before you turn thirty-five."

After Marla sat down, Michael gripped her hand and asked, "Does he treat you like an adult or like you just turned eighteen?"

Marla glanced at Michael, his face red and jovial, and managed to bite her upper lip. She had the urge to say Gabe was right. That Michael overdid drinking like he overdid everything. That he would drink himself into an early grave. That drinking made him obnoxious. But instead she managed a smile and said, "He's just worried about you, Michael."

Michael raised a finger. "There's more than enough worries to go around, darling Marla. That's the one thing *Gabe* does to excess." Michael's grin widened and his eyes filled with surprise. "Look who's here." He motioned towards the other side of the room where Sonny Keys stood behind a middle-aged guy in a wheelchair. Standing next to Sonny, a heavyset man with blond, curly hair beamed a friendly smile, eyes shifting around the room.

That must be Frank and Wyatt, Marla thought.

The hostess, a trim brunette, greeted them and led them to a table on that side of the room. Sonny slid a chair out of the way and the man wheeled himself to the table.

"Hey! Sonny!" Michael called and waved.

With the din of the crowd pervading the room, Sonny didn't seem to hear.

Michael cupped his hands. "Hey! Sonny! Detective Keys! Come over here!"

"Shhhhhhhhhhhhhh!" Marla couldn't take Michael's blustering manner anymore. "Quiet. Everyone in the place can hear you."

"Yeah. Everyone 'cept for Sonny. He didn't even look."

Marla stood. "No more yelling. I'll go get him. You two talk quietly."

"That's a good gal," Michael said, smiling, eyes gleeful. "And tell that waiter I need another beer."

Gabe met Marla's gaze and tilted his head. "We'll keep it quiet here."

Marla wove her way through the tables, admonishing herself to be patient. Her brother-in-law at times exasperated her. Although Gabe and Michael were twins, their personalities contrasted. Michael was self-indulgent, Gabe self-disciplined. Michael was overbearing, Gabe considerate. Both were intelligent and creative, but Marla was glad she'd fallen in love with a sensitive, empathetic man who respected her as a person as much as he loved her as soul mate. Because Gabe cared for his brother, Marla tried to go the extra mile in tolerating the occasional clash of Michael's objectionable behavior. Living on the Outer Banks, she hoped their influence on Michael would somehow reach him, open his eyes to his need to grow up and live more responsibly.

When she arrived at Sonny's table, all three looked up at her. Sonny, dressed in a black western-style shirt with white buttons and red roses embroidered above the pockets, reminded her of the country music fans back in the Ohio Valley.

"Hey, Mrs. Easton," Sonny said. "We must be wanderin' the same trail today. Keep runnin' into each other."

Marla leaned on the only empty chair at their table. "I'd call that a good thing for me, Sonny. You showed up like John Wayne in one of those old cowboy movies to save the day."

Sonny leaned back, chest expanding, raising his fists. "Listen here, Pilgrim, me and that outlaw almost came to blows today."

"That's good. That's good," the curly-haired blond man said. "That was from *Mclintock*. Right, Sonny?"

"That's right, Wyatt," Sonny said, patting the man's forearm. "Not the exact quote, but close."

"You sounded just like the Duke," Marla said.

"John Wayne's easy. One of my favorites."

"Are these your two friends you told me about today?" Marla asked.

"Yes, ma'am, this is Wyatt. He's a classic movie expert . . ."

Wyatt stood and stuck out his hand. "Glad to meet ya. Glad to meet ya. Any friend of Sonny is my friend."

Marla shook his hand. It was warm and soft. He wore an extra large white Hawaiian shirt with a blue hibiscus blossom pattern. "You know your movies, eh Wyatt?"

"Yes I do. Yes I do. Me and Sonny know our movies." He held up three fingers. "Cowboy movies, science fiction movies, and horror movies. We know all about those three kinds." He smiled, nodded, and sat down.

Sonny gestured towards the other man. "And this is Frank Nolan."

"Your favorite teacher?"

"That's right. The one who taught me the best way to learn vocabulary."

Frank, bespectacled with round wire rim glasses and wearing a tan polo shirt, was thin with muscular arms. His shoulder-length dark brown hair had streaks of gray. "I'd stand up, but that would take a minor miracle." Frank grinned and extended his hand.

Marla clasped it, not knowing what to say. He had a strong grip. Catching the hint of fun in his eyes, she realized he also had a good sense of humor, making light of his physical limitations. "It's a pleasure to meet you. Sonny told me you are a most excellent teacher."

Frank released her hand and clasped Sonny's shoulder. "Believe me. I've learned more from Sonny than he has from me."

Sonny's face reddened slightly as he glanced at his lap

"It's very nice meeting both of you," Marla said. "I hope you don't mind, but I need to steal Sonny for a few minutes. My husband and brother-in-law wanted to speak to him about something important."

"Can I come too? Can I come too?" Wyatt asked.

Sonny stood and patted Wyatt on the back. "No. You stay here and keep Frank company. I won't be long."

Wyatt frowned, picked up the saltshaker, and sprinkled some into his palm.

Marla led Sonny across the room to Michael's table where Gabe was examining a photograph. Two stacks of pictures sat in front of him on top of an opened manila envelope. Michael sat across from him staring at a larger print, probably an eight by ten.

Michael glanced up and said, "There's Detective Keys, the inimitable gumshoe. Have a seat, Sonny. We have some details to discuss."

Sonny and Marla sat down. A waiter, a scraggly-haired blond in his early twenties, came by with a tray of drinks and buffalo wings. Marla assumed Gabe had ordered for her, her usual Diet Coke. Sonny informed the waiter that he was with Frank and Wyatt across the room and would order over there. The waiter told them he'd be back to get their dinner order in a few minutes.

"Are these Sonny's photographs?" Marla asked.

Michael nodded. "I printed them out at home before I came here. Mostly five by sevens, but I enlarged the important ones. He laid down the eight by ten and dug into the wings. "Tell Marla and Gabe about your confrontation with Payne."

Sonny peered up from the stack of images he was examining. "I barely made it back to the kitchen sink when Payne came bustin' in. I must have scared him more than he scared me. He dropped his groceries like he'd seen a ghost. After he picked them up and put them away, he disappeared into his bedroom for a few minutes. Then he came out madder than hell, standin' over me."

"What was he mad about?" Gabe asked.

"Well, after I photographed his wife's bedroom, Michael called to tell me Payne was on his way. I panicked and rushed to the kitchen sink so fast I forgot to shut the door all the way. He must have noticed it when he came out of his bedroom. He said, 'Someone's been in my wife's bedroom and there's somethin' missin'.' Then point blank he asked me, 'Did you go in there?'"

Marla raised her hand to her mouth. "What did you tell him?"

Sonny blew a stream of air through pursed lips, cheeks puffing out then deflating. "Well, I hate to lie. I said something like, Mr. Payne, I could get fired for abusing my privileges as the maintenance man. My boss trusts me with these keys. That's why they call me the 'Keyman.' Then I asked him, 'Do you really think I'd take the chance of losing my job by wanderin' where I shouldn't be wanderin'?'"

Michael swallowed a mouthful of chicken. "That's how smooth the Keyman is. He didn't have to lie. He just asked a question."

"So, did Payne drop it?" Gabe asked.

"No. I could tell he wasn't convinced because he kept eyeing my stuff. Then he asked me if he could look in my toolbox. I said, 'Sure you can check my toolbox, my pockets, whatever you want.' He opened it up and looked through it. Didn't find what he was lookin' for. I asked him if he wanted me to check anything else. I knew my camera was in my right pocket, but I thought what the hell. Better go all the way with it. He told me what he was lookin' for wouldn't fit in my pockets."

"Wonder what was missing?" Marla asked.

Michael lifted the photograph in front of him and held it up. "This is what was missing. A Greek mask."

Marla examined the picture, an array of odd masks hanging on a wall with an empty space where one seemed to be missing. "How do you know they're Greek?"

"I know my Greek mythology. I've taken courses at the community college in Manteo. Believe it or not, I actually paid attention in class." He pointed to the one in the middle. "This is Zeus, king of the gods. You can tell by the crown. Next to him is his queen, Hera. She was also his sister. Guess they had some redneck tendencies, a little incest action going on."

Marla didn't think the comment was funny, maybe because of her stress-filled day or maybe because she'd had it with Michael tonight. She glanced at Gabe and noticed he wasn't smiling either.

Michael indicated the mask on the far left. "This, of course, is Medusa. She's got the famous snaky hairdo and stone cold stare."

Sonny said, "That was my guess. I remember seeing her in *Clash of the Titans*."

"Sonny, the movie man." Michael pointed to the mask with stubby horns and pointed ears. "How about this last one, Sonny? Care to guess who?"

"That one freaked me out," Sonny said. "I'd say he's some kind of demon or devil, or one of those mischievous imps that cause all kinds of trouble."

"Mischievous? Is that one of your vocab words?" Michael asked.

Sonny nodded. "Learned that one a while back. Use it all the time."

Michael grinned, eyebrows rising. "Well, you're wrong, Mr. Dictionary. This is Pan. Not a demon, devil, or dastardly spirit, although he was half goat. He's the god of flocks and shepherds, wilderness and hunting." Michael twittered his fingers in front of his lips. "Remember, he played a panpipe. He was also very *sexual*." He pronounced the last word emphatically.

Gabe pointed to the space. "What about the missing one?"

"Lots of Greek gods," Michael said. "Hard to say."

Sonny shuffled through the photos he'd been reviewing. "Look here. It's a close-up of the missing one. You can make out the shape because the paint's faded around it."

Marla took the picture from Sonny. "It has curled horns like a ram and a beard. Is it some kind of animal?"

"Curled horns? Let me see that." Gabe took the picture. Something clicked in his mind—the crime scene when Dugan Walton announced he'd found something unusual, a papier-mâché horn that had been torn from a larger piece. "This could be important. The killer may have been wearing this missing mask."

"Like Jason in the *Friday the 13th* movies," Sonny said.

"That's right." Gabe handed Sonny the photograph. "Find this mask, and I bet you find the killer."

Marla shuttered. The thought that a murderer may have been on her back deck last night raised goose flesh on her arms and neck. She wanted to change the subject. "What about Payne? Did he say anything else?"

Sonny rubbed his chin. "Well, after he couldn't find the mask he sort of apologized. Said sometimes his mind blanks out and he's not himself. Said when he's in these states he'll do things and not even recall doing it. Then he looked really baffled like he was tryin' to remember whether or not he went into his wife's room and took that mask. Knowing I went in there made me feel guilty, so I said, 'There's a lot of mischievous ghosts on this island. People see the shipwrecked spirits wanderin' around here all the time. Maybe one of them opened the bedroom door.' I was jokin' but I shouldn't a said that."

"Why not?" Marla asked.

"He got real spooky lookin' like Vincent Price in *Diary of a Madman*. Then he said, 'Believe me, Sonny, there are unseen things in this world few people understand. I know what I'm talkin' about. I've crossed over.'" Sonny shook himself like a dog shedding water. "I just wanted to crawl under the sink, fix the leak, and get out of there."

Michael placed a photograph in the middle of the table and stabbed it with his finger. "There's your ghost." The image, a photo from the scrapbook, displayed Loretta Payne posing on the gallery of the Cape Hatteras Lighthouse with her back to the railing, smiling seductively. "He knocked her down the steps and put her into that coma. Now he's haunted by her memory and can't deal with the guilt. He's crossed over all right. Who knows what he's capable of when he gets into these so called states?"

The waiter stepped up to the table and inquired if everyone was ready to order. Sonny excused himself and headed back to Frank and Wyatt. As Gabe and Michael placed their orders, Marla quickly glanced through the menu and decided on the linguini with red clam sauce, something light that wouldn't bother her stomach. After the waiter left she collected the photographs and stuffed them into the manila envelope. She didn't want to look at those images any longer. She needed a respite from the stress, the intrigue, the fear. A slight headache droned above her brow, and her throat felt dry. She reached for her Coke, sat back in her chair, and took a long sip from the straw. Closing her eyes helped block out the world, and the bubbly liquid cooled her insides. She drew in a long breath and let it out slowly. A familiar voice sent chills through her.

She turned in her chair to catch Tony Trenton staring at her from four tables behind her. When their eyes met, he blew her a kiss. She felt a nerve above her cheek twitching and her stomach tensing up. At his table two young men, one with long, thin blonde hair, and the other with short black hair, looked her way, grinning and nodding. Trenton must have been telling them about that morning's encounter. She checked to see if Gabe or Michael had noticed these punks eying her, but they were too busy munching on the chicken wings and licking their fingers.

She decided to wipe Trenton from her mind and avoid looking in his direction the rest of the night. That's what he wanted—her attention. Telling Gabe would only add stress to the evening. She'd keep it to herself unless Trenton threatened her in some way. Blowing a kiss didn't qualify.

Certainly he wouldn't try anything with her husband and brother-in-law sitting next to her.

"Let's go! Let's go! Let's go!" The strident voice booming from the restaurant's P.A. system startled her. "It's karaoke time! Who's ready to step up and belt one out?"

Half-hearted applause rippled through the crowd, and several hands shot up. Marla swiveled her head to see a stocky man with slicked back hair at the microphone on the small stage near the bar. He wore a large white t-shirt with the restaurant's logo and a cartoon sea turtle on the front. His hand, held above his head with finger pointing, shifted back and forth like a weathervane pushed by gusting winds. Finally it stopped, finger jabbing towards a pretty redheaded girl sitting near the front.

"Hurry and get up here, young lady. Let's see what kinda pipes ya got," he said with a raspy voice.

The girl, long legged and dressed in tight jeans and a low cut tank top, stepped onto the stage to loud whoops and cheers. Her smile flashed white teeth framed by full pink lips. Marla noticed the girl's model looks had captured the attention of all the men sitting around her, including Gabe and Michael. *Guys are so visually oriented. A little skin and a pretty face absorb their attention quicker than a sponge sucks up spilt milk.* Unfortunately, her voice didn't match her beauty. By the end of "My Heart Will Go On" lusty ogling turned to yawns and groans.

A short, squat guy mounted the stage next and sang "New York, New York" with a pitchy voice even worse than the redhead's. Marla was ready for earplugs, but then the third singer approached the mic, and Marla sat up. She could have sworn it was Dolly Parton—the platinum blonde wig, big boobs, hourglass shape, and beauty mark just below her bottom lip. Wearing black four-inch heels, she busted out of a blue silk, low V-cut top tucked tightly into a short denim dress. Applause erupted and several men in the audience hollered, "Dolly!"

When the music started, a country version of "I Will Always Love You," Marla listened carefully to discern whether or not she was in the presence of Opryland royalty. It didn't take long. The imitator's voice reminded Marla of a Minnie Mouse version of Parton. When she got to the high notes of the chorus, it sounded like she had overdosed on helium.

Michael began to giggle. At first he tried to hold it in, but it spurted out in short, rapid bursts. Marla shot a warning glare his way, but it only served to unhinge the little control he had. The Dolly Parton look-a-like kept singing, though her confident expression deflated into self-doubt. When she focused on Michael, who now was using his hand to stifle the sniggering, her eyes filled with fire. She continued to blaze him with her stare through the final note. She then put her hand on her round rump, pointed the microphone at him and shouted, "You think you can do better?"

"I'm sorry," Michael said. "I'm a little tipsy."

"Do you think you can do better?" she demanded. "Get up here if you got the guts. And I can certainly see you've got plenty of guts."

Michael stood and patted his belly. "Guts to spare."

Throughout the crowd people spurred him on: "Go for it!" "Show her what you got!" "Get up there, big boy!"

With a swagger, Michael cut through the tables, stepped onto the stage, bowed low, then reached up and took the microphone. The Dolly double stepped off the platform and strutted back to her seat.

"Please accept my apologies, Miss Parton. You are a breath-taking woman with two prominent features." He waited for the chuckles to subside. "Your voice and your smile." More laughter erupted.

He's got the crowd in his pocket, Marla thought. She guessed he'd sing an Elvis song. Michael resembled a combination of the young and old Elvis—heavy like the old one but with a youthful face. His dark, wavy hair added to the likeness, although he wasn't as pretty as Elvis. Three years ago at her wedding Michael had sung "I Can't Help Falling in Love with You." She had to admit, he had done a good job.

Michael peered at the stocky MC who was now behind the sound equipment. "Do you have any Elvis tunes back there?"

"A bunch"

"How about 'I Can't Help Falling in Love with You'?"

"Anything for the King."

I knew it, Marla thought. At her wedding he'd put just enough Elvis into the song to keep it entertaining, but now after he'd had a few beers she predicted he'd over do it.

The music started, and he immediately went down to one knee, upper lip twitching. Applause rippled through the audience. As he sang, he rose slowly, voice in low vibrato, slurring the words. His free hand reached out to the crowd, lyrically unfolding. His imitation was good but not great. The higher notes of the chorus caused him the most problems, so he overcompensated with gyrations, wiggles, and sweeping hand motions. At the end of the performance, he finished with his hands in the air, like a Baptist preacher offering a benediction to his congregation. To Marla, the crowd seemed generous in their approval.

The stout man in the turtle t-shirt slipped out from behind the equipment stand, pranced to the stage, and took the microphone from Michael's flaccid hand. "Wow! How about that rendition! Elvis is in the house!" The applause rose again.

Michael bowed and ambled back to the table.

"Anybody brave enough to follow that act?" the MC asked.

The crowd quieted, heads turning to scout out any volunteers. No hands went up.

From across the room a low chant began: "Keyman. Keyman. Keyman."

Sonny shook his head and waved his hand, a negating motion, towards Frank and Wyatt, but they kept up the chant, increasing the volume, pounding on the table: "Keyman! Keyman! Keyman!"

The MC said, "Sonny Keys, get up here and sing us a song!"

"No thanks," Sonny said. "Not tonight."

Michael, who had just sat down, stood up abruptly, cupped his hands around his mouth and shouted, "What's the matter, Sonny? Was the King too much for you?"

Marla saw what Michael was up to, egging Sonny on to have a little fun with him. She guessed once he got up there and missed a few notes, Michael would make wisecracks to get the crowd laughing.

"I've always heard you could carry a tune," Michael went on, "but I've never had the privilege of hearing you sing. If you truly are the Keyman, let's see if you can hit all the notes."

Frank and Wyatt started their chant again and the crowd joined in. Marla closed her eyes, dispirited by a sinking feeling deep in her chest. *Don't do it, Sonny. Stay in your seat. Don't let Michael amuse the crowd at your expense.*

Sonny stood, and the audience cheered. Behind her, Marla heard someone say, "This ought to be good—a moron at the mic." She knew immediately the insulting words came from Tony Trenton. Somehow she stopped herself from turning around and castigating him with a withering stare. That would only spur him on. He didn't need more incentive to humiliate Sonny. Marla decided to shoot up a prayer for her new friend that he'd get through the song without too much damage to his sensitive soul.

When Sonny arrived at the stage, he leaned and said something into the stocky man's ear. The MC nodded, handed him the microphone, and returned to the audio controls behind the sound equipment.

Sonny cleared his throat, the spotlight reflecting off his glistening, shaved head. "It's been a few years since I've sung here. Tonight I'd like to sing my mother's favorite song. She played it all the time on the stereo when I was a boy. It's from an opera called *Turandot*."

Murmurs and snickering pattered throughout the crowd. From the direction of Trenton's table a man's voice said, "The mama's boy is gonna sing an opera song." Someone else nearby complained, "Not opera. Let's hear some country."

The knot in Marla's chest tightened.

Sonny's eyes flicked around the crowd. They blinked several times, becoming watery. "I'd like to dedicate this song to my mother's memory. She passed away three years ago tonight. The song is called 'Nessun Dorma.'"

The murmuring and comments ended abruptly, silence falling like a thick curtain.

The title of the song struck a chord of memory with Marla. In college to fulfill a fine arts requirement, she'd taken a course on famous arias. The main character in this opera competed and won the right to wed a beautiful princess by correctly answering three riddles. However, the princess was not attracted to this homely suitor. The love-struck man offered the princess a way out: if she could guess his name by morning, instead of marrying him, she could have him executed. He hoped his willingness to offer his life as a sacrifice would change her mind. He knew if he could kiss her, she would love him.

The music began, strings cascading down the scale from mid to lower range, followed by the low, lonely moan of an oboe. Sonny gazed above the audience as if seeing into another world. The first two words he sang were the title of the song repeated twice: Nessun dorma. Nessun dorma. His voice was clear and on perfect pitch. Chills poured over her as she remembered her professor's interpretation: No sleep tonight. No sleep tonight. The next line flowed wonderfully in Italian as if Sonny could speak the language fluently. To Marla's ears it sounded like, "My meo mister O chuse en me. Il numb meo nessun supra! No! No!" *He would keep his secret. None would know.* The next line rose up the scale, challenging notes for even the greatest of tenors, but Sonny hit them with a depth of feeling Marla had never sensed in a live performance. Tears welled in her eyes as she focused on his ardent expression. She blinked and they streamed down her cheeks. She felt embarrassed, but she couldn't help crying.

As the song proceeded she felt the audience being swept up in the power of Sonny's virtuoso effort. When he hit a difficult range of notes, spontaneous applause broke out. Next to her Michael murmured, "That sonovabitch can sing."

Although the Italian words became hard to decipher, she knew he was singing about the princess seeing the night stars flickering with love and hope, about how his kiss would dissolve the wall between them and open her eyes to his devotion. As he approached the climax of the song, the part where he declares his love will achieve victory, Marla could barely breathe. Each "Vincero" rose higher, stronger, more powerful than the last: "Vincero! Vincero! Vincero!" His vibrato reverberated throughout the room, causing her whole being to tremble. The strings reached a crescendo in unison with his voice, and everyone in the restaurant rose to their feet, applauded thunderously, and cheered.

Gabe stuck two fingers in his mouth and whistled loudly.

Michael kept repeating, "That sonovabitch can really sing."

Marla wiped the tears from her cheeks, amazed at what she'd just witnessed.

Chapter 11

Their meals came shortly after Sonny finished singing. Marla couldn't remember tasting linguini and clam sauce so good and wondered if Sonny's performance had somehow affected her taste buds, left an afterglow that enhanced the savoring of each bite. She would never forget his expression, and the way his magnificent voice electrified not only her but also everyone who listened. The power of the moment flowed like a tidal wave that no one could withstand, not even Michael and his sarcasm or Trenton and his cruelty. Now she knew why Frank and Wyatt were so insistent in their chanting. By doing so they helped to unwrap a rare gift meant to be shared with others.

Marla took the last bite and sat back in her chair, satisfied and fatigued. Now that she'd finished eating, she wanted to go home. She glanced at Gabe and noticed he appeared very tired too. Michael, however, tapped his hands on the edge of the table, eyes shifting around the restaurant, head bobbing to the beat of "On the Road Again," the latest in a series of country songs selected by the karaoke crooners.

Michael raised his hand in an effort to get the waiter's attention. He probably wanted another beer, although he'd drunk a half dozen. He cupped his hands around his mouth, preparing to shout at the poor guy, but then slowly lowered them and said, "Look who's here." He pointed in the direction of Sonny's table.

Marla immediately recognized the man, Dugan Walton, a former classmate at Martins Ferry High School back in Ohio. Usually Marla saw Dugan around town patrolling in his deputy uniform, but tonight he was dressed in a red plaid shirt and blue jeans. The shirt almost matched the color of his hair, medium length on the sides but longer and parted to the right on top. His freckled face reminded her of a young Ron Howard in *Happy Days*, cute rather than handsome. He leaned on the empty chair at Sonny's table, a serious aspect to his demeanor as he spoke a few words. Sonny nodded, raised his hands in front of him, palms up, and responded. Marla wondered what they were talking about. Dugan reached across the table and shook Sonny's hand, tilted his head towards Frank, patted Wyatt on the back, and then headed towards them.

"Good." Michael picked up the manila envelope. "He's coming our way. I wanted to give him these pictures."

"Are you sure about that?" Gabe asked. "You might get Sonny in trouble for invasion of privacy."

"You kidding me?" He raised the envelope to chin level. "These babies could solve a crime. Good ol' Dugan will overlook a little amateur P.I. dabbling if he can get his hands on some hard evidence. Believe me, he wants to climb that law enforcement ladder and wear the big badge one day."

Halfway across the room Dugan altered course and headed between the tables to their right. To see where he was going, Marla would have to turn around, but she guessed he aimed for Trenton's table. She hadn't looked in that direction all night, not wanting to make eye contact with the creep and fan the flame of his warped libido. But now, her curiosity getting the best of her, she glanced over her shoulder. Dugan stood, hands on hips, glaring down at Trenton. Marla could hear them, but just barely.

"This is your chance to eliminate yourself as a suspect," Dugan said.

Trenton's eyes shifted from one buddy to another, then up at Dugan. "I know I'm not guilty. I've got nothing to prove. I didn't kill her."

Dugan held out his hands as if measuring a fish. "Listen to what I'm saying. We have DNA evidence. They did a rape test on the girl. If you don't come in and offer a DNA sample, then you become the prime suspect. We'll get your DNA sooner or later."

"But we had sex." Trenton's voice wavered. "She wanted it. It was . . . what's it called? Consensual."

Dugan pointed at him. "You had sex with her on the beach last night?"

Trenton shook his head emphatically sideways. "No. We made out in the late afternoon at my apartment. Right before she had the fight with her parents."

"Can you prove that?"

"Yeah." Trenton motioned towards his friends. "Me, Gator, and Chuck went fishing last night after her parents threatened me with a restraining order. Ain't that right, boys?"

"That's right," the blond said. "Drank beers and fished most of the night."

The dark-haired guy nodded in agreement.

"You need to come in anyway. If someone else raped her, they'll find both traces of DNA."

Trenton held up his hands. "Okay. Okay. I'll come in and let you take your sample. But I'm telling you the damned truth. I didn't kill that girl."

"That's all I'm asking," Dugan said, "a little cooperation."

Dugan pivoted and strode in the direction of the bar, heading away from Marla's table.

Michael stood. "Dugie! Dugie! Over here!"

Dugan paused and peered in their direction.

Michael waved him over. "You're just the man we wanted to see."

When Dugan reached their table he said, "Looks like a Purple Rider powwow—The Easton twins and Marla May Garehart."

Michael slapped him on the back and pulled out the empty chair. "Have a seat, Deputy Dugie."

"Hi Dugan," Marla said, extending her hand. "And remember, it's Marla Easton now."

Dugan shook her hand. "Of course. Good ol' Gabe got lucky."

"You're right on that account," Gabe said.

Dugan sat down, smiling. "Better to be lucky than good"

Michael held the manila envelope in front of him. "We were wondering, Dugie, how's the investigation going?"

The playfulness in Dugan's eyes faded. "We caught a break. I don't have all the details, but I heard the lab picked up some trace evidence from the rape kit, the rope, and that odd-looking horn I found today. It'll take some time, but if they can extract the DNA, then all we have to do is find a match."

"Think it's Trenton?" Michael asked.

"Maybe. Sounds like he's been working on an alibi, though. His two buddies over there swear he went fishing with them last night. But if his

DNA shows up on the rope, then he's in a super-sized dog pile of trouble."

"Who else are you checking out?" Gabe asked.

Dugan pointed to the front of the restaurant. "Sonny Keys."

"Why Sonny?" Marla objected.

"When I interviewed him, he said a few things that struck me as questionable. He had what I call a developing relationship with the girl. Ever since her family rented the apartment a few months ago, he has spoken to her regularly. Her parents told me he was always real friendly with her, telling her how pretty she was. He mentioned that to me too. Seems he was bedazzled by her looks. I'm guessing she must have flirted with him. You know how young gals can be with older men—like to see if they can get their motors revving. Sonny said he offered to walk with her last night, but she turned him down. No one likes to be rejected. Maybe he followed her, forced himself on her."

Michael snorted. "Yeah, and maybe the Pope's Presbyterian and Jerry Seinfeld is uncircumcised. Come on, Dugie, Sonny's a legend. He doesn't hurt people. He helps people."

Dugan's face remained stolid. "He doesn't have an alibi. Said he spent last night in his apartment watching movies."

"I can't believe you think Sonny committed murder," Marla protested. "He's naturally nice to people."

Dugan held up his hands. "I didn't say I think he did it. I said he's a suspect. It's my job to investigate suspects. Besides, he agreed to offer a DNA sample. Like I said, all we're trying to do is find a match."

Michael tossed the manila envelope, and it landed in front of Dugan, some of the photos spilling out.

"What's this?"

"Some pictures your suspect took today," Michael said.

"Huh?"

"I gave Sonny an assignment. Sent him into Martin Payne's apartment with a digital camera."

Dugan's eyebrows tensed and his nostrils flared slightly. "You shouldn't have done that."

Michael raised his hand. "Now don't get your rod and reel all in a tangle. Payne asked Sonny to fix a leaky sink. He just carried out some extra curricular activities while there."

Dugan shook his head. "Doesn't matter. There are legal issues here. Payne didn't give approval for these to be taken."

"No shit, Sherlock. That's the beauty of it. Before you slap handcuffs on me and Luciano Pavarotti over there, take a look at the photographs. I can guarantee you'll find a couple interesting ones."

His jaw clenched, Dugan peered across the room at Sonny, then at Michael. He slid the pictures out of the envelope and shuffled through them, glancing at most of them for only a few seconds. Halfway through he found one that caught his attention. After studying it for what seemed a full minute he set it aside and continued. By the time he made it through the pile, he had set aside three pictures. "Mind if I hang on to these ones?" He flipped them over. The first and second were of the masks, and the third showed the yellow towrope hanging in the bathroom.

"Anything to help," Michael said. "Why those three?"

Dugan pointed at the second photograph. "I found a piece of this missing mask at the crime scene. Its shape matches the outline on the wall where the sun faded the paint. And this other one looks like the same kind of rope used to bind the girl's hands. The lab guys found traces of DNA on the rope and the piece of mask."

Michael grinned. "Told you you'd be interested. Now how about a sample of Payne's DNA?"

Dugan nodded. "That'll be my first stop tomorrow morning, Payne's apartment."

"Good," Michael said. "In my humble opinion, he's your man."

"We'll see," Dugan said, rising. "Now, I need a drink and something deep fried from the ocean. It's been a long day." He smiled, gave an informal salute and walked towards the bar.

"Try the fried octopus balls! You'll love 'em!" Michael called after him.

"Geesh, Michael," Gabe said. "Do you have to say things like that so loud everyone can hear you?"

Michael finished off the last of his beer and set the bottle down with a clunk. "Brother Gabriel, you are a stuffed flounder. Everyone who heard me thought it was funny 'cept for you."

Marla raised her hand. "And me."

"All right. That's two out of a hundred. Pretty good average."

"I think you ought to come home with Marla and me. You've had too much to drink."

Michael thumbed towards the entrance. "What about my car?"

"Give Marla the keys. She'll drive it home. You ride with me."

Michael shook his head. "No. No. No. That's not going to happen."

Gabe leaned forward, eyebrows lowering, darkening his eyes. "I'm serious, Michael. You ought to know me by now." He jabbed his finger at his brother. "I will not let you drive like this."

Michael held up his hands. "Okay. Listen. I promise you I will not drink another beer. I'll hang out here for a couple more hours 'til I'm completely sober, then I'll drive myself home. You have my word."

"What are you going to do here for two more hours?" Gabe asked.

"Listen to the music. Sing another song." Michael pointed in the direction of the platinum blonde. "The King needs to apologize to the Queen of Country. Maybe we can make some sweet music together?"

Marla couldn't believe it. "You're going to hit on that woman you insulted?"

"I said apologize. That's step one. Making a pass is more like step three or four."

Marla imagined the Dolly double slapping her brother-in-law and smiled. By Michael's expression, she could tell he assumed his humor curled her lips.

Gabe said, "You promise you'll not drink another beer?"

Michael held up two fingers. "Girl Scout's honor."

"If you break the promise, do you promise to call me so I can come and get you?"

"Promises, promises, promises. Whatever it takes. You have my word."

Gabe left money for the bill and tip with Michael, and he and Marla headed for the door. They reached the foyer at the same time Sonny Keys and his two friends arrived, Frank leading the way, spinning his own wheels.

Marla put her hand on Sonny's shoulder. "You are an amazing man. Your song made me cry."

Sonny glanced at his feet, his face reddening. "Thanks, Mrs. Easton."

"Call me Marla, please. Mrs. Easton is what my friends called my mother."

Sonny looked up and smiled. "Okay, Marla. I'm glad you liked my singing. I haven't sung that song since my mother died. Tonight I did it for her."

"It was beautiful." Marla introduced Gabe to Frank and Wyatt.

Gabe shook their hands enthusiastically. "Did you guys know your buddy could sing like an opera star?"

"Taught him everything he knows," Frank said, grinning.

Wyatt began the chant again: "Sonny! Sonny! Sonny!"

Sonny elbowed him. "That's enough, Wyatt."

"Where you guys headed?" Gabe asked.

"Calling it a night," Sonny said. "We need to save some energy for tomorrow night."

"What's happening tomorrow night?" Marla asked.

Wyatt raised his hand as if he were in class. "Movie and bowling. Movie and bowling."

Sonny glanced at him and nodded. "Saturday night we usually take in a movie at the Cinema in Avon and then drive up to Nags Head for some late night bowling."

"*Friday the 13th Part Nine*. Right Sonny? Right Sonny?" Wyatt said.

Marla felt slightly repulsed by their choice. She couldn't imagine Sonny enjoying the violence and gore of that kind of movie.

"We're big fans of horror films," Sonny said, "the old ones and the new ones."

Frank rubbed his hands together. "Especially slasher flicks."

Marla eyed Gabe, but he didn't seem affected by their macabre enthusiasm. Maybe it was a guy thing. To change the subject, she turned towards Frank and Wyatt and asked, "Is Sonny as good at bowling as he is at singing?"

"Oh yeah. O yeah," Wyatt said.

"He bowled a 300 game two months ago," Frank chipped in.

Marla stared at Sonny, eyes wide. "A 300 game?"

Sonny held up his hands. "It was pure luck. I usually bowl around 180."

"That's about eighty points better than my average," Gabe said.

"Frank beats me half the time."

Marla eyed Frank. For a thin man he did have strong-looking arms. She tried to imagine how he would roll the ball sitting in his wheelchair.

Frank flipped his hand sideways. "I've got a wicked hook."

By now they were at the stairs. Sonny and Wyatt waved goodbye and followed Frank to the exit that led to the wheelchair ramp. Marla hesitated and watched them depart before descending the steps, impressed by their loyal friendship, the kind of rare commitment to one another that endures through the years.

* * *

Although they were tired, Marla insisted they make love. She was ovulating. Gabe didn't put up a fight. Usually *he* pressured her. He started

80

the same familiar way, his fingertip tracing the rim of her ear. She loved it. He didn't mind the lack of variety. Sex with Marla was a beautiful thing like making love to an angel. It seemed new every time, a precious gift.

They had both been virgins when they started dating seriously in high school. The attraction began back in junior high when they attended the same youth group at the Scotch Ridge Church. Their pastor, Byron Butler, was conservative when it came to teaching about dating and waiting. His philosophy basically stated those who commit themselves to purity before the wedding and faithfulness after discover the best kind of sex because it becomes not only physical but also spiritual. Gabe and Marla believed every word, although they almost gave into their passions twice before their wedding night. Somehow they made it through. Gabe liked it that way, not having a sexual experience with another woman to make comparisons. He knew Marla felt the same. Maybe that's what made making so great with his wife—knowing they were special in each other's eyes

With patience, focusing on her pleasure, he traced her jaw line and then lightly across her lips. She gripped his hand and sucked on his fingers. This drove him crazy. He had to tell himself to keep it in first gear. Step by step he did everything she enjoyed, the gentle crisscrossing of his finger on her neck, the long strokes up and down her body, the deep kissing. At that point it became harder for both of them to keep it slow. Sometimes they did, sensing every touch, drawing out every pleasure, bringing each other near the edge and then backing off. But tonight they caught fire. They wanted each other now, rapidly, an explosion of bliss.

When it was over, they lay in each other's arms, breathing hard, gently touching each other's face, and confessing love. Gabe rolled onto his back, and Marla rested her head on his chest, her arm across his belly. Gabe realized he had never been so happy in his life. He feared losing Marla. Does God get upset when you love someone too much? When that person becomes the center of your world? He thought about the Bible story of Abraham and Isaac, how God tested Abraham by calling upon him to sacrifice Isaac. Would Gabe pass that kind of test with Marla? He doubted it and hoped God would never ask him for that kind of sacrifice.

"You're brother drinks too much," Marla said after several minutes of silence.

"I know. He needs help."

"He needs a good woman."

Gabe pulled Marla tight against him. "He can't have you."

Marla twirled Gabe's chest hair. "Believe me, I don't want him. He's so sarcastic and obnoxious, especially when he's drunk."

"Maybe he'll fall in love with Polly Darton."

Marla giggled. "That lady was at least fifteen years older than him."

"I don't think he cares."

"That's his problem: He doesn't care. He doesn't take care of himself, and he's not too worried about anybody else."

Gabe combed his fingers through her dark brown hair, pulling it back from her face. "Don't be too hard on him. He wanted you and me to come down here and live next to him, didn't he?"

"That's because he's lonely and selfish. He can't stand sharing you with me."

Gabe chuckled. "You sound jealous."

Marla shrugged.

Gabe realized Michael's quirks often irritated Marla. She didn't want to move into the same apartment complex with Michael, saying she needed space. But the rent was so reasonable and the view of the ocean so spectacular, that it didn't take much for Gabe to convince her. Together they could be positive influences on Michael, demonstrating what love is all about, offering daily reminders of living responsibly. Gabe hoped so, anyway. So far he hadn't seen much progress. His brother hadn't changed a bit.

Marla turned over and lay on her back. "Isn't Sonny Keys the most unusual man you've ever met?"

"He is amazing."

"He has a learning disability yet seems very wise. He takes care of Wyatt and Frank with that gentle sense of humanity. And he's so good at things. I've never heard anyone sing like that before."

"Some people with learning disabilities have exceptional talents. They can be good at math or remembering dates. With Sonny it's opera. Then again, maybe it sounded so good because we haven't heard that much opera music."

"What do you mean?"

Gabe clasped his hands behind his head. "We don't know exactly how it should sound."

"Come on, Gabe. It was magic. And he bowls like a pro."

Gabe never imagined that Sonny Keys could become a rival for his wife's attention. Sonny was almost ten years older than both of them, a little over weight, and bald. Today's rescue probably had enamored Marla, giving her a new admiration for the man. "Well, he does look like Yul Brenner. I could see why you'd be infatuated with him."

Marla elbowed him in the ribs. "I'm not infatuated with him. He's just different. There's one thing I don't understand, though. Why would a kind, compassionate man like Sonny be a fan of slasher movies. It doesn't make sense. All that blood and violence."

The words came into Gabe's mind and out of his mouth before he could stop them. "Maybe he's a serial killer."

"That's not funny."

The phone on the nightstand rang, sending an eerie jolt through his body. He let it ring again, then picked it up. "Yeah, Gabe here."

"Don't yell at me or say I made a promise." He recognized his brother's voice.

"You didn't stop drinking?"

"Beer? Yes. But Miss Parton wanted a brottle—a blottle—a bottle of wine. How could I not oblige her?"

He sounded more intoxicated than when they'd left him. "Where's Miss Parton now?"

"Dru—dri—drank my wine, then left me cryin'."

"So you're alone?"

"Naturally."

"All right. I'll be there in fifteen minutes. Don't do anything stupid like trying to drive home."

"I prom—promised not to do that."

"That's one you better keep." Gabe hung up and glanced at Marla.

She pulled the sheet up to her chin. "Your brother's more trouble than a two year old in toy store."

"At least he didn't drive home drunk."

She turned onto her side. "Try not to wake me up when you get back."

Gabe's clothes sat in a pile on the floor next to the bed. He quickly dressed and stepped into his flip-flops. He grabbed the keys off Marla's dresser and started for the front door. Tonight he wanted to have a serious talk with Michael. In December they would turn twenty-eight. In Gabe's estimation, Michael's time to grow up and become a man was past due. Why did his brother lack self-discipline? How come he couldn't say no to excesses and impulses? He had such potential, blessed with more talent than Gabe. Michael could become a nationally renowned painter, a published writer, a brilliant teacher. But he always settled for the easiest path. His moderate success as an artist on the Outer Banks had curbed his

83

ambition to reach for the outer limits of his ability. Paintings sold. More than enough money flowed through the door. Why should he sweat and toil? Eat, drink and be merry. What a waste, Gabe thought.

In contrast Gabe overachieved. He had a vision for himself and had determined long ago to follow a strict plan to achieve that vision. Mentally, physically, and spiritually, he wanted to become the best he could possibly be. His running, writing, and relationships helped him to stay on track. He may not have Michael's talent, but for damn sure he would get the most out of what he had. Running made him physically sharp. Writing pushed his mental capabilities to new frontiers, and his love for Marla kept him spiritually alive. Life was good. Now if only he could open Michael's eyes.

Gabe stepped onto the deck and inhaled the humid, salty air. He loved the smell of the ocean and sound of surf less than seventy-five yards away. He blinked his eyes, trying to adjust to the darkness as he descended the steps. At the bottom he peered into the night sky. A million stars blinked down at him. Their magnificence reminded him of making love to Marla. He closed his eyes, recalling the sensual details of their passionate union just minutes ago. A wide smile broke across his face.

When he heard footsteps coming his way, he opened his eyes to see a dark figure. Was it Sonny? His eyes had adjusted enough to make out the man's face. It wasn't a real face but rather a mask—a mask of a man with grapes and leaves tangled in his beard and a ram's horn sticking out of one side of his head. The other horn was missing. Gabe's heart jumped into his throat when the man raised a tire iron.

Chapter 12

Marla heard a far-off grunt and then an agonized groan. It wasn't loud enough to startle her but did concern her. Was it Sonny's or Mr. Payne's television? She sat up, remembering the Peeping Tom and the murder victim. The groan echoed in her mind, reminding her of when Gabe had slipped in the shower and banged his head a couple weeks ago. Fear sprang like a panther from the darkness, causing her heart to thud against her ribcage. She whirled her head to look at Gabe's Louisville Slugger leaning against the wall. When she stepped out of bed, she realized she was naked and rushed to the closet to grab a robe. She tried to control her jittery limbs as she funneled her arms into the sleeves, but the rush of adrenalin had overcharged her body.

God, please let this be nothing but random sounds in the night, she prayed. She picked up the bat and tried to hold it steady in both hands, but it trembled like a branch in a windstorm. Glancing at the pillow, she remembered Gabe demonstrating how to swing the thing effectively. She took a deep breath, squeezed the handle tightly, and marched towards the front door. Her body shook uncontrollably, but she managed to grasp the knob, fling the door open, and raise the bat in front of her. She peered into the darkness, listening for any kind of sound—nothing but waves spilling onto the shore, muted by the distance.

Her eyes adjusted to the darkness slowly. The silhouette of her car took shape in the driveway sending a shock through her. "Gabe! Gabe! Where are you!" Eyes wide, she stepped onto the deck and edged to the top of the steps. She scanned the immediate area. Now her vision became more acute, revealing another shape on the ground in front of the car. A body?

She descended the steps and approached the slumped figure cautiously. "Gabe?" Now close enough to recognize his blue t-shirt and jeans, she dropped the bat, fell to her knees, and placed her hands on his shoulder and hip. "Gabe, say something." *God, please let him be alive.* She slid her hand down his neck and across his face and felt wet, warm liquid. *Blood.* "Oh, God, no!" Reaching farther, she touched the side of his head. It dipped slightly like a dinged fender. *He's dying. Think. Think. What to do? Call 911. Hurry.*

She reached back to support herself in order to rise, but something slipped over her head and tightened around her neck. She leaned forward to regain her balance, grasping at what seemed to be a nylon rope. It tightened more, slightly choking her.

"Don't move." The voice was horrifying like a demon speaking through a possessed man. "You scream and I crush your windpipe right now."

It didn't sound human, as if it had been filtered through some kind of sound-altering device. Marla held as still as possible, trying to breath through her constricted throat. She had to keep it together if there was any hope of saving Gabe. Some kind of cloth, a blindfold, slid over her head. She felt latex gloves brushing her cheek. All went black.

The attacker tugged on the rope, making it harder to breathe. "Stand up."

She struggled to her feet, managing to gain her balance, the rope slackening, loosening slightly. "Please don't hurt me," she croaked. "I'll do whatever you want."

"That's a good gal. I hope you feel the same way once you find out what I want to do." He grabbed her shoulders and turned her halfway around. "Walk that way."

She placed one foot in front of the other, thinking at any moment she would trip over something. Her mind skipped like a broken record from Gabe, to each step she took, to what might happen to her, and back to Gabe again. The tip of her toe hit the top of the curb, and she knew she'd stepped onto the sidewalk in front of the apartment.

"Steady," the creepy voice said. "Get ready to lift your leg."

He's taking me back into the apartment. What's he want with me?

He pulled back on her shoulder and she stopped. "Climb the steps."

She nudged the top of the first step with her toe, planted her foot and rose to the next. When the reality of the man's intensions hit her, she almost collapsed, her legs feeling like gelatin. She had to stop and collect herself.

"Get moving." He shoved her slightly, and she lurched forward, somehow advancing to the top.

She thought about the murdered girl. Did he try to rape her then kill her after she put up a fight? Marla wanted to live. Maybe Gabe could be saved. She decided to comply with every command, get it over without resisting. Maybe he'd let her live, and she could get even another day. With new resolve she crossed the deck.

He stopped her and ordered her to step up again. Her left forearm brushed against the half-open door. In her mind she envisioned her kitchen and living room, guessing their destination was the bedroom. He stopped her again. She heard the door shut and the sound of the dead bolt being turned. The horror of being locked in the apartment with the killer threatened to unhinge her determination. An impulse to rip off the blindfold and spin free surged through her like a jolt of electricity.

He must have felt the surge because his hand tightened on her shoulder. "Don't do anything mischievous."

Mischievous. That was one of Sonny's vocabulary words. Could it be? She steeled herself and moved forward. He guided her through the kitchen and into the living room, where he jerked her shoulder to change her direction sharply.

When they entered the bedroom, a new thought flashed in her mind: *The bat. I could grab the bat and whack him.* Hope flamed like a sheet of paper thrown into a fireplace but burnt out quickly when she remembered she'd taken the bat outside and dropped it next to Gabe. She felt the latex glove against the back of her neck as he grasped the collar of her robe and pulled down, whisking the garment away. She stood naked, trembling, her stomach becoming a huge knot threatening to make her heave.

His finger traced a snaky line down her back, wedging in the crack of her butt. No man had ever touched her there before except Gabe. The killer's breathing accelerated, creating an odd whistling and gurgling noise. He shoved her into the bed, her knees colliding with the mattress. She fell forward.

"Turn over on your back." He sounded monstrous, inhuman.

She obeyed.

"Spread your arms and legs."

She heard him undoing something, then the slight whiz of friction, two things separating. She wondered if she could bear being raped. Would it destroy her? Cause a mental breakdown from which she could never recover?

She searched for some kind of strategy to endure. *Put your mind somewhere else. Escape from here. Go back in time.* She remembered a Sunday afternoon when she was thirteen years old. After a church service at Scotch Ridge, she and Gabe went for a long walk into the woods. On top of a hill they discovered a stand of maples and oaks that formed a circle. They slid between the trees to the opening in the middle. The sun's rays filtered through the leaves creating a spectral vision of shadow and light. She felt like she was in an outdoor cathedral, a place of healing and life. She and Gabe held hands, the rays spilling over them.

She tried to keep her focus on this memory, even when the monster tied a rope around her wrist and strapped her arm to the bedpost. He repeated the maneuver on her feet and other arm, lashing her spread-eagle to the bed. Then she felt the mattress roll and pitch as he crawled on top of her, hovering over her. His amplified breathing intensified. Something paper-like brushed against her cheek—the missing mask? Then she heard the sound of the mask sliding upwards. He kissed her and she tasted strong mouthwash. When he forced his tongue into her mouth, she almost choked.

Be strong for Gabe, she kept telling herself but couldn't help crying. When his hands groped her, she forced her mind back to that place in the woods. He didn't take long to penetrate her. She wanted to scream because of the pain and humiliation but kept her mind on the rays of light and memory of holding Gabe's hand. When he finished his final thrust, he no longer braced himself but allowed his full weight to press on her. Struggling to breath through compressed lungs, she thought he would crush her. Finally, he rolled off and sprang from the bed, the mattress bouncing. Within seconds she lay motionless, his seed spilling out. She wanted to die.

"I'll let you live this time." He walked to the front of the bed and grasped the rope tied to her right hand, shaking it. "I don't know if your husband's still alive. If he is, you better keep your mouth shut about what I just did to you or I'll come into his hospital room and kill him. Hear me?"

Marla felt too traumatized to answer, but he yanked the rope, and she managed to say, "Yes . . . yes, I hear you."

"You go have a rape test done and I'll kill both of you. Hear me?"

She nodded.

"I'm going to untie one of your hands and leave."

She felt the latex glove brushing her wrist as he worked the knot free. *What is he thinking? Of course, if the police find me tied to the bed, they'll know I've been raped. They'll get his DNA.* Her hand dropped to the bed. *He's letting me go. I'm going to live.* She spread her fingers and closed them to get blood flowing again.

"Remember what I said," the demonic voice commanded.

She nodded violently again.

His footsteps trailed away into the living room, fading into the kitchen.

Marla ripped off the blindfold and worked as quickly as possible undoing the knot on her other wrist. Please, *God, don't let Gabe die.* It took several minutes, but finally she managed to loosen it and pull the rope away. Untying the bindings on her feet went more quickly with the advantage of using two hands. As soon as the last knot fell away, she sprang towards the nightstand, snatched the phone, and dialed 911.

The operator answered, a female voice.

"Please," Marla pleaded, "send an ambulance as quickly as possible to 4626 Old Lighthouse Road. My husband was attacked. He's dying."

Chapter 13

Marla tugged on the sleeve of her sweatshirt, making sure it covered the marks on her wrist. She checked the other one and pulled the sleeve clear down to her knuckles. She stared at the white wall in the waiting room, the horrifying memories of the last hour assaulting her mind—Gabe's bloody head, the distorted, evil voice, the ropes, the rape, the frantic 911 call. Once she'd dressed, she'd rushed out to Gabe's side and checked his pulse. His heart was still beating, but just barely. It hadn't taken long for the ambulance to arrive, maybe ten minutes.

She didn't have much to say to the deputy who showed up shortly after the ambulance. He'd asked several questions while the medical personnel prepared Gabe to be transported. She kept her answers short: I heard a commotion. I came outside and found my husband on the ground unconscious. His head had been struck with some kind of object. I don't know who did it. Maybe a thief. That's all I know." Thankfully, they'd ushered her into the back of the ambulance and were on their way before the officer could press for details.

As the images faded, numbness crept over her, a draining of all emotion. She entered the insensate state of exhaustion. She became indifferent to the passing of time, as if asleep with her eyes open. Then she heard footsteps coming towards her and looked up, hoping to see the doctor. But it was the last person she wanted to see, Dugan Walton, still wearing his plaid shirt and blue jeans.

"Marla, I'm so sorry," he said as he sat down next to her. "The news came over the scanner while I was driving home. How are you holding up?"

His question brought a wave of emotion back into her chest, washing away the nothingness. She had to take a deep breath in order to respond. "I'm here."

He reached and grasped her hand. "I'm here too. I want you to know I'm going to do everything I can to find out who did this to Gabe."

She glanced down and saw that the scoring on her wrist had been exposed when he had turned her hand towards him. A chill iced through her, contracting her emotions. She pulled her hand away, wondering if he'd noticed the marks. She didn't look at him, thinking her rejection of his comfort may have bothered him.

"Are you all right? What happened?"

She closed her eyes. "I can't talk about it right now."

With his forefinger he slid the sleeve of her sweatshirt up her arm. "Someone hurt you."

She shook her head, lips tightening. They sat in silence for several minutes. She knew he wanted her to open up, give him details of the incident. The attacker's words kept coming back to her: "You go have a rape test done, and I'll kill both of you. Hear me?" As long as Gabe was alive, she'd keep quiet. If he died, she didn't care if she lived or not.

Dugan grasped her hand again. This time she didn't pull away. "Listen to me," he said. "I'm not going to ask you any more questions tonight. It's been a long day. You've been through hell. I'm not sure what happened to you, but your information could make a difference in this investigation. We could get the guy that attacked Gabe."

He squeezed her hand, and she squeezed back and nodded. "I understand, but please, Dugan, I need time. I'm not ready to talk about this yet."

"Okay." He released her hand. "But if that fiend did to you what I think he did to you, we may not have a lot of time."

She bit her lip. Tears welled in her eyes and spilled down her cheeks. Her body quivered as she sniffled and swallowed, fighting the urge to break down completely. Dugan put his arm around her and pulled her close. His compassion helped. She gathered herself, breathing deeply.

"I'll sit with you for a while."

"No. I'll be okay. It's been a long day for you too."

He lifted his arm over her head and patted her hand. "Since high school I've considered you and Gabe two of the finest people I know."

Dugan's words were unexpected. She met his gaze. "We always liked you."

"It's more than that. Growing up, I didn't get a lot of respect from people. I don't blame anyone really. In junior high I tried to impress everyone by exaggerating things. Actually I lied a lot." Dugan smiled.

Marla turned her hand over and intertwined their fingers. "You were just a kid like the rest of us."

Dugan nodded. "There were problems at home. My father didn't come around too often. Anyway, you and Gabe never made fun of me. By the time high school rolled around I'd grown out of it. But my classmates still had me tagged—Dugie Walton, Texas Ranger, the man with a lethal weapon for a body. You and Gabe never said a negative word to me. Always encouraging and friendly."

"Gabe and I knew you were different, serious about your dreams. Look at you. You're a lawman now, just like you said you'd be."

"That's true. I'm not where I want to be, but I'm working on it."

"Marla!" a familiar voice called from the doorway.

She glanced up to see Michael standing there, face red, Hawaiian shirt somewhat disheveled.

"Where's Gabe? Is he all right?" Michael walked in their direction and stood in front of them. He smelled of alcohol.

"He's in surgery. I haven't heard anything yet."

"I waited for an hour at the restaurant, and he didn't show up."

Dugan asked, "How'd you know to come here?"

"I finally drove home." He held out his hand and wiggled it. "A little drunk, maybe, but not totaled. There was a deputy snooping around the apartment complex. He questioned me—Who was I? Where was I? Why was I there? That sort of thing. I knew something bad happened. Then he told me about Gabe. I came right over."

Marla stared at him. She didn't feel like repeating the whole story. Besides, if Michael hadn't got drunk tonight, this wouldn't have happened to Gabe. Bitterness crept over her like a black veil. She cast her glance to the floor, not wanting to see his florid face, a distortion of Gabe's.

Dugan stood. "Now that Michael's here, I'm going to take off. Big day tomorrow. Lot's of work to do on this investigation." He leaned and touched Marla's cheek. "You going to be all right?"

She nodded. "Thanks for coming."

"We'll talk tomorrow, okay?"

"We'll see."

Dugan's eyes seemed tired but determined. He wouldn't look away, so she lowered hers. He lifted her chin, and she met his gaze again. "You'll feel better tomorrow. We'll talk then." He backed away, waved, and strode out of the waiting room.

Michael plopped down next to her and put his hand on her knee.

She felt like smacking him for being such a lush, such a self-centered fool.

"Fill me in," he said. "What happened?"

She glared at him.

He quickly removed his hand.

Her face felt like it would catch fire. "You are such a self-indulgent jackass."

"What? What'd I do?"

"You promised Gabe not to drink any more tonight, but you did anyway."

Michael held his hands out. "I'm sorry."

"Sorry doesn't help."

"Is he that bad?"

"That bad?" Marla closed her eyes, and the heat that flamed the surface of her face surged through her entire body. "Michael, he might die. All because of you." The words slipped out, although she knew they were only partially true.

Michael leaned forward, resting his face against his hands, elbows on knees. "The deputy didn't tell me much—just that Gabe had a head injury. He wasn't sure exactly how it happened. Do you know?"

"Yes I know. He was attacked."

Michael sat up. "By who?"

"The same man who murdered the girl."

"Are you sure?"

Marla nodded.

"Did you see him? Was it Martin Payne?"

Marla shrugged. "I don't know. I didn't see him."

"Then how do you know it was the same man?"

"Trust me. I know."

Michael gave her the strangest look, as if she'd a lost grip of her sanity.

"After Gabe left to pick you up, I heard a commotion out front. A fight. I found him beside our car unconscious. His head . . . his head had been bashed with some kind of weapon."

"My God," Michael gasped. "I guess it is my fault."

Michael's acceptance of responsibility shifted the weight of guilt to Marla's side. Did she put too much blame on her brother-in-law? "I'm sorry. I didn't mean to totally blame you for what happened."

"But I got drunk and called him to pick me up."

"But you didn't hit him, Michael. Let's drop it."

They sat in silence for many minutes. Michael watched Letterman on the television suspended on a bracket in the far corner of the room. A pile of news magazines lay on the table in front of her, but she didn't feel like reading. Her wonderful life had come to a sudden end like a car skidding through a roadblock and now teetering on the edge of a cliff. The incredible happiness of the last three years may be over. She realized at any second that car could fall into oblivion.

Echoing footsteps jolted her out of her reverie. She peered up to see a doctor walking towards her holding a clipboard. She recognized him—Dr. Shepherd, the one who introduced himself as the surgeon who would be working on Gabe. Her heart raced and a new jolt of fear surged through her. She stood, trying to read his expression. He wore black-rimmed glasses and sported a thick brown mustache. His surgeon's cap covered curly brown hair, his facemask dangling around his neck. He remained pensive, somber, obviously strained from the two hours in surgery where the life of a man depended on his skills.

Marla rose to her feet. "Is he all right, Doctor?"

Michael arose beside her.

Chapter 14

"He's stabilized," the doctor said, "but in a coma." He spoke in a low, somber tone. "He's on a respirator. We're keeping a close eye on him. I've ordered a brain scan. We should be able to get it done in the next couple of hours."

Marla struggled to interpret the few sentences, unable to gauge any degree of optimism in his voice. "So, he's going to be all right?"

Dr. Shepherd reached and clasped Marla's hand, seeming to measure his words. "There's still hope." He made eye contact with her again. "He suffered a severe blow to the head. We'll know more when we get the scan results."

Michael stepped forward. "You said he's on a respirator. Is that keeping him alive?"

"Yes. His heart stopped several times on the operating table. We brought him back, relieved the pressure on his brain, and connected him to the machines that help him breath and monitor his vital functions. Without those machines he would die."

The word "die" made what little stability Marla had left crumble beneath her. She felt dizzy, and the doctor must have noticed because he released her hand, gripped her shoulder, and led her to a seat. She rested her head against her palms.

Dr. Shepherd, leaning on his knees in front of her, said, "Take deep breaths. Close your eyes and try to relax."

After several minutes she regained some strength. She raised the courage to ask the question that weighed on her heart. "Give me the God's honest truth, Dr. Shepherd, please. What are his chances? I need to know what I'm facing."

"I really can't say, but we'll know fairly soon. Dr. Pearson, our neurologist, will take charge of the EEG. I don't want to raise your hopes too high or hit you with the worst-case scenario. Once we get the results we'll be able to answer your questions."

"Can I see Gabe?"

Dr. Shepherd nodded. "We've moved him to ICU for now. He'll be there for a short while until we're ready to do the scan."

"Can I come too?" Michael asked.

Marla almost protested but managed to keep her mouth shut. Michael was Gabe's own flesh and blood. He deserved time with him, especially if Gabe didn't make it through the night. Dr. Shepherd led them down several corridors to large gray double doors with ICU imprinted in block letters on each.

He hit a fist-sized button on the wall and the left door swung open. They entered a spacious room bordered by sectioned glass enclosures, each one housing a patient. The nurses' station to the left buzzed with activity: medical staff conferring about patients' needs, doctors giving orders, nurses scurrying back and forth between the rooms and the station. Because of the glass walls, Marla could see into the rooms, but most of the interiors were darkened, probably to allow the patients to sleep. She wondered where they had put Gabe.

Dr. Shepherd touched Marla's shoulder. "This is Nurse Magdelane."

Marla pivoted to see a thin woman, probably in her early fifties, her black hair streaked with thin lines of gray and tucked under her nurse's cap. Her smile seemed weary, evidence of long hours at a challenging job.

Dr. Shepherd excused himself, promising to let them know what's going on as soon as the scan results were analyzed.

"I'll show you to your husband's room," Nurse Magdelane said, her voice more amiable than Marla expected. She turned left at the nurse's station and walked to the last cubicle. Like the others, the room was dark. A red light blinked and beeped with a steady beat in the upper right corner. The bandage covering most of Gabe's head glowed, reflecting a small florescent light above the bed. The steady rhythm of inhale and exhale from the respirator added an ominous tone to the surroundings, as if Darth Vader loomed in one of the murky corners.

"I'll check back in a few minutes," Nurse Magdelane said before departing.

Michael moved to Marla's side. She didn't know where to put her hands; there were so many tubes and wires. Finally she placed her right hand gently on his chest, feeling the rise and fall of his lungs. Just touching him brought a flood of tears. Michael grasped her shoulder and drew her near. His arm felt so much heavier than Gabe's. She didn't protest his compassion, knowing he must be hurting nearly as much as she. *Why did this happen to us? Why?* Gabe was a beautiful man, a kind and loving soul. She would never find anyone like him again. How could God let this happen to someone so good? And what did she do to deserve being raped?

With his free hand Michael reached and clasped Gabe's hand. Marla noticed their hands matched perfectly. They wore the same ring on the third finger. Why hadn't she noticed this before? She knew Gabe's grandmother had given Gabe the silver band for his high school graduation. Now it made sense. She'd given a matching one to Michael. When Grandma Easton had died two years ago, Gabe had taken it hard, weeping profusely at the funeral. With his thumb and forefinger, Michael wiggled Gabe's ring, inching it up his finger.

"What are you doing?" Marla whispered.

Michael sniffed and swallowed. "Exchanging rings."

"Why?"

"Grandma Easton always told us when you exchange precious gifts you exchange a part of yourself." His arm dropped from her shoulder. He removed his own ring and slid on Gabe's, then placed his on Gabe's finger. "I know it probably doesn't make much sense to you, but if I could somehow put my life into him, I would. I want his life be a part of me."

Marla had to agree that it didn't make much sense, but Michael's way of thinking rarely made sense to her. She didn't like the idea that he took Gabe's ring without her permission but now wasn't the time to obsess over something so small. Knowing Gabe could slip away at any moment made her contention about Michael's ring swap seem insignificant.

Instead, she focused on her husband and the wonderful years they'd shared together: as innocent adolescents, happy-go-lucky teens, idealistic college students, and the last three years—a young married couple exploring the depths and wonder of their love. She remembered the last time they made love, less than three hours ago. Could they have conceived? She was ovulating. Suddenly Michael's words made sense to her. Right now on a microscopic level a part of Gabe's life may be alive within her, united with a part of her to form a new being. She sent up a prayer, asking God to make that possibility a reality. Laying her free hand on the lower part of her stomach, she imagined an embryo within her, alive, forming, growing to become a perfect baby nine months from now.

A muffled voice over an intercom in the outer room sent a horrifying iciness through her. Its electronic distortion reminded her of the rapist's voice. Her heart raced and she pulled her hand away from her belly. What if he impregnated her? The thought of bearing that monster's child turned her stomach. She raised her hand to her mouth and closed her eyes. Is there a test to determine the father of a baby before it's born? Then she remembered Gabe had a sperm count done three days ago. If she's pregnant and his semen couldn't produce a child, then the rapist would be the father. She didn't believe in abortion. *Could this be an exception? Stop it. Quit thinking about it. Don't worry about things that may not have happened.*

"You know," Michael broke the silence, "I asked you and Gabe to move to the Outer Banks because . . . because I'm a lonely man."

Marla opened her eyes and eyed at Michael, his solemn expression a rare occurrence replacing his usual sardonic demeanor.

"I missed hanging out with my twin brother. Of course, I missed you too."

"You don't have to lie, Michael. Ever since Gabe and I started dating seriously, you have resented me for monopolizing his time."

"No, Marla, you're wrong. I admit I get jealous, but that's because I'm so selfish. I know you two have something special. You love each other. Sometimes I wish I could find someone like you and discover what love is all about."

"Maybe you will."

"I don't think so. I'm not like Gabe. He's a better man than me. I admit it. He loves you so much because he has that capacity. He's selfless. I'm not. I'd have to change if I were to find a woman worthy of that kind of love."

"That kind of love is worth changing for."

Michael met her gaze. He bobbed his head slowly, and his eyes sparked as if her words got through.

The door swung open, and Marla swiveled to see Nurse Magdelane enter with two orderlies, young men in their twenties dressed in pale green scrubs. "Dr. Shepherd just called," Nurse Magdelane said. "The neuroimaging department is ready for your husband. They'll be doing a

EEG scan. The staff there will answer any questions and guide you through the paper work. You can follow us down."

After talking briefly with Dr. Shepherd and the technicians, Marla filled out insurance papers and release forms. Dr. Shepherd introduced Dr. Pearson, a neurologist, to her and Michael. A short, balding man, Dr. Pearson promised to have the scans analyzed within two hours. He seemed kind and caring, skilled at dealing with tragedy. After walking them to the waiting room, he assured them they would talk again as soon as he knew more.

Marla slumped into a cushioned chair next to Michael and stared at the television stationed on a stand directly in front of her. Conan O'Brien sat at his desk interviewing Julia Roberts. Wildly gesturing, O'Brien muttered indecipherable words with an Irish brogue. The audience laughed loudly, but to Marla their enjoyment served only to accentuate her pain. She closed her eyes in an effort to shut out the world. Her head became heavy, and she leaned it on the back of the chair. The audience's applause and laughter faded. Her mind emptied, forming a dark corridor. From far away she heard footsteps approaching, echoing down the hall. Her vision blurred. A figure drew near, the footsteps increasing in volume. She tried to focus but couldn't make out the person's face. Was it Dr. Pearson already? She felt so tired. It took incredible effort to lift her head and blink her eyes.

"Marla, it's me," the person said. She still couldn't see clearly but he sounded like Gabe.

"Gabe?"

"I'm here."

"Come closer. I can't see you. Everything's blurry."

"I've been trying to find you."

"Find me?" *Where am I? At the hospital, of course.* "I've been waiting for your test results."

"I'm afraid I didn't do well."

"How could that be? You're out of the coma. I want to hold you." She reached but her hands swept through the blur like one trying to embrace smoke.

"I want to come back to you." His voice receded.

"Why can't I touch you?"

"I'll find a way to come back to you."

"I love you." She felt someone tugging on her elbow.

"I love you too."

She blinked and forced her eyes open to see Michael's wide face. Had she been talking to Michael or Gabe? "Did you see him?"

"Who?"

"Gabe. He was right here."

Michael shook his head, his eyes incredulous.

"I must have been dreaming."

Around 2:00 A.M. Dr. Pearson entered the waiting room, his large wire rim glasses reflecting the light, making it hard to read his eyes. Marla and Michael stood. The doctor held a clipboard in his hands, glancing at it as he approached. He cleared his throat.

Gabe's words echoed in Marla's mind: *I'm afraid I didn't do well.*

Dr. Peason took off his glasses and rubbed his eyes. "I'm sorry." He slid his glasses back on. "I don't have good news."

Marla nodded. "He's not there."

Dr. Pearson's brow furrowed. "Not there?"

"Gabe's gone."

He put his hand on her shoulder. "Yes. There was no activity in the brain."

"But he's trying to come back to me."

The doctor tilted his head. "What?"

"Is he still alive?"

"The machines are keeping his body alive, but his brain's dead."

"Is it my decision?" She took a deep breath and let it out slowly. "You know, to pull the plug."

"Of course." He moved closer and slipped his arm around her shoulder. "But I would recommend it."

She stepped away from him. "I'm not ready to do it yet."

Dr. Pearson bobbed his head. "I understand. You need time to absorb all of this. Go home and catch up on your sleep. Come back tomorrow and we'll talk about it."

Michael asked, "Is there any hope at all?"

"Almost none, barring a miracle."

Michael's lower lip quivered. "Almost none means there is some."

The doctor frowned, his eyes empty of any encouragement.

"Let's go home," Marla said. "I'm too tired to think." She wanted to go home and sleep. Would Gabe come to her again in a dream? She needed his guidance, some kind of sign to help her decide what to do.

Marla insisted on driving Michael's car. She knew he hadn't drunk for several hours, but she still didn't believe he was completely sober. Michael didn't complain. The news about Gabe had sent him into a dazed state. The headlights cut through the thick night, the yellow double lines on the road unreeling before her from the blackness. No cars appeared ahead or behind, houses and businesses had left few lights on, and the silence made it seem like they were driving under water. *Is this what death is like? Darkness. Silence. Nothingness. Emptiness.* She gripped the wheel harder just to feel something.

Halfway home Michael started sniveling. The sniveling turned into weeping. She glanced sideways as he wiped the tears away with his fingers.

Michael sniffed hard, swallowed, and sighed. "I can't believe he's gone."

Marla didn't respond. She didn't want to accept that reality either.

"He was the best person I knew," Michael said. "Everything that I'm not."

Marla kept silent, tacitly agreeing with her brother-in-law. Gabe was a much better man than Michael in every important aspect of life—attitude, generosity, compassion, self-sacrifice, dedication, commitment.

"The other morning on the beach he came up to me," Michael went on. "He was concerned about my health—my overeating and drinking. He wanted me to begin a training program with him. Meet with me in the mornings, start with walking, build up to running. You know what I told him?"

Marla shook her head.

"Leave me alone. Let me squander my life if I want to. You're Mr. Discipline, the runner, the writer, the dreamer, the worker. I'm Mr. Ease and Pleasure. He wanted to help me. He cared about my health more than I do."

"That's the way he was, Michael. He was concerned about you. That's one reason we moved down here. He thought we could be a good influence on you, set an example, maybe get you to grow up and become responsible."

"Gabe always told me I was the talented one. But it came so easy for me. He said I could be a world-class painter or a published writer." Michael sniffed again and wiped his nose with the back of his forearm. "I was satisfied to put in a couple hours a day, collect my check from the galleries and piss my life away."

"You're right about him," Marla said. "He was a man of vision. He could see your potential. He had big plans for himself and for us. More importantly he had the discipline and drive to go after those dreams. That's what he wanted you to catch. He knew he couldn't take what's inside of him and put it inside of you, but he wanted you to catch it."

Michael nodded. "And I more or less told him I'd blow my own nose. Let me be."

Marla slowed the car, put on the blinker, and pulled into the apartment complex driveway. She wanted to crawl into bed, fall asleep, and never wake up again unless Gabe was lying beside her.

"I'll walk you to your door. Who knows if that maniac is still around or not? I swear, Marla, I'll keep my eye out for you. Call me if you hear any strange noises."

That possibility rekindled fear within her. "I will. Thanks." She handed Michael the keys and they exited the car and headed towards the front steps. At the door as Marla turned the deadbolt, Michael asked if she wanted him to check inside the house. Remembering the ropes tied to the bedposts, she told him not to bother. She'd be fine. For now she didn't want Michael to know what happened to her. She didn't want to think about tomorrow, about deciding Gabe's fate, or reporting the crime and going through a rape test. Sleep was all she wanted. A chance to escape this night's horror. A chance to see Gabe even if only in a dream.

When she entered the bedroom and saw the ropes, waves of anger beat back her fears. With each cord she untied, the level of rage towards the murderer increased. Now she wished she would have dove for the baseball bat on the ground by the car and taken her chances. If he'd killed her, so what? Gabe's spirit was gone, no longer indwelling his body. She had nothing to lose. Gabe's Louisville Slugger? Where was it? She had laid it by the front steps while waiting for the emergency squad to get there. The officer asked about it, but she had told him it was hers. She imagined swinging the bat and cracking open the skull of the rapist. She hated violence, but the vision empowered her. She wanted to kill the creep who violated her and took away the life of the man she loved. If he'd come back tonight, she wouldn't hesitate. She'd kill him or die trying.

After placing the ropes in the bottom drawer of the night stand, Marla walked towards the front door. She wanted that bat. Tonight she'd sleep beside it, her hand on it. She flipped on the porch light and peered out the window, seeing no one on the deck. She turned the deadbolt, undid the lock on the knob, and opened the door. Oddly, she wasn't afraid. Did a craving for vengeance have that much power? She crossed the deck and descended the steps. The porch light didn't illuminate the landscaping in front of the deck adequately. Marla scoured the ground around the plants and decorative stones but couldn't see the bat.

From behind she heard slapping, the sound of wood rapping someone's palm. She whirled to see the silhouette of a man holding a bat. He said, "Are you looking for this?"

Chapter 15

The porch light delineated his form, revealing an ominous black figure with glowing edges. He stood about six feet tall, husky, legs spread and muscular arms. Marla's legs threatened to collapse, and her heart pounded into her throat. Then she focused on his bald dome.

"Sonny? Is that you?"

"It's me." He moved closer, extending the bat handle to her.

She grabbed the bat, remembering how the rapist used the word "mischievous." Could it have been Sonny? She gripped the handle tightly just in case he tried to come at her. But why would he give her the bat, if he planned on attacking her? It didn't make sense, but she still wasn't ready to trust anyone.

"You look frightened," he said.

"I am." As she spoke she couldn't keep her voice from trembling. "I've had a horrible night."

"No need to be afraid of me."

She tried to swallow but her throat felt like stale bread. "I can't help it, Sonny." In the weak light she managed to see his eyes lose their focus and the corner of his lips turn down. She wondered if he felt wounded knowing he scared her.

"I'm sorry," he mumbled. "A neighbor told me an ambulance took Gabe to the hospital, but I don't know any details. What happened?"

"Someone attacked Gabe."

Sonny straightened up, eyes becoming incensed. "Who? Tony Trenton?"

"We don't know."

"Is Gabe all right?"

The question pierced Marla to the core of her being. She couldn't answer, her throat tightening. Her eyes welled with tears, and she wiped them away with her fingertips. She shook her head sideways, took a deep breath, and blew it out audibly.

Sonny edged closer but didn't try to embrace her or even pat her on the back. Marla was glad. She didn't want any man touching her. She cleared her throat. "Gabe's in a coma."

Sonny raised his hand to his mouth. "Holy Joe Moley. I'm so sorry. I had no idea things were this bad. After I dropped off Frank and Wyatt, I went for a long walk on the beach. Must have walked four miles or so. By the time I got back the excitement was over. Fred Parsons from down the road told me about the ambulance. What did the doctors say?"

"They administered an EEG scan to check for brain activity." Marla sniffled, struggling to continue. "Nothing."

Sonny's bottom lip trembled. "He's . . . he's dead?"

"His body's alive, but his spirit's gone."

"Dammit! Why didn't I stick around? I could've helped him."

"It's not your fault, Sonny. Michael was drunk. He needed a ride home from the restaurant. Gabe left to go get him. That's when it happened."

"Yeah, but . . ." Sonny placed his hands on his hips and stared at the sky. "I should have been watching over this place. That's my job—making sure everything's secure."

"You're the maintenance man. No one expects you to fend off killers."

"But that girl was strangled yesterday. There's a murderer in this neighborhood." He put his hands on the sides of his head. "I should've been here."

Marla observed him carefully, looking for some hint of guile in his mannerisms or speech, but he seemed sincerely upset, furious with himself for his perceived irresponsibility. "I understand you feel awful. We all do. But please don't blame yourself."

Sonny met her gaze, his brow tensing. "I swear to you, Marla, I won't let anything like this happen around here again. I'll patrol this property reg'larly. Every hour on the hour. I'll make sure no strangers come snoopin' 'round here. You can count on me. If that killer comes back . . ." He raised his fists. " . . .I'll put a hurtin' on him."

Sonny's fury sent nervous tremors through her. He'd flashed the same anger when he confronted Tony Trenton. Was he capable of that kind of lethal violence? She felt the weight of the bat in her hand and remembered her craving for vengeance—the vision of the bat cracking the head of the killer. A cold wave flowed over her, dousing the sparks of fear. *I'm capable of it. I'd do it without thinking twice.*

Chapter 16

With the bat by her side, Marla slept for about five hours. But she did not dream. Gabe did not come to her to offer guidance about her decision, nor did the killer intrude in a nightmare to violate her again. It was as if she had died for five hours, left this world, and then, with the morning sun slanting through the blinds, had been rudely re-deposited into her body, awakened to face the brutal world again.

By 9:00 A.M. she'd taken a quick shower, threw on jeans and a t-shirt, stepped into a pair of flip-flops, gobbled a breakfast bar, and washed it down with a glass of milk. She didn't fix her hair or put on make up. She didn't care. Getting back to Gabe was all that mattered. Besides, he'd complimented her natural beauty many times, saying she didn't need makeup. If only he'd say that today. As she headed out the door she hoped for a miracle.

In the hospital room she stood by Gabe's bed, holding his hand. The machines beeped, whirred, and respired their mechanical rhythms. His hand felt warm and alive, but looking at his head, she knew all hope had almost perished. All she could do was pray. So she prayed. She'd never prayed that long and hard in her life. But would it do any good? Would

God listen to her? Did he care that the love of her life may never speak to her again?

By noon she felt prayed out and exhausted—mentally, physically, and spiritually. Still holding his hand, she leaned on the bed railing and closed her eyes. Vividly, she remembered the dream from when she'd fallen asleep in the waiting room. She heard the footsteps walking down the corridor and Gabe's voice saying, "I'm here . . . I've been trying to find you . . . I want to come back to you."

She rose up and squeezed his hand. "Come back to me, my love. Please, come back to me."

Speaking the words aloud brought a flood of memories. Her mind drifted five years into the past to a country road near Mount Pleasant, Ohio. Marla and Gabe had pedaled up and down rolling hills for almost an hour on a long bike trek. They'd pulled off the side of the road near a cemetery to sit in the shade of an immense elm tree and share a bottle of water. After finishing their drink and resting a few minutes, they'd decided to take a stroll through the graveyard and check out the more interesting monuments.

Somewhere near the middle an angel had caught Gabe's eye, and they cut through the rows of stones to get a closer look. The large monument stood about seven feet high. The bottom half consisted of a square block of granite that served as a pedestal for a kneeling angel. Her surface had endured a century of exposure to the elements, creating a weathered texture of grays and off-whites. Hands folded and head bowed, she faithfully prayed over the buried bodies of a deceased couple. Her long tresses flowed over her shoulders and down her back between two exquisite wings. Unfortunately, a portion of the right wing had been broken off at the top, giving Marla the impression that the poor thing was now earthbound.

Gabe's hand had shot out and grabbed hers, a reflexive movement. "Look at the names," he'd said.

Marla had read them aloud. "Gabriel Early—husband . . . Martha Early—wife." She gasped and read them again. "Gabriel and Martha. That's almost the same as ours."

"Look below the names," he'd said.

"In life, in death, and beyond the bounds of this earth, I will always love you."

Gabe had lowered himself to his knees, very similar to the angel's position.

"What are you doing?" Marla had asked.

He'd reached and grasped her hand then gazed into her eyes. "In life, in death, and beyond the bounds of this earth, I will always love you." He'd inserted his hand into his pocket and pulled out a ring, a diamond ring. Holding it up for her to see, he'd said, "Will you marry me?"

Marla had almost collapsed, she felt so weak in the knees. She'd stared at the ring, only moderate in size but so unexpected that it seemed to glow like a two carat diamond. After regaining some composure, she'd dropped to her knees. "Yes. Yes. Yes. I will marry you."

He'd slipped it on her finger, and she drew it closer, lost in its beauty and the significance of the moment. Then they'd embraced in front of the monument that memorialized the life and love of the buried couple, invoking a renewal or resurrection of their love, one that would last beyond the bounds of this earth. Passionate kissing had followed, so passionate that Marla gave into the flames of desire, wanting Gabe to make love to her for the first time right in the middle of a graveyard. They'd managed to remove each other's tops, but then Gabe had slowed down.

"We can't go through with this," he'd said. "Remember what Pastor Byron taught us about God's best design for a couple?"

Marla had remembered. Pastor Byron had said that true love can wait until marriage but lust can't. She'd marveled at Gabe's self-control in that moment of sexual heat. If it had been up to her, they would have consummated their love right there under God's big blue sky six feet above that couple who had pledged to love each other into eternity. She believed God would have forgiven them. They were human beings caught up in the flames of desire.

Owing mostly to Gabe's idealism, they'd waited until their wedding night to make love for the first time. Looking back, Marla had to admit Pastor Byron was right: Their life together had been wonderful. Was it because they had waited?

On the ride home Gabe had talked about his ideas of true love. Obsession and infatuation with someone didn't carry much weight in his opinion. Of course, they were obsessed with each other, but he said that would pass. Contrary to the notions of romantic movies and soap operas, living on a love-struck cloud didn't guarantee the deeper, more lasting benefits of love. He knew the emotional high of falling head over heels for each other could never last. According to Gabe, their characters would ultimately determine the quality of their love. He believed if the contents of their hearts were filled with compassion, kindness, gentleness, patience, forbearance, and forgiveness, then they would forge a love that would last beyond this world. Who they were was more important than the fickle fluctuations of emotion. Marla had to agree. Gabe's character brimmed with those traits.

As they had pedaled home, they came to a challenging hill. Marla had kept up at first, but her legs had become heavy, and Gabe slowly had pulled away. The hill had seemed more like a mountain, a least a mile long, and Gabe would disappear around a turn, making Marla frustrated. She had yelled at him several times to wait for her, but he had kept going. Finally, exasperated and exhausted, she had given up hope of catching him. She had stopped the bike, stepped off, and begun walking it up the hill. That's when he came back to her. She had refused to talk to him at first or even look at him but then had realized she was being foolish.

"Why didn't you come back to me when I yelled at you?" she had asked.

Pushing his bike beside her, he had extended his arm and touched her cheek. Their eyes had met. "I wanted to make it to the top without stopping. But I always intended on coming back to you."

Now, as Marla stood beside the hospital bed, she wondered again if he would return. "Please come back to me, my love. Give me some kind of sign."

She squeezed his hand one last time and was about to let go when he squeezed back. The response made her jump. "Gabe! Gabe! Can you hear me?"

She held his hand lightly, wanting him to tighten his grip on her again. Nothing. She squeezed his hand and waited. Seeing the green nurse's button on the bed railing, she pushed it.

"Can I help you?" a female voice said over an intercom.

"My husband, he just squeezed my hand. He must be coming out of the coma."

"I'll be right there."

His eyelids were closed, and the respirator continued to methodically pump air in and out of his lungs. She gripped his palm and rubbed his shoulder. "Gabe, can you hear me? If you can, squeeze my hand again."

A nurse entered the room, a hefty brunette with bushy eyebrows. "Tell me what happened," she said with a nasally voice.

"He squeezed my hand."

She nodded and checked the lights and flashing numbers on the equipment bank to the left of the bed. She grasped his other hand. "Mr. Easton, can you hear me?" She leaned closer to his head.

"Call him Gabe, " Marla said. "No one calls him Mr. Easton."

"Gabe, can you hear me? If you can, squeeze my hand." She loomed over him, very still, focusing on his face for almost a minute. Then she shook her head and glanced at Marla. "Are you sure it wasn't just a nervous twitch?"

"Yes, I'm sure." Marla's voice became strident. "I squeezed his hand, and he squeezed mine back."

She nodded. "I'll get the doctor." The large nurse pivoted and marched out of the room, her footsteps trailing down the hall.

Marla sent up a quick prayer, thanking God for the sign for which she'd been asking. She held tightly to Gabe's hand just in case he signaled her again. After several minutes she heard footsteps approaching.

Dr. Shepherd entered the room followed by the nurse. "I'm afraid this is a false alarm," he said.

"What do you mean? How could it be?"

He came to the side of the bed opposite her. "What you felt was probably an involuntary reflex. Even brain dead patients will move sometimes. Their muscles contract and relax. It's not unusual."

She glared at him. "But I squeezed his hand and asked him to respond to me. That's when he squeezed back."

"I understand. Probably coincidence. We know there's no activity in Gabe's brain. But his body continues to function. These kind of nerve related tics and movements happen all the time."

Marla struggled to keep her temper under control. "But, Doctor, you told me I need to make a decision. I'm trying to do that. I've been praying for a sign from God, and Gabe squeezed my hand. Now you're telling me it's a coincidence? I should go ahead and pull the plug anyway?"

Dr. Shepherd combed his fingers through his curly brown hair, took a deep breath, and blew it out. "No. I don't want you to do anything until you are sure about it."

"Is it possible Gabe is back? Could he have regained his mental functioning?"

He shook his head. "It's very unlikely."

"I want another brain scan done."

Dr. Shepherd glanced at the nurse and shrugged.

Marla walked around the bed and faced them. "He gave me a sign. I will not take him off those machines unless I have proof positive that there's no activity in his brain."

He reached and patted her shoulder. "Okay. We'll do another EEG scan. I know you're hoping for a miracle. I've seen a few in my years of practice. But very few."

Marla didn't care what kind of odds Dr. Shepherd gave Gabe. A sign was a sign. She wouldn't make any hasty decisions, even if it took months.

She stayed by Gabe's side and held his hand for several hours until she became incredibly hungry. With dizziness coming on and a slight headache threatening to turn into a migraine, she knew she had to get something to eat. She decided to head down to the basement level and check out the hospital's cafeteria.

When the elevator's doors parted, there stood Deputy Dugan Walton. Seeing him reminded her of another decision she needed to make. Dread sunk into the core of her bones as the memory of the rapist's threat echoed in her mind. She steeled herself, knowing she had to deal with it.

His eyes brightened. "Marla, I was hoping to catch you here."

Marla nodded. "I was heading down to get something to eat. Want to join me?"

"Of course. I could use a cup of coffee and a sandwich."

Marla shuffled into the elevator and hit the "B" button. As the doors closed, she glanced at Dugan.

He met her gaze, his eyes laden with concern. "How are you holding up?"

"I haven't given up hope."

"Good."

"I think the doctors have, but I haven't"

Dugan rubbed his chin and dipped his head, giving Marla the impression he was undecided about Gabe's chances.

The elevator doors parted, they exited, and followed the signs to the cafeteria. It was a sunless room, lit by intermittent fluorescent lights across a white-paneled ceiling. The floor, a burnt orange tile, and pale green walls didn't help to add vitality to the place. At least they didn't have to wait in a long line. Marla's stomach felt like it had collapsed in upon itself. She played it safe and selected a turkey hoagie with plenty of cheese, lettuce, and tomatoes. She usually drank Diet Coke but opted for a large coffee, hoping the caffeine would jumpstart her or at least give her enough zip to get through the rest of the afternoon.

They sat down at a booth in the back, a good distance from the few people scattered at various tables around the room. The sandwich was just what she needed, and the coffee, although strong, warmed her insides and, within minutes, jolted her wide-awake. Dugan dug into his ham sandwich and fries like he hadn't eaten since sunup. Between bites she filled him in on all of the details of the last two days concerning Gabe's condition. Dugan asked a few general questions but let Marla do most of the talking.

The words poured out. She admired and trusted Dugan. Confiding in a long-time friend helped relieve the incredible stress pressing upon her.

When a lull in the conversation occurred, Marla thought about Dugan noticing the cuts on her wrists the night before. She knew he wanted to broach the subject and wondered how much she would tell him. She stared at the scoring on her wrists and then met his eyes.

"I know what you're thinking," she said.

Dugan nodded. "Did the guy that attacked Gabe force himself on you?"

She closed her eyes and shuttered. "Yes. He raped me."

"I'm sorry, Marla." Dugan patted her hand.

She stared into her lap, shame washing over her.

He scooted closer to the table and grasped her hand. "Listen carefully. We can get this guy. We can put him away for life. He'll never harm another innocent person again, if you are willing to help."

A tear trickled down her cheek, and she wiped it away with her fingertips. "I want to help, but . . . but . . ."

Dugan squeezed her hand tighter. "You can tell me."

"But the rapist threatened to kill Gabe and me if I reported what happened."

"We can protect you."

She sniffed, snagged a napkin from the holder, and wiped her nose. "I guess I'm not as concerned now. Dr. Shepherd wants me to take Gabe off the machines. But I'm not willing yet. I asked for another brain scan. If he is brain dead, I don't know what I'll do."

"Did the rapist use a condom?"

Marla shook her head sideways.

"You're sure he didn't?"

"Of course I'm sure."

"If you are willing to let a staff member here administer a rape kit test, I guarantee you we will catch this guy."

Finally, Marla glanced up at him. "How can you guarantee me that?"

"We found three distinct traces of DNA at the crime scene from three different individuals. The traces came from three sources: the rope, the mask, and the rape test on the girl."

"Three different people?"

Dugan bobbed his head.

"But wouldn't the DNA from the rape test identify the killer?"

"Not necessarily. I'm guessing that DNA belongs to Tony Trenton. He confessed he had consensual sex with the girl that afternoon. The killer may not have raped her. She managed to free her hand and rip the horn off his mask. I believe that's when he strangled her. That's why any evidence we get from you is so important."

"What do you mean?"

"I think it will match up with the DNA from one of three sources. If it matches the DNA from the girl's rape test than we know Trenton's probably the killer. If it matches the specimen from the rope or the mask, then we have the same DNA from two crime scenes. All we have to do is find the suspect with matching DNA. I've got the list narrowed down to three people—Trenton, Martin Payne, or Sonny Keys."

"But what if the DNA from my test doesn't match those three?"

Dugan pulled his hands away and folded them under his chin. "Then we'll keep looking. We'll find him."

Marla eyed her empty plate, the desire for revenge seething within her. Or was it a longing for justice? She'd take both. "Last night I slept with Gabe's Louisville Slugger next to me. If that monster came back, I would've crushed his skull."

"Do you have a gun in the house?"

"No."

"Have you ever shot a gun?"

"Yes. My uncle took me into the country a few times to shoot his pistol and hunting rifle. I'm not afraid of handling a gun."

Dugan rubbed his chin, an approving look in his eyes. "We'll step up our patrols in your neighborhood. However, two of the suspects live in your apartment complex. You could stay at my apartment, if you'd like. I'm willing to sleep on the couch."

"I'm not going to run away from those three. Trenton scares me the most."

"Take the rape kit test then. If Trenton's the man, we'll put him in jail as soon as the results come back."

Dugan's words made sense. Now she felt it her duty to follow through on any course of action that would help convict her husband's attacker. With all she'd gone through in the last two days, a rape test couldn't make things worse. Maybe it was their only hope.

Dugan led the way to the elevator. They stopped at the first floor, exited, and walked through the maze of hallways to the emergency room. There he introduced her to Nurse Cummings, a medium built redhead, probably in her late thirties. She took Marla into a private room to administer the test. It was the size of a small bedroom with white walls and ceiling. White cabinets lined the wall opposite the examination table.

The first question Nurse Cummings asked was if she had taken a shower or bath since the rape. Marla confessed she'd taken a brief shower that morning. The nurse seemed displeased but continued with the procedure. She took a blood sample, vaginal swab, anal swab, did a pubic hair inspection collecting several samples, and then asked for a urine specimen. Marla stepped into a small adjacent bathroom to oblige her.

After handing Nurse Cummings the cup, Marla hoped the humiliation was over. "Anything else?"

The nurse opened a drawer and pulled out a translucent orange bottle. "These are called 'Morning-After Pills.' Do you know what they're for?"

"Yes. To abort the baby in case the rapist impregnated me."

"I suggest you take one."

Marla had to think. After she and Gabe made love last night, she'd felt so confident she was pregnant. She wondered about the results of his sperm test. Then she remembered feeling so violated after the rapist rolled off of her, his seed dripping from between her legs. If she was pregnant, she couldn't be sure who the father was until she checked on Gabe's sperm test.

She took a deep breath. "No. I don't want one."

The nurse dipped her head slowly, eyes fixed on Marla. "Sure?"

Marla nodded.

She placed the bottle on the counter and then faced Marla. "All of this evidence will be turned over to the investigation team. I commend you on your courage to complete this exam." Nurse Cummings seemed to relax, her features losing that professional stoicism. "One more thing, Mrs. Easton."

Marla raised her chin.

"I truly hope they catch the scum-sucking bastard who did this to you."

Amen to that, Marla thought.

Marla decided to tell Dugan about the ropes she'd placed in the drawer of her nightstand. Since she'd committed herself to helping solve the crime, she wanted to hand over any evidence that may provide a break in the case. He appeared intrigued and offered to drive her home to pick them up and return her to the hospital. The trip wouldn't take that long, so she agreed. She could be back at Gabe's side within two hours.

On the way, Dugan mentioned the towrope found at the murder scene. His description matched her memory of the rope the rapist used—yellow-corded nylon that easily cut into the skin. Dugan believed it might provide another source of DNA. As Marla listened to him talk about the technical aspects of solving the case, she marveled at the transformation of an insecure ten year old into an intelligent, skilled young man, one on the fast track to becoming a successful investigator. More and more she felt convinced she'd done the right thing—defy the rapist's threats and make an all-out effort to contribute to his capture.

After entering the apartment, Marla led Dugan to the bedroom and gathered the ropes from the drawer. When she pivoted to hand them to him, he was facing the side of the bed staring at the covers. Then she noticed the bat handle sticking out.

"That's my security stick," she said. "It's better than a security blanket."

Dugan faced her, took the ropes, and placed them into an evidence bag. "Wait here. I've got something out in the car for you." He marched out of the bedroom and angled towards the front door.

Marla wondered what in the world he wanted to give her. Pepper spray, maybe?

Within a minute or two he returned with a black handgun. He held it out. "Smith and Wesson forty-five. It's a beauty."

The pistol's hard, angular appearance sent a chill through her. She brushed the textured handle with her fingertips. "You're giving this to me?"

"Yes, ma'am. It's a loan for your safety." He pointed at the bat. "If that's a security stick, then this is the whole damn lumber yard."

"Is it easy to shoot?"

"Sure." Dugan turned it over. "It takes a ten-round clip." He moved a lever and a cartridge popped out of the handle. "See." He shoved it back in with his palm until it clicked. "Here's the safety. Take it off if you want to shoot. Just point and pull the trigger." He gripped the barrel and offered her the handle.

She reached but hesitated. "Will it fire now?"

"The safety's on." He pointed. "Slide that little lever over if you ever need to fire it."

She grasped the handle. It felt lighter than she'd imagined, its surface cold against her palm. "It's not as heavy as my uncle's pistol."

"The barrel's stainless steel but the handle's made out of plastic."

Facing the window, she raised the gun, imagining an intruder breaking through the screen. "How do you aim?"

"You could use the sight on the barrel but at this range just point and shoot."

In her mind she pulled the trigger. Bam! The bullet entered the rapist's chest, crimson spreading across the front of his white t-shirt. *Take that you scum-sucking bastard.*

Dugan placed his hand on her shoulder. "Where will you keep it?"

She lowered the revolver. "Right under my husband's pillow."

Chapter 17

The rest of the week trudged by like a bad movie. Michael accompanied Marla to the hospital on Tuesday and Thursday but had to meet with gallery owners on the other days. Sometimes he'd show up on his own late in the afternoon. He wasn't much help anyway, always regretting his mistake of drinking too much that night, blaming himself for Gabe's encounter with the killer. Marla wished he'd drop it. What happened, happened. Dwelling on who's to blame only prolonged the pain of that night. She was tired of hearing it.

Then she had to put up with Michael's incessant pledge to protect her, to keep his eye out for anything or anyone who may be a threat. She never told him about the rape or the handgun under Gabe's pillow. She didn't need Michael to protect her. She almost wished the rapist would return, believing she wouldn't hesitate to put a bullet right between his eyes or at least empty the clip of that Smith and Wesson into his chest. She hated the monster for destroying her life.

She didn't need Sonny Keys to protect her either, but he was out there every day, ten times a day patrolling the grounds. Whenever she'd see him as she left for the hospital or came home, he would ask about Gabe and promise to do everything in his power to keep the apartments safe. Marla was ninety-nine percent sure Sonny didn't commit the crimes. How could someone that compassionate and caring perpetrate such evil? But that one percent still lingered in the back of her brain like a tiny red spot on a white tablecloth.

She was anxious to hear back from Dugan Walton about the DNA results. If Tony Trenton or Martin Payne or Sonny Keys had raped her, she would turn into a bulldog in court, determined to send him to the state penitentiary for the rest of his life. Hopefully, he'd be thrown into a cell with a big roommate named Brutus, who would exact revenge for her a thousand times over.

Earlier in the week Dr. Shepherd had reported that the latest brain scan again showed no activity. He'd sat her down and told her not to prolong the inevitable. She didn't want to hear it. God's sign was clear—Gabe had definitely squeezed her hand. Even if it was an involuntary reflexive movement, it occurred at the exact moment she'd appealed to Gabe to respond. He deserved more time. The dream she'd had in the waiting room the night of the attack hadn't faded. She could picture the scene in her mind and hear his voice as if she'd just awakened. If Gabe wanted to find a way to come back to her, she wouldn't eliminate an option by removing life support. That's for damn sure.

On Friday, after a long day at the hospital, she wanted to stop by the bookstore to see Mee Mee Roberts. Her boss had been so gracious, insisting Marla could have as much time off as she needed with pay. She didn't want to take advantage of Mee Mee's generosity and decided to come back to work next week on a part-time basis. When Marla entered the store, Mee Mee glanced up from a box full of books she'd been unpacking.

"Marla! I wasn't expecting you." She arose, stepped over the box, rushed to Marla, and embraced her. "I've been so worried about you."

"I had to come see you." Holding her tightly, sensing an outpouring of concern from Mee Mee, Marla fought back tears. Mee Mee'd become like a big sister to her and a more appreciated source of comfort than her brother-in-law. Marla closed her eyes and allowed herself a few moments of solace generated by a heartfelt hug.

They separated, and Mee Mee asked, "How are you holding up?"

"You know how they say to take it day by day?"

Mee Mee nodded.

"I'm taking it hour by hour."

"Be strong." Mee Mee cupped Marla's cheeks in her hands. "This is the dark night of your soul."

"But will it ever end?"

"It has to. You'll make it through, even if you have to take it minute by minute." Mee Mee led her to a couple of reading chairs by a large window. "Can I get you a cup of coffee?"

"No thanks. I've had six cups today already."

"How about a glass of Merlot?"

"Now that might hit the spot."

Mee Mee fetched the wine and glasses, filled the goblets halfway, handed one to Marla, and eased into her seat. Marla sipped the crimson liquid. It felt cooling, soft, and velvety as it went down. Sitting back in the cushioned chair, she took a deep breath and another drink. The wine loosened her tongue, and she caught Mee Mee up on all that had happened in the last few days. Mee Mee listened attentively, giving her a chance to unravel her thoughts and feelings. Every sentence, every word spoken helped to ease the stress that had built up. As the minutes flowed by, the tension in her chest lessened, and her shoulders relaxed as if a yoke had been removed.

After telling Mee Mee about the sign of Gabe squeezing her hand, she asked, "Do you think I'm crazy?"

"Of course not. Your heart will tell you what to do."

"But am I prolonging suffering by keeping Gabe alive?"

Mee Mee clasped Marla's hand and squeezed it. "Listen, Honey. You'll know when the time is right. It may be tomorrow. It may be months from now. Don't go pulling any plugs until your heart and your mind come to an agreement."

Marla nodded and took another sip. She told Mee Mee she would begin work again on Monday, at least on a part-time basis. Mee Mee insisted there was no hurry, but Marla said she needed to get back on the job—it would help her to have a diversion from all the turmoil she was facing.

A customer entered, and they both glanced up. He wore black slacks and a black polo shirt. It was Martin Payne. An alarm went off in Marla's brain. Dugan Walton considered Payne a prime suspect. She hadn't seen him around the apartments since the attack.

He nodded at them, a flash of recognition entering his eyes. "Mrs. Easton?"

Marla's heart sped up. "Good afternoon, Mr. Payne."

He marched towards them and stopped within a few feet. "I wanted to tell you how sorry I am to hear about your husband." His face appeared strained, dark bags under his eyes.

"Thank you for your concern."

Payne leaned towards her. "I hear he's in a coma."

Marla's eyes darted from Mee Mee back to Payne. "Yes. He's been in a coma ever since . . . ever since last Friday."

Payne's eyes widened. "Someone assaulted him?"

Marla tried to detect guilt in his expression but couldn't discern anything tangible. "Yes, sir. He suffered a terrible blow to the head."

Payne's eyes lost focus, as if he were looking beyond them into another realm. "I truly hope he comes out of it for your sake."

Thank you was all Marla could think to say. Silence followed, and Marla's and Mee Mee's eyes met. She sensed Mee Mee was on edge too. When she glanced back up at Payne, he refocused on her.

Finally, he said, "What do the doctors say?"

Marla couldn't imagine why Payne was suddenly interested in her. In the six weeks they'd lived next to him, he hadn't spoken more than a few sentences to her. Then she remembered his wife. *She's in a coma too. And he may have put her there.* "They don't give me much hope."

"Did they do a brain scan?"

"Yes, but . . . but there was no activity."

"And they want you to remove him from life support."

Marla nodded. The tension in Payne's face melted. Was that compassion Marla detected in his eyes?

"I know exactly what you are going through. It's a terrible position to be in. Have you heard about my wife?"

"She's also in a coma? No brain activity?"

Payne bobbed his head. "That right. It's been a year. A year of pure hell."

Marla was afraid to ask the question, but the words slipped out. "And you don't want to let her go?"

The lines in Payne's face deepened as the muscles beneath the surface tightened. "No. No. I will not allow them to remove life support," he said, his voice quavering. He took a few seconds to compose himself. "She wants me to end it, but I'm not ready."

"Who wants you to end it?" Mee Mee asked. "Your doctor?"

Payne shook his head. "I shouldn't have said it that way. I'm sorry. You wouldn't understand what I'm talking about." He rubbed his forehead. "It's been difficult. Sometimes I don't make sense even to myself."

Marla met Mee Mee's gaze again, sensing the uncomfortable feeling mounting.

"You see," he went on, "I still talk to my wife."

Marla sought words to dispel the uneasiness. "I talk to Gabe too. I know he can't hear me, but it helps to talk to him."

"No," Payne said. "You don't understand. I believe my wife hears me. She hasn't departed this earth yet. She's still here."

Marla's back turned to gooseflesh. She glanced at Mee Mee, who was staring at Payne with the oddest expression.

"I hope you don't mind me asking, Martin," Mee Mee said, "but does this have something to do with those books you've been ordering—the ones about walk-ins?"

Payne closed his eyes, nodding ever so slightly. "Please don't think I'm crazy. I've never mentioned this to anyone."

Mee Mee shrugged. "A lot of people believe this sort of thing is possible."

Payne opened his eyes, the intensity returning. "I know it is. I'm sure of it."

Marla sat quietly, not knowing what to say. Did he think Gabe was in this netherworld too? Obviously Payne had been under tremendous stress for months. Had he lost it? She eyed the nerve-frayed man. *Maybe I should take Gabe off those machines.*

Payne leaned closer to Marla, his eyes wide and anxious. "If you ever want to talk . . . if you want to learn what I've discovered, please don't hesitate to stop by. There is a way for your husband to come back to you."

"Martin," Mee Mee broke in, "I'm sure Marla appreciates your insight, but she needs time right now to adjust to all that has happened—a person can deal with only so much."

Payne straightened and edged back as if he realized he'd stepped over a boundary he shouldn't have crossed. "I'm sorry . . . I didn't mean to come on too strong, but I've been there, that's all. I know what you're going through." He backed away. "Forgive me if I've frightened you."

"Oh no," Marla said. "Thank you for your concern. We'll talk some day."

Payne backed away. "I . . . I need to find some books." He about-faced and sped to the back of the store.

Marla took a deep breath and blew it out audibly. "Thanks." Her voice could barely be heard. "That conversation was on the outskirts of reality."

Mee Mee wiggled her fingers. "Somewhere between the *Twighlight Zone* and the *Outer Limits.*"

"Yeah. Out there on the edge somewhere."

"You never know, though." Mee Mee patted Marla's hand. "Life is like an iceberg. We see the tip—that's what we understand, but there's a whole mountain of ice under the water we don't see."

Marla agreed. She struggled to comprehend what she *could* see—why it all happened. Martin Payne had struggled also, much longer than she, and it showed. But his words lingered in her mind: *There is a way for your husband to come back to you.*

When Marla pulled onto Route 12 to head home, she peered in her rearview mirror and noticed a Jeep parked on the side of the road. A black Jeep with its top down—Tony Trenton's Jeep? She glanced at the highway ahead and swallowed, hoping she was wrong. She checked the rearview again, and her heart double-timed. The Jeep had pulled onto the road. She sped up. The Jeep kept pace. The driver resembled Trenton. It had to be him. Was he trailing her?

She turned down a side street without putting on her blinker. Maybe he'd go straight. Before she turned right at the next road to double back, she checked the mirror and saw the black vehicle had followed, drawing closer. *What's he want? Is he after me?* She gripped the wheel and spun it, causing her car to slide around the corner. Her knees shook. She leaned closer to the wheel. Where can I go? Someplace with a lot of people. A store. A restaurant. She glanced at the buildings on each side of the street, looking for a parking lot. Nothing. She made the next right turn and saw the stop sign ahead—Route 12 again. Left would take her back to the bookstore. Right would lead home.

At the stop sign she eyed the mirror again and made sure it was Trenton driving the vehicle. The driver stopped almost on her bumper. No doubt about it—Trenton. He wore dark sunglasses and a flannel shirt with cut-off sleeves. His snide smile let on that he knew she recognized him. He raised his chin and scratched his two-day beard.

The attack on Gabe and the rape flashed across the screen of her mind. She hit the gas and turned right onto Route 12, back towards the apartments. "Okay, you son of a bitch. You want to follow me home? Then I've got something waiting for you there. Something that will blow your mind . . . right out of your skull."

During the mile ride home, Marla kept checking to see how far back Trenton lingered. He didn't tailgate like she had predicted he might, probably to avoid drawing attention to himself in case he passed a cop.

Could she really do this? *Oh, yes. Damn straight I will. If he's the one who tried to kill Gabe and brutally raped me, then he deserves to die. My life's a shell now. I've got nothing to lose. I'll kill him. Give me the chance.* The key to the front door hung on the same key ring as the car keys. She planned to sail into the driveway, jump out of the car, rush to the door, unlock it, and head straight for the gun in the bedroom. If he followed her in, she'd fire away. If he knocked on the door, she'd wait to see if he'd enter. That would be a bad decision on his part, one that would unleash the fury of a desperate woman wielding a Smith and Wesson.

Within two hundred yards of the driveway, she began to have second thoughts. *What if I panic? Was the gun's safety on? Now how did Dugan take it off? Will I be able to hold the gun steady and fire?* If he overwhelmed her, she couldn't stand to be raped again. She'd kill herself. One hundred yards to go. He closed on her. *Oh no. He's right on my bumper—less time to get into the house and grab the gun.*

She hit the brakes, turned the wheel, and whirled, skidding into the driveway. She clutched at the keys. They were stuck. She jiggled, jerked, and yanked them out of the ignition. Grasping the door handle, she thrust into the door with her shoulder. It flew open. When she stepped out of the car, she glanced back. The Jeep slid to a stop right behind her vehicle.

Marla slammed the door and raced up the steps. Frantically, she flipped through the keys. The house key. Where is it? The second time through she found it and poked it towards the keyhole on the knob. It wouldn't go in. Glancing over her shoulder she saw Trenton reaching for something inside the Jeep. The rope? She turned the key upside-down and managed to fit it into the slot. Her hands shook as she wiggled it, trying to get the lock to turn.

"Mrs. Easton," Trenton called.

Marla took a quick peek over her shoulder. He held something yellow and walked towards the steps. Not a rope. What was it?

"Mrs. Easton, could I talk to you?"

She gave up on the lock and spun around. "Don't come near me."

"Mrs. Easton. Please. I have something for you."

"Get out of here." She couldn't believe what he held in his hands.

He raised his leg to mount the steps.

A flash of white and blue soared from the right, colliding with Trenton like a like a lineman blindsiding a quarterback. The jolt threw Trenton's body to the ground, sending him sprawling into the mulch near the ferns.

At the bottom of the steps Sonny Keys, hands on hips, breathing like a bull, towered over him. He wore blue overalls and a white t-shirt.

Trenton rolled onto his back, hands fumbling with a mass of crushed daisies. "Why the hell did you knock me down, you idiot?"

Sonny crossed his arms. "You heard the lady. Get out of here!" he growled like a grizzly bear about to attack.

Trenton stood and brushed himself off. "I wasn't going to do nothing. Just give her some flowers."

"You deaf?" Sonny asked.

Trenton peered up at Marla, eyes appealing for her approval. "I just wanted tell you how sorry I was to hear about your husband." He held out the daisies, but they dangled in his hand like limp noodles.

Sonny turned to Marla. "You want him around here?"

Marla shook her head, then eyed Trenton. "Stay away from me. I don't want your sympathy, your flowers, or your smart ass near my front door."

Trenton threw the daisies into the mulch. "Geesh! What'd I do? Just trying to be friendly and helpful. Look what it gets me."

Sonny jerked his thumb towards the Jeep. "Get out of here."

Trenton's bottom lip curled up. After a sheepish glance at Marla, he hung his head, walked to the Jeep, climbed in, backed out, and drove away.

Sonny faced Marla. "Are you okay, Marla?"

She nodded, taking a deep breath. "Thanks, Sonny. That's twice you've gotten rid of that punk for me. I can't stand him."

Sonny smiled. "I trust him 'bout as far as I could shot put a rhinoceros."

"I don't know, Sonny. It wouldn't surprise me if you threw a rhinoceros halfway to the beach from here."

Sonny placed his hands on his hips, his chest expanding. He tilted his head. "Don't think I could throw one that far."

Marla grinned.

Sonny half saluted, half waved. "Have a good day, Marla."

"Thanks, Sonny. Same to you."

He marched across the front of the property then angled around the corner of the apartments.

Marla about-faced and grasped the key, still inserted in the lock. This time she turned it easily, and the door budged open. *Damn. I'm one hell of a bumbler in a crisis. God help me next time something like this happens.*

Chapter 18

On Wednesday morning Marla woke up nauseated. She hadn't been sick for years. Had it been all the stress? She stumbled into the bathroom and vomited. After about twenty minutes she felt better. Then it hit her: she was pregnant. It had been eleven days since she'd ovulated, eleven days since Gabe had made love to her, eleven days since she'd been raped. Until then she hadn't thought much about checking on Gabe's sperm-count test. Now she had to know the results. She called the clinic and asked for Dr. Green, insisting her inquiry was extremely important. Five minutes later Dr. Green picked up the phone.

"This is Marla Easton, Gabe Easton's wife."

"Yes, Mrs. Easton. How is Gabe doing?"

Marla inhaled deeply, trying to keep control of her emotions. "Not well. He's still in a coma."

"I read about the assault in the paper last week. I'm so sorry. This has to be the toughest trial of your life."

"It is." Marla didn't want to dwell on the desolate condition of her soul or the hopeless state of her circumstances. She got to the point of the call. "The week before last Gabe came in for a sperm analysis. Could you tell me the results?"

"Yes." The doctor paused for several seconds. "Again, I must tell you I'm sorry. Gabe had a low sperm count and the progression analysis of those sperm showed them to be slow moving or immobile."

"Does that mean he couldn't get me pregnant?"

"His chances aren't very good. Maybe one in a thousand. But there are a few things we could try if he . . . if he . . ."

Marla hung up before the doctor completed the sentence. She knew he was struggling to find another way to say: if he . . .survived. In all likelihood if she'd conceived, the rapist was the father. That is, unless Gabe somehow managed a one-in-a-thousand connection, like a blind man hitting an all-star pitcher's fastball over the fence.

She went back to bed and slept for several hours. At noon she forced herself to eat a bowl of chicken noodle soup to gain strength for another day at the hospital. By the time she got on the road it was almost 2:00 o'clock. Iron-gray clouds, edging in from the west, slowly extinguished the afternoon's sunshine. When she descended the front porch steps, strong winds tousled her hair, shook the branches, and fluttered the leaves of the magnolia and yaupon trees along Old Lighthouse Road.

Marla drove to the hospital in a haze, not wanting to face the white walls, tubes, needles, and beeping machines of that room, her husband lying there unmoving, unthinking, unfeeling. *Where are you Gabe? You said you'd come back to me.* She thought about Martin Payne's desperate state of mind, wanting his wife's companionship so badly he had slipped into an unstable world where she would haunt him now and again. Marla didn't want to enter that world, but anything was better than the ever-darkening skies of her life.

At Gabe's bedside she prayed. She hadn't prayed for several days. She'd become tired of praying, her faith teetering as she questioned God's inscrutable ways. But now she had reason to pray again. As usual, she held Gabe's hand. *God, if I'm pregnant, and this baby belongs to Gabe, please give me a sign. Is this how Gabe will come back to me? Through this baby? If it is, I can accept what has happened. You've given me a part of Gabe in exchange for him. I'll miss him, but I won't complain. God, please let this be his baby.*

She squeezed his hand. *Come back to me Gabe.* She thought about Martin Payne channeling his wife. At that moment it didn't seem so crazy. *Come back to me, Darling, even if it's through this unborn child. Give me some kind of sign. Squeeze my hand again.* She sat silently, waiting, listening, her hand ever so gently grasping, hoping for a response, a reflexive twitch. Nothing. Keeping as still as possible, she hovered over him for more than ten minutes.

She remembered the night they had stood under a canopy of stars on the hill above her uncle's farm. At first she felt uneasy, standing in a hayfield in need of mowing. She kept hearing the rustling of the grass. Was it some night creature or just the wind? Gabe sensed her nervousness, squeezed her hand tighter, and said, "Don't worry about what's down here. Look up." She heard his words, but her fears had so preoccupied her that they didn't register. Then he said it again: "Look up." When she did, the anxiety drained away, lost in the wonder of the stars. She'd never seen them so bright and glorious before, as if Gabe and she had risen above the cloying superficiality of the world and shared a glimpse of infinity.

At that moment by the hospital bed, holding Gabe's hand, she relived those precious memories. She shut her eyes, and his words echoed in her mind—*Look up. Look up. Look up.* Raising her head, she opened her eyes. There in the doorway stood a man, his form dark against the hallway's light. At first she didn't recognize him. When he entered, the small fluorescent light above Gabe's bed cast a pale glow on his features.

"Dugan?"

"Hi, Marla. How you holding up?" He was dressed in his gray uniform. When he removed his black ball cap, his red hair stood out against his pale forehead.

At first she'd felt stunned, hearing Gabe's instruction within her mind and looking up to see a dark figure, perhaps a messenger. When she'd recognized Dugan, her hope of some kind of answer didn't falter. Maybe Dugan had arrived to reveal something important. "I'm struggling, Dugan. I need some answers." She motioned to the chair beside her.

"I've been working hard for you. Uncovered a few things." Dugan circled the bed and eased into the chair.

"The DNA results?"

Dugan nodded. "My suspect list was right on the mark."

"How so?"

"We found traces of blood on the yellow rope and were able to extract a quality DNA sample."

"Tony Trenton's?"

Dugan shook his head. "Sonny Keys."

"No way." The thought of Sonny violently snuffing out a young woman's life sent a shockwave through her. "Sonny killed that girl?"

"I didn't say that. But there's no doubt about it. His DNA is on the rope. I questioned Sonny yesterday. He said it's the same rope he used to tie up a sapling in front of the apartments. He showed me a slash on his finger where he'd cut himself with a utility knife. Claimed he had tied the tree up the same day he'd cut himself. That night someone took the rope. He'd thought maybe a local kid stole it but now figures it was the killer."

"Do you believe him?"

"My heart says yes, but my head says not so fast. There're miles to go in this investigation. We can't overlook Sonny until we've analyzed all the evidence thoroughly."

"But he's so determined to protect me. The other day Tony Trenton followed me home and started to come towards me even after I told him to back off. Out of nowhere Sonny plowed into him. 'Bout turned him inside out. Trenton took off like a scalded skunk."

Dugan chuckled. "Still, Sonny might be obsessed with you and jealous of your husband enough to attack him too."

Marla inhaled a quick breath and fixed her eyes on Dugan. "Really? Do you really think he's capable of that?

"Maybe, but I doubt it. I'm leaning towards Tony Trenton. As we assumed, his DNA showed up on the rape kit test. 'Course he said it would. That night at the restaurant he confessed he had consensual sex with the girl. With his background, though, we know he's capable of violence against women. Problem with Trenton is his buddies are vouching for him."

Marla agreed with Dugan. Trenton didn't like to take "no" for an answer. He was a cowardly man who enjoyed overpowering women. "Isn't there anything you can do to undermine his alibi?"

Dugan leaned back in the chair and folded his hands on his lap. "We're trying. It takes time. Lots of interviews, finding people who may have seen Trenton that night, anything to disprove their claim he was fishing with his buddies. Until we ascertain stronger evidence, I recommend you file a restraining order against him. He comes near you again, and we'll arrest him."

That made sense to Marla. "How do I do that?"

"Follow me to the sheriff's office in Manteo, and we'll take care of it."

Dugan's willingness to help protect her sent a wave of appreciation through her. She placed her hand on his arm. "Thanks."

"No problem."

She withdrew her hand and asked, "Did you find anything else out? What about Martin Payne?"

Dugan bobbed his head. "Payne's still in the mix. We found his DNA on the horn of the mask. That's not a big deal, though. The mask did belong to him and his wife. It's not unusual for your property to contain traces of your DNA. The big question I had for Payne was: 'How did the killer get hold of the mask?'"

"What did he say?"

"He had no idea. Couldn't tell by talking to him if he was trying to be deceptive. Payne's not tied too tight to the pier. Unbalanced people can be dangerous, especially if they believe what's going on in their noggin."

"He came into the bookstore earlier in the week," Marla said. "He feels he has this connection to me now that Gabe is in a coma. Says his wife still speaks to him. He wants me to stop by for a talk about how Gabe's spirit can contact me."

Dugan rubbed his jaw and shook his head. "I wouldn't if I were you. I don't think he's the killer, but I can't count him out either. Like I said, crazy people do crazy things."

Again Marla agreed. Guilt may have played a part in Payne's instability. If he harmed his wife in a fit of anger, it's possible he grasped for any preposterous ideology that could ameliorate his feelings of shame and regret. Going to talk to him about this spirit world his wife inhabits would nurture the very thing keeping him off balance. "No. Whether he's wacko or not, I don't plan on going down that road. Talking to ghosts doesn't appeal to me. If Gabe's gone, he's gone."

Dugan coughed and cleared his throat. "Does that mean you've made a decision about removing Gabe's life support?"

Marla bowed her head and stared at her lap. "Not yet. I'm still waiting for some answers. Maybe soon, but I don't know."

"I have one more answer, not really an answer. A result—the results of your rape kit test."

Marla raised her head and met Dugan's gaze. Was this the message Gabe wanted her to hear? "You identified the DNA of the person who raped me?"

Dugan shook his head. "Bad news. We found only Gabe's DNA."

Marla's heart leaped. Gabe was the father? But the rapist ejaculated inside of her. "How could that be? I swear to you the rapist didn't use a condom."

"Are you sure he reached orgasm?"

"Of course I'm sure." She remembered that disgusting feeling of his seed dripping between her legs.

"Then the hospital technician must not have done an adequate job. She should have taken more swabs. Or if you took a shower or bath before the test, it may have compromised the results. Whatever the case, I'm sorry."

Marla didn't care about an incompetent technician or an unreliable test result. The possibility of Gabe being the father of her baby had ignited a flame of hope within her. *This must be the way Gabe will come back to me, through my baby.* Her heart soared until Dr. Green's words echoed in her mind: Gabe had *a one-in-a-thousand shot* of his sperm fertilizing her egg. Maybe Dugan had a point. The nurse might have failed to do a thorough job. She remembered taking a shower the morning before the test. The odds of her and Gabe conceiving put a damper on the new flame in her soul but did not douse it. For now she would hold on to that possibility as tightly as she could.

Marla followed Dugan Walton to the sheriff's office in Manteo and went through the paper work to file restraining orders against Tony Trenton. By the time she finished, it was nearly four o'clock. She didn't want to go back to the hospital, not with the most important question of her life unanswered: Was she pregnant?

In Avon she stopped at Beach Pharmacy. She had purchased a test kit there seven weeks ago when they'd first arrived on Hatteras Island. Of course the results had been negative, an outcome she had been conditioned to expect over the last year. She wanted to try a new brand today, if only to break away from the patterns of the past. After entering the small, homey store, she walked directly to the feminine-care aisle and examined her choices. She settled on a product called First to Know, one that claimed to detect the hormone levels in 95 percent of women three days before their expected period.

While Marla checked out, the charcoal gray sky that had grown darker with every hour finally reached its saturation point and released sheets of rain that splattered the store's windows. The world outside became distorted and warped as the droplets ran together and bent the fading light. With bag in hand, she rushed to the car, her bare skin stung and chilled by the downpour. She managed to unlock the car door and jump in before becoming too soaked. The ride home called for concentration and patience as the rain pelted the windshield, the wipers working overtime. But Marla had lost her patience, knowing she was only minutes away from a discovery that could totally alter her life unlike anything she'd ever experienced.

By the time she reached the apartment, the rain had let up. Both Martin Payne and Sonny Keys stood on their decks and watched her as she climbed out of the car and ran to the porch, as if they had been waiting for her to return. She gave a quick wave, and they both lifted their hands, Sonny from above and Mr. Payne directly below. Maybe they just wanted to watch the rain, she reasoned. Lonely people can be drawn to rain—the rhythm of the pattering, the softness of a muted world drained of color.

Inside the house she went immediately to the bathroom and reviewed the pregnancy test directions. "Remove the indicator from the wrapper and take off the cap. Okay. Hold the test stick pointed down in your urine steam for five seconds. No problem. I haven't peed for hours. Replace the cap and lay the test stick flat with the results window facing up. Easy enough. The results should appear in the window within three minutes: one line—not pregnant, two lines—pregnant. Three minutes to a possible life transformation." She took a deep breath. "Here's goes everything."

At that moment a queer feeling washed over her, one that seemed to intensify the chill from the rain. *What if she carried the rapist's baby? Would the child be a constant reminder of that night of horror? She didn't believe in abortion. Certainly God would understand her circumstances if she made that choice. But didn't Gabe tell her to look up? And when she did she saw Dugan, and he brought the news that only Gabe's DNA had been found?* She swallowed and unwrapped the test stick. *Why am I so flustered? I'm probably not even pregnant. If I am, then no matter whose baby it is I have to deal with it. Get a hold of yourself and get to it.*

She sat on the toilet and followed the procedure. After peeing on the indicated end, she set the test stick on the sink face up. Then she leaned on her knees, eyes closed, clearing her mind, allowing the minutes to slip by. She could feel her heart beating in her chest as she listened to the sound of her own respiration. The silence calmed her. The goose bumps on her skin began to fade. After several minutes, she knew the answer awaited within two feet of her reach.

She sat up and grasped the test stick. She blinked and focused on the results window. Within the oval display she saw two red lines.

Chapter 19

Marla sat on the recliner next to the bookshelf trying to finish the last few chapters of the latest Harry Potter novel. With her pregnancy dominating her thoughts, causing confusion and apprehension, she needed a break from the real world. She had opened the window facing the sea to let in a cooling breeze on such a warm night for late October. She had lost focus on the story several times because of a woman's voice coming through the window—Mr. Payne's mysterious female visitor. Was it the ghost of his wife? His voice would alternate with hers, making Marla curious about the content of their conversation. She lowered the recliner, arose, placed the Potter tome open facedown on the chair, and moved to the window. The breeze felt refreshing.

As she leaned on the sill, she listened intently. Mr. Payne asked the woman to be patient with him. The woman answered, her voice softer than Payne's, but Marla couldn't make out the words. She inched forward, placing her ear almost on the screen.

"I'm not ready yet," Mr. Payne said. "Please don't make me do it."

"I can't make you do anything," the woman said, louder this time. "It's your decision. I can only tell you what I want. You know what I want."

"Yes, you've made that clear time and again. I've been very selfish, but I can't let go."

"You must," she insisted. "It's the best thing for both of us."

Then Marla heard a man weeping, sniveling, trying to gain self-control. She sensed his agony and felt guilty for eavesdropping but couldn't force herself away from the window.

"Let's not talk about this anymore tonight," Mr. Payne said.

"Don't send me away, Martin. I'm tired of coming and going. You can't put this off forever."

A rapping at the front door made Marla jerk her head up into the window frame. "Ouch! Darn it." She backed away, rubbing her noggin. *Who could that be?* She glanced through the large open space of the apartment to the front door. Tony Trenton's face appeared in her mind's eye. When she'd returned from the pharmacy, she'd chain latched the door and turned the deadbolt. Because she'd filed restraining orders earlier that day, she could have Trenton arrested if he showed up again. She decided not to open the door until she knew for sure who it was.

Marla cautiously entered the kitchen to within a few feet of the door. "Who's there?"

Loud knocking startled her, causing her to step backwards, her heart pounding.

"I said who's there?" she yelled.

"It's me, Michael," came the muffled reply.

She inhaled deeply and relaxed. *Only Michael.* Marla wasn't in the mood to talk to Michael. Several times during the week he blubbered over his immature attitude in life and how his self-indulgence ultimately led to Gabe's horrible encounter with the killer. Marla had managed to keep her mouth shut but so badly wanted to agree: *Yes, you self-centered fool. Gabe is lying in that hospital room on life support because you can't grow up and become a responsible human being. It is your fault. You insisted your brother move down here near you because you need someone to lean on. Now look what has happened. You selfish sonovabitch.*

If Marla let Michael in tonight to sit and rehash the misery she'd been through over the last couple weeks, she knew she wouldn't be able to bite her tongue for long. She tried to think of an excuse. *I'm not feeling well. I'm tired. I've got a headache.* She turned the dead bolt and opened the door a few inches until the chain latch stopped it. The porch light brightened Michael's round red face. The smell of alcohol wafted through the opening.

"You've been drinking," Marla said.

"Just two beers. I swear."

"That's two too many."

Michael swiped his forehead. "I needed something to settle my nerves. I had a long conversation with Dr. Shepherd today. What he said hit me hard. Please, Marla we need to talk about this."

Dr. Shepherd, Marla thought, a man on a relentless quest to free up Gabe's hospital room. Twice this week he'd cornered her and reminded her that prolonging the inevitable will only deepen the pain. His insistence on facing the reality of Gabe's condition convinced Marla he tried to cloak what he considered a clinical formality as a mission of mercy. Marla wasn't buying it yet. Without one hundred percent proof that Gabe was gone for good or the child growing inside her wasn't his, she wasn't about to pull the plug or visit an abortion clinic.

"I don't feel like talking tonight, Michael. I'm tired and I've got a headache."

"Please, Marla." Michael closed his eyes and took of deep breath. "If you've got a good reason to keep Gabe on those machines you've got to tell me or else I'm going to flip out. I'm willing to listen. I'll even tell Shepherd to keep his damn opinion to himself and leave us alone, but I have to side with him unless you know something I don't."

I don't know anything. Just a dream of Gabe coming back to me. A one-in-a-thousand chance that I'm carrying his baby. That's all I know. I don't care about anything else. What you and Dr. Shepherd think doesn't matter to me. She stared at Michael, her mouth not moving but her mind rambling.

"Marla?" Michael took a deep, shaky breath.

Sensing her brother-in-law was about to cry, Marla unhooked the chain latch and opened the door. "Come in."

Michael entered, head down, sniffling. Marla felt a deep sense of pity for him. Although Gabe's brother, he wasn't half the man her husband was. Not even close. For all of Gabe's character strengths, Michael possessed a corresponding weakness. With Gabe in a coma, Michael had lost the person in life who had given him an odd sense of balance. He reminded her of an old man alone in the world or of the kid at school who wanted to be friends but no one could stand to be around him. She told him to have a seat at the kitchen table.

"I'm so sorry. I know you're getting fed up with me."

"Please, Michael, don't start your apologies again. Just relax. Can I get you something to drink? And don't ask for another beer."

Michael waved his hand. "Nothing then. You don't understand what's going on inside of me. I can't relax. The closest person to me in my life is gone, and I don't know what to do about it. Yet I can walk into that hospital room and stand right next to him. But it's not him. It's just his body."

Guilt edged into Marla's conscience. She'd sensed the same feeling several times but refused to allow it to get a foothold in her heart. She didn't want to face the possibility that she alone kept Gabe from entering his final rest. "All I can tell you is I'll know when it's time. Now is not the time."

Michael blinked and stared at her, his manner becoming less agitated. "He's gone, Marla." His voice had softened. "He's not coming back. You know it, and I know it. Dr. Shepherd is worried that the mental stress may harm both of us the more you postpone this."

A flame of anger rose into her cheeks. "I'm fine. Don't worry about me. If you can't deal with it, too bad."

He sniffed and swallowed. "I don't like it, but I'll deal with it. All I ask is that you tell me why. Give me a logical explanation."

Marla considered her words. She needed to tell him something, throw him a bone to keep him from applying his exasperating pressure. "I might be pregnant."

Michael's eyes widened. "With Gabe's baby?"

"Of course. Who else would be the father?" She maintained a defiant expression, not wanting Michael to notice her fear of other possibilities.

"But Gabe told me he went to the clinic to be tested."

Marla wondered if Gabe knew the results and had told Michael. He'd never mentioned anything to her. "So what?"

"Nothing really. I just assumed he was having problems."

"Gabe was fine in that department. Don't you understand now, though? If there's any chance whatsoever of Gabe reviving, I'm willing to wait it out. Nine months if need be. I dreamed Gabe would come back to me. If he doesn't come out of the coma, then I know it must be through our child. I'll wait until the baby's born before I make that decision."

Michael shook his head. "Marla, a dream is only a dream. The doctors are convinced Gabe is never coming back. Think of the medical bills. Think of the stress of traveling back and forth to see only the shell of the man we once knew. This isn't good."

Marla stood, her chair scooting backwards. "Shut up!" She pointed at him. "You don't have a say! Either support me or get the hell out of my life. Don't ever come in here and tell me to pull that damn plug again."

Michael held up his hands. "Okay. Okay. I won't." He arose and walked into the living room. "I'll keep my mouth shut." He paused by the window and peered out, the breeze tousling his wavy hair. After a minute's silence, he glanced over his shoulder and motioned for Marla to come closer.

"What do you want?" She asked.

He held his finger to his lips. "Shhhhhhh."

Marla paced towards him. "What is it?"

"Do you hear that woman's voice?"

"Yes. I heard just before you arrived."

Michael shook his head. "It's Old Man Payne channeling his wife."

"Channeling his wife?"

"You know." Michael raised his eyebrows. "The spirit world. He's nuts. This is what hanging on does to a person."

Marla listened, but the woman's voice was more distant now.

"Can't make out what she's saying," Michael said, inching closer to the screen. "I swear one night I heard her accuse Payne of pushing her down the lighthouse steps."

"Really?"

Michael held up his hand, palm facing her. "God as my witness."

"What did Mr. Payne say?"

"He didn't deny it. If I had a tape recorder, I'd go out on the deck and record the conversation just in case Payne confesses to attempted murder. Gabe has a cassette recorder, doesn't he? For his music?"

Marla nodded. "In the bedroom on his dresser."

Michael strode into the bedroom and returned with the cassette recorder, a black box about the size of her Harry Potter novel with a row of chrome buttons. Do you mind if I record their conversation?"

Marla had to admit she was curious. What if Michael caught Mr. Payne on tape confessing to the crime? Would they turn him in? "I don't care. It's up to you."

Michael walked to the back door, eased it open, and slinked onto the deck. The porch light was off, making it hard for Marla to see through the window. She did notice Michael's dark form pass by silently and heard the sound of a button being pushed. Listening intently, she tried to discern the see-saw of words between the masculine and feminine voices. She caught a few of them but not enough to make sense of the conversation. From the porch she felt Michael could hear every word.

After a minute or two she heard the sound of wood creaking and scuffing from the right side of the deck. What could that be? "Michael," she whispered. "What's out there?"

The noise continued. Michael whirled in the direction of the approaching clamor. Marla heard a clunk—someone jumping over the railing and landing on the deck? Then came stomps and a clash like the sound of football players colliding. She immediately thought Tony Trenton had climbed onto the deck, not expecting to confront Michael. She heard grunts, curses, and the sound of two men wrestling and pounding on each other.

He'll kill Michael. What can I do? The gun. I've got to get it. She raced into the bedroom and dove onto the bed, her hand sliding under Gabe's pillow. She grasped the cold handle and withdrew it. *Where's that safety?* She found the lever but had a hard time holding the thing steady enough to slide it into the off position. She could hear the ruckus continuing on the back porch—thuds, grunts, and the rattle of furniture. She backed off the bed onto her feet, her hand wavering with the gun, and rushed into the living room and opened the deck door.

The fracas had drifted towards the divider, which separated their deck from Payne's. *Now's my chance.* Marla shoved the screen open and stepped onto the back porch, the screen retracting against her rear end. Two large bodies grappled each other like wrestlers trying to get leverage, their jerky movements making it difficult for Marla to identify the attacker.

She raised the pistol. "Stop it! I've got a gun!" She reached inside the house and flipped on the porch light.

At that moment the assailant pulled Michael off balance and spun him into the railing. Michael held tight as he tumbled over the rail, pulling the man with him. Marla saw the flash of the porch light reflected off a bald head. The assailant flipped over the banister with Michael. Their plummet seemed to last forever, as if in slow motion, but then came the agonizing thud of bodies against the ground. Marla raced to the rail and peered over. Sonny Keys had landed on top of Michael.

"Sonny! What are you doing?" she shouted.

Sonny rolled off him and looked up. "I thought . . . I thought he was the killer."

"No. It's Michael."

To her left Mr. Payne's porch light came on, and his screen door flew open. "What's g-going on out h-here?" Payne's voice creaked with fear. From his hand a beam shot forth from a flashlight.

"Over here," Marla said. "Shine the light on the ground."

Mr. Payne hurried to the divider and directed the beam at Michael's face. Blood pooled on the sidewalk around his head. "What happened?" Mr. Payne asked.

Sonny stared into the light. "It's my fault. I thought Michael was the killer trying to break into Marla's apartment."

"He's hurt badly," Marla said.

Sonny touched the blood with his fingertips and held them in the light. "He's bleeding a lot. His head hit the sidewalk."

"Better call for help," Mr. Payne said.

Marla's hands shook so severely she thought she'd drop the gun. "I'll call 911. Someone help Michael. Stop the bleeding."

As she headed to the door, she heard Sonny say, "Throw me down a towel, Mr. Payne. There's a big gash on the back of his head."

Please, God, Marla thought, not another serious head injury. She entered the house, crossed the living room, placed the gun on the in table, picked up the phone, and dialed 911. The operator took the information and informed her an E-squad would be there within ten minutes.

She headed out the front door, down the steps, and circled to the back where she found Sonny applying pressure with a towel to the back of Michael's head. From the deck above, Mr. Payne directed his flashlight on them.

Marla knelt next to Sonny. "Is he breathing?"

Sonny put his ear next to Michael's mouth. "I think so. Just barely."

Marla grasped Michael's wrist and found a pulse. *He's alive.* She listened for the sound of sirens. *Hurry. Please hurry.*

"Is there anything I can do to help?" Mr. Payne asked.

Marla glanced up but couldn't see his face because of the brightness of the beam. "Just keep the light on us."

"Will do."

"I'm so sorry, Mrs. Easton," Sonny said. "I was making my nightly rounds and saw a man near your window. Thought Trenton was trying to break into your house. Why was Michael on your back deck?"

Marla's mind raced for an answer. "He thought he heard a woman's voice out back and went to investigate." She looked into the light. "Mr. Payne, did you have a lady visitor tonight?"

Mr. Payne cleared his throat. "I . . . I . . . I've been home alone."

Marla blinked, then lowered her eyes. *Home alone? It's true then. He does channel his wife. He's crazy like Michael said.* In the distance she heard a siren. *Thank God, they're almost here.* "Stay with Michael, Sonny. I'll go out front and meet the E-squad."

"Yes, ma'am."

Marla arose and hurried around the corner of the building. As she walked through the darkness on the side of the apartment, she sent up a prayer for her brother-in-law. Now she felt bad for scolding him about pressuring her. The incident seemed surreal: Twin brothers with similar head injuries? If Michael's condition were as serious as Gabe's, then she would be alone on the Outer Banks—no relatives to count on. *But I'm not alone.* She touched her belly, the thought of the baby dispelling the chill of isolation. *God help us make it through these terrible times.*

With blue and red lights swirling from the top of the vehicle and the siren screaming, the emergency squad screeched to a halt in the driveway. Marla waved her hands crisscrossing in front of her as two crewmembers jumped out of the rear and two more exited the cab of the yellow truck. A sheriff's car pulled in beside them, and Dugan Walton stepped out. Marla informed the first man, a stocky guy with curly blond hair, where to find Michael. He hurried around the corner of the apartment, short legs a blur of motion. Two attendants with a stretcher followed him, and a female, carrying a large case trailed behind. Before they were out of earshot, Marla heard one of the men say, "What's with this place? They're dropping like rotten apples out here."

Thinking of Gabe, she cursed the man, but could she blame the guy for saying it?

"What happened?" Dugan asked as he caught up with Marla.

"A terrible mix-up. Sonny mistook Michael for the killer and threw him off my back deck."

"What? How could he make that kind of error?"

"It was dark. He thought he was protecting me."

"You just don't throw someone off a ten-foot porch unless you're sure they mean you harm."

Marla wondered if Dugan had zeroed in Sonny as a suspect. "But Tony Trenton followed me home earlier this week. Remember? Sonny must have thought Michael was Trenton. He feels responsible for me."

"He's over doing it, wouldn't you say?"

Marla had to agree. Throwing Michael off the back deck was over doing it.

The EMTs worked expeditiously on Michael, stopping the bleeding, stabilizing his neck, easing him onto the stretcher, securing him, and giving him oxygen. Within ten minutes they surrounded the stretcher and prepared to lift him. Because of Michael's girth, Dugan helped at the head and Sonny at the foot. On three they heaved, straining, but managing to pick him up. Marla borrowed Mr. Payne's flashlight and led the way to the emergency vehicle.

After they placed Michael into the back of the E-squad, the head EMT asked Marla if she wanted to ride along. Marla decided to follow in her car. She didn't want to be stuck at the hospital without transportation.

He shrugged and closed the door. She wondered if she appeared callous. She cared for Michael, but he wasn't her husband. As the siren blared and the truck sped away, she felt a pang of guilt. Should she have ridden with Michael? Emotionally she didn't feel attached to him, but a sense of obligation to Gabe's twin nagged her conscience.

As she turned to hurry back into the apartment and find her keys, she overheard Dugan questioning Sonny. They stood at the bottom of the front steps under the glare of a spotlight.

"Before you attacked Michael, did you try to identify him?" Dugan asked.

"No. It was dark. I figured he was the murderer. Everything happened so fast."

Dugan put his hands on his hips. "Why would you assume someone standing on Marla's back deck was the killer? Is it out of the question for Marla to have guests or relatives over for a visit?"

"No."

"Then why?"

"Because . . ." Sonny's voice cracked. He swallowed. "Because of what's been happenin' around here lately."

"So because crimes have been committed in this neighborhood, you have the right to bodily manhandle anyone who you think just might be a killer?"

"No. I don't have that right. I'm sorry. It was a mistake."

"Sorry doesn't solve the problem, Sonny. I've got to take you into custody. Michael may not survive what you just did to him. Do you know what manslaughter means?"

Sonny lowered his head. "Yeah. Killing someone without meaning to."

"Close enough." Dugan reached for the handcuffs and unhitched them from his belt.

"You're arresting me?"

"That's right. Turn around and put your hands behind your back."

Marla cut between them. "Don't be ridiculous. Sonny meant no harm to Michael. It was a case of mistaken identity. There's a murderer on the loose around here."

"We'll let someone with more authority than you or I make that judgment. Step aside please, Marla." Dugan reached and pressed his hand to her shoulder.

Marla stood firm. "Dugan Walton, I don't believe you're doing this." She felt a hand patting her back and realized Sonny was comforting her.

141

"Don't worry about me, Marla." Sonny's voice was low and gentle. "I'll be fine. I'm sorry for what I did to Michael, but I'd do it again if I thought you were in danger."

Chapter 20

Marla dreaded heading back to the Outer Banks Hospital in Nags Head. She'd spent several hours there earlier that day at Gabe's bedside. It was a nice place, a modern facility with friendly people, but her time in her husband's room, the hallways, and waiting rooms had been the darkest days of her life. Stepping into the emergency entrance brought back the horror of the night she'd arrived in the back of the e-squad with Gabe. Two weeks had passed since then, but it felt like a lifetime of loss. Now Michael may be gone too.

What a terrible night. Michael had felt compelled to go out onto the deck and record Martin Payne's schizophrenic dialogue. Marla wondered about the tape recorder. Was it still on the deck? Had Michael recorded anything that may have implicated Mr. Payne as a suspect in harming his wife?

And poor Sonny. He thought he had done the right thing by climbing onto the porch and subduing the man standing near the window. Michael probably fought back, mistaking Sonny for the killer. What a mess. Sonny was a loyal friend to a fault, and because of his blind devotion, he now sat staring out the bars of the Dare County Detention Center. Or was he such a tragic hero? *Could Dugan Walton be right about Sonny's obsession with me? Did it harbor a dark side, a murderous inclination?* Marla didn't believe it. Sonny may be extreme in his devotion and impulsive in his reactions, but he wasn't a murderer.

Marla entered the waiting room and informed the receptionist, a plump woman with thinning red hair, she had come to see Michael Easton. The lady told Marla to have a seat and she'd let her know about Michael's status in a few minutes. Marla prepared for a long night. In her experience at this hospital "a few minutes" usually stretched into hours.

Five minutes later, to Marla's surprise, the receptionist called her to the window and asked, "Are you a relative?"

"Yes. I'm Marla Easton, Michael's sister-in-law."

"Michael's in surgery. I'm not sure how long he'll be there. As soon as Dr. Chambers finishes, he'll let you know Michael's condition."

Marla nodded and thanked her. She hoped Michael would make it through without permanent brain damage for his sake and Sonny's sake. The terrible thud of Michael hitting the ground reverberated in her mind. After two weeks of agonizing over Gabe, she didn't want to think about the possibilities or add the pain of losing someone else.

She plopped down in the chair and glanced at the magazines on the coffee table in front of her, hoping to find something to keep her interest for a while. Under a stack of *People* she found one called *Motherhood*. She flipped through the pages and ran across an article entitled "Enjoying the Simple Pleasures." Reading the first few lines immediately drew her attention. The article talked about having fun with your family through the common experiences of life: telling stories, looking through picture albums, enjoying a backyard picnic, going for a walk in the country, visiting the library together.

Marla imagined a scene along Hatteras beach five years into the future. She held the hand of a little dark-haired girl. Gabe grasped the girl's other hand as they walked along the firm sand next to the water's edge. Occasionally they stopped to look for shells. With great exuberance, the blue-eyed child picked up a sand dollar and showed it to Marla. All three of them touched the round white sea urchin, creating a sense of unity and awe. The girl asked her daddy to keep it safe for her, and Gabe placed it into his breast pocket. Marla noticed darkening clouds on the horizon and suggested they head back. When she turned to face home, she saw three sets of footprints trailing in the wet sand, and the surf rushing up the slope in its unrelenting effort to erase them.

Her mind wandered through other possibilities: she and Gabe riding carousel ponies beside their daughter on the merry-go-round, picnicking in the park, celebrating a birthday, picking flowers in a meadow. But the dark clouds always appeared, hastening a premature ending to their family time. Marla wondered if these kinds of visions lifted her up emotionally to a height from which she would eventually fall even harder. Maybe she should give up the hope of the one-in-a-thousand chance of bearing Gabe's child or the one-in-a-million odds of Gabe emerging from his coma. Should she face the facts and put hope to death?

As she pondered cold reality, she heard footsteps, glanced up, and saw Dr. Chambers, a young bespectacled colleague of Dr. Shepherd, approaching. He had a kind face with slight dimples on his cheeks and a notch in the middle of his chin. Marla stood and tried to discern the seriousness of Michael's condition by the tall doctor's expression. The lack of cheer in his brown eyes told her something was wrong.

He shook his head, his lips tightening before he spoke. "Marla, I'm so sorry to see you having to go through another trial like this. I've never understood why some people receive an unfair portion of disaster."

"Is Michael dead?" Marla couldn't keep the question from escaping.

"No. But we're not sure how badly his brain was damaged. We relieved the pressure and began immediate treatment to keep inflammation down. We'll do a CAT scan to see how much damage has been done and then an EEG. I hate to say it, but Michael may be in as much trouble as Gabe."

Marla hung her head, and the tears spilled down her cheeks. She didn't understand why this flood of emotion overwhelmed her. Michael could be such an irritating man. Did she care for him more than she realized or was it caused by the culmination of everything she'd been through? Dr. Chambers placed his hand on her shoulder, and she moved closer to him, leaning her head on his chest. As she wept, he patted her back.

After several minutes, the crying subsided, and she stepped away and blinked. "When will you know how badly he's hurt?"

"We won't do the EEG until tomorrow morning. He's unconscious, of course, in a comatose state. They'll move him to ICU after the CAT scan. We'll keep a close eye on him. I suggest you go home and get a good night's rest. There's nothing you can do here. Come back tomorrow when we know more."

Marla agreed. She wanted to drive home, crawl in bed, and sleep. Her problems wouldn't disappear. They'd be waiting for her tomorrow. She couldn't escape them or solve them. All she could do was temporarily set them aside, gather strength, and face them another day. She headed out the emergency room entrance and into the parking lot.

After starting her car, she checked the time on the radio: 10:37. The drive back to Buxton would take about an hour. If she could climb into bed by midnight and sleep five or six hours, she could return to the hospital by eight in the morning.

As she drove along the two-lane road that traversed the narrow spine of the southern Outer Banks, she felt utterly alone. Crossing the bridge onto Hatteras Island, she gazed at the span as it rose into the night sky. She wondered why the engineers designed the bridge to rise to such a peak like the back of a brontosaurus in the Smithsonian. The appearance of the road ascending into the ominous heavens and the wind off the sea buffeting her little Cobalt sent a jolt of apprehension through her. An illogical fear gripped her that the downhill portion of the bridge had been swept away and she would drive over the crest and disappear into the abyss of clouds or drop into the ocean. Although she knew the thought was silly, she couldn't shake the uneasiness. She slowed the vehicle and eased over the top. Upon seeing the span descend to the island, she scolded herself for allowing her imagination to override her sensibility. To make it through the months ahead, she needed to trust what she knew to be the truth and refuse to give fear a foothold.

When she turned onto Old Lighthouse Road, she realized the two people who had been watching over her for the last two weeks were gone. Ironically, they eliminated each other in their efforts to protect her. Her imagination kicked in again. She envisioned the rapist in the shadows under the deck, waiting for her to arrive. Remembering his violent manner and creepy voice sent chills through her. She held tightly to the steering wheel, leaned forward, and took a slow, deep breath. *Don't let your imagination overrule your sensibility.* She tried to think logically, but that didn't help. *It is possible. He could be there. Maybe he knows Sonny and Michael are gone.* Her heart sped up as she pressed the brake, slowing the car even more. She turned left onto the gravel road that led to the dunes, the ocean, and her apartment.

Someone had parked a mid-sized SUV off the road near her driveway. She didn't recognize the vehicle. Her headlights brightened the parking area under the front deck, and she pulled into the space next to Michael's old Pontiac. She wished she'd brought the gun with her. Before turning off the engine and headlights, she swiveled her head and examined what she could see—the side of the laundry room, the huge posts supporting the house, the outside shower stall, and fish-cleaning table. *What if he is hiding on the other side of Michael's car, waiting for me to get home?* Her hands shook as she turned off the engine and extracted the keys.

She stepped out of the car and listened before shutting the door, ready to jump back in if need be. Hearing nothing, she closed the door and pivoted to take off for the steps. That's when she saw his black form at the bottom of the stairway. He held something in his hand in the shape of a mask with the broken-off horn. *No. Please, God, no.*

She backed into the car, her keys poking through her fingers like a weapon. Could she poke out his eye?

He stepped forward. "Marla?"

She recognized the voice. "Dugan? Dugan Walton?"

"Yes. It's me."

"Dammit You scared the hell out of me! Give me some kind of warning next time you creep up behind me. "

"I'm sorry. I came around the side of the building when I heard the car pull up."

She placed her hand on the middle of her chest. "My heart feels like it's going to explode."

"I figured you'd stay at the hospital tonight."

She shook her head and took several deep breaths. "I couldn't stay there another night. What are you doing here?"

"Sonny wants me to believe he's innocent. He gave me his keys and told me I could tear his place apart looking for evidence."

"And you found that?" Marla pointed to the mask.

Dugan nodded and held it up. "It's the mask that was taken from Loretta Payne's bedroom wall." He pointed to the missing horn. "I'm sure the piece of the mask from the crime scene will match up."

"But it doesn't make sense, Dugan. Why would Sonny insist you search his apartment to prove his innocence if he knows the mask is there?"

Dugan tapped the bulbous nose of the mask. "I didn't find this in his apartment. Figured I'd be wasting my time searching there. Sonny gave me his key ring and told me which key opened his apartment." Dugan reached in his pocket and pulled out a key ring loaded with keys. "There's a shed out back with a padlock on it. I sorted through the keys and found about a half dozen used for padlocks. Little bit of trial and error and voila—the lock opened. Inside the shed on a top shelf behind a couple cans of paint I found the mask. Guess what was on the shelf below?"

"I have no idea."

"A large spool of yellow towrope. Same kind used on the dead girl and you."

147

It still didn't make sense to Marla. Everything pointed to Sonny except his character itself. He was kind, loyal, and willing to sacrifice himself to help someone else. At times violent, maybe, but only out of necessity to protect the weak. "Do you really believe Sonny's the killer?"

"He seems obsessed with you. Perhaps he's so obsessed he doesn't want anyone else to be near you. He eliminated Gabe and now Michael, the next closest person."

"Michael was never that close."

"From your perspective, perhaps, but not Sonny's."

"I think you're wrong, Dugan." Marla walked around him, and stood at the bottom of the steps. "Sonny's not a killer. He's got the heart of a hero."

"You may be right, but I've got to go on evidence. Hero or not, the evidence points to him."

Marla stared at the ground and shook her head. She couldn't think of anything else to say in Sonny's defense. Finally, she blew out a long breath through puffed cheeks and said, "I'm tired, and I've got a long day tomorrow. Good night, Deputy Walton."

"You don't have to call me Deputy Walton. We've been friends a long time."

Marla headed up the steps. "Good night, Deputy Walton."

"Okay. I get it. Good night, Mrs. Easton."

Feeling a little guilty for her sudden formality, Marla stopped halfway up the steps and watched him walk towards the SUV. He was just doing his job. No sense in turning on the cold air of resentment. Then a thought occurred to her. "Hey! Dugan!"

He about-faced and raised his chin.

"The key to the padlock, is it one of those common keys with a number on it?"

"I think so." Dugan pulled out the key ring and opened the door to his car to get a better look at it. "Yeah. 9357."

"Some of those padlocks you get at the hardware store only have about ten or fifteen different keys that unlock them. If a person has several padlocks at home, chances are one of his keys would work in his neighbor's lock."

"That's true. You think someone else has a key that fits the lock on Sonny's shed?"

"It's possible. I'm guessing those things wouldn't be that hard for someone to pick either."

Dugan nodded and bounced the keys in his hand. "Someone who's trying to pin the murder on Sonny?"

"Makes sense to me." Marla observed him, noticing how he studied the keys in the glow from the car's interior light. Maybe she did find the right words in defense of Sonny.

Dugan jammed the keys into his pants pocket. "I'll keep that possibility in mind."

"Thanks, Deputy Walton, I mean Dugan."

Dugan smiled. "You're welcome, Marla."

She climbed the remaining steps, inserted her key, and opened the front door. As she shut the door and locked it, she considered the prime suspects and others in the neighborhood who would know about Sonny's stash of yellow towrope in the shed out back. Tony Trenton would have no idea about the shed or the rope. The only time he ever came around, Sonny sent him whimpering away with a handful of crushed flowers. She entered the living room and slumped into the recliner next to the bookshelf. Martin Payne would definitely know about it. She remembered the photograph Sonny took of Mr. Payne's bathroom and the yellow towrope hanging across the tub. Were the rumors true? Was Michael right about Mr. Payne pushing his wife down the lighthouse steps? Did he follow up that violent act by killing the girl? Marla guessed it was possible. Maybe Sonny gave Mr. Payne access to the shed whenever he needed supplies.

Marla recalled her two encounters with Mr. Payne at the bookstore. He was unstable, believing he could channel the spirit of his wife. Then she remembered the tape recorder. *Michael was recording Mr. Payne's strange dialogue with his wife when Sonny attacked.* She stared at the door that opened onto the back deck. *It must still be out there.*

Marla sprang to her feet, crossed the room, and opened the door. The ocean breeze coated her with the mist of the humid night. The waves beyond the dunes slapped the sand and rumbled along the shore. The porch light had been left on, casting an amber glow across the deck and plastic furniture. She turned and eyed the divider between the decks. There at the base sat the recorder. Michael must have put it down or dropped it when he turned to face his attacker.

As Marla approached the recorder, she peered over the divider into Mr. Payne's living room window. Through the blinds she could see him sitting in a chair with a book on his lap. If he looked out the window he would spot her. Should she retreat, turn out the porch light, and then return for the recorder? *No. He may notice the light going out. Just ease over to the recorder, bend down, and pick it up.* Carefully she edged closer to the divider, alternating her focus from Mr. Payne to the recorder. He seemed consumed by what he was reading, probably one of those books about "walk-ins." With one last look at Mr. Payne, she bent and picked up the recorder. When she straightened, he was staring at her.

He arose from the chair and walked to his back door. Marla wanted to escape but realized how suspicious fleeing would appear. As the door opened, she placed the recorder behind her back. Feeling her heart pounding into her throat, she swallowed and tried to appear calm.

Mr. Payne approached her, lines of anxiety or perhaps concern etching his face. "Is everything all right, Mrs. Easton?"

Marla nodded, her mind scrambling for the right words but no sentences formulated.

"I saw you through the window and wondered how Michael was doing?"

"Michael? He's not doing very well." She tried to hold his gaze, so he wouldn't become curious about what she held behind her back. "He's still unconscious."

"I'm sorry to hear that. Michael and I weren't close neighbors, but my wife got along well with him. Are the doctors hopeful?"

Marla shook her head. "Dr. Chambers scheduled a EEG for tomorrow morning. He warned me that Michael might be in serious trouble."

"Most unfortunate. I know you've been through a lot. You don't need another tragedy in your life."

Marla nodded. "Well . . . thanks for your concern. I've had a long evening and a difficult day awaits me tomorrow. Good night, Mr. Payne." She turned to go, shifting the recorder to her front.

"Mrs. Easton?"

Marla halted. "Yes."

"Remember earlier this evening when you asked me if I had a lady visitor?"

Marla gently placed the cassette recorder on the table in front of her and turned around. Her hands felt sweaty so she slid them over the pockets of her jeans and then clasped them in front of her.

Mr. Payne leaned on the divider. "I didn't tell you the whole truth."

"Someone *was* visiting you?"

"Technically, no. I was alone." He stared at her feet, blinking several times. "My wife, Loretta, walked in to me tonight."

"Walked in to you?"

"Yes. She comes back to me and I allow her to take over my body. That's how we keep in touch."

Marla swallowed. *He is bonkers.* She wanted to end the conversation and lock herself in her apartment.

Mr. Payne met her gaze. "I can tell by the way you're looking at me you think I'm crazy."

"I . . . I . . . I don't know much about this kind of thing . . . the spirit world and talking to the dead."

Mr. Payne straightened. "Loretta's not dead. Neither is Gabe. We've kept their bodies alive. Their spirits remain with us, free to wander in this realm until we let them go."

"Do you mean until we pull the plug and allow them to die."

Mr. Payne nodded. "I'm not the only one who experiences this kind of thing. I was reading a book tonight written by a lady whose husband regularly walks in. He's in a coma just like my wife."

Marla's fear had somewhat relented, giving way to curiosity. "What does your wife talk to you about?"

He rubbed his hand over the salt and pepper stubble of his jowl. "Lately she has been insisting that I take her off life support and let her rest in peace."

"Why don't you?"

"I'm not ready yet. There's something I want her to tell me, but she refuses."

"Why won't she tell you?"

His eyes bore into her. "She's worried I may do something rash."

That's all Marla needed to hear. "I see. Mr. Payne, it's been interesting talking to you, but I need to get to bed. Like I said, I've got a long day tomorrow. Good night."

His eyes softened. "I hope I didn't frighten you. The only reason I shared this with you is because of Gabe's condition. I know what you're going through."

Marla forced a smile. "Thank you, Mr. Payne. I appreciate your concern." She turned, picked up the recorder, and headed for the door, listening for any sounds of Mr. Payne climbing the divider and coming after her. She heard none.

"Good night, Mrs. Easton."

Once inside she locked the door and turned the deadbolt. Relief washed over her now that she was out of the odd man's presence. Why would his wife be worried about Mr. Payne doing something "rash"? Was he capable of murder? And who would he kill? She examined the cassette

151

recorder and noticed it had played to the end of the tape. She put her finger on the rewind button and pressed it. *Maybe I'll get some answers here.* The recorder whizzed back to the beginning and popped up the rewind button. Marla hit the play button.

The woman's voice was distant but audible. "I tried to tell you, but I knew you wouldn't listen. I was afraid you'd become violent, and you did."

"I've told you I'm sorry a hundred times. I can't take back that moment I pushed you. I wish I had fallen down those steps, and you were alive and well, but I can't change what happened."

Her voice became softer. "If you would have just listened to me."

"But I thought you were having another affair."

"I promised you I'd never do that again, even if you couldn't . . . meet my needs."

Several moments of silence followed, and then Mr. Payne spoke, his voice harsher. "You had to bring that up, didn't you? My inadequacies—not meeting your needs."

"I'm sorry. I didn't mean to humiliate you. But it's true. I was through with affairs and willing to be celibate."

"But the stains I found on your sheets. How can you explain those away?"

"Listen to me, Martin. I've never told you this before because, knowing your temper, I was afraid of what you might do. Those stains weren't from a lover. Don't you remember the marks on my wrists and ankles? I tried to tell you at the top of the lighthouse that day, but you wouldn't listen."

At that moment the clamor of footsteps and bodies colliding interrupted their conversation. Marla heard again the struggle between Michael and Sonny and the commotion that followed. Not wanting to relive that night's calamity, she hit the stop button.

As she sat in the quiet of her living room, Loretta Payne's words echoed in her mind: *Don't you remember those marks on my wrists and ankles?*

Chapter 21

Marla managed to head out the door by 8:00 A.M. the next morning despite the heaviness that had pressed upon her as she lay in bed listening to the strident beeping of the alarm. Remembering she carried a new life inside her had helped her to gather strength and shake off the chains of depression. As she drove up Route 12 through the lonely stretches of the national seashore preserve between Buxton and Nags Head, she considered Loretta Payne's final words on the tape: *Don't you remember those marks on my wrists and ankles?* Horrifying memories of the night Marla had been tied up like an animal and raped tried to infiltrate her thoughts, but she repelled them. Steeling her spirit, she focused on the implications of what she had heard. Talking with Mr. Payne and listening to the conversation on the tape convinced Marla that the rumors were true—Mr. Payne had pushed his wife down the Cape Hatteras Lighthouse steps. Was he crazy enough to kill the girl, attack Gabe, and rape Marla? She didn't think so.

In all probability, this "walk-in" mania was Mr. Payne's delusional means to deal with his guilt. However, it implied his innocence in the other crimes. At the top of the lighthouse steps he had confronted his wife with the evidence of another affair—the semen stains he'd discovered. She'd tried to tell him about the rape, but the pain of being cuckolded in the past and perhaps the humiliation of his impotence blinded him. In a rage, without taking the time to weigh her words, he struck out at the woman who exposed his inadequacies. Now his life was consumed with seeking her pardon. *No. He's not the rapist or the murderer. How could he be if he's impotent? His wife's revelation of being raped pointed to someone else. But who?*

Now Marla had another decision to make. Should she tell Dugan Walton about the tape—evidence implicating Mr. Payne's culpability in his wife's injuries? Would Dugan consider it the ramblings of a madman or could he see the underlying truth? She had stuck the tape in her purse in case she ran into Dugan. Perhaps the best approach would be to hand it to him without commentary and allow him to sort out the ramifications. Legally, this kind of evidence may not even be permissible in prosecuting a suspect. Poor Mr. Payne. To Marla, more and more he seemed like a victim rather than a criminal.

Taking a break from her reverie, Marla observed her surroundings as she drove along the two-lane road. To her left passed salt marshes, thickets, maritime woods, and grasslands, beyond which the wide Pamlico Sound stretched to the unseen North Carolina mainland. To her right the undulating rhythm of the dunes topped with sea oats and grasses went by with an occasional glimpse of the Atlantic Ocean. The ribbon of sand that composed these barrier islands always gave Marla an otherworldly sensation, one that caused her to look inward and reflect on life. Living on the Outer Banks meant living on the edge of sand and water. At some points a mere fifty yards of land separated the sound from the ocean. Often it made her feel small and vulnerable, knowing a destructive storm could quickly develop and sweep over this narrow strip.

The insecurity of living on the edge of nature's wrath had its upside too. Temporary things lost their importance—houses, cars, jewelry, money—things that lack eternal significance. The invisible aspects of soul and spirit and relationships with people and God grew in priority. Maybe that's why she noticed so many churches in Buxton, Frisco, and Hatteras. People living on the Outer Banks were constantly reminded of their need of eternal assurance. Could that be a part of the reason Martin Payne had embraced this "walk-in" phenomenon? Had living in this precarious environment attuned him to the spiritual realm? What if it were true? The thought sent a prickling sensation up Marla's back to the base of her skull. What if the spirits of those released from their living bodies could possess people and communicate their thoughts and desires? *Don't be ridiculous, girl.* She shook her head to escape the track of reasoning on which this surreal environment had placed her.

Ahead she noticed the rising bridge that spanned Oregon Inlet between Hatteras Island and Nags Head. Although the sky was clear blue and the wind had subsided, the same fear from the night before rose up within her. *Believe what you know is true*, she told herself. *The downhill side of the bridge will be there. You won't disappear into the heavens or drop into the depths of the sea.*

At the hospital she decided to stop in and see Gabe first before checking on Michael. She followed her regular route to the second floor and nodded at the familiar faces of nurses and attendants along the way. When she entered Gabe's room she noticed the blinds were not quite closed, the bright morning sun sending a pattern of light rays rippling over Gabe's form under the white sheet. The repetition of light and shadow created an ethereal effect, giving Marla the odd feeling she had stepped into a sacred place.

She reached for Gabe's hand and squeezed it. "Good morning, Luuvums." He felt warm and alive. She touched his cheek and noticed several days' growth of beard. "They haven't been shaving you regularly, have they?"

Gabe lay motionless, except for the rise and fall of his chest, each breath relying on the respirator. His newly acquired facial hair gave him the appearance of a character from the Bible—a disciple or perhaps Lazarus?

"Things haven't been easy for me lately. Your brother Michael is in ICU. He had a terrible fall from our back deck last night. He's in a coma like you." She knew Gabe couldn't hear a word, but telling him gave her comfort. She wondered if he, Michael, and Loretta Payne could communicate with each other, three spirits no longer confined by a conscious body. She dispelled the silly thought from her head. "I don't know what to do, Gabe. Things are so confusing. I wish you could somehow tell me, somehow come back to me and let me know."

She thought about the baby growing inside her, lifted Gabe's hand, and placed it on her belly. "I haven't told you yet, but I'm pregnant. I've been afraid to mention it. I pray to God it's your child. The odds are stacked against us, but I keep hoping. The last time we made love I thought for sure we conceived. I guess time will tell. Hoping a part of you is inside me keeps me going."

She recalled her ponderings on the ride to the hospital. "Your brother was right about Martin Payne. He did push his wife down the lighthouse steps. I've got proof, but I don't know what to do with it because I feel sorry for the man. I miss your wisdom and advice. You'd know what to do. I don't think Mr. Payne is the one who attacked you. He's more mixed

155

up than me. Keeps his wife alive because he channels her spirit. He believes if he takes her off life support, then she'll be out of his life for good."

Marla's own words smacked her like an unexpected wave at the seashore. She was keeping Gabe alive for a similar reason—he had spoken to her in a dream, telling her he would return. Feeling hypocritical, she said, "Am I imprisoning you? Do you want to be set free like Loretta Payne?"

Feeling shaky inside, she took a deep breath and let it out audibly. "Help me Gabe. If you're going to come back to me, do it soon." A tear slid down her cheek. She stared at the ceiling. "God, I can't take much more of this. Is Gabe with you up there or still down here with me?"

A silhouette appeared in the doorway, startling Marla. "Mrs. Easton?" a low voice said.

Marla couldn't make out his features. "Yes?"

The person stepped into the room. A stray ray of sunlight shooting through the blind lit the face of Dr. Shepherd. "I need to talk to you about Michael."

His voice did not sound encouraging. Marla swallowed, released Gabe's hand, and faced him. "Do you have the results of the EEG?"

Dr. Shepherd approached her, nodding. The light reflected off his black-rimmed glasses, giving his thick mustache and curly brown hair a golden sheen. "He's breathing on his own, but . . . but . . . the scan showed very little brain activity."

"But there's some?"

"There's always some. Even in patients who are brain dead. Michael has slightly more activity than Gabe. Most neurologists would look at the results and say there's very little hope."

Marla's heart sank, and her legs felt weak. "What's *your* opinion, Dr. Shepherd?"

He peered at the ceiling as if he were trying to see through the building into heaven. He lowered his head, their eyes meeting again. "If I had to put a number on it, I'd say Michael has a one-in-a-thousand chance of coming out of the coma."

One-in-a-thousand, Marla thought. *The same odds of her conceiving Gabe's child. That's strange.* Marla bobbed her head slowly, trying to take it all in. "What do you recommend?"

Dr. Shepherd shrugged. "Like I said, he's breathing on his own. Until his condition changes, there's nothing we can do but wait and see."

Marla felt an odd sense of relief. No decision had to be made. Just wait and see. Did she really have any input on Michael's life anyway? His parents were deceased. He was single. Maybe she did, but it didn't matter for the time being. "Can I see him now?"

"Of course. We're keeping him in ICU for the next few days to keep a close watch on him."

"Thank you, Dr. Shepherd."

He reached and grasped her shoulder. "Hang in there, Mrs. Easton. I'll be here to help you through all this. You've been sailing a stormy sea and the winds have picked up another notch or two. But you're young. Remember, there'll be a lot of life to live beyond this valley."

For Marla it was difficult to imagine life beyond this valley. The mountains were too steep and the way too demanding to spend time dreaming of a brighter tomorrow. It took all the strength and will power she had to place one foot in front of the other. If she could keep taking one step at a time, maybe she'd make it through.

Her next step was to check on Michael. She hadn't seen him since they hauled him away in the E-squad. She felt a little guilty for not staying the night at the hospital or checking on him earlier. But how could she manufacture devotion for someone who had constantly rubbed her the wrong way? She cared for her brother-in-law but more out of duty than sentiment.

After thanking Dr. Shepherd, Marla walked to the elevator and hit the down button. It opened immediately, and she entered the empty cubicle, feeling a little claustrophobic. Being alone didn't help. ICU was on the first floor near the emergency room. When the doors parted, she stepped out quickly. She'd spend some time with Michael and then head over to the Dare County Detention Center in Manteo to visit Sonny. Maybe she'd run into Dugan there and give him the cassette tape. Maybe not.

She didn't look forward to returning to the Intensive Care Unit. Within its walls Marla had spent the most heart-wrenching hours of her life. She paced down several hallways, making the familiar turns and ended up in front of the large double doors. She hit the oversized button to her left and the doors opened. After taking a deep breath, she walked in and nodded at a couple nurses who recognized her. Nurse Magdelane, the middle-aged, thin woman who had been so helpful with Gabe's time there, approached without hesitation.

The salt-and-pepper-haired nurse grasped her hand. "Marla, it's good to see you again, but of course, not under these circumstances."

"Thanks. Nice seeing you again too."

157

"You must feel emotionally exhausted after what you've been through these last two weeks."

Marla nodded, her eyes watering at the display of compassion. "Emotionally and physically I've been worn threadbare. But I'm still here."

Nurse Magdelane hugged her. "You poor girl. God be with you."

They separated, and Marla wiped tears from her cheeks.

Nurse Magdelane's expression became solemn, her lips tightening. "Michael's room is on the far left."

Marla couldn't believe it. "The same one Gabe was in?"

She nodded. "Weird how things can go, isn't it? Twins ending up with the same kind of injury and placed into the same ICU room? How strange the coincidences of life can be."

Marla wondered about that possibility. *One in a thousand? No. More like one in a trillion. But isn't that how tragedy works? People are at the wrong place at the wrong time and collide with the wrong set of circumstances.* She felt like she had ended up on the wrong end of the luck spectrum where all the wrong roads crossed. Nurse Magdelane led her to the room and patted her gently on the back as she entered.

Michael appeared to be sleeping peacefully, his thick dark hair springing out from under a white bandage that capped the top of his head, his wide face tranquil. She stood close to the railing, deciding whether or not to hold his hand. After so many hours spent with Gabe in this same unconscious state, it seemed normal to talk aloud to Michael, even though she knew he couldn't hear a word.

"Good morning, Michael, you poor son of a . . . gun. I'm so sorry this happened to you. You never expected to end up here when you invited Gabe and me to come down to Buxton and live next to you, did you?"

Marla shook her head, trying to muster some tenderness. "We've rarely gotten along, but I surely never wanted to see you like this. It doesn't seem fair . . . to any of us." She had to take a deep breath and swallow at the thought of life's lack of fairness, staving off a lump that tried to form in her throat. "But who said life's fair, huh? If you hadn't called Gabe for a ride that night, he'd still be with us. If you hadn't felt compelled to record Mr. Payne's conversation with his wife, you'd still be with us. But now you're both somewhere else."

Again the knot rose in her throat and she gulped it down. "Are you with Gabe now? Somewhere beyond this world keeping him company? You always wanted his attention, but I got in the way these last few years." She fought off an urge to become bitter. "Forgive me." She reached and grasped his hand. "I didn't mean to use those exact words. I know you two were close all your lives."

She drew nearer and examined his eyes. Had they opened slightly? She squeezed his hand. "Can you hear me?"

His head turned ever so slightly towards her, causing her heart to jump. She glanced at her hand pressing on his and wondered if she caused the movement. *Take it easy now. It's just that I'm leaning on the bed.* Her heart slowed, but when she examined his eyes again they appeared even wider than before, almost half open.

"Gabe?" *Dammit, I mean Michael.* She blamed the slip on force of habit from spending so much time at Gabe's bedside. She lowered her head to within inches of his face.

"Sweetcheeks," he mumbled.

Marla raised up, gasped, and squeezed his hand tighter. "What did you say?"

His eyes closed.

"Michael! What did you say?"

Marla stared at him. Was this a dream? No. She was wide awake. She felt the metal railing in one hand and Michael's soft skin in the other. This was real. Across the bed on the other railing she spotted the green nurse's button. She leaned over Michael, resting on his substantial gut, and pressed the button.

Within thirty seconds Nurse Magdelane darted into the room and sped to the bedside. "Is everything all right?"

The words rushed out of Marla's mouth like water out of a pump. "Michael just opened his eyes and spoke. I swear he turned his head, barely opened his eyes, and said, 'Sweetcheeks.'"

Nurse Magdelene lightly patted Michael's cheek. "Michael. Wake up. Can you hear me?"

He lay unmoving.

The nurse glanced at Marla. "He said, 'Sweetcheeks'? Who's 'Sweetcheeks'?"

When the realization struck Marla, it almost knocked her over. *I'm Sweetcheeks. But Gabe is the only one who calls me that. No one else even knows about that nickname.* Marla shrugged. "That's w-what my husband c-calls me."

Nurse Magdelane gave her an odd look. "Stay here and watch him. I'll get a doctor."

Marla bobbed her head and refocused as the nurse exited the room. Michael appeared exactly as he did when she first arrived—unconscious, unmoving, tranquil. She tried to reason how in the world he would know

159

Gabe's pet name for her. Maybe Gabe allowed it to slip out when they were goofing off together or having a heart to heart talk. But Gabe wasn't the kind to make personal details public, even to someone as close as his twin brother. The more she thought about it, the more the incident spooked her. She let go of Michael's hand and took a step back. Peering out the door, she hoped the doctor would get there as soon as possible.

One in a thousand, she thought. For several seconds the mystery of life overwhelmed her. Why was she here? Who was she? Where did she come from? What was her purpose? She had experienced those odd moments a few times in the past, times when she seemed to step out of herself and see her circumstances from a distance. She became an observer, watching a stranger battling through difficulties and thinking how temporary and small and insignificant she and her problems were compared to the universe and the eternal realm that couldn't be seen. She couldn't deal with those transcendent states for long because they disturbed her, pushed her to the edge of sanity, threatening to whisk her away from the realities of life.

She stepped back to the bed and gripped the railing. "Michael. Wake up!" She shook his shoulder, but he lay unresponsive. She leaned to get a good look at his eyes. A weird urge came over her. *Do it. Say it.* "Gabe, are you there?"

His eyes remained closed, but his head nodded. Was she shaking the railing?

Dr. Shepherd and Nurse Magdelane hurried into the room. Marla straightened and stepped away from the bed.

Dr. Shepherd's eyes bore into her. "You heard him say something?"

Marla nodded, her eyes widening. "He called me Sweetcheeks."

"You're sure?"

"Yes. And he opened his eyes, just barely, but he opened them."

The doctor took his thumb, raised Michael's eyelid, and shone a penlight into his eye. "Check his pulse and blood pressure."

Nurse Magdelane sped to Marla's side of the bed, placed a blood pressure wrap on Michael's arm, pumped the air bulb, and took a reading. "One thirty over eighty-five."

Dr. Shepherd checked his other eye. "I don't see much change." He clasped Michael's cheeks with both hands. "Michael, can you hear me!" He shook his face slightly. "Michael!" Nothing.

"I couldn't have imagined it, Doctor Shepherd," Marla said. "Right before you came in he nodded his head."

The doctor eyed Nurse Magdelane. Her lips tightened and eyes narrowed in what Marla considered an acknowledgement of Dr. Shepherd's doubt. She lifted Michael's gown, placed her stethoscope on his chest, and studied her watch. "Heartbeat is normal."

Dr. Shepherd ambled to their side of the bed. "You've been under a lot of stress lately, Mrs. Easton. It's easy to mistake a patient's involuntary sounds or movements for actual words or intentional gestures."

Marla shook her head. "I know what I heard. I know what I saw."

The doctor's shoulders slumped as his eyes dropped to the floor. He inhaled audibly and said, "All right, then. If you're sure, we'll do another EEG. Maybe we got an inaccurate reading on the first one."

"Believe me," Marla said. "I'm sure."

Marla needed to get away from the hospital while they tested Michael again. She decided to drive to Manteo and visit Sonny at the detention center. It wasn't that far away, maybe ten minutes. Michael's temporary emergence from the coma and reaction to Marla addressing him as Gabe rattled her. In his condition how could he come up with Sweetcheeks? It didn't make sense. Michael always called her "Marla" or once in a great while, "Sis". She didn't like it when he called her "Sis" because she didn't want him to get too comfortable around her, but she never complained. Thinking about Martin Payne's walk-in obsession dissuaded her from believing Gabe could take over Michael's body. That was too far out there. Besides, if it did happen, how could it be proven? It couldn't.

Driving over the bridge that crossed to Roanoke Island, Marla recalled she was entering a historically significant area—the location of the Lost Colony. Sir Walter Raleigh attempted to organize a permanent settlement on the island in the late 1500's, but three years later they disappeared without a trace. Marla always found their story incredible, something the tabloids would make up. *I'll fit right in here. I've never felt more lost and alone in my life.* She wondered what it would be like to disappear, never to be seen again. Is not existing better than suffering? Then she thought about Sonny sitting in his cell. Knowing she would bring a little joy into his day shooed away her gloomy clouds of self-pity.

The Dare County Detention Center was located on the north side of the island near the regional airport. Marla didn't have any problem finding it, a modern building of geometric design composed of beige block with blue trim. To Marla, it looked more like a Ramada Inn than a jail. The receptionist, a young woman with short black hair dressed in a light-blue uniform, directed Marla to the holding cells. There, an attendant, an older man with a tanned and wrinkled face, led her down the corridor. Most of the barred rooms she passed were empty, but a few contained prisoners quietly reading or watching television.

When Marla reached the end of the hall, she peered into the last chamber and observed Sonny sitting on his bed with a small magazine stretched across his lap, intently studying its contents.

He glanced up and jumped to his feet. "Mrs Easton, I never expected a visit from you."

Marla couldn't help smiling. "You know I told you to call me Marla, Sonny. Good friends should be on a first name basis. Right?"

"Of course. I forgot."

Marla asked the attendant to allow her to enter the cell. He obliged and then locked the door behind her.

"Have a seat," Sonny said, motioning to his bed, which was neatly made, a white sheet stretched tightly over a thin mattress. He leaned against the wall, his face beaming, eyes bright and hopeful.

Marla pointed to his magazine. "What're are you reading?"

He held up a *Reader's Digest* with an image of a couple tow-headed boys on the cover. "I've been studyin' this month's *Word Power.*"

"Always learning new words, aren't you?"

"Yes ma'am. I missed one out of twelve."

"Which one?"

"Nictitate."

Marla had never heard the word before. "I give up. What does it mean?"

Sonny winked at her.

Was he dallying with her? When he winked again, this time sporting a wide grin, she realized he was giving her the definition. "To wink at someone?"

Sonny nodded. "That's right."

"Thought maybe you were flirting with me."

"Nope, nope, nope." His expression sobered. "I'd never do that. You're a married woman."

Marla sensed sincerity in his tone. "I know, Sonny, I'm just kidding."

His smile returned, his face reddening.

"How're you holding up in here?"

His bottom lip stiffened. "I'll be fine. Got an appointment with a bail bondsman today. Hopefully, I'll be out of here soon, at least for a while. Is Michael all right?"

Marla shook her head. "He's still unconscious, although . . . although I could swear he spoke to me this morning. They're running another test on him. I'll know more when I get back to the hospital."

Sonny bobbed his head slowly. "How 'bout . . . Gabe?" He lowered his eyes.

Marla took a deep breath and swallowed. "I haven't given up hope, but the doctors don't expect him to ever come out of the coma."

"I'm truly sorry, Marla."

Marla couldn't speak and battled back the urge to cry. *Don't lose it, girl. You're here to cheer Sonny up, not break down in front of him.*

Sonny cleared his throat. "If Michael . . . if Michael regains consciousness, do you think he'll press charges against me?"

Addressing the question helped to stabilize her. "Michael has always spoken highly of you. I doubt if he'll press charges. He knows the circumstances. You were just trying to protect me."

"I hope you're right."

"Sonny, I need to ask you something. Last night Deputy Walton showed up at the apartments. He had your keys."

"That's right," Sonny said. "I gave them to him. Got nothing to hide."

"Did you tell him he could look in your shed out back?"

He rubbed his chin. "No. But that's fine, if he wanted to look there."

Marla stood and waited for Sonny to meet her gaze. "He found something in the shed that may incriminate you."

Sonny straightened. "Incriminate? That means to prove someone's guilty."

Marla nodded.

"What did he find?"

"The killer's mask. Does someone have the key to that shed besides you?"

Sonny peered at the ceiling and shook his head. "No one. But it's just a padlock. It's easy to find matching keys."

"That's what I told Deputy Walton. I think someone is trying to frame you."

"Why me?"

Marla shrugged. "Do you have any enemies?"

Sonny's eyes widened. "Only one: Tony Trenton."

Maybe, Marla thought. Footsteps echoed down the hallway as someone approached. She glanced up to see Dugan Walton, ball cap in hand, his red hair somewhat molded by the shape of his hat

Dugan waved. "Hey, Marla." He unlocked the cell door and swung it open. "You've got a phone call at the front desk."

"Thanks, Dugan." She peered into her purse, saw the cassette tape, and reached for it.

"Morning, Sonny," Dugan said.

Sonny stepped towards Dugan. "Heard you found the killer's mask in my shed."

Dugan nodded.

"I swear I didn't put it there."

Dugan shrugged. "I'll be back in a minute to talk about it, Sonny. Got to escort Marla down the hallway."

Marla encouraged Sonny to stay strong and then headed down the corridor, the cassette tape held firmly in her hand. The caller had to be somebody from the hospital. She had left word with them that she'd be at the detention center.

Dugan caught up with her. "Whadaya got in your hand?"

She held up the tape and shook it. "Something you might be interested in."

"A recording?"

"I wasn't sure whether I should give this to you or not. It's quite strange. Michael was recording this when Sonny attacked him. That's all I'm going to say. Listen to it and see what you think." She handed him the tape.

"Interesting."

They entered the lobby, and the receptionist held up the phone. "Nurse Magdelane from the Outer Banks Hospital. Says it's urgent."

Marla rushed to the desk and grabbed the receiver. "Yes, this is Marla Easton."

"Marla, could you get back here as soon as possible?"

"Of course. Why? What happened?"

"Michael's conscious, and he's asking for you."

Chapter 22

On the short drive back to the hospital Marla dealt with a whirl of thoughts and scenarios. Michael's emergence from the coma brought relief, but the fact that he referred to her as Sweetcheeks bewildered her. There had to be an explanation. Certainly he knew about the pet name, probably overhearing it when he was hanging out at the apartment, but why would he use it? A person regaining consciousness doesn't call someone else a name he'd heard once or twice in the past. Marla reasoned that Michael wasn't thinking clearly, latching on to names he'd linked to her somewhere in his cache of memory. Once she got to the hospital, everything would settle logically into place. Bottom line—thank God he's okay. No funeral arrangements or long hospital stays to worry about. Gabe's circumstances burdened her enough.

Along with those thoughts she juggled Sonny's suspicion of Tony Trenton. No doubt Trenton was Sonny's enemy after the two confrontations he'd had with him over her. But Trenton had no access to Loretta Payne's bedroom. How could he get hold of the mask? *Wait a minute.* Loretta's Payne's words echoed again in her mind: *Don't you remember those marks on my wrists and ankles?* Did Tony Trenton tie her up and rape her?

It all made sense. According to the tape, Loretta Payne had several affairs, seeking sexual fulfillment her husband could no longer provide.

Living only a quarter mile from the Citgo station, she must have stopped to have her tank filled by Trenton on a regular basis. Was she flirtatious? Marla didn't know much about her character but guessed she would have been. Women who go through several men know how to attract them. It wouldn't take much of a scent to get a hound dog like Trenton on her trail. It may have started as playful banter at the gas station, but then one day he showed up at her door when Martin Payne wasn't there or maybe he broke in and waited for her. Perhaps she even let him in, trying to be cordial. He probably wore pants with deep pockets to conceal the ropes. Once inside, he'd taken what he wanted the way he wanted it. The pervert. Maybe he thought she would like the ropes. Then he removed the mask from the wall to disguise himself or for added effect. But she didn't like it, so he tied her up anyway and raped her. Then he threatened to kill her if she reported it. And he'd follow through, no doubt. The dead girl on the beach offered proof of that.

With DNA evidence from the murder victim's rape kit test pointing directly at him and a record of mistreating women, Trenton decided to use the mask to get the investigator's focus off him and onto another possible suspect. After Sonny manhandled him a couple times, Trenton zeroed in on him to take the rap. He picked the lock on the shed and planted the mask. Then Dugan came along and found it, just as Trenton had hoped. A surge of adrenalin charged through Marla, the energy extending through her foot and gas pedal. She glanced at the speedometer. Sixty miles an hour in a forty-five zone. She hit the brake and slowed the vehicle, amazed she might have solved the crime.

She couldn't wait to meet up with Dugan and offer her hypothesis. Could he have come up with the same line of reasoning? He had the evidence. But it was Sonny's revelation that got Marla thinking: Trenton was his only enemy. He had to be the one. A terrible notion hit Marla like a shovel in the face. If Trenton was the killer and rapist, then she might be carrying his child. She glanced at her belly, feeling sudden nausea that threatened to make her upchuck her breakfast. She *did not* want to give birth to that man's baby. Unfortunately, the odds favored Trenton—999 to1.

Marla wondered if some kind of test could be administered to determine the DNA of a fetus. If so, she'd have it done to find out who impregnated her. If Trenton was the father, she could opt for an abortion and let the authorities use the DNA evidence to prosecute him. She hated the thought of terminating the pregnancy. *God, please let it be Gabe* After all she'd been through, Marla believed she deserved a miracle.

Marla entered the hospital and checked at the front desk to locate Michael, thinking they might have placed him back in ICU to keep an eye on him. She was right. The receptionist relayed that Dr. Shepherd had left a message for her that he'd be waiting with Michael there. Marla navigated the hallways to the entrance, smacked the large square button on the left wall, and strode into the intensive care unit, almost colliding with the not-fast-enough opening doors.

Nurse Magdelane grasped Marla's elbow and ushered to the last cubicle on the left. "Everyone is so excited. We were getting ready to transport Michael to neurology for the EEG when he sat up. I almost peed myself, and Nurse Johnson screamed. It's really a miracle. Dr. Shepherd hadn't given him much hope of regaining consciousness."

Marla grinned. "I told you he called me Sweetcheeks, opened his eyes, and nodded his head."

"I know. I know," Nurse Magdelane said as they entered the room. "I shouldn't have doubted you."

Michael sat propped against the raised bed with a wide smile. "I'm back." He spread his arms.

A wave of amazement flowed over Marla. *He wants a hug?* She didn't like hugging Michael, but she wouldn't begrudge him one today.

She approached the bed and leaned to embrace him. He pulled her tightly against him, an affectionate hug. Before she could back away he planted a wet kiss on her mouth."

"Michael, take it easy," Marla said, breaking away from the lip-lock and his heavy arms. She felt her face flush.

"Huh?" He looked puzzled. "You're the third person who's called me that today." He waved his hand over his belly. "And when did I gain so much weight?"

Dr. Shepherd stood on the opposite side of the bed, shaking his head. "He's a little mixed up. Not quite sure who he is. But he knows you. That's a positive."

Michael appeared confused. "How could I forget my wife?"

Marla stared at him, searching his features for some indication of a put-on or even deception, but all she saw was confusion. She stepped to the rail. "Listen to me. I'm not your wife. I'm your sister-in-law. You are *not* Gabe. You are Michael."

He leaned against the back of the bed, his eyes narrowing, mouth open. "I don't understand." He examined his hands and patted his gut as

167

if to insure it was his own flesh and not some pillow stuck under his gown. "Does someone have a mirror I could borrow?"

Marla reached into her purse, pulled out her compact, opened it, and handed it to him. *Is this Michael's way of dealing with his guilt—trying to resurrect Gabe? Is that why he called me Sweetcheeks or is he just mixed up?*

Michael studied his face in the small round mirror and rubbed his hand over his wide jowls. His eyes strained with incredulity and met Marla's. "I don't know what to say. Something happened in the darkness. I can't remember exactly what. But I waited for so long—then a door opened, and I saw a sliver of light. I thought I was coming back to you, but it's not me. Where's Michael?"

"I told you," Marla said. "You are Michael."

He peered into the mirror and nodded. "I look like Michael."

Marla turned to Dr. Shepherd. "Is this normal? To not know who you are?"

"His mind may be jumbled a bit," Dr. Shepherd said. "That's not so unusual. Also, keep in mind he is a twin, and twins have a deeper bond than regular siblings. Give him some time. Things will fall into order."

Marla swallowed, more like a restrained gulp, and eyed Michael. He looked hurt, as if he showed up at a party to find out someone had mistakenly sent him an invitation. Mr. Payne's walk-in claims lingered in the back of her mind but with no real conviction. Guilt drove Mr. Payne to believe in something so far out on the fringe. Marla would plant her feet on the solid ground of reality. *Believe what you know is true.* Perhaps guilt drove Michael to that extreme too. Time would tell. It would take irrefutable evidence to convince Marla walk-ins were possible.

Dr. Shepherd informed them he wanted Michael to stay a few more days for observation and further testing. Michael, somewhat out of character, said very little. Marla did her best to respond to the technical information the doctor presented. After he and Nurse Magdelane left, an uncomfortable silence permeated the room. Marla moved closer to the railing, trying to think of an excuse to leave.

Michael reached and grasped her hand. "Listen to me, Sweetcheeks. It *is* me. Don't you remember I came to you and told you I'd come back to you?"

Marla strained to be patient but wanted to pull her hand away and get out of there. "That's enough of this kind of talk, Michael. Gabe came to me in a dream, not you. I told you all about the dream a few days ago. That's what you're remembering—things I have told you and things Gabe has shared with you. I don't hold you responsible for Gabe's condition. There's no need to feel guilty anymore. You don't have to try to bring him back to me like Martin Payne brings back his wife."

Michael blinked and tears rolled down his cheeks. Marla had rarely seen him cry before. He shook his head, unclasped his hand from hers, and wiped the wet streaks away with his fingertips. "I'm sorry. I don't want to upset you."

"I'm fine. You just need some rest. That's all. This has been a traumatic experience for both of us."

Michael sniffled and stared at his hands.

Marla reached and patted his shoulder. "I've had a long day. You should get some rest."

He glanced up, eyes watery. "You're leaving?"

"I'll be back tomorrow morning. By then you'll feel much better. Things will have cleared up. We'll talk then."

Michael took a deep breath and let it out haltingly. "I wish I knew what to say to convince you."

Marla held up her finger. "No more of this, Michael, please, or I won't come back tomorrow."

Michael nodded and lowered his head.

"I'll see you in the morning." Marla headed for the door, glad to be on her way.

As she reached the doorway, Michael called out, "Marla."

She turned and faced him.

"I love you."

Michael had never said *that* to her before. She forced a smile, turned, and feeling like her heart had moved from her chest into her throat, hurried towards the ICU exit. Yeah, she loved Michael because he was her husband's brother but didn't want to feed any errant flame that had started in a boggled mind.

As Marla crossed the parking lot to her car, she noticed a sheriff's vehicle driven by a redhead turning off the main drag. *Dugan must be looking for me.* She stepped towards the entrance lane and waved, catching his eye. He pulled into the nearest empty parking space.

"I'm glad I ran into you," she hollered as he got out of the car.

"How's Michael doing?"

"He's a little mixed up but seems to be okay. The medical staff thinks it's a miracle."

"That's good news for a change."

Marla bobbed her head, thinking even good news comes with complications.

Dugan held up the cassette tape. "After listening to this, I wanted to talk to you."

"What'd you think of it?"

He raised his eyebrows. "This guy has gone bonkers. I think you should be very careful around him."

"I feel sorry for him."

"I feel sorry for his wife."

Marla had to admit Dugan had a point. "Yes, of course, she was victimized twice. Don't you think?"

Dugan shrugged. "I don't know what to think. How can I take seriously anything a man says when he's possessed by his wife's spirit?"

"I know he sounds crazy, but it's his way of dealing with the guilt."

"I'll give you that," Dugan responded. "From what he said on the tape it's easy to conclude he pushed his wife down the lighthouse steps."

"Right." Marla paused, struggling to phrase her words in a way to help Dugan see the truth behind the bizarre. "He's using himself as a medium to reconnect with his wife out of his need to be pardoned."

Dugan nodded. "You're probably right, but the world he's creating is outside of reality. That's why I can't use anything on this tape as evidence."

"Don't you see, though, just because he creates it doesn't mean it's all fantasy. I think he uses it to deal with the awful truth."

Dugan placed his hands on his hips. "Give me an example."

"Obviously—his wife accusing him of pushing her down the steps."

"Okay, I can see that, but only because he knows what he did. The accusation really didn't come from his wife. She's in a coma."

"That's not all," Marla said. "How about what she said at the end of the tape? Her wrist and ankle injuries indicate someone raped her."

Dugan shook his head. "But, Marla, Payne didn't know that beforehand. A brain-dead woman cannot possess her husband and reveal she'd been raped."

"I know. I know. If he knew she'd been raped, he wouldn't have pushed her. What I am saying is Mr. Payne remembered his wife had ligature marks on her wrists and ankles. Maybe the murdered girl's injuries opened his eyes. Something helped him to figure it out. This channeling thing is just his way of expressing it."

A new look came into Dugan's eyes, a light of comprehension perhaps? "So you're saying he knew about his wife's injuries but didn't put one and one together until recently?"

"Exactly. Back then he found evidence of what he thought was another affair and overreacted. Once his rage passed and he could think more logically, he realized he may have been wrong. He kept remembering the marks on her wrists and ankles. Then he heard about the dead girl and how she'd been tied up and raped. But what can he do about it now that his wife was in a coma?"

A smile crept across Dugan's face. "Bring her back to confirm what he has concluded?"

"Right. I believe if you find the man who raped Loretta Payne, you'll find the one who killed the girl, attacked Gabe, and raped me."

Dugan raised his chin and looked directly in her eyes. "You think you know who that person might be?"

Marla nodded. "Tony Trenton."

"Any evidence or just a gut feeling?"

"The mask. Someone planted it to point the finger of suspicion at Sonny. Today I asked Sonny if he had any enemies. He said he only had one—Tony Trenton. Loretta Payne must have known Trenton. Maybe she got her gas at the Citgo station. It's not far from where she lived. She discovered a little bit of flirting with Trenton isn't a good thing. Once he has a woman in his sights, she becomes his sexual prey. Somehow he got into her house, put on the mask, and raped her."

Dugan blew out a long exhale through pursed lips. "That's stretching it."

Marla's confidence in her speculation of the events faltered slightly. "Why? Doesn't it make sense?"

"You're assuming too much. There are no witnesses connecting Trenton and Loretta Payne. She may never have gotten her gas at the Citgo station. Let's say you're right, though, and he did enter the house and rape her. What's his motive for taking the mask? It would link him to the crime."

Marla's mind raced, sorting out the possibilities. "To hide his identity, maybe. Or some kind of fetish. Don't serial rapists take souvenirs, something to remind them of their conquests?"

Dugan tilted his head. "That's a possibility, but why wouldn't Loretta Payne report the rape?"

"Because he threatened to kill her like he threatened to kill me."

Dugan stood silently for what seemed a full minute. Finally, he said, "I guess I could question Trenton about Loretta Payne. At least find out if he knew her or ever pumped gas for her. Even so, it'll be hard to prosecute him."

"Why?"

"Because his two buddies swear he was with them the night the girl got killed."

Marla had forgotten about that. Trenton had an alibi. She guessed his witnesses lacked credibility, but maybe her theory did too in the eyes of professional crime investigators. Marla shrugged. "At least the cassette gives you another lead or two to follow up on."

"Do you mind if I keep the tape?"

"It's all yours. Hope it helps."

"This makes me want to question Martin Payne again too. He may know something about the relationship between Trenton and his wife. By the way, I wanted to tell you to be careful around Payne."

"I'm not too worried about him."

Dugan knotted his brow, his eyes darkening. "I would be if I were you."

"He's a psycho but not a murderer or rapist."

"Did you ever see *Psycho*?"

Marla remembered watching the black and white Hitchcock flick at a friend's house one night when she was ten or eleven years old. The shower scene had horrified her, but the image of Bates dressed up as his mother, wielding the knife, haunted her so much she didn't sleep well for a week. She'd wake up imagining him hovering over her, wearing that gray wig, ready to plunge the knife into her. The memory sent a shiver through her. "Of course I've seen *Psycho*. Hasn't everyone?"

"You just called Martin Payne a psycho. Most killers are mentally unbalanced."

Marla swallowed to steady her voice. "I'll be careful around him."

Dugan raised a finger like a teacher emphasizing an important point. "Never allow yourself to be alone with that man. You might be wrong about Trenton. Payne could be the killer. He has no alibi, and this tape confirms the rumors about what he did to his wife. It's clear he's a schizo."

"I don't plan on stopping over his house for a cup of coffee in the near future." Marla studied Dugan's face to see if her comment lightened his mood.

"I hope not. Whatever you do, don't let him into your house when you're alone. You never know what personality will possess him next."

Dugan's words helped to muddle her already cloudy vision of the crimes and culprits. *Maybe Payne is dangerous. For all I know, Sonny Keys could be the killer, and I'm doing all I can to set him free.* She glanced at Dugan and said, "I'll see ya later. I need to go home and crash. I'm tired."

"Take care of yourself, Marla." Dugan walked away, angling towards the hospital entrance.

"Where you going now?" Marla called.

"To see Michael. Need to find out whether or not he's pressing charges against Sonny Keys."

Marla gazed skyward and noticed a lone seagull floating on the breeze against a brilliant blue sky. *He won't press charges. Not if he thinks he's Gabe. Gabe would never press charges against someone who was trying to protect me.*

For the next few days Marla made her regular trips to the hospital. She'd stop to see Gabe first, and then, fighting a sense of uneasiness, she'd force herself to visit Michael. She had to warn Michael several times not to even mention Gabe's name. He needed to know she wasn't buying this "walk-in" business. If he had to deal with the guilt of his responsibility in contributing to Gabe's condition, he'd better find another way. Living in the same apartment complex with Martin Payne provided enough contact with the spirit world. Michael responded by clamming up, making Marla's visits uncomfortable but brief. She tried to give him the benefit of the doubt because of his head injury, hoping he'd snap out of it by the time they released him.

As Marla predicted, Michael refused to press charges against Sonny. Dugan Walton managed to orchestrate Sonny's release soon after Michael's decision. Sonny's presence back at the apartments gave Marla a greater sense of security, even if he remained a suspect in the investigation. Marla had pulled him aside and instructed him not to be so aggressive in his commitment to protecting her. As usual, his face reddened and he apologized for what he did to Michael.

When Michael came home at the end of the week, Sonny became his attentive caregiver, helping him up the steps, getting his groceries, taking out his trash, and visiting him every morning and evening. Marla was glad because she decided to limit her time with Michael. She wanted to maintain a friendly but cautious relationship with him, at least until he recovered from his head trauma and regressed to the old, self-indulgent, borderline-alcoholic brother-in-law she knew best. He seemed to sense her trepidation and backed off his insistence Gabe had taken over his body. But still, his eyes had that anxious look, as if he struggled to keep this exchange of personalities to himself.

One late afternoon about a week after Michael had returned, Marla pulled into the driveway after putting in a few hours at the bookstore. She stepped out of the car with a bag of groceries and heard the sound of an acoustic guitar being strummed. *That's odd.* It had been a month since she'd heard that kind of music—the kind Gabe loved and played. She peered up at the apartment above hers, Michael's apartment, and spied him sitting on the deck strumming away on a guitar very similar to Gabe's. Did Michael have a key to her apartment? *How dare he take Gabe's guitar without permission.*

"Hey! Michael!" she shouted.

The music stopped, and he looked down.

"Where did you get that guitar?"

Michael stood and leaned the guitar against the railing. "At a garage sale down the road, near the bookstore where you work." He grabbed the neck of the guitar and held it up. "Not bad for fifty bucks, huh?"

Marla remembered passing the yard sale that morning and felt ashamed for jumping to conclusions but tried not to show it. "I didn't know you played guitar."

"I don't. I've just had this desire to fiddle with one lately. It seems to come easy to me."

By Michael's smile, Marla could see he seemed elated that she had paid some attention to him. She didn't want to overdo it. "Have you tried painting at all lately?"

He shook his head. "Can't seem to get into painting."

"That's how you earn your living down here."

Michael set the guitar down. "I might have to get a real job."

That'll be the day, Marla thought. "Talk to you later," she said and ascended the steps to her apartment. *A real job. Right.* If it wasn't easy, Michael wouldn't do it. Inside, she set the groceries on the counter and pulled an orange out of the bag and set it on the butcher block. As she opened the utensil drawer to find a knife, she wondered if Gabe's guitar was still in the bedroom. Would Michael lie about something like that? She set the knife down on the counter and headed for the bedroom.

The guitar leaned against the wall collecting dust, exactly where Gabe had put it over a month ago. Don't be so suspicious, she told herself. Seeing the guitar reminded her of that love song Gabe had written her. Alhough she'd only heard it once, the melody and lyrics played often in her mind: *Do you believe in love so good, it lifts you to the sky, makes you want to laugh, makes you want to cry. I do. I do. Because I found you, I'll never be the same, ever since you came into my life.*

She sang the song to herself as she returned to the kitchen. On the table she noticed the packet she'd picked up earlier in the week at the hospital. It contained information about DNA prenatal paternity testing. She had put off reading it because she didn't want to face the probable results: the child she carried belonged to the rapist. She hadn't heard from Dugan Walton in a while and wondered if he had questioned Tony Trenton and Martin Payne about the possible relationship between Trenton and Loretta Payne. Staring at the packet, she loathed the thought of the baby being Trenton's. She reprimanded herself for not wanting to face reality. *Believe what you know is true.* She possibly held the key to prosecuting a killer and rapist.

She opened the packet, extracted a brochure, and skimmed down until she reached a vital paragraph. *This is not an invasive test . . . uses only the mother's blood and DNA samples from the alleged father.* That shouldn't be a problem, Marla thought. She remembered Dugan had successfully persuaded the prime suspects to offer DNA samples. She read on: *The test can be administered as early as 13 weeks into the pregnancy.* She was about seven weeks in—another six to go. *Fetal DNA is plentiful in the mother's bloodstream. DNA profiles are prepared for the mother, alleged father, and fetal cell population. The mother's DNA profile is compared to that of the fetal cells. Any markers not present in that of the mother have been inherited from the biological father.* Seems simple enough, Marla thought. *Accuracy rate for the test is 99.9%.*

A loud rapping at the door startled her. *Who could that be?* She folded the brochure and placed it back into the manila envelope. Maybe Dugan Walton had finally made some headway in the investigation and stopped by to talk to her. Good. She could tell him about her pregnancy and willingness to go through a paternal DNA test. She grasped the knob and swung the door open to see Martin Payne. He had dark bags under his eyes, his salt-and pepper hair disheveled.

"Mrs. Easton, I have to talk to you." His voice wavered.

"Sure." Marla' mind scrambled, remembering Dugan's warning, searching for the right words. "Give me a minute. I'll be right out."

"No," he said gruffly.

"Excuse me?" Marla reached to pull the door shut.

He placed his hand against it. "Please. I'd rather talk inside. It's very important."

Her heart shifted into high gear. "I can't talk right now."

He stepped forward, nudging her backwards into the apartment, and pulled the door shut behind him. He leaned towards her, his dark eyes barely visible below his thick brows. "You're in grave danger," he said.

Chapter 23

Marla backed into the kitchen table and raised her hands. "Don't come any closer."

Martin Payne's eyebrows rose slightly, giving him the appearance of an offended Irish terrier. "I'm not going to hurt you. I came to tell you something very important." He glanced over his shoulder at the closed door. "I didn't want anyone else to hear."

Marla didn't know what to think. Was he dangerous or just an oddball or both? The closest weapon, a butcher knife, lay on the counter to her right next to an orange. She edged in that direction, trying to remain calm. "Tell me what you need to tell me but keep your distance, please."

"Okay." He folded his hands in front of him at belt level. His wrinkled blue polo shirt and gray slacks gave him the appearance of a used car salesman. "But you have nothing to fear from me. It's someone else you should be worried about."

Marla had managed to slide over to the counter, catching a glint of the knife's chrome handle in her peripheral vision. "What are you talking about? Who wants to hurt me?"

"I don't know. She wouldn't tell me who."

"Who wouldn't tell you?"

"My wife."

Marla figured as much. Mr. Payne wanted to deliver a message from the beyond—something he dreamed up in the world he created to deal with his guilt. "I must be frank with you, Mr. Payne. I don't believe your can speak through you. She's in a coma."

"Listen to me!" He charged forward and stopped within inches of her. "You're wrong. She can speak through me."

Think before you open your big mouth. Think. Think what to say. She slid her hand towards the knife, hoping he didn't notice the movement. She tried to breathe slowly. "I'll listen, Mr. Payne. Go ahead and tell me what your wife said."

He straightened, giving her more room. "She told me that the man who violated her also violated you. But he's not finished with you. He's going to come back."

Mr. Payne's words stunned her. How did he know she had been raped? Unless . . . unless he did it. But wasn't he impotent? She couldn't be sure of anything. Maybe she could turn the tables on him and find out. "Could I ask *you* a question, Mr. Payne?"

"Of course." His eyes became serious, his upper lip disappearing under his mustache as his facial muscles tightened.

"Did the same person who raped your wife also put her into a coma?"

He bowed his head, his focus dropping to the floor. "No. I . . .I . . ."

Does he want to confess? Her fingers touched the handle of the knife. "Did you push your wife down the Cape Hatteras Lighthouse steps?"

The front door opened. Sunlight slashed across Mr. Payne and into Marla's eyes. She squinted at the dark figure in the doorway.

"I hope I'm not interrupting anything, Marla, but do you have any granola bars?"

She recognized Micheal's voice, so similar to Gabe's. "Come in, Michael. I'll have to check."

Mr. Payne backed away and gazed at Michael. Marla dropped her hand to her side, the knife quivering slightly on the counter.

Mr. Payne turned from Michael to Marla. "Remember what I told you."

"How could I forget something like that?"

He nodded and said, "I must be going now." He skirted around the kitchen table and cut between Michael and the open door.

Michael watched him depart then eyed Marla. "I didn't mean to barge in, but that guy worries me. From my deck I saw him leave his apartment

178

and walk across the yard and up your septs. I thought I'd better stop down."

"Thank you." Marla could feel the thumping in her chest diminishing. "I'm glad you did. He's a strange man. Do you remember when you taped him on the back deck?"

Michael stared at her blankly, shook his head, and said, "No."

Marla could have guessed that answer. *Does he still think he's Gabe?* "Anyway, you recorded Mr. Payne channeling his wife, you know, when she 'walks in' to his body and takes over."

He knotted his brow. "She takes over? And becomes him?"

"You knew all about that. You're the one who told me. I gave the tape to Dugan Walton because it contained some information that may help with his investigation."

"For instance?"

Marla inhaled deeply, debating whether or not to go into it. She would try to keep it short and sweet. "For instance, Loretta Payne denied his accusation that she had an affair and told him she'd been raped."

Michael rubbed his chin and glanced at the ceiling, as if trying to make sense of the information. "Why did he stop over to see you just now?"

"To inform me of his wife's latest revelation: Apparently, I'm in grave danger. The same man who raped his wife is after me."

Michael's eyes widened. "Do you think it could be him?"

"It's possible. I don't know. Let's drop the subject. Talking about it makes me nervous." She walked along the counter and placed her hand on the handle of a cupboard door. "Did you really want a granola bar? Gabe has a box of them up here."

"I've been craving them lately, but that was just an excuse to stop down. Besides, that box in the cupboard is empty."

"Empty?" Marla opened the cupboard, pulled out the granola bar box, and shook it. No sound or extra weight. She faced Michael, her voice on edge. "How did you know it was empty?"

"I'm sorry. I meant to throw it away before you found it."

She couldn't recall Michael scavenging her cupboards for food in the last month. She always got on Gabe's case when he left empty boxes in the cupboard. "Did you take the last one recently?"

Michael appeared confused, glancing around the kitchen. "I don't remember exactly when."

That's odd. Marla walked across the kitchen, collapsed the box, and dropped it into the trashcan. Then it occurred to her that Michael wouldn't crave granola bars. Twinkies or Milky Way bars, but not granola bars. She glanced at him and noticed he had lost a few pounds. Maybe he was trying to change his habits. "Thanks again for looking out for me. I don't think Martin Payne would have hurt me, but you never know."

"Are you going somewhere?" Michael asked with anxious eyes. "I was hoping we could talk."

"I'm hungry. I might head down to Burger Burger and get something to eat or else just throw on some eggs. When we do talk, I don't want to rehash this thing about Gabe taking over your body. You don't want to end up like Mr. Payne, right?" She hoped to put an end to this foolishness here and now.

Michael nodded, releasing a long exhale, the air slightly whistling through his lips. "Do you mind if I get something out of the bedroom before I leave?"

"What do you want from my bedroom?"

"A pair of shoes."

"A pair of Gabe's shoes?"

"Yeah."

Gabe would have lent Michael anything he needed. No sense quibbling over a pair of shoes. "I guess so. Do you know where they are?"

"Of course." Michael slipped into the bedroom and reappeared in less than a minute carrying a pair of running shoes. "Thanks, Marla. I appreciate it."

"Why those shoes?" Marla asked.

Michael opened the front door. "Sauconys—the only kind I run in."

His words echoed Gabe's oft-repeated sentiment about his favorite shoes. Marla wanted to reprimand him for maintaining this Gabe facade. Instead she said. "That's funny, Michael. I thought running was against your religion."

He smiled and met her gaze. "You don't realize it yet, Marla, but I've been born anew. A completely different man." He stepped into the sunshine and closed the door.

Marla wanted to scream: *Stop it!* She knew Michael. He'd never be able to keep up this charade. His character was too weak. The indulgent life he enjoyed had sunken its claws too deeply into him. In time he'd be back to drinking beer at nine o'clock in the morning and cramming junk food into his face all day long. Pleasure and pain had shaped Michael's life. Granola bars and running were Gabe's pleasures but Michael's pains. Michael couldn't change his character overnight. Emulating Gabe would be too tall a task for him.

On the way to the hospital the next morning, Marla scoured her brain to recall any memory of Michael rummaging through her kitchen cupboards for food. Nothing came to mind. That bothered her. How could he know that box was empty? Ever since the attack, she had always kept the doors locked. Gabe must have given him a key without informing her. That possibility bothered her too. Gabe knew how she felt about Michael, about their personality conflict. Would he really give Michael a key without her permission? She doubted it.

She thought about Michael playing the guitar and asking for Gabe's running shoes. Was it possible? Could Gabe's spirit have entered his twin brother? Maybe Michael's brush with death made him step out of his own skin and reconsider his approach to life. Maybe he admired Gabe's example so much he believed that only by being Gabe could he make the drastic changes required to become the new man he wanted to be. But what if he stepped out of his own skin while unconscious, and Gabe slipped in? *Don't go there.* Marla gripped the wheel and gazed at the bridge rising ahead crossing from Hatteras Island over to Nags Head. *Believe what you know is true.*

As she neared the hospital, she considered the prenatal paternity test. She still didn't want to believe that cold reality: in all probability the baby within her contained the paternal DNA, which could convict the man who raped her, attacked Gabe, and killed that poor girl. Believing in that truth killed hope. But it did offer justice. Maybe justice was more important than hope. She counted the weeks since that night—seven. Seven weeks pregnant. The brochure stated the test could be administered after the thirteenth week. Six weeks from now she could bring a killer to justice by volunteering to take a simple test. Hope would either die then or seven months later when the baby came due. Keeping hope alive at the expense of justice failed her commitment to truth. She decided to have the test done in six weeks.

She entered Gabe's hospital room to see two men standing on the other side of the bed, holding hands with heads lowered. She couldn't believe it. Reverend Byron Butler, the minister who had officiated their wedding, and Dugan Walton were praying for her husband. The preacher was dressed like a vacationer in blue jeans and a yellow T-shirt with three dolphins skimming over green waves. Byron Butler had been her pastor since she was a little girl back in Martins Ferry, Ohio. Gabe and she first met in the youth group his wife, Lila, had organized at the Scotch Ridge

181

Church. She wanted to shout out a greeting but controlled the urge to avoid interrupting their prayer. She padded to the opposite side of the bed and waited quietly for the Amen.

Pastor Byron, a thin middle-aged man about six feet tall with wire rim glasses and receding brown hair, lifted Dugan's hand and said, "Lord, we believe in miracles. All things are possible with you. Into your hands we commend Gabe's body and spirit. We ask that you bring him back to us or perform the ultimate healing of taking him home to be with you for eternity. According to your will and by the name of Jesus we pray. Amen."

When Pastor Byron raised his head and glimpsed Marla, he widened his eyes and smiled, tear tracks glistening on his cheeks. "Marla May Garehart. I haven't seen you for months. Come here and give me a hug."

She hurried around the bed and embraced the preacher. Holding him tightly, she couldn't keep from crying. He had always been an anchor in her life. Her father had abandoned the family shortly after her youngest brother, Stephen, was born. She had looked to Pastor Byron as someone she could count on to be there week in and week out, preaching God's love and compassion from the pulpit and offering a proper example of a dedicated father and servant to his congregation. When her mother battled lung cancer, Pastor Byron stood by their side through it all until the day she died shortly after the wedding. She thanked God her mother hung in there to see her and Gabe united in marriage. Her brothers, Stephen and Jacob, joined the Marines and headed for Iraq a year later. Both had signed up for a second tour of duty. With no family to support her on the Outer Banks but Michael, Pastor Byron's arrival bolstered her spirit.

Leaning back, she gazed at his face. She had talked to him on the phone several times since the incident but never expected him to make the ten-hour drive. "What a surprise. It's such a long trip from the Ohio Valley. Thank you so much for coming."

"I'm sorry it took this long, but I couldn't get away from ministerial duties until now. I'm staying a couple days in Avon with Dugan. Lila's taking care of everything back in Martins Ferry."

"God bless her," Marla said, remembering the great times she had with all the kids in the youth group. Lila had maintained a balance between fun and spiritual growth. Marla and Gabe's attendance had made a big difference in their lives. She knew Dugan appreciated their ministry also and regarded Pastor Byron as a father figure.

Pastor Byron stepped back and put his arm around Dugan's shoulder. "This young deputy here was kind enough to take me out to breakfast this morning and then bring me to the hospital."

Dugan's freckled face broadened with his smile. He patted the preacher on the back. "It's about time I bought breakfast for the man who always told me I'd be a lawman one day. He was right."

"Not just a lawman." Pastor Byron drew Dugan closer. "You will be a first rate detective, one of those top CSI guys. Mark my word. The criminal element in these parts is in big trouble."

Dugan shook his head and laughed.

Pastor Byron released Dugan and took Marla's hand. "How are you holding up, young lady?"

"As best as can be expected, I guess." She lowered her eyes then glanced at Gabe's pale face. "I'm not sure what to do, Pastor Byron. The doctors say let him go, but I don't feel it's time yet."

The preacher nodded. "I know it's a tough decision. Is there a particular reason you're holding on?"

"Yes." Marla's eyes shifted from Pastor Byron to Dugan. "I'm pregnant."

Dugan's jaw dropped. "How long have you known this?"

"About five weeks. I haven't told anyone until now."

"That's one reason you moved down here, isn't it?" the preacher asked. "To start a family?"

The question was difficult because it made her face the harsh facts of probability. Her new determination to confront the truth helped her formulate words. "Our hope was to start a family, yes, but . . . but . . . chances are the baby isn't Gabe's."

Pastor Byron straightened, his eyes filling with disbelief. "I don't understand."

Dugan stepped forward. "Let me explain. This has to be difficult for Marla. On the night of the attack, after Gabe had been knocked unconscious, the perpetrator subdued Marla and forced himself on her."

Pastor Byron squeezed her hand. "You've been through hell these last six weeks, haven't you?"

Marla nodded. "I kept hoping Gabe was the father. When the rape kit results came back and found only Gabe's DNA, I didn't know what to think. But then I received word from Gabe's doctor that his sperm count was low."

Dugan said, "The technician must have botched the rape kit test. She didn't take enough samples."

Marla sniffed, swallowed, and met the preacher's gaze. "Odds are the rapist impregnated me. I need to come to grips with the truth."

The preacher let go of her hand and rubbed his chin. "But there's still a chance that Gabe might be the father?"

"A long shot," Marla said.

Pastor Byron reached out and raised Marla's chin. "Miracles still happen."

"That's why I didn't want to take Gabe off life support. I keep hoping, praying, believing for miracles—Gabe coming out of the coma and helping me to raise our child. But now I have something else to consider. At thirteen weeks I can take a prenatal paternal identification test."

"That's right," Dugan said. "And we have all the DNA samples of the prime suspects for comparison."

Marla dropped her focus to the floor. "Six weeks from now I'll take the test. If the baby belongs to the rapist I want to end all of this."

"What do you mean: end all of this?" Pastor Butler asked.

"I'll seek justice. Hopefully, the evidence will put the killer on death row. Then I'll let Gabe rest in peace. I know you don't want to hear this, Pastor Byron, but I'll probably get an abortion."

The preacher closed his eyes and hung his head. "You're right. I don't like hearing those words. You know where I stand on abortion."

Marla's lower lip quivered, but she held steady. "You have to admit, these are special circumstances."

Pastor Byron put his hand on Marla's shoulder. "I'm not going to pressure you about this. It's your decision if it comes to it. Just keep your options open. I know several childless couples who would love to raise that baby. One person's curse can be another's blessing."

No pressure, eh? Marla thought. "Of course, I'll keep that in mind. The decisions confronting me lately seem to be at the difficult end of the spectrum." Imagining the baby already born and in the arms of a young couple pierced her to the center of her being. She didn't want to break down and cry again. The only way to hold together would be to change the subject. The most pressing thing came to mind first—Michael's strange personality change. "There's something else I wanted to mention to you, Pastor Byron. It has to do with Gabe and Michael. Does the Bible say anything about the possibility of someone's spirit taking over someone else's body?"

The preacher shrugged. "That's the thrust of the whole New Testament—the Spirit of Jesus entering into a believer's life and taking over, making us like Christ."

Marla shook her head. "No, I don't mean God's Spirit."

184

Pastor Byron scratched his chin. "There're many incidents of evil spirits possessing people. Jesus and the disciples cast demons out wherever they went. But I don't see how that would relate to Gabe and Michael."

"You heard what happened to Michael, right?" Marla asked.

"Yes. Dugan told me all about it. His recovery sounds like a bona fide miracle."

"I agree," Marla said, "but ever since Michael came out of his coma, he has claimed that Gabe's spirit has taken over his body."

Dugan crossed his arms. "That's news to me."

Marla touched Dugan's elbow. "I know. You've been busy with the investigation. I haven't talked to you much in the last two weeks."

The preacher raised his hand and waved it in a dismissive gesture. "Impossible. There are no incidents in scripture where one man's spirit has taken over another man's body. Hebrews 9:27 states, 'Man is destined to die once, and after that to face judgment.' Some cults believe it's possible but not mainline Christianity. You don't get a second chance, a reincarnation—you are born, you die, and then you face judgment."

"But what if you don't die?" Marla asked.

"What do you mean?"

Marla pointed to Gabe. "Neither Gabe nor Michael is dead."

"Technically, you are correct." The preacher's voice became less dogmatic, slightly hesitant. "Still, the scriptures don't back it up."

Dugan asked: "What do you think about Michael's claim, Marla?"

"I think Michael feels guilty about what happened that night. He drank too much at the restaurant and called to ask Gabe to come get him. Now he blames himself because his overindulgence led to Gabe's crossing paths with the killer. It's his way of bringing Gabe back."

Dugan nodded. "Similar to what Martin Payne does when he channels his wife."

"Exactly, but . . ." Marla considered whether or not she should go into Michael's mysterious behaviors: knowing her pet name and about the empty granola box, playing guitar, and borrowing Gabe's running shoes.

"But what?" the preacher asked.

"Michael knows things that only Gabe should know."

"Like what?" Dugan asked.

"For instance, when he came out of the coma he called me by the pet name Gabe always called me—Sweetcheeks. And yesterday he told me about an empty box in the cupboard, one that Gabe should have thrown away after taking the last granola bar."

185

"That's easily explainable," Dugan said. "Somewhere along the way he's overheard the pet name, and when you weren't looking in the last four weeks, he tried to snatch a granola bar, but the box was empty."

The matter-of-fact manner of Dugan's conclusion made Marla feel foolish for giving Michael's claim an ounce of credibility. She nodded, feeling the heat of embarrassment in her cheeks.

Pastor Byron cleared his throat. "Michael's a good guy, but he's always had an odd side to him. I'm not saying he's trying to deceive you. Maybe the bump on his head mixed him up. Besides that, most twins sense one another's thoughts and feelings."

"Perhaps," Dugan said, "but this switch-a-roo won't last. I've known them both most of my life. Michael's no Gabe. He always wanted to be more like Gabe but didn't have the self discipline."

"You're right," Marla said. "I'm sure this is just a phase." Marla reached and patted the preacher's shoulder. "I just needed to hear what my pastor thought about it."

"That's easy," Pastor Byron said, his authoritative tone returning. "If God's word doesn't back it up, then it can't happen."

Marla felt better after talking with Dugan and Pastor Byron. Their opinions helped solidify any unstable ground beneath her feet. Gabe wasn't coming back to her through Michael. The weirdness of it caused her to shudder. She needed to give up on grasping at improbabilities and gather strength to face the tough road ahead. There would be lonely times and perhaps difficult legal proceedings. The decision to abort the baby or carry it full term only to give it up for adoption would require more courage than she'd ever mustered in her life. Deep inside she felt the beginnings of an inner strength taking hold: She'd do what had to be done, seek justice, and start her life over.

She walked Dugan and Pastor Byron to the parking lot. The wind had picked up, scudding puffy clouds, like cotton balls, across the cerulean sky. They reached the squad car and faced each other. The temperature must have been near sixty degrees, but the breeze raised goose bumps on her arms, so she crossed them and rubbed her forearms. "One more question before you take off, Dugan. Any more progress in questioning Trenton again?"

Dugan squinted into the sun. "Just yesterday we caught a break. We questioned the girlfriend of one of Trenton's buddies, Dalton Phelps. She claimed Dalton was with her that night at her apartment. If her statement pans out, then Trenton and his buddies are lying. We're still following it up. Hopefully we can get enough evidence together to lock him up until the paternity test. I know that would make you feel better."

"No doubt about that." Six weeks, Marla thought. *If Trenton is the killer, this could all be over in six weeks.* Knowing Trenton was behind the bars of the Dare County Detention Center would help her sleep better, but until that happened, Sonny and Michael would watch out for her. She remembered the gun under Gabe's pillow. *And I'll watch out for myself.*

Marla hugged Pastor Byron and promised to keep him updated on a regular basis concerning her circumstances. As the car drove away, she waved, thinking her world has changed inconceivably since the days she and Gabe sat in the pews of the Scotch Ridge Church. She returned to Gabe's hospital room and sat for another hour, listening to the beeping and rhythms of machines keeping her husband alive. Six more weeks of this, she thought. It seemed like an eternity.

On the way home, two miles from Buxton, she glanced to her right to see two kite boarders taking advantage of the brisk winds. At the end of August when she and Gabe had first arrived, she'd often see fifteen or twenty enthusiasts zipping across the Pamlico Sound pulled by the colorful kites, which resembled small parachutes. Gabe occasionally had run the five miles to Avon, turned around and stopped on the way back to watch them. He had told her he wanted to try it if their financial status improved. Kite boarding was an expensive hobby. Today's kiters must have been fanatics, wearing black wetsuits for insulation from the cold water. The forty-mile-an-hour gusts lifted them ten to fifteen feet into the air. Their daredevil acrobatics made Marla shiver.

She redirected her focus to the road and swerved to miss a runner. *Gabe!* The determined expression, the hair, the running form—just like Gabe's. She almost came to a stop and peered into her rearview mirror. The runner, a wider version of Gabe, turned and waved as he slowed to a walk. He headed across the public parking lot towards the sound. *I can't believe it. He ran two miles? He's never run two miles in his life.* Marla kept glancing into the mirror to watch Michael Easton as he ambled towards the shoreline and gazed into the sky at the yellow and red kites.

Chapter 24

Five weeks. Marla placed an empty cereal bowl into the sink, turned, and leaned against the counter. At two months pregnant, her stomach protruded slightly. Not many would notice, but she did. She dipped her hand inside her gray sweatpants and pressed it against her lower belly. Her skin felt warm, as if the baby generated a wonderful heat in the safety of her womb. *Five weeks and I'll find out.* Tony Trenton's face appeared in her mind, and she whipped her hand away from her stomach. She hated the thought of the child being his. Every day she struggled with the decision of carrying his child to full term and giving it up for adoption. In five weeks she'd make that decision. Pastor Byron would be greatly disappointed if she opted for an abortion. But it wasn't his body. No one raped him. Of course, he would say it was God's body on loan to her.

Would she be able to live with the guilt? Guilt did strange things to people. Martin Payne and Michael Easton provided regular reminders of that truth. In the last two weeks Marla had tried to avoid conversations with either. Michael seemed resigned to the fact that she wasn't interested in his transfiguration into Gabe. He went about his business and didn't bother her. Unfortunately, that troubled her even more. She noticed him running every day, getting thinner. Often she heard him strumming the guitar on the deck above her, singing songs Gabe enjoyed singing. He sounded just like his brother. She wished he would go back to painting, getting drunk regularly, and overeating.

Martin Payne had come to her door twice in the last two weeks. She had spied him through the peephole and didn't answer. Life was strange enough without him adding to the mix. What a disturbed man. Even if his wife could communicate with him, how would she know Marla was in danger? Could she read the rapist's mind? Did she haunt the rapist's bedroom and enter into his dreams? No. Martin Payne was madder than a monkey on a merry-go-round.

Marla walked to the front door, opened it, and stepped onto the deck. Below in the yard, Sonny Keyes raked leaves. December had arrived, the days becoming shorter and colder. Most of the week had been blustery with temperatures in the forties, but today the sun shone brightly and the wind had calmed—a good day, really, to tidy up the yard. Marla checked the thermometer nailed just below the porch light. Mid fifties. Her gray hoody felt adequate to keep her cozy, especially in the sunshine. She wanted to take a long walk along the beach up to Cape Point and back. The waves, wind, sand, and blue sky would help calm her. She needed the calm to sort things out.

"Nice day, eh, Sonny?" she called, hands spread on the porch railing.

The husky man raised his shaved head and smiled broadly. "Good mornin', Marla. Beautiful day for the middle of December. Big plans today?"

"Just a walk along the beach. How about you?"

"Got plenty of work to do around here all day. Tonight me, Frank, and Wyatt are headin' to Nags Head."

"Bowling?"

"You guessed it."

Marla had noticed Sonny was a creature of habit. Saturday night was bowling night with his friends. On Friday and Sunday evenings they headed off to the movies at the cinema in Avon or watched DVDs at his apartment or Frank's house. During weekday mornings he tended to outdoor chores of all the properties he maintained in Buxton and in the afternoons worked inside on plumbing or other repairs. He still made regular rounds of their apartment complex. Marla could set her watch by them. He never said a negative word about anybody except for Tony Trenton. Even though Dugan Walton still considered Sonny a possible suspect, Marla trusted him completely.

She peered a hundred yards down the access street where it met Old Lighthouse Road and spotted Michael rounding the corner at a good pace.

"Can you believe Michael? I thought he'd give up this running kick by now."

Sonny pivoted and stared down the narrow stretch of asphalt. "He's a changed man thanks to me." He shifted his focus to Marla and winked.

Marla chuckled. "Yeah, you must have knocked some sense into him."

"Guess it ain't funny. I almost killed him."

"Doesn't seem like Michael any more, does he?" Marla asked.

"No. He's turned into Gabe."

Marla expected that answer, but it still bothered her. "Do you think he's putting on an act?"

Sonny leaned on the rake and shook his head. "If he is, it's an awful good one. He doesn't tell me dirty jokes anymore. 'Course, I don't miss that. He's not lazy like he was, askin' me to run errands for him all the time. He used to be a slob. Now his apartment's neater than a master plumber's toolbox. To tell the truth, I don't miss the old Michael much at all."

"I do," Marla said without hesitation.

"Why's that?"

Marla tilted her head towards the street, signaling Sonny that Michael had arrived within earshot. She wanted to say, "Because there's only one Gabe," but didn't get the chance.

Sonny acknowledged her signal with a nod, turned, and waved.

"Hi, Sonny," Michael slowed to a stop, leaned on his knees and glanced at his watch. He rose up and saluted Marla. "Good morning."

"Hi, Michael." Marla eyed him. He must have lost thirty pounds in the last four weeks. Another thirty and he'd match up perfectly with Gabe physically. "How far today?"

"Six miles in under fifty minutes. I'll be back in shape before you know it."

Since when have you been in shape? Fifth grade? She looked away, not wanting to encourage his Gabe fantasy.

Michael slapped Sonny on the back. "Yard's looking good, my friend. You do a great job around here, ya know?"

"That's what you've been telling me these last couple of weeks," Sonny said.

"Marla, I haven't seen you much lately."

Marla glanced up to see Michael smiling at her, wondering what he would say next.

190

He took a couple steps towards her. "Sorry, I've been busy, working on a few things. Is there anything I can do for you? I haven't been much help."

The question surprised her. She didn't mind him keeping out of her business, at least the old Michael. The new Michael she didn't trust . . . yet. Recently she noticed his absence at the hospital. "I'm handling things all right. Just curious, though. Why haven't you stopped by the hospital to visit Gabe?"

Michael averted his gaze, his eyes darting from his feet, to Sonny's rake, to the pile of leaves. He took an audible breath and looked up. "I don't feel right walking in that room anymore. It's hard to explain. Something has happened, and I'm trying to deal with it. I'm working through these weird feelings, but I just can't go in there and look at myse— . . . and look at Gabe lying there lifeless."

"I'm not complaining," Marla said. "I just thought it was odd that you quit coming all together. Gabe doesn't know if you're there or not anyway."

Michael's eyes seemed to plead for Marla to understand. "I can assure you that Gabe isn't there, and I'll drop it at that. But please, if there's anything I can do for you, let me know. I'm trying not to bother you, because I know . . ." he glanced around the yard as if searching for words. "I know you would rather not have to deal with what I'm going through. That's okay, but I don't want you to think I'm ignoring you."

Marla tried to weigh these unexpected sentiments. In the past Michael couldn't care less what she thought or how she felt. He said and did whatever he wanted. Something *was* happening to him. "I'll let you know if I need anything."

Michael bobbed his head. "Great. Well . . . got to get going." He thumbed towards the steps. "Working on a few things. Hope to get a new job." He turned and hustled up the upper deck stairs.

"Michael!" Marla called after him.

He halted halfway and faced her.

"What kind of job?"

"I want to write. Last week I sent my résumé to the *Outer Banks Sentinel.*"

Marla nodded. *Interesting. He's in for a shock. Writing stories for the Sentinel will be ten times harder than putting twelve or so hours a week in on a few canvases. Good luck on that one.* In the back of her mind, though, Marla had to admit she was beginning to admire this new Michael.

Just as she started down the steps she heard Mr. Payne's door open. She wanted to shift into high gear, get around the corner of the house and head to the beach before Mr. Payne could see her.

"Mrs. Easton!" Mr. Payne hollered as she scurried across the sidewalk.

Shoot. She slowed to a stop and turned around.

He stood at the top of his steps looking more haggard than before, dark circles under his eyes, his blue Polo shirt soiled with coffee stains and his gray slacks badly wrinkled. "I have something very important to tell you. It can't wait."

Marla met his stare, determined not to be intimidated. "Go ahead. I'm listening."

He motioned to her door and tilted his head towards Sonny. "Could we go inside? This is a private matter."

"Absolutely not." She walked over to Sonny and put her hand on his shoulder. "Sonny is the one person I trust around here."

Sonny straightened, holding his rake like a soldier at attention.

"If you have something to say to me, I want Sonny to hear it too."

Mr. Payne's thick eyebrows tensed, but then he blinked several times, his jaw losing its rigidity. "Okay. I guess I have no other choice."

Marla maintained her unflinching stare.

He rambled down the steps, waddled to where they stood in the yard, and looked in her eyes. "I have a message for you from someone very close to me." He shifted his focus to Sonny and then back to Marla. "Do you know who I'm talking about?"

"Yes." Marla sensed Mr. Payne didn't want to mention his wife's name in front of Sonny. "What does she want to tell me?"

"She visited me again the other night, maybe for the last time." His eyes flashed that anxious, edge-of-insanity look. "She's very afraid for you."

"No need to worry," Marla said. "I'm fine. Sonny and Michael keep their eye out for me."

"Don't be so sure." His voice took on a harder edge. "She says he's very near. Closer than you think. Don't let your guard down. Watch over you shoulder. He's out to get you. Maybe even kill you."

This guy has lost it. Marla glanced at Sonny, and he raised his eyebrows. She dropped her hand from Sonny's shoulder and raised a finger. "Listen to me, Mr. Payne. I don't need this nonsense in my life right now. You need help. More help than I or any one around here can give you. I suggest you see a psychologist. As for these messages from you know who, I'm putting an end to them right now. Do you understand me?"

Mr. Payne straightened, his mouth twisting into a childlike scrawl. Finally, he said, "Can't you see I'm trying to help you?"

"Not any more. You're the one who needs help. I have contacts at the hospital. If you would like, I could ask around and find a good doctor for you."

Mr. Payne shuddered involuntarily as if a jolt of electricity went through him. Without a word, he about-faced, marched up his steps and into his house, and slammed the door.

"Whewwee," Sonny said. "That's the worst I've ever seen him. A few more waves and his ship's goin' under."

Marla felt a tension that had started in her lower back and spread through her shoulders. She tried to shake it out and relax. "He scares me."

"I can see why."

"Do me a favor would ya, Sonny?"

"Anything."

"I'm heading out for a long walk on the beach. If he follows me, could you keep your eye on him."

Sonny waved his hand in front of him, an "S" motion. "I'll tail him like a hound dog on a rogue black bear."

Marla smiled. Sonny had a way of keeping her loose.

The walk from the apartment to Cape Point was about a mile. Mee Mee Roberts had filled Marla in on the uniqueness of this jutting arrow of sand into the sea at this spot on Hatteras Island. Two major Atlantic currents caused the formation, the Labrador Current from the north and the warm Gulf Stream from the south. Their collision created turbulent waters and caused an unusually diverse collection of sea life from both southern and northern currents. Fisherman loved the possibility of catching a variety of fish there, and Marla expected to see a few anglers standing in the surf when she arrived. To her surprise and satisfaction, the Point was deserted. She wanted to be alone. She stood and gazed at the waves as they rushed into each other, boiling and seething in the middle like a divine stew.

She thought about her life and the turbulence she'd experienced in the last two months. Would it be never-ending like the roiling waters in

193

front of her? She hoped not but could see no relief in the near future. An abortion might cause a psychological upheaval. Keeping the baby would prove incredibly challenging. Maybe Pastor Byron was right. Maybe she should give birth to the child and then give it up for adoption. But how could that be easier? She couldn't imagine giving away her baby after carrying it nine long months. If only Gabe were here to help her.

She turned from the ocean and faced the shore. Cape Point was a great place to find interesting shells. Immediately she spotted a large conch left behind by that morning's high tide in the midst of smaller shells, seaweed, and detritus. She hurried over and picked it up. It was perfect, white with marbled tans throughout its surface. The top of it spiraled with unusual knobs—no broken pieces and definitely one of the heaviest shells she'd ever found. She held the opening to her ear to listen to its mimic of the ocean. Mee Mee would be impressed. What did Mee Mee call these kinds of shells? Lightning Whelks?

Marla guessed her arm would actually get tired carrying it home. What a find! She heard a far off car engine and about-faced to peer down the shore. A black vehicle rumbled along the beach. Probably a fisherman heading for the Point. She focused on the headlights, grill, and windshield—a Jeep. Her heart jumped. *Tony Trenton drives a black Jeep.* Suddenly Martin Payne's words came back to her: *She says he's very near. Closer than you think. Don't let your guard down. Watch over you shoulder. He's out to get you. Maybe even kill you.*

Her mind reeled with escape possibilities. If she headed south along the shoreline, he would easily catch her in the Jeep. Would he follow her into the cold sea? Could she survive the clashing currents and freezing water? No way. She stood on the largest section of wildlife and seashore preserve on Hatteras Island. Behind her, sandy paths crisscrossed acres of dunes and marshes interspersed with small ponds. She could try to take off over the dunes and make it to the large campgrounds about a half mile away. But would anybody be camping this time of year? It didn't matter. She had no other options.

She spun around and sprinted across the wide beach. Looking to her right, she noticed the Jeep about a hundred yards away. Now she wished she would have kept in shape like Gabe had always encouraged her to do. The sand swallowed her feet with every step. Her pace slowed as she plowed towards the nearest dune, a fairly challenging hill covered with sea oats. She took a quick peek over her shoulder. The Jeep had veered from the shoreline, aiming directly for her. *He's coming after me.* Her breathing accelerated as she strove to lift her knees higher. She heard the engine closing in on her as she reached the base of the dune. Leaning into the slope and pumping her arms helped her ascend, but her legs already felt tired.

At the top she heard the engine conk out and Trenton's familiar voice: "Hey! Stop! Come back here!"

She scanned the down slope in front of her. Which way to go? To the left the grasses and bushes thickened and to the right another large dune rose up. She decided to go straight towards a pond about fifty yards away. Several trees loomed on the edge of the pond, their spidery branches leafless in the December chill. A large turkey vulture perched on a branch just ahead of her. Her foot caught on an old log, and she tumbled into the sand. The whelk shell flew out of her hand, landing a few feet in front of her. *Pick it up. Maybe use it as a weapon.* She lunged and grabbed the shell. Her harsh breathing made it hard to hear anything. She stumbled to her feet and swiveled her head to see Trenton appear at the top of the dune. *God, don't let him catch me.* A new surge of adrenalin shot through her, propelling her forward. The vulture took flight in a flurry of wing beats.

"Marla! Stop! I need to talk to you!" Trenton yelled.

"You stay away from me!" Marla screamed. Beyond the pond, she noticed a narrow path cutting through the grasses and turned onto it. Her feet didn't sink in as much, making it easier to run. She hoped the path led to the campground. It had to be at least six hundred yards away. Could she run that far? Ahead she could see a wider path, a sandy road the rangers probably used to get to Cape Point. Turning right onto it would lead back to the seashore. She turned left and tried to run in the tire tracks. She glanced behind her. Trenton trailed by about thirty or forty yards. *He's getting closer.* She felt like crying but knew giving into to that urge would make it harder to breathe.

It occurred to her that Trenton had the advantage on the road. All he had to do was run faster than she. At least cutting through the weeds and over the dunes would create more obstacles for him to negotiate. She veered to the right through a thick patch of growth and aimed between two large mounds of sand. She managed to fight her way through the tangles of bushes and grasses and paused momentarily to catch her breath at the base of a dune where the vegetation had cleared. She turned to see if Trenton followed. He did, although the denser growth hand slowed him. How much farther could she go at this pace? She crossed another narrow path and took off towards an even thicker patch of trees and grasses. Her only hope was to lose him among the dense vegetation ahead of her.

She ducked under a tree limb and filtered into a patch of cattails, their tops tattered and bursting with fluffy seeds. Needing a rest, she crouched among the grasses and listened, trying to stifle her harsh breathing. She heard the sounds of dry weeds being trampled. By inhaling through her nose she managed to keep quiet. Her feet felt wet and cold; her old Nikes had sunken slightly into the marshy ground. Peering through the cattails she detected movement about ten yards away.

"Come out, come out wherever you are," Trenton said with a singsong tone. Then his voice became more serious. "Come on, Marla, I'm not going to hurt you. I just want to talk. This is important."

Marla gripped the whelk shell. She felt certain he wanted to kill her out here on this remote section of the island. Maybe he'd rape her again too. She wouldn't give up without a fight. She thought of Gabe lying in the hospital bed with the terrible head injury. As the footsteps neared, she stared at the knobs on top of the shell. *Wait 'til he gets closer. Surprise him. Get even for Gabe.* Ten feet away . . .five . . . three—She shot up and swung the shell, crashing it onto his forehead. It broke in half, and he stumbled backwards with a loud, "Oooffff." He tripped and landed on his rear end. Blood poured into his eyes from a large gash just below his hairline.

He swiped his hand across his face and stared at the blood on his fingertips. "You bitch! I'll slap you silly when I get a hold of you!"

Marla charged out of the cattails and aimed for a narrow deer path. She felt recharged. Maybe the campground was only four hundred or so yards away. *Look for the access road.* She sprinted along the path, but it didn't take long for her legs to grow weary again. An extreme sense of helplessness welled up in her chest. She felt doomed as she slowed to a jog, panting like an exhausted collie. When she glanced over her shoulder, the shock of seeing Trenton's bloody face not far behind sent a new jolt of energy through her. He looked like a red-faced demon released from the depths of hell. Fifty yards ahead she saw a clearing. Could that be the trail to the campgrounds? She forced herself to pick up her pace. Her stomach cramped and she felt like puking.

By the time she reached the clearing and turned onto the trail, she could hear his loud breathing as he closed in on her. She wasn't going to make it. Her legs turned to Jell-O. The sand lost its firmness causing her feet to slide when they landed. She lost her balance and fell forward. Struggling to catch her breath, she lay facedown in the sand.

A shadow passed over her. "Get up, you bitch," he said between huffs.

Slowly, she rolled over and eyed him.

He leaned over her. Blood dripped off his chin onto her ankle. He reached down and grabbed her forearm. "I said get up!"

He pulled her to her feet, and she struggled to find her balance in the soft sand. Finally, she stood straight.

"Look what you did to me!"

She stared at the ground.

He reached and clasped her jaw, raising her head, forcing her to look at his face. "You about killed me." The gash on his forehead was deep and raw. It seeped blood profusely.

If this was the end, she wanted to die courageously. "Let go of me, you bastard."

He released her chin but still clung to her forearm. He raised his fist in front of her face. "I ought to knock the hell out of you."

To the left of Trenton's head, a large stick appeared. It tapped him hard on the shoulder.

"Let her go," a female voice said.

Trenton's eyes widened. He slowly turned, stepping to the side.

There stood Mee Mee Roberts, holding a long, intricately carved walking stick. She raised it like a batter at home plate. Mee Mee was all of five feet two inches and a hundred and ten pounds but wiry and strong. Her eyes burned with an intense fire. "Get away from her," she growled. "I'll split your head like an overripe melon."

Trenton stepped backwards and raised his hands. "I wasn't going to hurt her."

Mee Mee twisted slightly, her arms and the stick coiling behind her head. "The hell you weren't."

He stiffened, leaning away from her, inching backwards. He pointed to his forehead. "Look what she did to me."

"You deserve a lot worse," Mee Mee said.

"I just wanted to ask her to cut me a break, but she wouldn't stop and listen."

"Cut you a break?" Marla said. "You haven't cut me any breaks."

"What the hell are you talking about? I tried to help you when your car broke down. I brought you flowers to offer my condolences after what happened to your husband. Both times you sicced Sonny Keyes on me."

Marla stepped towards him and pointed at his chest. "Explain this. I've sworn out a restraining order against you, and yet you chase me through these dunes. You hunt me down like an animal, drag me to my feet, and grab my face." She rotated her forearm, his finger marks still glowing red on her skin. "You're going to jail, you bastard."

"What have you got against me?" His voice sounded strained like a man on the verge of tears. "That damn deputy keeps questioning me and my buddies. I didn't kill Julia Hungerman. And I sure as hell didn't attack your husband and rape you. You know that. Why don't you tell him? Get him off my back."

"How do I know you didn't rape me?"

Trenton's face twisted into a confused expression. "What do you mean?"

"The man who raped me wore a mask. He blindfolded me. I never saw his face. I think it was you."

His eyes widened. "You never saw him? I guess that makes sense. No wonder Walton hasn't arrested me for rape. You think it was me, huh? But you can't prove anything."

"You're wrong. I can prove it. I'm pregnant and the rapist is the father. In five weeks I'll know for sure if you did it."

Mee Mee stepped closer, the stick poised over her shoulder. Marla knew immediately she shouldn't have revealed the fact of her pregnancy. If Trenton was the murderer, now he had motivation to eliminate both Marla and Mee Mee. And this was the perfect place to do it.

But Trenton's shoulders loosened and his arms dangled at his side. He grinned and said, "Really? You're pregnant? Couldn't your husband be the father?"

Marla just stared at him. She didn't want to say any more.

Trenton chuckled. "He couldn't put the puck in the net, could he? His fish couldn't swim." He shrugged, shifting his focus from Marla to Mee Mee and back to Marla. "Then I've got nothing to worry about." He kicked at the sand, shook his head, and strolled down the narrow access road towards Cape Point.

They watched him disappear around a turn. Then Mee Mee dropped her walking stick and wiped her hand across her forehead. "What a Cro-magnon."

Marla embraced her. "Thank you so much," Marla couldn't hold back the tears any longer. Between sniffles she said, "If you didn't show up, he would have killed me."

Mee Mee patted her back. "Keep strong, gal. He might come back."

Marla broke the hug, alarmed by Mee Mee's words. "Why would he come back?"

Mee Mee leaned to see beyond Marla, focusing where Trenton had rounded the turn. "If he's the murderer and knows you're pregnant with his child, then now's the time to get rid of you and any other witnesses."

"But why would he leave and come back?"

Mee Mee's expression became grave. "To get a gun. He probably keeps one in his car."

Marla panned the top of the dunes, gripped Mee Mee's shoulder, and said, "Let's get out of here."

"Follow me." She picked up her staff and held it in the middle like a warrior carrying a spear. "I know the paths here like the back of my old surfboard. Been walking them for more than twenty years." Mee Mee turned in the opposite direction and took off running at an easy gait. "Try to step in my footprints. Makes it harder for him to track us."

Marla concentrated on her stride, doing her best to land in the sandy dips Mee Mee left behind. The pace was manageable, but the terrain became challenging when Mee Mee followed a maze of narrow paths through marshy ground, loose sand, and trampled weeds.

After about five minutes, Mee Mee stopped, faced Marla, put her finger to her lips, and tilted her head. "Hear anything?" she whispered.

The wind rustled through the trees and dried grasses around them, but Marla couldn't hear any out-of-place noises—car engines, tramping sounds, a shotgun being pumped. She shook her head.

"I think we're safe. We can walk from here. The campground is only a few hundred yards away."

Thank God, Marla thought. She was tired of running. Mee Mee kept a brisk walking pace, but Marla didn't mind. "That's what I call good timing. Why were you heading out to the Point today?"

"Needed some fresh air and an aerobic workout. Ally, my best friend, stopped in the bookstore and said she'd watch the place for a couple hours. Besides, this is the best time of year to find shells."

"You should have seen the one I found."

Mee Mee slowed her pace and glanced over her shoulder. "Really?"

"A big lightning whelk. Not worth much now, though."

"What happened to it?"

Marla couldn't help smiling. "Let's just say it left a big impression on Tony Trenton."

Mee Mee burst out laughing. "On his forehead?"

"That's right. Something to remember me by whenever he looks in the mirror."

Mee Mee waited for Marla to catch up and then slapped her on the back. "You are a tough kid, you know that? You're becoming a real Hatteras gal."

"A Hatteras gal?"

Mee Mee nodded. "That's right. You've got to be tough to live on this island as a single woman for any length of time. Independent. Self-sufficient. Hard-nosed."

Marla reached and clasped her hand on Mee Mee's walking stick. "Can I see this?"

"Try it out. I carved it myself."

Marla examined the carvings—symbols of birds, stars, arrows, fish, animals, the sun, and moon. "What are these?"

"Algonquian Indian symbols. They lived on this island long before the whites ever arrived. They were a hardy people. Survivors. Some of their descendants are still around."

"Wow." Marla ran her fingers over the carved lines. "I can relate to survivors." Walking with the staff felt empowering. After covering another couple hundred yards, the trail opened to a large deserted campground. Marla held the stick in the air. "I need to get me one of these, just in case I decide to *stick* around and be a real Hatteras gal. Can this thing part the sea?" She handed the staff back to Mee Mee.

"I haven't tried that yet, but it sure works like a gem on the heads of Cro-Magnons."

Mee Mee walked Marla all the way back to Old Lighthouse Road. They saw no sign of Tony Trenton along the way. Marla thanked her again, gave her a hug, and told her she'd see her at the bookstore on Monday.

What a strange morning, Marla thought as she ambled down the access road to the apartments. Trenton had appeared relieved when he'd heard Marla was pregnant with the rapist's child. Did he think the prenatal paternity test would prove his innocence, or did he have more malevolent plans? Maybe he figured killing her and Mee Mee was too risky—two against one. Maybe he didn't have a gun in his car. Now that she carried irrefutable evidence of the identity of the rapist and murderer within her womb, he might do the deed at night with no one watching, silently breaking into her apartment and killing her while she slept. Not if Marla could help it. She'd add a few more scars to his body—bullet holes.

Hearing music, Marla glanced up. Michael sat with his back towards her on his upper deck, strumming his guitar. The song sounded familiar, his voice a copy of Gabe's: "Do you believe in love so strong, it melts your fears away. Makes you want to sing. Makes you want to pray."

How does he know that song? Gabe wrote that for me. She upped her pace until she reached the bottom of the steps and then hesitated to listen: "Do you believe in love so good, it lifts you to the sky. Makes you want to laugh. Makes you want to cry." Marla didn't know how Michael acquired the words and melody to Gabe's song, but he'd better have some answers. As she dashed up the stairs, he sang the chorus: "I do. I do, because I found you. I'll never be the same, ever since you came into my life."

At the top of the steps she hollered, "Stop it! Quit singing!"

Michael, his eyes filling with hurt, placed the guitar against the railing. "What's the matter? Did I do something wrong?"

"Where did you learn that song?"

Michael shrugged. "I don't know. It just . . . it just came to me."

Chapter 25

That song was Gabe's gift to her. At first Marla felt like slapping her brother-in-law for even singing it. But as she glared down at him, she realized he resembled Gabe more than Michael. His physical appearance actually had a calming effect on her, the way Gabe's presence and nearness used to ease her mind when she came home after a stressful day in the classroom.

"Does the song bother you?" Michael asked. "I won't sing it ever again."

Marla slumped into a cushioned deck chair across from Michael and studied his eyes. "The song just came to you? You somehow snatched the words and melody right out of the air?"

"No." Michael twirled his finger near his temple. "It plays over and over in my mind. I had to get out the guitar and sing it. I couldn't help it."

Marla leaned forward on her knees. "Do you know the second verse?"

"Yes. I haven't sung it yet, but the words are up here." He pointed to his forehead.

"Sing it to me."

Michael picked up the guitar and played a couple introductory chords. Then he sang with Gabe's mellow, wonderfully textured voice: "Do you believe love will last beyond the here and now? At the end of time, love will live on somehow. Do you believe love is more than words on a page, more than just a scene acted on a stage? I do. I do, because I found you. I'll never be the same, ever since you came into my life."

As Michael picked through the finishing chords, a tear broke over Marla's eyelid and trickled down her cheek. Gazing into his eyes, Marla sensed she was peering into Gabe's soul. Michael was gone. She stood slowly, her eyes fixed on his.

He placed the guitar to the side and rose. "I'm sorry. I didn't mean to make you cry." He reached and traced the tear track down her cheek with his fingertip.

The light touch upon her skin generated wonderful warmth through her despite the chilly afternoon. "Don't be sorry. I asked you to sing the song. You didn't miss a word." His forefinger lightly glided along the rim of her ear and then her jaw line. The pleasure of it made her suck in a quick breath. He continued, drawing his finger gently across her lower lip. "Gabe?" she whispered.

He nodded.

She clasped his hand and wanted to kiss his fingers but, instead, gently pushed him away.

"I'm sorry, Marla. I don't know why I did that. I couldn't help myself. It just seemed like a natural response."

She shook her head. "Don't apologize." Her focus dropped to his chest and blurred slightly. She closed her eyes and took a deep breath, trying to regain clarity. *Am I losing my mind? There's got to be some way to prove or disprove this strange interchange of body and spirit. Of course. Gabe's novel.* After blinking several times, her vision cleared. "Come to dinner tonight at my apartment at six o'clock."

"I'll be there."

"There's something I want you to do before you arrive."

"Whatever you want."

Marla released his hand and stepped back, bumping into the deck chair. "Before the attack, Gabe had written several pages in the next chapter of his novel."

Michael glanced skyward for a few seconds then down again. "I remember. It's a story called *Journey to the Eastern Light*."

"That's right. This afternoon I want you to write that chapter and bring it to me when you come to dinner."

"I'll do my best."

"I'll see you then."

Michael stepped closer, perhaps intending to hug her, but Marla raised her hand to stop him, a sign to let him know she wasn't convinced yet. But she had to admit, Michael had changed. Had Gabe taken over his body? How could she believe something so fantastic? Somehow she'd find out tonight.

When Marla entered her apartment, she did all she could to put Gabe's possession of Michael out of her mind. She knew she needed to call Dugan Walton. Not only had Tony Trenton violated the restraining order, he'd chased her through the dunes at Cape Point and manhandled her, leaving marks on her arms and roughly squeezing her jaw and cheeks. The marks had faded, but it didn't matter. She had a witness—Mee Mee Roberts. Hopefully, the Dare County magistrate would consider his actions serious enough to hold him in jail for the next four weeks until the prenatal paternity test could be completed. Marla felt certain Trenton was the rapist and murderer. Mee Mee probably had saved her life today. Now she hoped Dugan could keep him penned up until he was no longer a danger to her.

She dialed Dugan's cell phone number, knowing he could be anywhere in the county. He answered after three rings and explained he'd been called to Avon to investigate a domestic violence incident and now headed back to Nags Head with a drunken husband handcuffed in the back seat. Marla reported her encounter with Tony Trenton and asked Dugan to call Mee Mee Roberts if he needed a witness to verify her statements. Dugan felt sure this violation would be enough to keep Trenton in jail for the next four weeks and hopefully longer. At least he'd do all he could to convince the sheriff and judge to keep him locked up for Marla's protection.

After thanking Dugan, she hung up and headed for the bedroom. Gabe kept his work-in-progress, a thick spiral bound notebook, in the top drawer of his dresser along with other important papers and items—his wallet, watch, keys, and old coins. He preferred writing the first draft of his novels in longhand and then completing rewrites on the computer. That way he could carry the notebook with him wherever he went, just in case his schedule afforded some idle time during the course of the day.

She pulled the notebook out and flipped through it to find the last written page. Then she turned back several pages to locate the beginning of the chapter. At the top of the page headed "Chapter Six," she began to read. The narration told about a man riding up to a gas station on a bicycle. Marla remembered Gabe talking about his main character, Gordon Silvers, an old fellow on a cross-country bike trip to raise money for the homeless. As he climbed off his bicycle and pulled a bottle of water from its holder on the bike frame, a black motorcycle gang, about a dozen or so men, pulled up to the pumps.

Below that paragraph she noticed a heading and outline:

Notes for the rest of the chapter:

A.   *Members of the gang look in Gordon's saddlebag and find the donations.*

B.   *Gordon explains his mission. He worries they might rob him. He also tells them he plans on crossing the street to visit the large Presbyterian church and ask for donations during their service.*

C.   *Gang leader informs Gordon that the gang will guard the money while he's in the church. Gordon thinks he has lost everything now.*

D.   *Gordon enters church and returns within ten minutes. To his surprise, the gang and his money are still there.*

E.   *He tells the gang the ushers escorted him to the back of the church for sitting in the wrong pew and informed him he would not be allowed to solicit funds during the service, so he left.*

F.   *The gang accompanies him back into the church and spreads out in the congregation.*

G.   *During the collection the gang leader stands up and proclaims a special offering will be taken for Gordon's homeless fundraiser.*

H.   *Half of the gang members collect the offering and the other half form an impromptu choir and sing Amazing Grace.*

I.   *They exit the church and the gang leader collects even more money from each of the gang members.*

J.   *Gordon watches them ride away, amazed at God's mysterious ways. He counts the donations—over $2000.*

Marla couldn't help smiling. Gabe hadn't completed the chapter but the outline was wonderful. *What a great storyline! So creative.* Michael wouldn't be able to reproduce something like this in a million years. Only Gabe could write this story. This would be the test Michael had to pass. She would accept nothing less. She felt like a Doubting Thomas, demanding to touch the scars of the risen Christ, but she refused to enter into any kind of closer relationship with Michael unless she knew for sure Gabe had taken over his brother's body. She could not permit any doubts. Michael had to write the chapter exactly as outlined by Gabe. If he couldn't do it, the charade was over.

Marla thought about that night's dinner. She wanted to cook something Gabe loved but Michael despised. That shouldn't be difficult. Gabe loved fresh fruits, vegetables, and lean meats. Michael craved hamburgers, French fries, and Twinkies. She headed to the kitchen and selected a cookbook from the cupboard next to the refrigerator. Several years ago Gabe had requested a certain kind of big salad for the evening meal. What was it? She thumbed through the book, trying to remember. Michael had barged in that night as he sometimes did, hoping to get free food. Marla's hand hesitated, recognizing a familiar page. *Here it is—Spinach and Beet Salad with Chicken.* Gabe had generously welcome Michael to share the meal with them, but when Michael had seen the spinach and beets, he took off for McDonald's to pick up a super-sized Big Mac meal. Marla had facetiously informed Gabe she had discovered the secret to getting rid of his brother—health food.

Marla snatched her keys from the kitchen table. Conner's Supermarket, a half mile down the road, would have everything she needed. As she headed out the door, she noted how much her mood had changed. She had gone from heart-pounding fear during that morning's encounter with Trenton, to relief at the sight of Mee Mee Roberts, to anger upon hearing Michael singing Gabe's song, to amazement at the possibility of Gabe's return.

Now that she had reasoned things through, she felt more in control of her circumstances and emotions. She had come up with the perfect test. If Michael passed, they would take it slowly from there. She would be careful, observant, discreet. If he failed, she would cut him off. If he wanted to pretend to be Gabe, fine. Maybe it helped Michael deal with his guilt and overcome his indulgent lifestyle. But Marla wouldn't be a contributor to his fantasy.

* * *

Deputy Dugan Walton hoped his afternoon would go better than his morning. He hated domestic violence calls. They were the worst. They usually involved a husband who drank and bullied his way through life and a wife who took the brunt of it. They would arrest the husband and haul him off to jail only to discover the bruised and battered woman welcomed hubby home with open arms a few days later. This morning's confrontation fit the pattern. Dugan had been there twice before over the last six months. Both times the woman had dropped charges.

This time when he'd arrived, she waited on the neighbor's porch with a black eye. She had promised Dugan she would press charges, but he had his doubts. Dugan had entered the house and seen a slob of a man, unshaven and drunk, sprawled out on the couch in his boxer shorts, watching some kind of strong man competition on ESPN. When Dugan had told the louse he was under arrest, he stumbled to his feet and took a swing at Dugan but missed. Off balance, the man had fallen to his knees, and Dugan had taken full advantage, slamming him facedown to the carpet and cuffing him. On the forty-five minute drive back to Nags Head, Dugan had endured a maelstrom of cursing and insults. The highlight of the trip had been the call from Marla. Tony Trenton had made a crucial mistake, and Marla had survived thanks to Mee Mee Roberts. Dugan looked forward to arresting the son of a bitch.

Trenton lived in Buxton at the end of Rollison Road in an old house trailer near the shoreline of the Pamlico Sound. Cinder blocks suspended the structure about five feet off the ground. Overhanging cedars shadowed the trailer, and green mold spotted its dirty white siding. Dugan parked the squad car, a white Impala, behind Trenton's black Jeep in the gravel driveway. He exited the vehicle and walked to the steps. Junk littered the ground—an old hose, buckets, tools, engine parts, trash. A storm door with a torn screen hung open, but the entrance door was completely closed. Dugan mounted the creaky wooden stairs and rapped on the door. He heard footsteps and decided to check out the window to the left. Trenton's face appeared and quickly disappeared. Not a good sign, Dugan thought.

He waited about a half minute, listening carefully, and then knocked again. "I've got a warrant for your arrest, Trenton. Better not cause any problems. You're in enough trouble already." Dugan heard rambling sounds at the back of the trailer. *Shit. He must have jumped out a back window.*

Almost tripping, Dugan double-timed down the steps and sprinted around the end of the trailer. In the rear he spotted Trenton jumping off a dock into a small motorboat. Trenton threw off an anchor line and pulled a chord on the outboard motor. It sputtered. Maybe the motor wouldn't start. Dugan charged down the dock, but the engine came to life on the second try. Dugan skidded to a stop and pulled his Smith and Wesson pistol. "Hold it right there!"

Trenton revved the engine and the boat curled away, generating waves that teetered the dock. The unsteady footing made it difficult for Dugan to aim, but he zeroed in on the motor and pulled the trigger. The gun fired with a loud crack. He missed. Trenton raised his middle finger as the boat sped away.

"Same to you!" Dugan hollered. He watched to see what direction Trenton would go. He'd do his best to give headquarters a bead on the bastard. Trenton headed straight out. Was he going to cross over to the mainland? That's more than twenty-five miles. Or would he cut back as soon as Dugan walked away? He could head down to Ocracoke, crossing into Hyde County, or even cut back to Frisco. Lots of places to hide along the way, especially if he had connections—fishing buddies, relatives, or old girlfriends.

"Dammit!" Dugan wanted to fire a shot right at the slimeball's head but had little chance of hitting him now. Besides, he couldn't justify shooting a man for resisting arrest on a charge of breaking a restraining order. However, Trenton's fleeing added weight to the rape and murder suspicions. Why would he run if he were innocent? The boat now looked like a dot on the middle of the sound. Dugan figured he'd better call in and let the boss know, just in case Sheriff Johansson wanted to send the Coast Guard out to look for him. He marched back to his vehicle, kicking at the junk strewn along the way.

At the garbage cans in the driveway he halted and peeked inside. A few skin magazines lay on top. He reached in and thumbed through the first one. It was filled with hardcore pornography—women with pained expressions being dominated by muscular men. *What a pervert.* Dugan wondered if he should take the magazine as possible evidence but then figured he didn't have the proper paperwork. Besides, this stuff was so commonplace nowadays he could probably find similar magazines in a third of the trashcans in America. He shook his head and got into the vehicle.

Now that Trenton had escaped, Dugan figured he'd better tell Marla. She lived less than a mile away. He'd drive over. After putting a call in to the sheriff's office, he backed out of the driveway and headed for the main road. He looked forward to seeing Marla. He had had a crush on her since junior high but never let it show. Gabe had always been a good friend, and he respected that. Now that Gabe wasted away in a coma, Dugan's attitude remained the same: he had no right to let on he had feelings for her. He would keep their relationship platonic until the day Gabe died. Even then he would take it slowly. She probably wasn't attracted to him anyway. He wasn't ugly, but he definitely looked more like Richie Cunningham than Arthur Fonzarelli.

When Dugan turned onto Old Lighthouse Road, he noticed Michael Easton walking towards him carrying a notebook. He hadn't talked to Michael in a while and wondered how his recovery from the head injury was going. He slowed to a stop and powered down the window.

Dugan waved. "What a small world. Here comes a fellow Purple Rider from my old hometown." Michael's sudden weight loss stunned him. His blue sweat outfit hung on him like clothes on a scarecrow.

Michael hurried to the car. "Hey, my friend, Dugan." He stuck out his hand. "Once a Rider, always a Rider."

Dugan shook his hand. Michael's greeting surprised him. Usually Michael addressed him with a slight hint of disrespect—Deputy Dugie or Dugie Walton—Texas Ranger. "You okay? You're looking mighty slim."

"Feeling good. Just trying to find myself again."

Dugan wondered if he still struggled with his identity or amnesia or whatever it was. "Back to painting your seascapes yet?"

Michael shook his head. "Nope. Just got a phone call about a new job. Starting Monday I'll be reporting for the *Outer Banks Sentinel.*"

"Really? I thought writing was Gabe's thing, not yours."

Michael shrugged. "People change." He held up his spiral bound notebook. "I've been writing all afternoon. Seem to have a knack for it now. I'm heading down to the coffee shop for a caffeine jolt. Want to join me?"

"No. Got things to do." Dugan patted the steering wheel. "Well, don't lose too much weight. You'll have to buy a whole new wardrobe."

Michael winked. "Can't do that until I get my first paycheck."

Dugan smiled, waved, and shifted his foot from the brake to the accelerator. As he pulled away, he glanced in his rearview mirror. *Michael still thinks he's Gabe. Or he's pretending to be. But why?* He refocused on the street, turned left onto the access road, and gazed at the apartment complex ahead of him. Marla came out the front door of the right-hand lower apartment with a garbage bag heaved over her shoulder. *That's why. The bastard's in love with his brother's wife.* The thought sent a twinge of guilt through him. He had to admit he had a crush on her too.

By the time he pulled up, she was dumping the bag into a large plastic trash can under the deck. He stepped out of the car and lifted the brim of his ball cap slightly. "Hey, Marla. Getting some chores done around the house?"

Marla cast a glance at him and waved. "Somebody's got to take out the garbage."

Her words troubled him a little, reminding him she no longer had a husband to do that job. Not much he could to about it, though. "Good to see this morning's run-in with Trenton hasn't slowed you down."

Marla walked to where he stood at the bottom of the steps. "Life goes on. Garbage piles up." She smiled. "I can't sit around and watch the paint peel off the walls because a killer's on the loose."

Dugan nodded. "I've got bad news for you. Trenton's still on the loose."

Marla's expression lost its gaiety. "Didn't you get a warrant to arrest him?"

"I did." Dugan patted the pocket on his brown nylon field jacket. "Son of a bitch took off on me, though."

Marla placed her hands on her hips. "He got away?"

"That's what I came to tell you. He's out on Pamlico Sound somewhere. Jumped out a back window and managed to take off in a fishing boat. Couldn't pursue him in the water."

Marla let out a long sigh. "What now?"

"Sheriff Johansson is letting the Coast Guard know. Course all our officers will be alerted to keep an eye out. Hard to say what direction he'll go."

Marla laid her hand on her cheek. "Where does that leave me?"

"You've got to be careful. Never know about a guy like Trenton. It's risky, but he might try to come at you again. Don't go for any long walks alone."

"I don't plan on it."

"I'll definitely spend more time on this end of the island."

"Thanks." Marla reached and touched the side of his arm. "I appreciate it."

Dugan enjoyed her touch but realized it was purely a friendly gesture. "Have Sonny and Michael been keeping an eye out for you?"

"Sonny's been making his rounds. Haven't seen much of Michael, but he's coming over for dinner tonight."

"Really?"

Marla nodded.

"His idea?"

"No."

That surprised Dugan, knowing Marla's personality conflicted with her brother-in-law's. Then again, Michael wasn't acting much like Michael nowadays. "He's family, I guess. It's good to be with family."

Marla's deep blue eyes took on a serious aspect. "It's more than that, Dugan. He's changed."

"I know. Just saw him heading to the coffee shop with a notebook. He's almost as skinny as Gabe."

Marla hesitated, her eyes studying his. He could tell she wanted to say something but was measuring his trustworthiness. Finally she said, "Weird, isn't it? He's just like Gabe."

"Seems to be." Dugan didn't want to comment too much, knowing the wrong words may convince her not to open up to him.

"This morning I overheard him playing guitar and singing a song Gabe wrote for me. Gabe was the only one who knew the words to that song. How could Michael know that song unless Gabe is somehow . . . in some way . . ." Marla let out a sigh, her lips tightening.

Dugan put his hand on her shoulder. "Remember, he lives right above you. He could have been out on the upper deck, listening while Gabe wrote the song."

She clasped her hand over his. "Do you think he's trying to deceive me?"

Dugan shrugged, lowering his hand and losing contact with hers. "Hard to say. The head injury might have mixed him up. All that he knows about Gabe may have become jumbled with his own identity. The song could be a part of the mix."

"But why? Why sing that particular song?"

Dugan rubbed his chin. "I have a theory. Maybe Michael's in love with you."

Marla's mouth dropped open. "Since when? We've never gotten along."

"Since junior high. He could never compete with his brother—Gabe's too good at everything he does. So he repressed his feelings until now." Dugan's words echoed in his mind, reminding him of his own repressed feelings towards her.

Marla shook her head. "I don't think so. A girl can tell when a guy likes her—body language, eye contact, subtle ways of flirting. Michael never gave me any of those signs."

"I'm just saying it's possible."

"If that's true, then he's being very deceptive."

Dugan rubbed his hands together. "That's the way I see it."

Marla stared at the ground and then met Dugan's gaze. "There is another explanation. It's far out, but maybe Gabe's spirit did take over Michael's body."

"Don't go there, Marla."

"Don't worry. I'm going to put Michael through a foolproof test. That's why I invited him over for dinner."

Dealing with criminals for the last few years, Dugan wondered if anything could be foolproof. "What kind of test?"

"Gabe was writing a novel. He kept the work-in-progress in a spiral bound notebook in his dresser. He had a detailed outline completed for the next chapter—Chapter Six. I told Michael to write that chapter and bring it with him tonight."

"I saw Michael carrying a notebook down to the coffee shop just before I arrived. He told me he'd been writing all day. Must have been working on that chapter."

Marla nodded. "If it doesn't match up exactly with Gabe's outline, I'll tell him to quit wasting his time. I'm not interested."

"And if it does?"

Marla took a deep breath and blew it out. "Then we'll see what happens."

Marla's foolproof test seemed reasonable to Dugan. Gabe probably wrote the outline the day of the attack. He doubted Michael's attempt would even be close. Marla was a smart gal. She would send him packing. Dugan glanced at his watch. "I'd better get back to Nags Head. Reports to fill out. Leads to follow. Criminals to chase." He glanced at the ground and shook his head. "Sorry Trenton got away."

Marla managed a smile. "Hey. I know you did your best. You always do."

She stepped forward and hugged him. He hesitated before embracing her. The display of affection had caught him off guard. She'd never hugged him before. Her hair smelled of summer flowers. Her cheek brushed his briefly but its softness remained in his mind. They stepped back from each other, and he felt his face flush. His mind scrambled for something to say. "Well . . . let me know what happens with Michael."

"Will do. Let me know what happens with Trenton."

"You'll be the first to know."

"Thanks."

Dugan tipped his ball cap, pivoted, and strode towards the vehicle. *Get a grip on yourself, Bozo. It was just a hug from a friend who's thankful for your efforts.* Dugan decided to maintain a cool mental state, not allowing his emotions or imagination to get carried away by one simple act of appreciation. It wouldn't be easy. The softness of Marla's cheek still lingered in his memory.

Chapter 26

Michael arrived right on time at six for dinner, carrying a black spiral bound notebook very similar to Gabe's. Marla felt tempted to seize the notebook, tell Michael to help himself to the salad, retreat to her bedroom, and read until she knew for certain the words were counterfeit. Her hopes had soared that afternoon, but as the hours passed, reality sobered her: Gabe's highly detailed outline could not be duplicated short of a miracle. If this was a pipe dream, she wanted it to end—now. But she didn't grab the notebook and run to the bedroom. When Michael offered it to her, she told him to put it on the coffee table in the living room and she'd read it after dinner. She would follow the plan.

She picked up the spatula. "Have a seat, Michael. Everything's almost ready."

Michael slid out one of the oak chairs and sat down. "Smells good. What's cooking?"

Marla stirred the strips of meat in the sauté pan. "Chicken. It's part of a spinach and beet salad."

"My favorite," Michael said.

His response caused Marla to do an about-face and catch any hint of forgery in his expression. "Your favorite? Really? You're a spinach and beet fan?"

"Sure."

Marla remembered how fast Michael had rushed out the door to head to McDonald's the last time she'd served the dish. "Hmmmmm." She lifted the chicken slices out of the sauté pan and lowered them onto the salads. "I've got beer in the fridge or fresh coffee."

"Coffee sounds good. Would you like me to get it?"

Another test passed, Marla thought. Coffee instead of beer and an offer to help to boot. "No. Sit still." She carried the salad bowls to the table. "You take yours black, don't you?" She examined his demeanor.

He shook his head, eyes narrowing and lips tightening as one imagining a bitter taste. "Cream if you don't mind. Have any of that hazelnut flavor?"

Marla was impressed. So far Michael knew the details of Gabe's preferences. She had set three bottles of dressing on the table—French, ranch, and Italian. After pouring the coffee and adding cream, she delivered the mugs and sat directly across the table from him, watching to see which dressing he would choose.

Instead of reaching for a bottle, he met her gaze.

"Go ahead," she said. "Eat."

"Could we pray first?"

Marla hadn't even anticipated the question. She should have. Even in restaurants Gabe would always take her hand and pray for the meal. "Please do."

Michael reached across the table and opened his hand. Marla stared at it for a second before placing hers in his. He clasped her fingers gently. "Dear Lord, we thank you for this day and each other, for this food set before us, and the possibilities of life you have also set before us. May the food be blessed and the possibilities embraced. Amen."

Marla knew Michael had heard Gabe say that prayer before, but he repeated it word for word with Gabe's tender tone in his voice. Not even thinking, Marla squeezed his hand and he squeezed back. Then she looked in the depths of his eyes and saw that spark she'd seen so many times before at the dinner table.

He released her hand, smiled, and lifted the ranch dressing from between the other bottles. Right again.

After sprinkling some Italian dressing over her salad, Marla picked at the strips of chicken and spinach leaves, avoiding the beets. She never did like beets. As she ate, she kept her eyes on Michael, hoping to see some hint of revulsion as he consumed his salad. Instead she saw pleasure exuding with every bite.

"This is good," he said. "You spiced up the chicken the way I like it."

The way Gabe liked it. "How are the beets and spinach?"

"Delicious." He speared a beet and savored it before chewing and swallowing.

After finishing his dinner, Michael bubbled with excitement about his new job, writing for the *Outer Banks Sentinel*. He had received a call that afternoon from the editor-in-chief, who instructed him to report on Monday to begin as a beat reporter.

"I know it's not much, reporting on school board meetings, town council, and the like, but I'm anxious to get started. It's in my blood."

"You always told Gabe writing was too much work."

Michael shrugged. "I don't know what to tell you, Marla. I'm not who I was." His eyes focused on the empty bowl before him.

"What about your seascape painting? You made a lot of money so easily selling your canvases down here."

His eyes fixed on her. "Can't you see? I can't do that anymore."

Marla nodded her head slowly. "I need to be honest with you."

"Of course. Why wouldn't you be?"

"This morning I told you to write the next chapter of Gabe's novel."

His smile returned. "I worked on it all day—six hours of writing. I can't wait for you to read it."

"Listen carefully." She took a deep breath, closed her eyes, and then opened them, intently locking eyes with him. "Gabe had created a detailed outline for that chapter. I know exactly, almost paragraph by paragraph what he wanted written. I know his style, the voice he uses as he writes. I've been editing his work for years. If what you have written doesn't match up exactly with his outline and his style, then this is over. No more pretending to be Gabe. You're good at it. Tonight you've matched him perfectly. At times I've felt like I was sitting across from my husband."

Michael leaned forward, his elbows on the table. "It's me, Marla." His voice trembled. "It's really me."

Steady. Her heart had risen into her throat. She could feel it pounding. *Keep control. Stay cool.* "If you're so sure, then you should have no problem agreeing to my terms."

"What do you mean to your terms?"

"If your chapter doesn't match up with his outline and style, then this is over. We don't see each other again. I'll probably look for a new apartment or perhaps move off the Outer Banks, back to the Ohio Valley or Pittsburgh or Nashville. Someplace away from you and everything that happened here."

Michael placed his palms flat on the table. "Fair enough. I agree with you."

"Why are you so agreeable? You have very little chance of proving your claim short of a miracle."

"I know my story. The scene of that chapter came back so clearly to me today. I wrote for six hours. The words flowed." He tapped his forehead. "If what's happening up here is all an illusion, I want to know too. I don't want to live a fantasy. If that head injury has thrown me off psychologically, making me think I'm Gabe, then I need to get back on track. But I don't think that's the case. I entered my brother's body. Don't ask me how, but that's what happened."

Marla bobbed her head. "Okay then. No sense in wasting any more time. I'm ready to read your chapter." She scooted out her chair, arose, and walked to the living room. Glancing over her shoulder, she noticed Michael had remained seated, eyes anxiously studying her. "You don't have to stay in the kitchen. Have a seat in Gabe's recliner." She picked up Michael's black notebook and settled onto the soft cushions of the wicker couch.

Michael skirted around the furniture until he reached the recliner on the other side of the room next to the bookshelf. "Are you sure you want me in here with you? I don't want to be a distraction."

"You're fine. Just don't get your expectations too high. Like you said—no sense in living a fantasy. In a few minutes we'll know."

Michael sat on the recliner and leaned on his knees.

Marla opened the notebook to the second page with the words "Chapter Six" printed at the top.

She read the first two sentences: *On the outskirts of the north side of Phoenix, Gordon pedaled along a two-lane highway. Several hundred yards ahead he saw a BP station and wondered if it would be open on a Sunday morning.* So far so good she thought.

Marla read faster, spurred on by the accurate start but anticipating a fatal error sooner than later. A mention of a Presbyterian Church across the street and Gordon's intension to solicit funds there accelerated her heartbeat. At the bottom of the page she read about the black motorcycle gang rumbling into the gas station. This was becoming uncanny. She stopped reading and eyed Michael. He sat in the recliner, head down, eyes closed, as if he were praying. How many times had Marla observed Gabe sitting in that same chair? And now because of Michael's weight loss, he and Gabe looked identical. Could it be possible? She read on.

The interactions between Gordon and the gang members matched the outline exactly. She slowed her pace, looking for some variation, some misdirection, but the story kept unfolding according to Gabe's plan: Gordon's inhospitable experience at the church, the gang's invasion of the sanctuary, the special collection for the homeless, the impromptu choir singing "Amazing Grace." It was all there. Marla's heart raced as she picked up her reading pace. She reached the last page—the final goodbye and departure of the gang. Gordon counted the donations tallying over $2000 and almost fainted with amazement. Marla knew exactly how the character felt. She closed the notebook and laid it on the coffee table, her head spinning. After shutting her eyes for several seconds, she opened them and focused on Michael. Or was it Gabe?

Michael's eyes met hers. "Well, was I close?"

Marla swallowed. She wanted to stand, rush to his arms, and tell him she believed—Gabe had come back to her just like he'd promised in her dream. She wanted to tell him how much she loved him and missed him, and now they could live out their lives together. But she hesitated. There was one more test he had to pass.

She stood, walked to him, and held out her hand. He peered up, eyes questioning the gesture. He took her hand and she smiled and stepped back as he rose to his feet. She reached and took his other hand. "The writing was perfect. Better than I expected, actually. I think it's your best writing yet."

"Really?"

"Really. But there's one more test you have to pass."

"Whatever you want."

She let go of his hands and unbuttoned his dark blue shirt. "Make love to me." Her fingers raked through his chest hair.

His eyes widened as he smiled. "I'd love to make love to you. It's been too long."

He reached for her ear, lightly touching its rim. That's how she loved Gabe to start. His index finger slowly traced the outside of her earlobe, along her jaw line to her chin, and across her lips so gently several times. Her respiration increased. She grasped his hand and kissed his fingers, hoping for him to say the right words.

"Marla," he whispered.

"Yes, Gabe."

"You don't know how badly I want to make love to you, but . . . but . . . we can't go through with this."

"Why not?"

217

"We're not married in the eyes of God yet."

Those were the words Marla wanted to hear—Gabe's idealistic standard even in these circumstances. If he were indwelling his brother's body, it would still be ethically wrong to Gabe to consummate their love for each other.

Marla stepped away from him. "You just passed the final test. I believe you now."

*　*　*

Mee Mee Roberts didn't usually carry a pistol with her on her walks out to Cape Point, but with Tony Trenton still on the loose, she thought her Beretta sub-compact semi-automatic would be a nice supplement to her walking stick. Fiercely independent, Mee Mee had lived on the Outer Banks running her bookstore for twenty-five years. In the winter months she made a habit of beachcombing out on the Point. That's when the good shells showed up. The winter storms and winds created enough wave power to lift the bigger conches over the sandbars and onto the beach. Tourist numbers dropped off from November through March, eliminating most of the shell-hunting competition.

Three weeks ago she had surprised Trenton as he manhandled Marla out in the middle of a usually deserted seashore preserve. Something had moved her to head out to Cape Point that day. Was it a push from God or just her own sixth sense? She wasn't sure. She *was* sure she would have bashed his brains in if he hadn't desisted. Too bad he had gotten away from Deputy Walton later that day. His at-large status made the usually invigorating walk somewhat uneasy, but Mee Mee refused to allow fear to dictate the direction of her life. If she did, she would have moved off the Outer Banks years ago. It could be a fearful place. She had learned to stand strong against stiff winds. Tony Trenton wouldn't budge her.

Mee Mee had noticed that same independent streak growing in Marla. When she and Gabe had first arrived, Marla seemed like the sheltered type, dependent upon her husband, unprepared to face the world alone. Like tragedies sometimes do, the loss of Gabe forced her to dig deeper inside of herself for the strength to stand against the onslaught of tribulation. In the last twelve weeks Marla had grown, toughened up, developed the fiber of the live oaks along the seashore preserve that withstood the constant battering of the sea breeze.

Mee Mee worried a little about Marla's new attraction to her brother-in-law, Michael. Were they falling in love or just becoming good friends?

Marla insisted he was a different man than the self-centered guy Mee Mee had met a couple years ago when he'd first arrived. Marla had kept mum about any romantic vibrations, but Mee Mee knew something was happening.

Next week Marla would take the prenatal paternity test. If the baby belonged to Trenton, would she keep it? How would Michael feel about that? Sooner or later Marla would open up to her. Time and patience. Mee Mee never pushed anything. She had learned to be a good listener over the years. Good listeners waited until the burdened are ready to share. She knew Marla had to sort through a lot of issues.

Mee Mee's thoughts about Marla were interrupted by male voices carried on the wind inland from the sea. She didn't recognize the voices, but she thought she heard one of them say something about "breaking in" to someone's house. Those weren't good words to overhear. She halted, not wanting to be seen. Ahead of her a patch of sea oats and a couple of myrtle trees grew in front of a dune. Through the grasses she could make out two figures seated at the base of the dune. Two fishermen on the way back from the Point had probably plopped down for a break. Were they plotting a robbery? About fifteen feet ahead she spied a medium-sized cedar along the trail. If she could make it there undetected, she could listen in.

She bent low and edged forward, crouching like an army scout nearing an enemy encampment. After ducking behind the cedar, she laid her walking stick beside her, reached into the pocket of her parka, and grasped the pistol. With the gun in hand but still concealed in her pocket, she felt safer. She tilted her head and listened.

"We haven't hit Frisco yet," a raspy voice with a strong southern accent said.

"We will. We're workin' our way down the island." The other voice was lower.

"But people are gettin' nervous in Buxton. We've already swiped three ATVs around town. Everyone's keepin' things locked up tight and the law has cranked up their surveillance—more patrols and whatnot. Besides, we haven't even cashed in yet. When are we gonna unload 'em?"

"Tony knows someone who wants them—a thousand bucks a piece. Not too shabby for a few hours work."

Mee Mee realized who the men were: Tony Trenton's friends—Gator Watts and Chuck Barton. Everyone knew everyone in Buxton. She'd read about the theft of the ATVs in the *Sentinel* a couple months ago. Were they planning another heist?

"A thousand bucks apiece?" The raspy voice said. "But they're worth four or five thousand each."

"They're stolen goods, Gator. You know that."

"I know. I know. That reminds me. I can't keep them in my gramp's garage much longer. He's only got a couple nuts and bolts left rolling around in his head, but you never know what he might say to someone."

It occurred to Mee Mee she had just heard enough incriminating information to put these two in the can for years. But how should she handle it? *Sit tight. Stay hidden. After they leave I'll call the sheriff's headquarters on my cell phone. The authorities can take it from there.* She noticed how much she trembled. Was it the cold or her nerves? Had to be both.

"Tomorrow night Tony's bringing the buyer over to pick them up," Chuck Barton said. "The dude's got his own boat. We'll use the dock behind your grandfather's garage."

"What time?"

"'Bout midnight."

Mee Mee couldn't believe what she had just heard. Now she knew where the most wanted man in the county would be at midnight tomorrow. She glanced over her shoulder at the trail behind her, feeling vulnerable, her backside exposed. What if they walk right by here? Would they notice her? She was in good shape. She could take off running right now. Those boys were young, though. They might catch her. Her parka was a bright yellow—easy to spot. When she refocused on the grasses and dune, she saw Gator Watts rise to his feet and then reach down to pull Chuck Barton up.

"Let's go, Chucko. I could use a couple beers."

"I'm with you." Chuck bent down and picked up fishing rods and a tackle box. They faced the cedar where Mee Mee hid and then walked directly towards her.

Her body tensed with fear. *Stay perfectly still.* As they neared, she saw how easily they would spot her unless she shifted her position around the tree, keeping it between her and them. The trick would be to do it soundlessly.

They approached more quickly than she'd hoped. As she tried to shuffle her feet to move her back side out of view, she accidentally kicked her walking stick. It rolled towards the path. *Crap!* She held her breath.

"What the hell was that?" Gator said.

"Someone's behind that tree," Chuck Barton said.

No sense in trying to hide now. Mee Mee stood and stepped into the open. She did her best to remain calm. "Afternoon, boys."

"That's the bookstore lady," Gator said.

"I'm surprised you recognized me," Mee Mee said. "I didn't know you could read."

Gator's brow knotted as his bottom lip pushed out.

"How long you been hiding there listening to us?" Chuck Barton asked.

Mee Mee slid her hand into her pocket, feeling the cold handle of the pistol. "Long enough."

Gator pointed at Mee Mee. "You heard what we were talking about?"

"Heard a few things."

Gator and Chuck glanced at each other, their eyes narrowing. When they refocused on Mee Mee, their facial muscles tensed.

"Shit," Chuck said. "Now what're we gonna do?"

"Can't let her go," Gator said. "She's knows about the ATVs and meeting up with Tony."

"That's right." Keeping the gun in her pocket, Mee Mee slid her finger around the trigger. "You boys are in enough trouble already. Don't get any foolish ideas."

"Shut up, bitch!" Gator barked, his long blond hair swaying forward. He tucked it behind his ears with a swoop of his hand. "You're the one who's in trouble."

"What're you going to do? Kill Me?" She tightened her grip on the pistol's handle.

Chuck Barton rubbed the dark stubble on his chin. "We can't kidnap her. Where would we keep her?"

Gator shrugged.

"I've got a suggestion," Mee Mee said, surprised at her own courage. "You two head on home without causing me any hassle and go break the news to your families."

"What news?" Gator asked.

"That for the next few years you're going to be wearing orange jumpsuits."

Gator's eyes caught fire. "I'm gonna twist her neck like a scrawny Sunday chicken" He thrust his hands towards her, surging forward.

Mee Mee didn't have time to pull the gun out and warn him. She shot through her pocket just as his hands reached her neck. The bullet twisted him sideways. He hit the ground screaming: "My shoulder! My shoulder! She shot me. Dammit! She shot me!"

Mee Mee pulled the Beretta out of her pocket and pointed it at Chuck Barton's face. "Take one step towards me and I'll blow your damn head off."

Barton raised his hands, eyes wider than a spooked horse's. "D-d-don't shoot me. P-p-please don't do it."

Gator quivered on the ground in a fetal position, his blood soaking the shoulder of his tan hunting jacket. He groaned and gripped his shoulder with his other hand.

Mee Mee pulled her cell phone out of her other pocket and flipped it open. "You want me to call 911 and get you some help?"

"Please," Gator groaned, and Barton nodded his head rapidly.

Mee Mee dialed the numbers and hit the call button. After the dispatcher answered, Mee Mee said, "This is Mee Mee Roberts out near Cape Point. We're going to need an emergency vehicle out here and a couple deputies to make an arrest."

"What's the nature of the injury," the dispatcher asked.

"Gunshot wound to the shoulder."

"Where's the shooter?"

"You're talking to her."

Chapter 27

Marla's hand shook as she tried to apply her mascara. She took a deep breath and steadied one hand with the other. Her ten o'clock appointment at the Outer Banks Hospital in Nags Head for the prenatal paternity test was approaching fast, and she wasn't even dressed yet. It was hard to focus, knowing what was at stake today. She was glad Michael offered to drive her to her appointment but worried how he'd react if they discovered the baby belonged to Tony Trenton. Would he want her to give it up for adoption?

Now that Gabe had possessed Michael, Marla hoped he would want to raise the baby with her, even if it was Tony Trenton's. She never thought she would go through with bearing Trenton's child, but feeling the baby growing inside her for thirteen weeks had changed her attitude. God worked in strange ways. She had been taught that God often took the bad and turned it into good. Maybe this was God's way of giving her and Gabe a baby. It had to be one of the strangest ways to do it short of a virgin birth.

Hoping against hope, she imagined the doctor informing her baby belonged to Gabe. No news could be more wonderful. Gabe's return through Michael and the blessing of their conception would rank right up there with Jesus turning water into wine and raising Lazarus. Michael had insisted they not go to bed with one another until they were married. To anyone else it would sound confusing, but Marla understood. That's just how Gabe was—incredibly idealistic. If the baby belonged to Gabe, there would be no doubt. They would get married as soon as possible and raise the baby together. The probability, though, was she would give birth to Trenton's child. How would Michael react? She had to put it in God's hands.

After finishing her makeup, Marla squeezed into her now tight-fitting jeans and an oversized OSU sweatshirt. It was a cold, mid-January day with a brisk breeze that made twenty degrees feel like ten below. Michael called from his cell phone to inform her he'd warmed up the car. She told him she'd be out in a minute or two. She found her warmest coat, a puffy, black nylon one, good against the wind with plenty of thick lining.

The dash to Michael's old blue Pontiac chilled her to the core, but the car's toasty interior and Michael's smile brought instant warmth. He appeared excited, face slightly flushed under his green toboggan.

"This is a big day," he said.

Marla averted her gaze. Gabe was always the optimist but often disappointed when reality hit. Did she need to throw ice water on his glowing hopes? Didn't he realize the odds? "One way or the other," she said.

"How's that?"

"You know what I'm saying. We have a one in a thousand chance this child belongs to Gabe . . ."

"You mean to me," Michael interrupted.

She met his stare. "Of course. To you when you possessed Gabe's body. But the other side of the odds—the 99.9 percent chance—will convict a murderer . . . your murderer."

Michael's expression sobered. "I'd rather my murderer go free, if it meant I conceived that baby."

"I'm just saying be prepared for the worst. Even bad news will accomplish an important purpose. Besides, the baby is the innocent one here."

Michael backed the car out of the driveway. "Does that mean you want to keep it even if it's Trenton's baby?"

Marla shrugged. "I don't know what I'll do." His tone didn't sound good to her. Maybe she'd assumed too much. Gabe was gracious but perhaps not gracious enough to raise his killer's child. "If I do decide to raise this baby, you're under no obligation to help me."

"Hold on now." He hit the gas and headed towards Old Lighthouse Road. "I didn't say I wouldn't help raise this child. Remember that day we rode bikes out past Mount Pleasant?"

"Yes."

"Do you remember walking through the cemetery and finding that gravestone?"

"Of course." Marla remembered like it was yesterday. Michael remembering was another confirmation of Gabe's return. "What about it?"

"There was an inscription written on that stone that I repeated to you."

"I know," Marla said. "Can you repeat it again?"

"I'll never forget it: *In life, in death, and beyond the bounds of this earth, I will always love you.*"

A lump formed in Marla's throat and she swallowed to gain composure. "Why did you mention that?"

"If you love that baby, no matter who it belongs to, I'll love that baby because I love you. In life, in death, and beyond the bounds of this earth. We'll raise that child together. Love will make it ours."

Marla didn't know what to say. The lump in her throat grew and wouldn't allow words. She blinked back tears, thinking how Gabe's love had always been unconditional. Her fear of his rejection of Trenton's baby subsided. In its place came the warmth of the kind of love she'd felt that day in the graveyard—a love that knew no limitations or raised no requirements. Michael took one hand off the steering wheel and extended it to her. She grasped it and squeezed tightly. Now she felt confident they would unite to raise this child no matter who the father was.

At the hospital the test didn't take long. Dr. Halsey, an OB-GYN on duty, performed the procedure transcervically, extracting a DNA sample from the placenta through the vagina. The sheriff's office already had Tony Trenton's DNA on file for comparisons, and, of course, the hospital had access to Gabe's DNA whenever needed. Dr. Halsey, a roly-poly man with thinning gray hair, explained how the DNA patterns would be compared between the child, mother, and father, resulting in a 99.99 percent accuracy identification rate. He would contact her with the results in about a week.

Marla dressed and headed to the waiting room. Michael stood as soon as she entered, a look of surprise on his face.

"I thought I'd be waiting an hour or more," Michael said, smiling.

Marla shook her head. "Didn't take long at all. We've got plenty of time before lunch. I'd like to go up and see Gabe."

His smile drained away. "I'm right here, Marla."

"I know you're here. But you're up in that hospital room too, as long as that heart is still beating."

"Okay. I'll go with you, but you know how I feel about standing there watching myself in that condition. It gives me the creepiest feeling."

Marla took his hand and led the way to the elevator. "Maybe it's time."

"Time for what?"

"Time to say goodbye to the old you."

The elevator opened, and they entered. "I told you before, I don't want any part of that decision. You'll know when it's time."

"We can't get married while he's still alive. You won't even go to bed with me."

Michael grasped her shoulders and met her gaze. "You know it wouldn't be the right thing to do. Not in God's eyes or even man's eyes."

"But what about my eyes?"

Michael dropped his hands to his side and shrugged. "You know how I feel."

The elevator doors separated. "The only way to make it right in your eyes is to pull the plug," Marla said.

"Or wait until the body finally gives out, however long that may take with life support."

They entered the hall and walked silently towards Gabe's room. At his bedside they held hands, seemingly mesmerized by the rhythm of the machines. Finally Marla said, "One more week."

"And then what?"

"By then I'll know who the father is. I've always said I'd wait at least until then."

Michael squeezed her hand. "You know I'll support you in whatever you decide."

* * *

Dugan Walton sat at his desk and signed the last in a series of reports due by the end of the day. He felt jazzed to be ahead of schedule on a Friday. Hopefully, nothing would interfere with this afternoon's meeting at the Outer Banks Hospital. Marla Easton had called him that morning to tell him Dr. Halsey was ready to disclose the results of the prenatal paternity test he had administered a week ago. Marla wanted Dugan there, knowing the results could convict a murderer.

Thanks to Mee Mee Roberts the suspect of that murder sat in a cell down the hallway. This morning when Dugan had passed by, Trenton complained about his stomach. He'd been moaning and groaning for hours. Dugan figured it was a ploy to get some time away from the detention center—a trip to the hospital's emergency room or at least a visit to the infirmary. Dugan didn't buy it and hoped Sheriff Johansson wouldn't believe that kind of baloney when he came in later that afternoon. With robbery, violation of a restraining order, fleeing arrest, and possibly murder hanging over his head, Trenton needed to get used to staring at those gray walls. Dugan looked forward to getting his hands on the test results. He wanted to put Trenton away for a long time.

He hadn't seen much of Marla for a couple weeks and missed her. Was she still falling for Michael's body snatcher claim? He hoped not. Marla was a smart girl. Gabe possessing his twin brother seemed like a case right out of the *X-files*. Surely she would come to see the absurdity of it. Because of Michael's head trauma from the fall, Dugan gave him some slack. But, obviously, twins share so much genetically and environmentally, it would be easy to get identities confused after a severe bump on the noggin, especially considering Michael's guilt over Gabe's unfortunate encounter with the killer. Sooner or later they would both come to their senses. Maybe by then Marla would realize how much Dugan cared for her. He decided not to obsess over it. Beautiful women rarely noticed him. If Marla and he were destined to be together, it would happen sooner or later. If not, he wouldn't force anything. He'd move on.

Dugan rolled his chair back, stood, and stretched his arms towards the ceiling. His stomach growled. He had time to get a bite to eat before heading to the hospital. He turned and walked to the locker to get his coat. On the way out he could drop off the paperwork with Daisy, the sheriff's secretary. He opened his locker and lifted his black bomber jacket off the hook. Peering into the mirror on the locker door, he combed his fingers through his unruly red hair. He didn't want to wear his knit cap to the meeting. It tended to compress his locks, making him look like Bozo the clown. His ears would have to endure the cold. Footsteps echoed down the hall, getting louder. He closed his eyes, thinking the last thing he wanted to do was fill out more papers. Daisy had probably sent someone his way to make a complaint against a neighbor or file a report about stolen or vandalized property. The footsteps stopped at his door. He didn't want to turn around.

"Deputy Walton?" a woman's voice said.

"Yes, I'm Walton." He finished adjusting his hair and closed the locker door.

"I want to report a rape."

Dugan straightened, his heart shifting into a higher gear.

He pivoted and faced the woman. There in the doorway wearing a blue Polo shirt and gray, baggy slacks stood Martin Payne. Dugan craned his neck to see if a female stood behind him or just out of view beside him, but clearly, no one else accompanied him. "Excuse me, Mr. Payne, but I thought I heard a woman's voice."

"You did. I'm Loretta Payne."

Female impersonators had nothing on Martin Payne. Just hearing the voice coming from a man's mouth gave Dugan the weirdest feeling. Payne's eyes were panicky like a cat stuck in a tree. His hair was disheveled and his shirttail half hung out of his pants. He'd lost it. Dugan decided to play along in hopes of calming him. "Come in. Please sit down."

Payne entered and slumped into the wooden chair across the desk from him. His eyes darted around the room as if he were tracking a pesky fly.

Dugan slung his jacket over the back of his chair and sat down. He cleared his throat, and Payne blinked, finally focusing on him. "You say you want to report a rape?"

"That's right." Payne wrung his hands, his eyes shifting back and forth across the desktop. "Do you have a cigarette? I'm dying for a smoke."

"No sir . . ."

Payne glared at Dugan.

"I mean, ma'am."

Payne took a deep breath and let it out audibly. "I was raped by the same man who killed that poor girl. He tied me up just like he tied her up."

If Dugan closed his eyes, he could swear he was talking to a woman. "May I ask when this rape occurred?"

"A year ago last September."

"About sixteen months ago?"

"That's right."

"And why are you waiting until now to report it?" Dugan knew this answer should be a doosie.

Payne leaned on the desk, his hands gripping the edge. "I've been in a coma. However, at times my husband allows me to possess him. Today I finally overpowered him."

"What do you mean by that?"

"I took over. And I'm not letting him back in until I do what he never had the guts to do. For more than a year I begged him, but he was too weak, too guilt-ridden. He couldn't let me go."

For a moment in Payne's eyes, Dugan glimpsed the essence of Loretta Payne, as if her spirit hovered there, just beyond the glistening irises where some say you can see one's soul. "What did you want your husband to do?"

"Set me free."

* * *

"I'm stoked, Marla. This could be the start of something big," Michael said, one hand gripping the steering wheel and the other gesturing wildly. His excitement impaired his driving as he drifted too close to the center line, and then overcompensated, almost running off the road.

Marla was happy for him, but his hyped state added to her anxiety over finally getting the test results. "Would you please slow down? I'm nervous enough as it is." Marla wanted to make it to her appointment with Dr. Halsey safe and sound. She'd been waiting for this day for a long time.

"Sorry about that." Michael hit the brake and the car's speed dropped to a reasonable level. "Lighthouse ghosts. Do you believe it? I'd never thought I'd be writing about lighthouse ghosts. I know it's just a Sunday feature for the next five weeks, but it might turn into a book."

"A book? Is there enough material for a book? There are only five lighthouses on the Outer Banks."

"I don't know. We'll see. That's why I want to stay overnight at every lighthouse. Get the full spooky atmosphere of each one. Tonight's Bodie Island. Are you sure you don't want to hang out with me all night. It'll be fun."

"I'm almost four months pregnant. The last thing I need is some Bodie Island banshee scaring me into a miscarriage."

"You're right. You're right. I'm sorry. Not thinking straight right now."

Marla reached and touched his elbow. "It's wonderful you're getting this opportunity to write about something fun and unusual for a change, but could we talk about it later. It's hard for me to think about anything else but the paternity test results."

"Of course. Forgive me. Sometimes I get obsessive."

"You've always been like that, Gabe."

Michael glanced over and smiled. "Thanks for calling me Gabe."

Marla couldn't help calling him Gabe. The more time spent with him, the more she'd become convinced of the interchange of spirits. More than anything she sensed Gabe's unconditional love. Today's paternity results may test that love, but Marla wasn't worried. She could count on Gabe. She placed her hand on her belly and rubbed gently. For the rest of the ride to the hospital, Gabe talked about their new life together, getting married in the near future, and raising the baby. Marla knew he'd do his best to love another man's child, but wouldn't it be incredible if the baby was his?

At the hospital a white-haired, older lady at the information desk directed them to a conference room on the second floor. She told them Dr. Halsey would meet with them as soon as he finished up in the delivery room. On the way to the elevator Dugan Walton caught up with them. He had an odd look on his face, as if he'd just learned something that caught him off guard.

"Hey, Dugan," Marla said. "Glad you could make it."

When Dugan's eyes met hers, his concerned expression faded, replaced by his usual smile. "Wouldn't miss it. The results could be a big help for us in your husband's case."

Michael extended his hand. "How's it going, Dugan?"

They shook hands and Dugan said, "Good as can be expected. How've you been feeling, Michael?"

"Never better. Feel like a new man."

Marla noticed the look of skepticism in Dugan's eyes and how his smile had faded when he'd greeted Michael. She didn't like the air of doubt he displayed. Of course, she had to give him some leeway. He hadn't seen what she'd seen in Michael.

Once they entered the elevator Dugan said, "Strangest thing happened at the sheriff's office today."

Marla immediately thought of Tony Trenton. Did Trenton make a confession? Try to escape?

"What happened?" Michael asked.

"A woman stopped in to report a rape that had occurred sixteen months ago."

The elevator doors opened and they entered the hall.

"Someone we know?" Marla asked.

"Yes. Loretta Payne."

"Loretta Payne? You've got to be kidding," Michael said.

The three paused in front of the nurse's station and Dugan met Michael's gaze. "Well, it was one of the strangest interviews I've ever conducted. Actually, Michael, you may have some insight into this. It was Loretta Payne speaking through her husband, Martin Payne. Do you believe that's possible?"

Michael rubbed his chin, eyes drifting upwards and then refocusing on Dugan. "After what I've been through, I'd say yes, it's possible."

Dugan nodded slowly. "Interesting. She said the man who raped her is the same man who killed the girl and raped Marla."

Marla felt a cold chill shoot through her. "Did she say who it was?"

"Yes, but I'm not at liberty to divulge that information right now. Besides, it may be irrelevant."

"Why would it be irrelevant?" Marla asked.

"Because Martin Payne is probably insane, right?" Michael said.

"Possibly," Dugan said, "but insanity doesn't disprove his accusation, or should I say hers. The test results could, though. If that's the case, then we'll know Payne is crazy. If the results confirm Loretta's story, then maybe there's something to this possession thing."

They started walking again towards the conference room. Marla found it difficult to shake off the bizarre sensation Dugan's revelation had stirred within her. She didn't know what to conclude. If Payne was crazy, does that mean Michael's crazy too? Walk-ins are impossible and anyone who makes these kinds of outrageous claims is unbalanced? No. She'd seen and heard the proof many times in the last few months. Gabe had possessed Michael's body. His behavior and personal knowledge afforded no other logical explanation, regardless of Payne's mental state.

In the conference room they sat in black leather chairs around a table made of dark wood. The crème-colored walls were broken by several framed seascapes. Marla noticed Michael staring at the canvas on the opposite wall, a thickly painted sunset with impressionistic blue-green waves poised to crash on a sandy shore. How unusual, she thought. He hadn't been interested in painting since the tumble from the deck, but this one seemed to captivate him.

231

Dugan shifted in his seat to see the artwork behind him. "Nice painting, huh?" Dugan asked.

"Very nice," Michael said.

"Have you done any lately?"

Michael shook his head. "Too busy writing. Painting's not my thing anymore."

"Right," Dugan said with a dubious smile.

Marla felt uncomfortable. Wanting to change the subject, she asked, "What's up with Tony Trenton lately? Any news about his trial?"

"The judge is waiting on the paternity results before he decides whether or not to set bail. I'm guessing the trial date will be scheduled soon. Trenton doesn't like being penned up. This morning he was complaining about his stomach. I ignored him."

"Why?" Michael asked.

"He's faking it. Just wants out of the cell—a trip to the infirmary or even the emergency room if he can swing it."

Marla didn't like hearing that. The last thing she wanted to deal with was the possibility of Trenton escaping. "The sheriff won't believe him, will he?"

Dugan shrugged. "I hope not. Depends on his acting skills. Sheriff Johansson may bring in a doctor to check him out. Then it's the doc's call."

Marla shuddered. "I pray they don't let him out of that detention center."

The conference room door opened and Dr. Halsey entered, still wearing his blue scrubs and cap. He had a round face and a thick gray mustache. "Sorry to keep you waiting. I know how important these results are to you." He held up a clipboard. "We've gone over these DNA patterns several times to make sure of our conclusion." He shook his head, took a deep breath, and blew it out. "You may be surprised at the results."

Chapter 28

"There's no doubt. Gabe Easton is the father," Dr. Halsey said.

Marla gasped.

Michael shot out of his seat, his jaw dropping. "I knew it. Deep inside I knew no one else could be the father."

Marla jumped to her feet and wrapped her arms around Michael. He lifted her off the ground. "It's a miracle," she said. "It's a miracle from God." She glanced towards Dugan and noticed he sat still, observing her and Michael as if taking mental notes, or was a hint of jealousy in his eyes?

Dr. Halsey placed a chart on the table, and they drew near and leaned over it. The doctor pointed at a series of dotted graph-like images. "This is the baby's DNA. Here's Marla's. If we remove Marla's, we're left with a clear set of markers for the father's." He pulled another printout from the clipboard. "This is Trenton's. No match. Not even close. But look here." He placed another DNA code chart next to the one of the baby's with the mother's markers removed. "Perfect match. I'm 99.99 percent sure Gabe is the father."

"Does that clear Tony Trenton as a murder suspect?" Michael asked.

"Of course not," Dugan said.

"Why not?" Michael asked.

"The technician may have botched the rape test. Somehow missed swabbing a sample of Trenton's seminal fluid." Dugan rubbed his chin. "It's just going to make things a lot harder if it is Trenton."

"I don't care," Marla said, tears streaming down her cheeks. "I'm carrying my husband's baby. That's all that matters to me right now. If Trenton is the murderer, I'm sure you'll find more evidence."

Dugan shrugged. "I'll do my best."

"This calls for a celebration," Michael said, his arm still draped around Marla's shoulders. "We're stopping at the wine shop in Avon on the way home."

Dr. Halsey peered over his reading glasses. "I'm very happy for you, but not too much wine for the pregnant lady. A glass at the most. Anyway, I've got to get back and check on a mother that just delivered. She refused pain medication. The baby came hard and fast. It was brutal, one of the most excruciating deliveries I've seen in a while."

With a wide smile, Marla patted her belly. "Thanks for the preview of what I'll be facing in the near future, Dr. Halsey. Hopefully my delivery won't be that bad."

Dr. Halsey offered a dismissive wave. "No worries. We'll do a spinal on you. You won't even flinch," he said as he headed out the door.

The pain that awaited her in childbirth didn't concern her much now. The news of the father's identity, Gabe's one-in-a-thousand shot, had sent her soaring. She could sense Michael was elated too. But Dugan seemed to drift away, eyes studying the floor as if he'd lost a precious coin. "Are you all right, Dugan? You don't seem too enthusiastic about the news?"

Dugan quickly glanced up and met her gaze. "I'm sorry. I'm happy for you, for both of you, really. It's nice that you two have made a connection, especially with the baby coming. It's fitting when you think about it."

Michael pulled Marla snuggly against him. "What do you mean by fitting?" Michael asked.

"I think Gabe would have wanted it this way. You two were identical twins, right?"

"That's right," Michael said, his eyes questioning the gist of Dugan's thinking.

Dugan lifted his palms as if balancing a large orange in each hand. "I've heard identical twins share everything from the cradle to the grave. You're probably the best man to take Gabe's place."

Marla couldn't gauge the degree of sincerity in Dugan's voice. Did she detect a hint of resentment? Envy? Or even sarcasm?

"I'll do my best to help," Michael said.

"Well," Dugan said, "I've got to get going. Now that the DNA evidence won't convict Trenton, I better explore other possibilities before they decide whether or not to let him out on bond."

Could that be it? Dugan's disappointed because he'd hoped to nail Trenton with the DNA evidence. If that was the case, Marla could understand his disappointment. He'd worked so hard on the case for months. She reached and patted Dugan's shoulder. "We'll walk you to your car."

Through the hallways, into the lobby, and out the front entrance, Marla and Michael held hands. Dugan trudged in front of them not saying much or even looking their way until Marla broke the uncomfortable silence by mentioning their need to brace themselves for the bitter cold. Marla wondered if Dugan's silence stemmed from romantic inclinations he might have towards her. If so, seeing her and Michael giddy about the baby and each other had to be difficult for him. Perhaps Marla would have been interested in Dugan at some future point, if Gabe hadn't come back to her. But Gabe had returned, and they were ecstatic about raising their baby together.

In the parking lot, standing next to Dugan's vehicle, they watched an emergency squad pass by, siren blaring, and come to an abrupt stop at the emergency entrance. A sheriff's vehicle, an exact copy of the car Dugan had driven, pulled in beside the white and yellow van. Dugan eyed the officer as he exited his car and strode to the back of the E-squad. An attendant flung open the back door and two assistants appeared in the opening. They lifted a stretcher on which a large man lay wearing an orange shirt. The helper on the ground unfolded retractable wheels, and the two inside moved the stretcher forward until the back wheels could be lowered.

"It's him," Dugan said.

Marla stared at Dugan. Did he know the man? When she refocused on the gurney, she realized the orange shirt was standard jail apparel. "Is it Trenton?"

Dugan nodded. "I was afraid he'd pull something like this."

"What's he up to?" Michael asked.

"My guess is he's faking an appendicitis attack to get time away from his six by eight cell. Hopefully Deputy Benson will keep a close watch on him."

He better, Marla thought as fear stabbed through her, causing every muscle in her body to tense. "Do you think he'd try to escape?"

"Wouldn't put it past him. He's not comfortable at all in the slammer. Don't know if it's claustrophobia or just total loss of freedom, but jail is pure hell for him."

As the attendants pushed the gurney towards the entrance, Trenton turned his head and gazed at Marla. His eyes lit with recognition, and his stare froze her. A deep dread iced over her fear, the same feeling she had on the night the rapist had blindfolded her and the day Trenton had chased her near Cape Point. Gathering her strength, she forced herself to turn away and look in the opposite direction. Michael put his arm around her waist, and his warmth helped her battle against the anxiety that threatened to overwhelm her.

Marla reached and grasped Dugan's elbow. "Promise me you won't let him escape."

Dugan straightened. "I haven't been assigned to guard him."

The implausibility of Marla's demand suddenly crystallized in her reasoning. Dugan wasn't Supercop. How could she expect him to focus solely on being her protector? He had his own responsibilities, his own life to live. A wave of embarrassment flushed her cheeks.

"My shift's about up." Dugan shrugged. "I guess I could call the sheriff and request to relieve Deputy Benson. That would mean overtime, but Sheriff Johansson might approve the extra hours."

Marla raised her hand. "No. Forget I said that. I have no right to expect you to be totally responsible for Tony Trenton. I guess . . . I guess just seeing him freaked me out. I'm sure Deputy Benson will do a good job."

Dugan bit his lower lip, looking somewhat defensive. "I'll hang out here for another hour or so on my own time to make sure he doesn't pull a fast one."

"You don't have to."

"I want to."

Dugan's offer gave her some relief. "Maybe you can find out if he's really sick."

Dugan nodded. "I'll check with the emergency room personnel. They'll let me know if he has a fever or any other serious symptoms."

"Thanks, Dugan," Michael said. "You've been a good friend through all of this."

Dugan smiled, but his eyes lacked their normal warmth. "You two heading home now?"

Marla shook her head. "We're going up to Gabe's room for the last time."

"I see," Dugan said. "Tough decision, but I think it's the right one. Gabe isn't in that hospital room. Just his shell."

"We know," Marla said, and then peered up at Michael. "But that doesn't make it any easier."

Michael shook his head. "No, it doesn't."

"Of course not," Dugan said.

Marla grasped Michael's hand. "I wanted to wait until I found out the identity of the father. Knowing a part of Gabe lives on in me helps me to face this final goodbye."

Dugan bobbed his head slowly, his eyes scanning the ground at their feet. "Marla?" He looked up, their eyes meeting. "Gabe was always a good friend. Say goodbye for me too, would ya?"

Marla let go of Michael's hand, stepped forward, and hugged Dugan. Hesitantly, Dugan wrapped his arms around her but then held her close.

"He thought you were a great guy," Marla said through her tears. "He believed in you."

"I know," Dugan sniffed. "And I'll always remember that."

The walk to Gabe's room strained Marla emotionally as if a heavy weight had been hung around her neck, pressing on her heart. She kept reminding herself Gabe had returned to her through Michael, but that fact didn't lessen the difficulty of the task before her. The body in that room had once been alive, energetic, warm, and beautiful. Gabe was the only man she had ever loved—emotionally and physically. She carried the baby of that union within her womb. But to give her relationship with the new Gabe a chance to grow and flourish, she had to set the old Gabe free.

As Michael and she proceeded down the hallway, their footsteps echoed off a distant wall, a ghostly sound that gave Marla an odd chill. The florescent lights sapped the colors from the surroundings, giving a pallid cast to the receding corridor. At the entrance to the room they hesitated, their eyes meeting. Marla wondered if Michael sensed the same haunting reverberation deep within, as if doubt had gained a foothold, causing an emotional and physical disturbance. But his expression seemed resolute, chin firm and eyes dauntless.

They entered the room and walked to Gabe's beside. The machines hummed and beeped, the respirator keeping up its steady rhythm. Gabe's emaciated body no longer resembled him. A dark beard now covered his gaunt face, and his hair had grown over his ears. He looked like an Old Testament prophet, who had just completed a forty-day fast. Marla glanced

237

up at Michael. He had lost more than fifty pounds since recovering from his head injury. He had become Gabe, lean and muscular, so much more like him than the pitiable body that lay in the bed next to them. She shifted her focus back and forth several times between them. This was the right thing to do. The dying Gabe needed to be released so that the living Gabe could take his place. They could be husband and wife again.

"It's me, but it's not me," Michael said, his voice sounding distant, as if he were standing outside the room.

"Do you miss your brother?" Marla asked.

Michael inhaled deeply and blew out the air audibly. "Yes. I miss him. He had so much talent, so much potential, but too many unhealthy indulgences. I'd hoped we could help him by coming here, but now he's gone."

Marla struggled to maintain Michael's chain of reasoning. Gabe was speaking through Michael about Michael no longer being with them. "Michael's gone," she said as she placed her hand on the middle of his Michael's back, "but his body's still alive and well. So he's not totally gone."

Michael gripped her shoulder and pulled her close to him. "I disagree. The spirit is what gives life. The body is shaped by the spirit but it's not the person."

That made sense to Marla. Michael's body no longer belonged to Michael. It had been possessed by Gabe and shaped by Gabe. Gabe's body belonged to no one. It had become an abandoned house that no one would ever live in again. "I'm ready."

Michael nodded. "If you're ready, I'm ready."

They turned away from Gabe's body, walked out the door, and headed towards the nurse's station. It's funny, Marla thought. I'm not sad at all. How can I mourn over someone who is walking beside me? It's true. Michael's gone, but I don't really miss him.

It didn't take long for Gabe's body to expire once the machines were turned off. Michael and Marla held hands and watched him die. His breathing quickly became ragged, his legs jerked several times, and then his heart stopped, the monitor beeping erratically and then a long steady tone. To Marla, watching the body die was unsettling, even repulsive. But then silence fell like January snow in the dead of winter.

Chapter 29

When Marla opened her front door to let Michael in, she noticed the large snowflakes drifting through the glow of the streetlight near the driveway. A gust of cold air rushed in from behind him. He quickly stepped inside and pulled the door shut.

Marla clasped her thick robe snug against her, crossing her arms. "I don't believe you're still heading over to the Bodie Island Lighthouse to spend the night."

Michael glanced up, that look of disappointment in his eyes, the one Gabe always had whenever she disapproved of one of his obsessive endeavors. "Are you still worried about Trenton escaping from the hospital?"

"No," she said with slight irritation in her voice, although she still felt uneasy about the circumstances. Dugan had called earlier to let her know that Trenton had a high fever and an increased white blood cell count. The emergency room doctor had informed him that Trenton may have a bad case of the flu or perhaps appendicitis. The doctor had mentioned further tests, but Dugan didn't stick around because the tests could have taken hours. Instead, he had instructed Deputy Benson to keep a close eye on things. On the phone Dugan had sounded fairly confident she had nothing to worry about, but Marla still grappled with an uneasy feeling. Was it intuition or just her imagination?

Michael set a wine bottle on the kitchen table. "I could postpone the lighthouse ghost article until next Sunday's edition."

"No." This time Marla tried not to sound so irritated. "I'll be fine."

"This wine will help settle your nerves."

A good glass of red wine sounded perfect to Marla. "Dr. Halsey said one glass shouldn't harm me or the baby."

"That's right," Michael said, removing his coat. He slung it around the back of the kitchen chair. "One glass of wine—a toast to our new life."

His words warmed her. She patted her slightly protruding belly. "And our new baby."

Michael drew near and embraced her. She held him tightly, getting a whiff of Gabe's favorite aftershave, Old Spice. "Unbelieveable, isn't it?" he said. "I knew Trenton wasn't the father. Deep inside, I knew it."

They released each other and stepped back. "I wasn't so sure," she said. "The news almost floored me. One-in-a-thousand chance. Gabe hit a homerun run that night."

"More like a grand slam." Michael's smile widened, or was it Gabe's smile.

"If it's a boy, should we name him Gabriel?"

Michael tilted his head, his lips curling slightly. "I think I'd like to name him after my brother."

This new start was confusing. Was he speaking as Gabe or Michael? "You know Michael always rubbed me the wrong way."

"I know, but I loved him."

Marla took a deep breath, slid out a chair and sat down. "No sense in discussing it now. The baby's not due for another five months. Besides, it might be a girl."

"You're right," Michael said. He walked to the drawer next to the sink, opened it, and retrieved a corkscrew. "Let's pop the cork on this bottle of wine."

Marla stared at Michael's back as he removed the cork and poured the drinks. She wondered if some day she and Michael would conceive. Maybe they'd have two boys, Michael and Gabriel. That would please both of them

Michael carried the glasses to the table and sat down. He slid hers across the oak surface, the bubbles rising through the crimson liquid. He lifted his goblet. "Grow old with me, the best is yet to be."

"Robert Browning?"

Michael nodded.

She raised her glass, clinked his, and sipped. It tasted so good, warming her insides. It would be tempting to drink two, but she would deny herself that pleasure for the baby's sake.

Michael raised his glass again. "And here's a wish: may I get a glimpse of a ghost tonight."

Marla shook her head. "Just so I don't see any."

"You'll be fast asleep," Michael said. "You're not used to drinking wine."

"That's true."

"Seeing one could be one helluva break for me, even if only in my mind. Could you imagine the number of readers an eyewitness ghost story would generate?"

Marla shuddered. "I could never stay in that lighthouse all night by myself. You must be desperate for readership."

Michael gulped his wine, downing more than half the glass. "Desperate isn't the right word. More like spirited."

Marla took another drink, bigger this time. "If you see a ghost, you'll be spirited all right."

Michael chuckled and downed the rest of his wine. "Hate to drink and run, but I've got to get going. Oliver Thomas, the lighthouse keeper, promised to let me in at eleven thirty. I don't want to be late. Besides, ya never know when the dead'll show."

That's exactly what Gabe would have said—always on time, brimming with anticipation. Marla waved her hand. "Don't let me hold you up. Like you said, I'll probably be out before you know it. Just make sure you stop here first thing tomorrow morning and let me know what happened."

Michael slid his chair out. "You'll be the first to know about any paranormal activity I encounter." He stood and slipped on his coat. "I'm taking the wine bottle with me. Can't let a pregnant lady be tempted."

"Just so you don't drink any more." Marla regretted the words as soon as she said them.

Michael's eyebrows raised, his mouth opening slightly, his hand rising to his heart. "You pierce me with your unkind insinuation."

"I'm sorry. Take it with you. I'm not worried about you backsliding. How can you? You're no longer Michael."

"My brother was a drunk. I can see how you'd be worried."

"No. I mean it. I trust you."

Michael set the bottle on the table. "I'll leave it here."

"I'm not worried." Marla walked to him and hugged him. "Let's trust each other."

Michael pulled her tightly against him. "We will." They leaned back and gazed into each other's eyes. He gently traced the rim of her ear with his finger, drew it across her jaw line to her chin and then lightly over her lower lip. They kissed, a long, soft kiss.

Marla didn't want Gabe to go but knew she couldn't insist he stay. She had always given him freedom to pursue his passions.

He released her, backed away, and glanced at his watch. "Sorry, Sweetcheeks, I've got to get going."

"I know," Marla said. "I know."

After Michael left, Marla picked up the remote, plopped down on the couch, and turned on the television to catch the eleven o'clock news. She felt incredibly tired but wanted to make sure a convict hadn't escaped from a local hospital. Once her head sunk into the pillow, though, she struggled to keep her eyes open. Was it the effects of the wine? The news anchor babbled on about a breaking story, but Marla couldn't stave off the overwhelming drowsiness. She sunk into the blackness of a deep sleep.

When someone tugged on Marla's arm, she tried to open her eyes. Her eyelids felt so heavy, as if they'd been glued shut. She attempted to draw her legs up so she could turn onto her side but couldn't. Was there something on her ankles? She heard heavy breathing. Someone gripped her wrist. She managed to pull her arm away.

"Dammit," a monstrous voice said. "Give me that hand, you bitch."

With a concerted effort, she opened her eyes and saw the horns and beard—the mask of the Greek god. What was his name? Dionysus? *This must be a nightmare.* "God, no. Please, no. Let this be a dream."

"'Fraid not. I'm all too real." The odd tone of his distorted voice sounded as if it came from the depths of hell.

"No, please. Don't do this to me again."

"If you want to live, you better keep quiet."

Marla wanted to scream, but she thought about her baby. Could she endure this one more time for the sake of her child? "Please don't hurt me. Do what you want but please don't hurt me."

He placed his hands on the pillow near each side of her head and lowered himself, the grotesque mask coming within inches of her face. "I intend to." She could smell alcohol. Was it wine? Now she wished Michael would've taken the bottle with him. The killer stood up. "Hold your arm still while I tie you up and stretch you out."

Both of her feet and her left arm had been lashed to the bedposts. Now he wrapped the cord around her right wrist like a cowboy tying up a calf. After knotting it, he yanked her arm towards the other bedpost. She let out a yelp, and he raised a hand and slapped her.

"I said keep your mouth shut."

She wanted to wail but forced herself to stifle her sobs.

As he wrapped the end of the rope around the bedpost, Marla heard a distant voice, Sonny Key's voice: "Mrs. Easton! Are you all right? Is there someone in there with you?"

The killer stopped tying the knot, straightened and raised his index finger to his papier-mâché lips. "Be very quiet," he whispered.

"Marla Easton! This is Sonny Keys! Deputy Walton asked me to check on you. Can I come in? I have my master key."

The monster shook his head sideways. "Don't say a word."

Sonny yelled, "I hope you don't mind, but I'm coming in!"

The murderer grabbed the brass lamp from the nightstand, yanked out the plug, and sidestepped to the edge of the bedroom doorway. Marla glanced at the bedpost and noticed the knot hadn't been tightened.

Sonny's footsteps neared. Marla screamed, "Watch out, Sonny!"

The masked man swung the lamp towards Sonny's head, but Marla's warning caused Sonny to raise his hands in time to block the blow. With Sonny off balance, the murderer lunged against him, knocking him to the ground. By leaning to her right, Marla could see the monster on top of Sonny, one hand around Sonny's neck and the other holding the lamp high above his head. Sonny's face reddened. His hands struggled to pry off the killer's choke grip. The killer struck at his head, but the lamp glanced off Sonny's arm and hit the floor.

With a powerful thrust, Sonny heaved his torso upwards. The masked man fell to the side, his elbow plowing into the dresser. Sonny used his opponent's loss of balance to gain the advantage. Like a skilled wrestler, he rolled over and clamped his arms around the killer. They rammed into the dresser several times, causing bottles to tumble off. Now they were hard to see, just below the end of the bed.

Marla yanked on the rope again and again. No luck. She tried to shove the yellow cord in different directions towards the post to loosen the knot. That seemed to be working. From below the bed came grunts and curses. She kept plying the rope. If she could somehow reach the free end with her teeth, she could unravel it, but she couldn't stretch that far.

243

The masked man broke free and tried to stand, but Sonny tackled him. They rolled on the floor near the doorway, punching and gouging. Marla frantically jiggled the rope. The knot loosened more. *Please, God, please. Help me get this thing undone.*

The killer managed to pull away again. Sonny lunged to grasp his legs, but he kicked Sonny's arms and crawled through the doorway into the living room. Sonny scrambled to his feet and disappeared through the doorway. Marla heard the sounds of things falling and crashing. Did Sonny tackle him again? She shook the knot, zigzagging it the air. *Almost there. Come on. Come on.*

The sound of glass breaking was followed by a loud "Oooofffff." That could have been the large glass vase near the bookcase. But who got hit?

"Sonny!" she called. "Are you okay?" She heard heavy breathing but no other sounds.

Back to the knot. She yanked it as hard as she could. The cord slipped through, and the knot fell away. Quickly, she began unlooping it from the bedpost, but stopped, leaving one loop in place. She held her arm as if it were still secured. Hearing footsteps, she glanced at the door. The man in the mask entered. He wore a black sweat suit. His hands were bloody. He stared at her, his eyes like dark pools through the mask holes.

Keep your cool. Remember the baby. "Please don't hurt me." Marla said.

"I just got even with your maintenance man," the distorted voice said.

Marla remembered Sonny's two altercations with Tony Trenton. "Did you kill him?"

"Don't know. Busted his head awful good. Now it's your turn."

"I won't resist you. Do what you want. Just don't hurt me or my baby."

He took several steps forward, hovering over her. "But that's what I came to do—hurt you bad. Real bad."

Marla's mind searched desperately for something to say, something to change his diabolic intensions. "I'm sorry I ran away from you at Cape Point. You scared me. But you really are a desirable man."

He put his hands on his hips and laughed, throwing his head back. Then he leaned forward, his breathing sounding so creepy through the device attached to the mouth hole. "You don't understand. I have no choice. I have to kill you and your baby. But first I'm going to enjoy you." His blood-splattered hand reached slowly towards the neckline of her nightgown. He focused on her breasts.

Striving to use as little movement as possible, she lifted the last loop off the towrope off the bedpost. His fingers curled around the collar of her nightgown and pulled it towards him, exposing her cleavage. She whipped the cord across his face, and it split the mask in two.

He stumbled backwards, the halves of the mask separating and falling away.

Chapter 30

"Michael!"

"Damn you, Marla. I just put the finishing touches on that mask."

"You? It can't be you."

"I'm back. Gabe couldn't keep me away."

It didn't make sense. "But you were at the restaurant that night."

"Exactly what I wanted you to think. I called from just outside the apartment using my cell phone. I waited in the shadows for my dear brother to come get me. I knew he would. He loved me too much."

"The wine. You drugged me, didn't you?"

"Yes. I needed you to sleep several hours—enough time for me to meet with Oliver Thomas at the Bodie Island Lighthouse. He thinks I'm still there. Great alibi, huh?"

Marla wanted to keep him talking, anything to delay his attack. "Why, Michael, why? What possessed you to do this?"

"Don't you remember? Gabe possessed me. That was the plan anyway."

"Why did I ever believe it?"

Michael took a step forward. "Because he did possess me. After I regained consciousness in the hospital, the plan crystallized in my mind. It was perfect. I knew my brother so well—his songs, his writing—he told me everything about your relationship. All I had to do was allow him to take over, like one of those method actors—Robert DeNiro or Daniel Day-Lewis. I kept telling myself to let Gabe take control: What would Gabe think? What would Gabe say? What would Gabe do? I yielded my soul totally to my brother."

If only she could keep him talking. Every second improved her chances. "But why did you want to become Gabe?"

"That's easy. I wanted what he had—his discipline, his drive, his body, and most of all I wanted you."

"Me?"

"That's right." He raised his hand and pointed towards the window. "I lost count of the number of times I stood on that deck at night and watched you two humpin' away."

A shudder rushed through Marla. The thought of Michael violating her and Gabe's most intimate moments together sickened her. She forced herself to gain control. "You could've had me. I would've married you. I thought you were Gabe. Why this? Why now?"

Michael stepped forward and grasped the end of the rope. "Because of Dugan Walton."

Marla wanted to pull her arm away and hit him again with the cord, but this time she knew she lacked the element of surprise. He stretched her arm towards the bedpost and looped the rope several times. She wasn't ready to give up yet. "Dugan Walton? I don't understand." She heard a groan emanate from the living room. *Sonny Keys is still alive.*

Michael released the rope, marched to door, stopped, and scooped the brass lamp off the floor. As he stood, Sonny dove through the doorway, plowing into Michael's knees. Michael fell backwards, the lamp flying out of his hand.

Marla eyed the bedpost. Michael never had time to tie a knot. She quickly unwound the cord by making circular motions in the air with her hand. Below the bed she heard gurgling noises. She saw Michael's head and shoulders rise above the end of the bed. He was choking Sonny, his eyes widening with each thrust against Sonny's throat. She twisted to reach the other bedpost. Untying the knot with one hand seemed impossible, but she tried to shove the end of the rope through the tightened plait without much success.

Sonny made horrible noises—like a small animal being tortured. How long could he go without air?

With her ankles still tied to the bedposts, she shifted on the bed as best she could to find the right angle to work on the knot. No use. Her free hand dropped to the pillow beside her, and she pressed down to shift her torso again. That's when she felt it—the gun. In the excitement she'd forgotten about the gun Dugan had given her. She reached under the pillow, grasped the handle, and whipped it out.

"Stop it!" Marla screamed.

Michael paid no attention. He gritted his teeth and bore down more on Sonny's neck.

"I'll shoot!"

Michael leaned back and shifted his focus to her. "No, Marla, no." He held up his hands.

"Sonny, are you all right?" Marla asked.

Silence.

Michael glanced at Sonny, a look of confusion on his face. "What happened to Sonny?" He panned the room. "How did I get here?"

Sonny must be dead, Marla thought. She tried to hold the gun steady, pointing it at Michael's chest.

Michael stood. "Marla, what are you doing? It's me, Gabe."

"Stay back."

"I tripped and fell at the lighthouse. That's the last thing I remember." He took a step closer, his eyes growing slightly wider. "Something must have happened to me when I was unconscious."

Could he be telling the truth? Impossible. It's another lie. "I said stay back."

He raised his hand, offering his palm, and took another step. "Sweetcheeks, where did you get that gun?"

No. Don't let him get to you. It's not Gabe. Now her hand shook like a tree limb in a thunderstorm, the barrel of the gun wobbling in odd circles.

"Put it down, Marla. It's me."

Marla shook her head. "It never was you."

Michael surged towards her. The gun exploded before he could slap it from her hand.

He grasped his stomach, his mouth opening as if he wanted to scream but couldn't. He removed one hand from the wound and extended it towards her. It dripped blood. "Why did you shoot, Sweetcheeks? It's me. I came back to you." His eyes rolled up into his head, and he slumped on top of her.

He lay across her hips, his head on her belly, his blood soaking into her nightgown just above her knees. Marla shoved him with her forearm, but he was hard to move. She didn't want to put the gun down.

She lay still, listening, and heard breathing. But it didn't come from Michael. A groan rose from the floor and the sounds of someone rolling over. "Sonny, are you all right?"

A bald head and wide shoulders appeared above the end of the bed. Bruises covered Sonny's neck and blood oozed from cuts on his face. "I'm sorry, Marla. I must have passed out when he choked me."

"Don't apologize. You saved my life. Could you get him off me?"

Sonny stumbled to his feet, wavered slightly, and rubbed his neck. He placed his hand on the bedpost at the foot of the bed to steady himself. After taking a deep breath, he wedged himself between Michael's legs, lifted them, and tugged the body off Marla until it slid off the bed and thumped onto the floor.

Marla glanced at the smear of crimson that stretched from the bottom of her nightgown, across the sheet to the edge of the mattress. "Untie me, please, Sonny. I've got to get out of this bed."

"Sure thing." Sonny pivoted to loosen the knot on the post at the bottom of the bed. "Dugan called me earlier this evening and told me to keep an eye out for you tonight. He told me to call him if I saw anything suspicious."

"Did you call him?"

"Yeah, as soon as I saw someone climbing your front steps. Then I came down and knocked on your door. Dugan should be getting here any minute." Sonny unloosed the rope from the post and quickly untied the knot around her right ankle.

She felt tingling in her foot as blood circulated freely again. "Who did Dugan think would show up? Trenton?"

Sonny shrugged as he picked away at the knot on the other post. "Don't know. He didn't say. But he asked me to stay up as late as I could and watch out for you. He knew something might happen."

"I'm glad you did."

Sonny made short work of the other knots.

Relieved of the tension of the ropes, she placed the gun on the mattress beside her, drew her knees to her chest, and rubbed her legs. "Take the gun, Sonny, and keep your eye on him. I've got to get out of this bloody nightgown." She scooted to the side of the bed opposite of Michael's body.

Sonny picked up the gun and waved it towards Michael. "Should I roll him over and see if he's still alive?"

Marla shook her head. "I wouldn't. If he's alive, he might try something." Marla stood and walked to her dresser.

She heard the sound of the front door opening.

The familiar voice of Dugan Walton called, "Marla! Sonny! You in there?"

"Yes. In the bedroom!" Marla yelled back.

Dugan rushed into the room and stopped abruptly when he saw the blood splotch on Marla's nightgown. "Are you all right?"

"I'm fine. It's not my blood." She pointed to the body facedown next to the bed.

"Is it Michael?" Dugan asked.

Marla nodded.

Dugan shifted his gaze to Sonny. "Did you shoot him?"

Sonny studied the gun in his hand and shook his head sideways. "Not me."

"I did," Marla said.

"Is he dead?" Dugan asked.

Marla shrugged. "Don't know and don't care."

Dugan pulled a cell phone out of his pocket, called 911, and asked for an ambulance and an investigation team. He walked to the body, turned Michael over and tried to find a pulse on his wrist and then his neck. "He still has a slight heartbeat."

A tinge of fear edged through Marla even though she felt sure Dugan and Sonny would protect her. She stared at Michael's face, thinking he still resembled Gabe. "How did you know it was Michael?"

Dugan stood and rubbed his chin. "This may sound a little out there in Lulu Land, but I took Martin Payne's visit very seriously."

"When he channeled his wife, Loretta, in your office?" Marla asked.

Dugan smiled. "That's right. Remember I told you and Michael that she named her rapist?"

"Yes. But you wouldn't tell us who she named. Was it Michael?"

Dugan bobbed his head. "I know you can't put much stock in a crazy man's ranting, but I let the possibility stew for a while. Then I studied Michael's expression when I told the story. I saw something in his eyes, a slight panic, a momentary hint of anxiety when I said she named her attacker. Of course, that wasn't the clincher."

"What was?" Sonny asked.

"Remember when I asked him if he and Gabe were identical twins?"

Marla really couldn't recall. "What difference does that make?"

Dugan glanced down at Michael and then back to Marla. "Identical twins have the same DNA. When Dr. Halsey told you Gabe was the father, I considered the odds. Yeah, Gabe may have had a one-in-a-thousand chance, but Michael's odds were much better—999 out of a thousand. I'll take those odds to court any day."

Marla's legs felt like gelatin. She gripped the bed's footboard to steady herself. *Michael's the father? Please, God, no.*

Dugan gripped her elbow. "Steady there, gal."

How could she go through with this pregnancy? "I wasn't expecting this, Dugan."

"Sorry, but I had to tell you."

A groan arose from the floor. Michael stirred. "Marla," he gasped. His eyes opened. Blood trickled from the corners of his mouth.

Marla focused on him.

Sonny pointed the gun at Michael's chest.

"Listen to me, Marla. I'm dying," he sighed.

Marla steeled herself. "What do you want?"

"It's me. It's really me. Don't . . ." he took two raspy breaths. "Don't get . . . an abortion."

"Give it up, Michael. I don't believe you. Why would I want to give birth to your child?"

Michael raised his head. "Because . . . because . . . there's still a chance . . . a chance that I'm the father." His head fell backwards, and air hissed out of his lungs like a tire going flat.

Marla edged nearer and noticed his eyes remained open, staring but not seeing.

* * *

They walked for more than a mile along the beach in the early morning July sunshine. Gulls floated and screeched above them, suspended by the robust breeze. Marla carried a cloth beach bag and, of course, the walking stick Mee Mee had carved for her several years ago. The waves, probably at least four-footers, plummeted and crashed, sending foamy water up the bank in front of them. The dark-haired boy ran ahead and splashed through the wash as it drifted back into the sea. She had promised Gabriel earlier in the week that they would walk to Cape Point to look for shells on his fifth birthday. He didn't mind the hike. In fact, he loved exercise and often persuaded Marla to go outdoors and play with him.

"Look, Mommy, look!" Gabriel lifted a white shell with spiraling brownish squares above his head.

"Good job, sport. That's a nice size Scotch Bonnet."

251

"You mean like a hat?" He placed the shell on top of his head, wavering to keep it balanced.

"Don't drop it. Mee Mee would love to see it."

When Gabriel lowered his head, the shell slid off, and he caught it in front of him with cupped hands. "Can we take it to Mee Mee's store after we finish looking for shells? I could trade it for a book."

"Yes. She's expecting us. I think she has a birthday present for you."

"All right!" He walked to Marla and extended the shell. "Could you hold it for me?"

"Sure." She held out the bag, and he deposited it.

Gabriel stared up at her, his brown eyes wide, his mouth forming an almost perfect "o".

"What is it, sport?"

"Did you and Daddy go for walks on the beach when he was alive?"

Marla took a deep breath and braced herself to maintain control over the swell of emotion that rose into her throat. There were moments when the pain of Gabe's loss returned with great potency, though not nearly as often during the last couple of years. "When we first moved here from Ohio, we walked on the beach almost every day."

"You lived in Ohio?"

Marla nodded.

"Why didn't we move back there after Daddy died?"

Marla lifted the walking stick and jammed it into the sand. "I'm a Hatteras gal now."

Gabriel reached with his forefinger and traced one of the animals etched on the stick. "Am I a Hatteras boy?"

"Indeed you are, sport. We're survivors, just like the Algonquian Indians who lived here long ago before we arrived."

"Can I carry the stick, Mommy?"

Marla leaned the walking stick towards her son. It was at least two feet taller than he, but he grasped it in the middle, jerked it out of the sand, and took off running down the beach like a young brave who had just been given his first spear.

Marla watched him run. *I'll find a way to come back to you.* Gabe's words echoed so loudly in her memory it seemed he was standing next to her.

"I believe you," Marla said.

About the Author

Joe C. Ellis, a big fan of the North Carolina's Outer Banks, grew up in the Ohio Valley. A native of Martins Ferry, Ohio, he attended West Liberty State College in West Virginia and went on to earn his Master's Degree in education from Muskingum College in New Concord, Ohio. He has been employed by Martins Ferry City Schools for the last thirty-three years where he currently teaches art and computer graphics at Martins Ferry High School. He also has been lay preaching for the Presbyterian Church U.S.A. for the last twenty-one years. He pastors two churches in the Martins Ferry area, the Scotch Ridge Presbyterian Church and the Colerain Presbyterian Church.

His writing career began in 2001 with the publication of his first novel, *The Healing Place*. In 2007 he began the Outer Banks Murder Series with the publication of *Murder at Whalehead* and in 2010 *Murder at Hatteras*. The popularity of this series continues to grow with his 2012 installment, *Murder on the Outer Banks*.

Joe credits family vacations on the Outer Banks with the inspiration for these stories. Joe and his wife, Judy, have three children and three grandsons. Although the kids have flown the nest, they get together often and always make it a priority to vacation on the Outer Banks whenever possible. He comments, "It's a place on the edge of the world, a place of great beauty and sometimes danger—the ideal setting for murder mysteries."

One of Joe's passions is distance running. *Murder on the Outer Banks* opens with a 5K footrace in which an older man runs to victory against much younger competition. In the last year (2011) Joe has posted 5k times and half marathon times at the national class level for his age group. Because running definitely keeps him younger physically and mentally, he enjoyed writing a novel with these themes as important threads in the plot. Joe hopes to continue to write stories set on the Outer Banks and run along its beaches for many years to come.

Novels by Joe C. Ellis

Ohio Valley Mystery Series:

The Healing Place   ISBN=978-0-9796655-1-6
The First Shall Be Last   ISBN=978-0-9796655-2-3

The Outer Banks Murder Series:

Murder at Whalehead   ISBN=978-0-9796655-0-9
Murder at Hatteras   ISBN=978-0-9796655-3-0
Murder on the Outer Banks   ISBN=978-0-9796655-4-7

US $15.95

ISBN 978-0-9796655-3-0
51595

9 780979 665530

CPSIA information can be obtained at www.ICGtesting.com
Printed in the USA
LVOW11s1427110916

504132LV00002BA/430/P